WOMAN DOWN

PRAISE FOR COLLEEN HOOVER

"*Verity* delivers the grand slam of thriller twists."
—*The Washington Post*

"Talk about a word-of-mouth page-turner we're still not over . . . Cue the seductive mystery that has one of our all-time fave twists. Run, don't walk."
—theSkimm on *Verity*

"Feel free to send Hoover your increased electric bill because you're going to be keeping the lights on late to stay up and read this one."
—*E! Online* on *Layla*

"What a glorious and touching read, a forever keeper. The kind of book that gets handed down."
—*USA Today* on *It Ends with Us*

"An emotional masterpiece about loss and hope, grief and forgiveness, and how the power of love can heal."
—Popsugar on *Reminders of Him*

"*Confess* by Colleen Hoover is a beautiful and devastating story that will make you feel so much."
—*The Guardian*

"Betrayals, secrets, and shifting family loyalties keep the pages turning in this excellent contemporary from Hoover . . . This is Hoover at her very best."
—*Publishers Weekly*, starred review, for *Regretting You*

"*It Ends with Us* tackles [a] difficult subject . . . with romantic tenderness and emotional heft. Packed with riveting drama and painful truths, this book powerfully illustrates the devastation of abuse—and the strength of the survivors."

—*Kirkus*, starred review

"Hoover is as unafraid as ever to explore the darker and more vulnerable aspects of love, expertly demonstrating the soul-deep trust required to reach happily ever after."

—*Publishers Weekly*, starred review, for *It Starts with Us*

"Hoover joins the ranks of such luminaries as Jennifer Weiner and Jojo Moyes, with a dash of Gillian Flynn. Sure to please a plethora of readers."

—*Library Journal*, starred review, for *November 9*

"Hoover builds a terrific new-adult world here with two people growing in their careers and discovering mature love."

—*Booklist*, starred review, for *Ugly Love*

OTHER TITLES BY COLLEEN HOOVER

Reminders of Him

Layla

Heart Bones

Regretting You

Verity

Without Merit

Too Late

November 9

Confess

Ugly Love

Hopeless Series

Hopeless

Losing Hope

Finding Cinderella: A Novella

All Your Perfects

IT ENDS WITH US SERIES

It Ends with Us

It Starts with Us

MAYBE SOMEDAY SERIES

Maybe Someday

Maybe Not: A Novella

Maybe Now

SLAMMED SERIES

Slammed

Point of Retreat

This Girl

WOMAN DOWN

A novel

COLLEEN HOOVER

This is a work of fiction. Names, characters, organizations, places, events, and incidents are either products of the author's imagination or are used fictitiously. Otherwise, any resemblance to actual persons, living or dead, is purely coincidental.

Text copyright © 2026 by Colleen Hoover
All rights reserved.

No part of this book may be reproduced, or stored in a retrieval system, or transmitted in any form or by any means, electronic, mechanical, photocopying, recording, or otherwise, without express written permission of the publisher.

Published by Montlake, Seattle

www.apub.com

Amazon, the Amazon logo, and Montlake are trademarks of Amazon.com, Inc., or its affiliates.

EU product safety contact:
Amazon Media EU S. à r.l.
38, avenue John F. Kennedy, L-1855 Luxembourg
amazonpublishing-gpsr@amazon.com

ISBN-13: 9781662539374 (hardcover)
ISBN-13: 9781542025614 (paperback)
ISBN-13: 9781542025621 (digital)

Cover design by Caroline Johnson
Cover image: © Larysa Vdovychenko, © Sviatlana Barysevich / Getty

Printed in the United States of America

First Edition

*For Lauren Levine. Without you,
there would be no there there.*

Dear readers,

Some of you might remember the short story "Saint" from the *One More Step* anthology years ago. For those who don't, you're about to meet it in a much bigger way.

That anthology has since been unpublished, but some of you guys never stopped asking for more of the story. You have somehow managed to keep a little story alive in your hearts, even when it wasn't officially available. There's nothing more inspiring for me as a writer than when a reader tells me they want more from characters I created.

I wanted to give these characters the space they deserved, and truly build out the world I'd only briefly touched upon when this short story was called "Saint."

I took the short story some of you read and poured my heart and soul into expanding it. It has taken me three years to release a book since *It Starts with Us*. Not because I've been rewriting "Saint" for those three years, but because I've been trying out new things outside writing. And frankly, I needed some space from a career I was beginning to find more stressful than normal.

But that changed when I dove back into this story. Working on this book gave me back that same joy I felt while writing the original short story. I've changed the title and some character names and locations, added scenes, added and changed characters, and even written in new little twists here and there that had no room in the short version. I wanted those of you who have already read it to get what felt like an entirely new and different book with the same underlying story and tones as the short story. I genuinely enjoyed every single second of bringing it to life in this new, complete form.

Just please keep in mind that while writers do take from their own lives, and some of the themes may mirror those of my own life in ways, this is in no way a replica of my journey or my morals, nor is it a reflection of how I feel about my peers or this industry. This is simply a fun journey the characters took me on and nothing more. Please, I beg of you, do not try to make ties between my personal life and this story, as there are none. I'm just a writer writing about a writer—I am in no way advocating for or defending the character's behavior or thoughts.

It was a joy to put a new spin on "Saint." I hope you're ready to get dizzy and enjoy this fun, sexy, sometimes creepy thrill of a ride!

With so much love,
Colleen Hoover

CHAPTER ONE

"Hey, hey! Kellie here. Your fiction therapist with a minor in messy behavior. Welcome back to *And What Now, Readers?* The podcast where your favorite book drama gets lovingly dissected and lightly roasted."

"And I'm Micah, your literary, and sometimes television, gossip sommelier."

"*Sommelier?*" Kellie laughs. "You don't even drink wine."

"Who needs alcohol when you can get drunk on shit like we have for you today?"

"Oh, I love how spicy this is," Kellie adds.

"It's more than spicy. It's full-on scorched earth. We're talking about Petra Rose today, darling of book clubs and Tumblr mood boards, whose reputation has erupted into literary flames."

"And if you somehow missed it while scrolling your feed, or, I don't know, *breathing*, the internet has *completely* turned on the formerly adored author. And not gently," Kellie says.

"Nope. The international bestselling author of *A Terrible Thing*—"

"That's probably the worst book title of all time," Kellie interrupts.

"Truly," Micah says. "It's like she was asking for this backlash. *Begging* for it. Anyway, the novel basically launched a thousand

#TeamAsh-versus-#TeamCaleb debates. It was at the center of total fandom fallout in the best way. Until it wasn't. Kellie, want to do the short-recap honors before we announce our surprise guest?"

"Well, it won't be short, but my pleasure. Let's rewind for those of you new to the alphabet. *A Terrible Thing* is, by readers' standards, not such a terrible book. It is a deeply emotional and beautifully crafted novel about Elise and her journey through love, trauma, identity, along with a pinch of fun. You get a little bit of everything in this realistic romance, so it's honestly shocking how huge the book got without it having a single dragon or wizard. But it's because it wasn't just sexy, cheap romance. It was character development, moral complexity, fan fiction GOLD."

"We get it. You liked it. Get to the good stuff," Micah says.

"It used to be my favorite book," Kellie says defensively.

"It can still be your favorite book."

"Not after this," Kellie says. "Okay, so the love triangle. Elise, Ash, and Caleb. You'd truly have to have been on a five-year trek in the jungle not to have at least seen an Ash-and-Caleb meme. Whole subreddits were devoted to that emotional tug-of-war. But then? Then the movie adaptation happened."

Micah groans. "Calling that an adaptation is a stretch."

Kellie says, "But this adaptation had promise and a high budget. It was a majorly hyped-up movie that the studio and author were being very oddly hush hush about. We weren't even getting cast updates, outside of two of the main characters. There was zero mention of our beloved character Caleb. He was nowhere to be found when the trailer dropped. Just—*poof*. And that was enough to almost start a war when the trailer dropped without a single clip of him in it. But people still showed up for the movie despite the early concerns spreading throughout TikTok."

"And the concerns expressed on this podcast," Micah says. "You talked about it every day."

"Fine, I was team Caleb. Anyway. They CUT him. Cut the entire triangle. Restructured the story to make it all about Ash and his connection with Elise. And fans were not happy. Not even team Ash fans, because what the hell were they supposed to do with all the merch the author sold them? Team Ash wasn't even a thing that made sense after that monstrosity of a movie. It made it seem like wearing a #TeamAsh shirt meant you were not team Elise, but we were *all* team Elise. We were betrayed, Micah. BETRAYED."

"Yes, like screaming-in-the-rain-while-covered-in-red-wine-stains levels of betrayed," he says.

"Let's not discuss that night. I was upset."

They both laugh.

"Okay, okay," Kellie says. "We all know how Hollywood works and how most authors don't get a say in how their adaptations turn out. There are a lucky few who do, but for the majority, it's not up to them. And Petra initially took that classic 'don't blame me' route. She posted to Insta with something like '*Hey, besties, I had no creative control. I was just as shocked as you all were.*'"

"And honestly, we were so ready to believe her," Micah says. "For about five seconds. Until—*cue dramatic music*—an old text exchange leaked between Petra and one of the producers. Not only did she know about the change, she *liked* it."

"Yes, what was it she said in that conversation?" Kellie asks.

"I have it here. I shall read it," Micah says. "'*You're right, there's a lot out there about him being unrealistic. I'm fine with that character being cut. Might make it a stronger film with Caleb and the love triangle out.*'"

"That '*stronger film with Caleb out*' line sent people into orbit," Kellie says. "Like, *stronger*? STRONGER? You don't just erase half an entire fandom and call it a decluttering session!"

"The backlash was immediate," Micah says. "TikTok, Reddit, X—*formerly Twitter but let's be real, still just Twitter*—all blew up with hashtags like #CancelPetra and #ATerribleAdaptation and

#ATerribleAuthor. Which is why I stand behind *A Terrible Thing* being the worst novel title ever. Too easy to roast."

"So easy," Kellie says. "And now there are fans literally burning their copies of *A Terrible Thing*. We are in a full literary rebellion. They feel personally betrayed, *as do I*. She lied to us. She chose the industry over the intimacy that made her book matter, and the fandom that made her a star. She erased everything that made us love this book in the first place. And then blamed it on a few critiques she received, despite hundreds of thousands of readers who praised it."

"Oof. That hit like a Caleb monologue in chapter twenty-eight."

"Don't talk about that monologue, Micah. I'll cry literal tears."

"My bad. But it was such a good monologue. Would have been great to SEE ON THE BIG SCREEN, HOLLYWOOD PEOPLE WHO ARE LISTENING TO THIS!"

"There aren't any Hollywood people listening to us, Micah. We have two thousand subscribers."

"Two thousand loyal listeners who we would never betray like Petra did her readers."

"And look at how it turned out for her. She focused on the few who didn't matter and now has even the most loyal supporters turning their backs. She flipped on us all. It makes me wonder if Petra Rose even believes in her characters or if she's embarrassed by her own writing."

"Well, she has been quiet," Micah says. "Not a single social media post in almost a year, outside her own fan club."

"Which I hear is dwindling. I wouldn't know, I left that fan club six months ago," Kellie says.

"Hopefully the silence is a sign that she's studying how to write a storyline that she actually *believes* in. Which is wild, considering this is the same author whose lines people literally tattooed onto their bodies."

"Speaking of, I've seen a few videos of people having her quotes removed," Kellie says.

"Sad. We used to quote her and now we just . . . *hate* her."

"*Hate* is a strong word," Kellie says.

"This is an honest podcast."

"True. We hate her. So much so, we've pulled a million strings and rescheduled three other bookings to bring you this special guest today. Not sure why he agreed to our little podcast, but we couldn't be more appreciative. We might even climb to two thousand and one subscribers after this."

"Yes, dream big," Micah says. "Ladies and gentleman, we welcome you to join us in conversation with none other than Allister Jones, the producer of *A Terrible Thing*."

"He's not quite off the hook for that adaptation, but at least he's brave enough to talk about it. Welcome, Allister!"

"Thank you so much for having me," Allister says. "That was quite the recap."

Fuck.

That.

Guy.

I turn off the podcast as soon as I hear his voice. My heart is pounding so hard and my stomach is churning.

I have to pull my car over to the side of the road because I feel very close to puking.

"Oh, God." My fingers are trembling on the steering wheel. I move my hand to the door in search of the button to roll down the window. As soon as it's far enough down for my head to stick out, I breathe in the fresh, pine-scented air and close my eyes, repeating slow breaths until my stomach begins to ease.

I can't believe I actually thought exposure therapy would help me heal.

Listening to that podcast just now was the worst few minutes I've lived through since my texts with Allister leaked.

I open my eyes and lean my head back against the headrest. I inhale a few slow breaths, attempting not to focus on the fact that Allister is probably out there doing a tour of podcasts and interviews, and I'm being forced to shut myself away in a grimy cabin and write a book I've been attempting to write since this whole movie fiasco started, just so I don't lose my house now that my sales have taken a nosedive.

"You did nothing wrong," I say to myself as I pull slowly back onto the highway. "You did nothing wrong. What the world thinks of you isn't who you are."

I've repeated this mantra since Nora made me promise to say it at least five times a day. But I just feel like I'm repeating a lie out loud, and that feeling doesn't leave me refreshed and ready to skip along and tackle my day.

I've been unable to function since all this started. I feel like a fraud. I feel like everything I've built has crashed down around me and I'm buried in rubble that no one even cares to dig through because they aren't even curious if I'm suffocating to death. They only want to know who will show up at my funeral after I *do* suffocate to death.

I wonder who would show up at my funeral. I have friends and family who would be there, but I realize now that all the "friends" I've made in my years of being in the book world weren't friends at all. Other than Nora, everyone has ghosted me. And I don't blame them. They can see that my reputation has tanked my sales, so any sort of public support my way might fuel TikToks that would tank *their* sales. This is a career, and as much as I've always hoped the friends I've made in this career would also be my friends outside this career, I'm beginning to realize we're all just unhappy coworkers trying to survive until we retire.

I've been driving for two hours now, the white lines of the highway blurring into an endless ribbon beneath my tires. I'm still not entirely sure if I'm running toward the sanctuary of the cabin or fleeing from the chaos of everything else. It's always a little of both, I suppose, a blend of aspiration and desperation. But I've never felt such an urgent need to escape my real life, to shed its skin and step into something new, as I do right now. My deepest desire is to dive headfirst into writing this book, to immerse myself so completely that not a single person or event from the outside world can penetrate the walls of my fictional creation.

My anxiety is at an all-time high, and writing is truly the only thing that eases it.

I just hope it works this time. This feeling of urgency, this desperate hope that I can redeem myself, won't go away unless I reach that cabin and commit myself entirely.

Writer's block clamped down on me like a suffocating trap that arrived precisely when my name started appearing in articles beyond the literary sphere.

It's a cruel irony, isn't it? One person's dream of widespread recognition can so easily become another's nightmare.

My phone vibrates in the cup holder, its screen flashing with yet another notification that induces my anxiety. I turned off notifications for social media after the vitriol began. The digital world, once a platform for connection, has become a relentless antagonist, and the only way to silence it is to cut myself off from it.

At least it means when I do get a notification, it's actually from someone who wants to talk *to* me and not *about* me.

I'm relieved to see Nora's name as the one flashing across the phone screen. I swipe it with my finger, and the call picks up over the car speakers.

"I hope you're calling to tell me you have extra Adderall and you're mailing me some," I blurt out.

"First of all," Nora says, "you don't have ADHD. *I* do. And second, you don't need drugs. You need intense therapy and a good fuck." She pauses. "From someone who isn't me. That was a suggestion, not an offer."

"Darn and darn," I sigh. "Well, you called at a good time."

"Why? Another panic attack?"

"I was listening to *And What Now, Readers?*"

"Petra! Goddammit."

I groan. "I *know*."

"That's why I was calling. I wanted you to avoid today's episode."

"But you told me exposure therapy would be good. I was exposing."

"I just meant exposure to going back on social media. Making a post. I didn't mean you should dig up everyone talking shit about you and listen to it all. *Good God*. I'm your friend, not Satan."

"So you listened?"

"I had to turn it off when Allister McFuckity Fuckface came on."

"Yeah, me too. I pulled over for a bit when I heard he was the guest. Felt like I was about to puke."

"I'm sorry. You almost to the rental?"

"Ten minutes away."

"Are you sure this is a good idea?" Nora's voice crackles through the speaker.

"Is what a good idea? Me, alone in the woods, trying to recover after being digitally flayed by the entire internet?" I keep my eyes on the road. Pines blur past, getting larger and more condensed until they begin to feel like they're threatening to swallow my car.

"It's not the *whole* internet," Nora says. "Just the vocal fringe with a financial agenda."

"Oh, right. The people making death threats were vetted and just deemed money hungry. I forgot." I smile despite myself.

"These people don't know you. They threatened to boil your dog, Petra. You don't even *have* a dog."

"Exactly. They'll probably buy me a new puppy and have it delivered to me with a cute bow and let me fall in love with it and *then* boil it."

The signal fades for a second and her voice becomes robotic, then cuts out altogether. "Goddammit." I pick my phone up and move it to the dash like that's somehow going to make for a better signal.

". . . serious," she says, her voice returning mid-sentence. "You've got a career, still. Sort of. You could write a groveling apology post in your notes app and post it to Instagram with those cute little heart hands and like one or two crying emojis."

"I'm not writing an apology to people who don't know the whole story but choose to take sides regardless."

She sighs. "Well, you have to get back online if you want to save your career. Maybe say your piece on a podcast."

"I can climb my way out of this hole without stooping to Allister's level. That's why I'm going to the cabin to write. I'll get revenge with my pen."

There's a long pause. "But . . . you use a laptop. Not a pen."

"*Pen* sounded more threatening."

"You're right. Revenge with your pen. Write the whole story and publish it as a work of fiction. It'll be a good outlet. Call me later when you're settled. I have an idea."

"No, I hate your ideas," I say.

"But it's actually a good one this time. I promise."

"Fine."

"Don't turn on another podcast. Listen to some Brudi Brothers or something. I love you."

"Love you too."

When I end the call, the podcast automatically cues back up. "She wasn't the easiest to work with," Allister says.

The words wash over me like boiling water over ice. I turn off the podcast again and focus on the road curving ahead of me. "Neither were you, Allister McFuckity Fuckface."

I don't hate a lot of people, but Allister is at the top of my list. And the bottom. And the middle.

He's my entire list, actually.

I slow down when my GPS tells me my turn is coming up. Somewhere down this road a cabin is waiting for me, along with a blank screen, a lot of silence, and hopefully whatever is still salvageable of my creativity.

CHAPTER TWO

I don't know that any part of my creativity will be salvageable if there are neighbors. I avoid booking places with neighbors, but there's a house on the same road as the cabin I'm staying in.

I looked up the satellite images for this place before I booked it just to make sure it's not near another cabin. I don't want to have to listen to someone else's loud children screaming at all hours of the day and night. The place where I'm staying looked to be secluded on this road, so I didn't notice the other cabin. It was probably swallowed up in trees when Google took the image.

The cabin I booked is tucked away at the end of the mile-long road I'm on, so I'm relieved to see they aren't right next door to each other. There's at least a quarter of a mile that separates the driveways.

I prefer no traffic and no neighbors. I get distracted easily. The fewer people I see and the fewer conversations I'm forced to have, the more focused I can be. I once booked a writing retreat and met the neighbors before I even made it in the front door. It was a group of women on a girls' weekend, and I ended up getting drunk with them every night and not getting a bit of work done.

It's not always a bad distraction, but any distraction would feel like a negative one this time around, considering I have so much riding on meeting this deadline.

Which is why I audibly groan as I reach the end of the driveway and see a human. A living, breathing human on the front porch of the property I'm pulling into.

With all the advancements in technology, there is absolutely zero reason the rental host for this cabin should be meeting me in person, but here he is. I don't even know him, and I already find him the most irritating thing in the world.

I take that back.

The shape of corgis is pretty damn irritating. There's something about a corgi that's just . . . *unfinished.* It's as if God started making the dog breed and walked away from them when he was only halfway into the design, leaving them in this weird limbo. Their bodies are too long for their stumpy legs, their heads too big for the rest of their bodies, like they might face-plant with every step. Anytime I see one, I can't help but feel like it's a cosmic mistake walking around on four legs.

If there were a corgi at this guy's feet, I'd question whether I had died and gone to hell.

The man's grin stretches, and I half expect his face to split open as if it can't quite contain all his teeth. There's a bounce in his step that reminds me of someone who's far too eager to please, as if he's trying to sell me on this booking that I paid for months ago.

Why am I in such a bad mood?

Oh yeah. The podcast.

I wipe the frown away as I put my car in park and grab my phone. I also bring my key chain with me—the one with the Mace on it. I've never had to use it, but I'm also rarely in situations where I'm alone with strangers.

My thumb brushes over the small canister as I slip it into my pocket, the cold metal comforting in its weight. I'm in the middle of nowhere, surrounded by dense trees that seem to swallow the road behind me, and even though I'm pretty sure I could take this guy down if things went south, I'm not sure anyone would hear me out here screaming for help.

Where's the bear when you need him?

I know from the guy's owner profile that his name is Louie Longsetter. What kind of name is Louie Longsetter? It sounds like a character from a sitcom, not the kind of person you'd expect to meet in the real world, with actual parents who said the name out loud and thought, *Yes! That's the one!*

I don't know that anyone named Louie Longsetter could even be dangerous.

But the way he's standing like he's been waiting for me longer than he should have been makes me second-guess that assumption.

I try to imagine a murderer named Louie Longsetter. I almost laugh at the absurdity of it, but as a woman about to embark on weeks of isolation, the thought that he could be a threat sticks in my mind, unwanted and uncomfortable, like a burr I can't shake off.

"Right on time!" he calls out, his voice too bright, too cheerful, as if I'm a guest of honor instead of just another renter. He jogs down the steps with an odd kind of buoyancy, heading toward me in a way that's both eager and unsettling.

I hate that I find cheerful people immediately unlikable. I'm aware that's a flaw within myself, but I have too many flaws to worry about polishing that one.

"Beauty of GPS," I mutter, popping the trunk with a little too much urgency. Louie Longsetter may not seem like the name of a murderer, but I'm pretty sure there was a serial killer named Pichushkin. Anything's possible.

Louie is beside me now, and he reaches into my trunk, his large hands wrapping around the handles of my suitcases. He yanks both out at once and lets them drop onto their sides on the gravel with a dull thud.

I wince, resisting the urge to snap at him. It's RIMOWA luggage—new, sleek, expensive, and so far, free of any scratches or scuffs. I received it for my birthday a few months ago, and this is the first time I've been able to use it. I've been proud that it's remained in pristine condition.

Until now.

I bend down quickly and lift one suitcase upright as I suppress a wave of irritation.

Louie, oblivious, mirrors my movements and sets the other suitcase upright, though I notice he's dragging it behind him as he heads to the porch. The wheels scrape against the gravel like nails on a chalkboard, and I flinch inwardly, lifting mine off the ground to carry it.

"You're *the* Petra Rose, right? The writer lady?" he asks, peering over his shoulder at me.

The writer lady?

I nod as I follow close behind, trying to plaster on a polite smile. "Yes, sir. Here to find inspiration. In the silence," I add.

There are groceries in the back seat I still need to unload, but I'd rather him not know that. I just want him to leave. I needed him to leave before I showed up. That's why rentals have door codes and self-check-in instructions.

We head up the porch steps, me holding my suitcase gingerly so the wheels don't scrape up the steps, while Louie drags the other behind him like it's an afterthought.

"I haven't read any of your books," he says, his voice almost apologetic, "but my wife said she thinks she's read one." He stops on the porch and fishes a ring of keys out of his pocket. "We did watch your movie, though. When I told my wife you were staying here, she made me promise to ask you about some character who was missing? Not sure what she's referring to. You know, I was thinking on my walk over here about what would make a great movie," he continues, handing me the keys.

Oh, God. Not this.

"My life," he says, cocking an eyebrow like I should be impressed. "I've lived one hell of a crazy life. It could make you millions."

I'm positive it wouldn't.

"If you need any ideas . . ." he starts again, clearly not getting the hint from my expression alone.

I cut him off, my smile stretched thin. "Fiction is the only thing I know how to write, unfortunately."

I've lost count of how many times people have offered their life stories to me after finding out I'm a writer. Everyone is convinced they're sitting on the next great American novel.

Maybe they are. I certainly haven't been.

"But if you heard my story . . ." he says.

"You know, if it's that good, you should write your *own* story," I say, not wanting to come off as rude. "No one knows it better than you, and you shouldn't be handing your ideas out for free." My voice is polite, but inside, I am willing him to leave.

"Dyslexic," he says with a shake of his head, his smile faltering slightly. "Very dyslexic. Not sure if you noticed that in my emails. Gotta be honest, when I recognized your name and saw you were the writer, I was kind of nervous to email you back. Thought you might laugh at my poor grammar."

"I would never. My father was dyslexic, and he was the smartest man I've ever known."

Louie smiles at that. "It's a hell of a thing to work through. Sorry your mother had to deal with that."

I pause, because I just told him it was my father. Not my mother. Does he have a memory issue? Hearing impairment?

He winks. "Gotcha. Little dyslexia humor."

I smile. "Yep. That one flew right by me."

"My wife says I woulda made a good actor. She's an actress. My wife. Sort of. Well, it's hard to explain, but she acts. In documentaries. Which I guess still makes her an actress, but . . ." He continues talking about his wife's career, or lack thereof, but I'm too distracted to listen because—*holy shit.*

The outside of this place does not do the inside justice.

The interior is far more modern than I expected—clean lines, smooth finishes, like it's been plucked straight out of a design magazine. The rustic exterior was just a facade—inside, everything gleams.

I was expecting creaky wooden floors, maybe the smell of old pine or the comforting musk of an extinguished fireplace. But instead, I'm greeted by sleek surfaces, harsh lighting, and the kind of clean, minimalistic decor you'd find in a city loft. The floors are polished concrete, gleaming beneath the recessed lighting that casts everything in a clinical glow. The walls are painted a crisp, sterile white, and large, abstract paintings hang in expensive frames, too curated and intentional for a place like this.

There's a charm to traditional cabins. The kind where you hole up with nothing but a roaring fire and the occasional scuttle of wildlife outside. I was hoping for the roughness of wooden, unsanded walls, and the sense of being tucked away in nature's arms, away from the world.

But this?

This feels like I've stepped into a tech startup's getaway house. Not a writer's retreat.

I let out a sigh and roll my suitcase toward the living room, the sound of the wheels echoing too loudly in the open space. I hear Louie following behind me, and can almost hear his pride as he watches me take it in.

"This looks nothing like the pictures online," I say, turning to face him.

"Just completed the remodel," he says proudly. "You're the first guest since we finished it, actually. We're pretty proud of her. My wife did most of the design herself. She's got an eye for this stuff."

That makes more sense. It explains the contrast between Louie and this house.

The living room furniture is completely sterile. A low black leather couch that looks more like a showroom piece than something you could sink into and read a book on. A glass coffee table that reflects the light in too many corners, its edges sharp enough to slice open a knee if you aren't careful.

Even the fireplace, which I thought might offer some rustic warmth, is just an elegant gas fixture behind a smooth modern facade. It flickers with a mechanical precision that makes me long for the uneven crackle of real wood burning.

I am such an ungrateful brat. *Who would be sad to stay in a place this gorgeous?*

It's just . . . there's no *charm* in it. No history. It's efficient, sure, but it doesn't feel like a place for inspiration. It feels like a place to execute tasks, to work, but not to *create*. I wanted solitude, yes, but I wanted to feel connected to the wilderness of this place, to the raw beauty of the woods. Instead, I feel like I've been dropped into a high-end Airbnb, too pristine for the kind of messy, creative process I imagined.

My writer's block has been so bad, I blame everything for it. I'm even prematurely blaming this beautiful house.

I sigh again. This might not be the retreat I hoped for, but considering my sour mood, I don't know that anything would be met with warmth from me right now.

"Really nice place," I say, giving Louie at least a fraction of the reaction he's probably hoping for.

"I'll tell my wife you love it," he says. "You know, we live just down the road. You probably noticed the house, actually. First and only other one on the whole road," he adds, his eyes fixed on me a little too long, as if waiting for me to ask for more details.

I nod, hoping that'll be enough to keep him from offering more.

"I know you're here to work," Louie continues, "but if you're not too busy, you could come over for dinner sometime this week. The wife would love to meet you. It's just the two of us, and we love having company when we can." His grin widens, and there's that gleam again in his eyes that makes him come off way too eager and forward.

Or maybe the word I'm looking for is *desperate*.

Or just lonely?

My mouth twists at the dinner invite, but I try to suppress it with a smile. I can't imagine anything worse than spending an entire meal making small talk with Louie Longsetter and his wife who *thinks* she read one of my books and is an actress, but not really an actress, but kind of *is* an actress. I'm already exhausted by the explanation of that, and I haven't even met the woman.

"Oh, that's really nice of you," I say, my smile feeling more forced with every passing second. "But I've got a lot of work to do. I'll text you if I find some free time?"

There's a flash of disappointment in his eyes, but he quickly recovers, nodding. "Of course, of course. You're here to write, after all. I just thought, you know, if you needed a break or anything . . ." His voice trails off, and he gives a little wave. "Well, I'm just down the road if you need me."

I nod again, tighter this time. "Thanks, I'll keep that in mind."

With another awkward wave, he turns and heads out the door toward the road. I close the door, lean against it for a moment, and stare back into the unnervingly modern space.

The backyard overlooking the lake isn't west-facing.

I always get a west-facing house for this part of the process. There's something about watching the sunset that lights a creative fire in me like nothing else. The way the sky burns with hues of orange, pink, and violet pushes me to write with a kind of urgency that feels both exhilarating and necessary.

That's how it's *supposed* to work, anyway.

But I booked so late this time around, I had to settle for an east-facing backyard view, and I feel the difference in every fiber of my insecure, untalented being. Sunrises just feel harsh and demanding, almost as if they expect too much from me too soon, and that's how I'm going to start each day here with these massive east-facing windows.

Maybe I could write in the primary bedroom, which is the next room I peek into. There's a window that faces west behind the bed, but it wouldn't offer views of the sunset through the dense trees.

"Almost forgot!"

Shit! I spin around at the sound of his voice, a yelp stuck in my throat. I bring my hand up to my chest, startled, but try to keep my anger at bay when I see Louie is standing in the doorway to my bedroom.

He waves a sheet of paper in the air. "Wi-Fi password and such. Forgot to leave the rules." He sets it on the credenza next to the bedroom door. "Like I said, first guest since the remodel, so I'm sure there's a thing or two I'm forgetting. Let me know if you have any trouble, or if any of the appliances don't work, or . . ."

"Thank you," I say sharply. "I can take it from here."

Louie nods, but half his teeth disappear in what would still be considered a smile on most people, though for him it's basically a frown. "Break a leg," he says. "Or . . . whatever they say to writers." He heads back toward the front door. "Break a pen? Break a keyboard?"

He's still muttering alternative phrases as he closes the door behind him. I hate that he knows who I am and what I'm here for. I shouldn't have booked under my business email, but I've been using it for so long, it would be too much trouble to change it to something that isn't my author name.

I can't get away from myself, or my recognizable name, even to a guy who is older than my father and lives in the middle of nowhere. No matter how much I try to hide from being Petra Rose, I'm here. I'm there. I'm *every-fucking-where*. On the cover of *People*, on the home pages of *E! News* and TMZ, on podcasts with only two thousand followers.

Whatever pays the bills, I guess. I'm sure I'd be doing the exact same thing if the writing didn't work out when it did.

Hell, I have the following—I should monetize my own platform and start shit-talking myself too. I'd probably make more money by *trashing* me than *being* me.

I always feared this would happen. The loss of anonymity. But I don't think I ever imagined it happening on this level.

When I first began writing, I did it purely for fun. It was a need. Something I could escape to when my real life got hectic. It was exciting, and readers were excited. I'd write about anything I felt like writing about. Hot MMA fighters, aliens attacking Earth, farmers falling in love with city girls. Seventeen books later, my name was out there and bills were getting paid and life was good. I felt like I was on top of the world.

Unfortunately, gravity pulls everyone back down again. And boy did I fall hard. It was like someone sliced a hole in my parachute and threw my descent on live television for the entire world to see.

Which is why I'm in the predicament I am in. Way too far behind on a deadline, and a house with a past-due mortgage. And the icing on the cake?

Writer's block.

CHAPTER THREE

Writer's block can suck a dick.

It's too dark outside and I am depressed and I have made zero progress. And I am so very hangry.

I've harrumphed my way through the last eight hours I've been in this cabin, frustrated by anything and everything. I become such a bitch when I'm not able to be productive. It's why I have to be alone when I write. I'm saving everyone I love from the wrath of me with writer's block.

I already miss the sunsets from my usual cabin, the slow descent of day, the way dusk allowed for reflection and peaceful contemplation there. But here, without the sunset, it's as if my inspiration is slipping away with the light, and I'm left grasping at shadows that refuse to form into coherent thoughts.

Yes, I am blaming the sun and lack thereof for my inability to write. Just like I've blamed the weather, my digestive health, Mercury in retrograde, caffeine, *men*.

I adjust my posture and lie to myself as I tap away at the keyboard, trying to convince my brain that I deserve every award I've ever been given, every positive review I've ever received, every book I've ever sold.

But the voice that tells me I'm just a lucky fraud is always the loudest. I hate impostor syndrome. I hate that I believe the negative reviews over the positive. I hate that I'm questioning whether or not I can actually write a realistic book.

I glance at the screen and read over what little I've written.

> The sterile scent of the interview room, a mix of old coffee and stale air, did little to calm the frantic beating of Reya's heart. Across the table, Detective Miller's voice was a low, steady rumble, asking questions about Sarah, about the last time Reya saw her. Each word felt like a fresh cut, tearing open the wound of losing her best friend. Yet, a part of Reya, a deeply unsettling and unwelcome part, registered the way the detective's uniform stretched across his broad shoulders, the dark intensity of his eyes as he scribbled notes. She hated herself for it, for the fleeting spark of attraction that flickered within her, a betrayal of Sarah's memory. How could her mind even entertain such thoughts when her world felt like it had shattered into a million pieces? The guilt was a heavy stone in her gut, compounding the grief she was already struggling to carry.

I stare at the sentences I just wrote, fully aware that my future self, probably still half asleep and fueled by lukewarm coffee, will declare them utter garbage and hit Delete.

This book isn't so much a manuscript as it is a digital graveyard of my fleeting literary aspirations. Every word feels like a temporary squatter on the page, just waiting for its eviction notice.

I'm never going to finish this. At this rate, I'll be stuck in this cabin-with-an-identity-crisis for an entire year, perpetually reworking the same five paragraphs while the cursor blinks at me like a tiny, judgmental oracle. If cursors could talk, mine would be chanting, "*You suck—give up,*" just to really drive the point home.

Not that being hermetically sealed in this cabin is actual torture. I do enjoy the solitude. Always have. It's why I rent these places, transforming into a temporary lakeside hermit multiple times a year, all to shed the suffocating skin of Sacramento. The city, bless its heart, often feels like a giant, noisy concrete hug I never asked for.

But here? It's quiet, peaceful, and the air smells like pine and fresh water. So, you know, *there's that.*

I need to embrace the power of positive thinking. Focus on the fact that these little escapes aren't just getaways; they're my mental therapy.

I push away from my desk, the cursor still blinking its silent judgment, and wander into the kitchen. The scent of stale coffee remains in the air, a testament to my earlier, more optimistic writing session when I was convinced caffeine could cure me. But then I was reminded how much I hate the taste of coffee.

I cross to the front door and open it to breathe in a rush of fresh air. Outside, the world is a kaleidoscope of greens and browns, but all I can see are shadows in the dark. I see something move in the distance, so I squint, trying to pull it into focus.

I freeze when it moves again.

A shadow. A figure.

My heart leaps into my throat, a cold, sharp terror seizing me. I press myself against the door, my breath catching. This cabin is supposed to be my sanctuary, my escape. Not a stage for some backwoods slasher film.

But as the figure steps into a patch of moonlight, my terror deflates into a puff of embarrassed relief. It's just Louie Longsetter.

He spots me standing in the doorway from his position by the lake and then gives me a friendly wave.

"Caught a raccoon in the trap!" he yells across the backyard. He holds up what looks like a floppy dead animal, and my sympathy for the poor creature seeps in. "Sorry if I scared you!"

I manage a weak, wobbly smile and a small wave back, my heart still trying to settle from its impromptu sprint. The lake is public—anyone can be out there—but I find it odd he would choose to be out there when he has a renter in this house. I hit the button to lower all the shades, and just as I'm about to turn away from the window, my phone buzzes, startling me again. I glance at the screen. Nora.

Shit. I forgot I was supposed to call her once I got settled.

"Hey," I say, my voice still a little shaky.

"Okay, so my idea," Nora says, her voice brimming with an almost frantic energy that buzzes through the phone line, a stark contrast to the quiet panic I just experienced.

"What now?" I ask, my brow furrowing. "Please tell me it's not another macramé owl kick. My office can't handle any more of your craft projects."

Nora laughs, a bright, unburdened sound. "Not a macramé owl, though that's not a bad idea. I was getting really good at those. No, I mean I have an idea to help your situation. But I need you to trust me."

I sigh, a long, weary sound. I know that tone. It usually precedes a suggestion that will be either incredibly brilliant or utterly terrifying. "Nora, what are you talking about?"

"Your private group," Nora begins, her voice dropping conspiratorially. "I think we should go live in it. Just us, and the few thousand people we have always trusted implicitly not to screenshot our bad hair days."

My breath hitches. "Go live? Nora, are you insane? I am traumatized by people online. What if someone shares it outside the group?"

"So what if they do?" Nora's voice is sharp now, cutting through my anxieties. "Honestly, Petra, you really have to stop caring so much. Do you think other famous authors care about social media? Do you think they obsess over every comment, every insult, every word they write that could end up a potential screenshot?"

There's a beat of silence on my end. Then, hesitantly, I say, "Um. Yes. Yes, I do think that."

Nora actually snorts. "Yeah, you're probably right," she concedes. "But it's time, Petra. It's been a year since you stopped doing the live videos with me. To the day."

The words hang in the air, heavy and significant.

A year to the day.

My mind reels. A whole year since the film adaptation of my last novel released. A year since my world turned upside down, since the public scrutiny became a suffocating blanket.

I, the author who used to churn out two books a year with effortless grace, haven't even been able to finish the one I started eighteen months ago, nor have I been able to face live questions since the last live video I did ended so badly. Why my publishers thought it would be a good idea to do a live stream with the biggest bookstore in New York City the day after the movie released is beyond me.

Well. It's not beyond me, actually. That's what publishers do. That's what authors do. It's standard publicity. Live streams just don't usually end in disaster with the author crying and running to the bathroom.

God, I'm still embarrassed.

I barely have time to react to the memory because Nora is switching to FaceTime. I see her face, and she's giving me a look through our phone screens. I don't really know what the look conveys; I just know I don't like it when I get it.

"Do this. *Please.* I think if you see that there are still people out there who believe in you, it'll inspire you."

"Nora, they're going to be mean."

"You're right, they probably will be, but you won't see it because you aren't going to look at the comments. Leave it to me, okay?" she says. "I'm going live. You can hang up if you want, but I don't think you should."

I'm reacting like someone is asking me to bury a body for them. It's freaking Facebook, for Christ's sake. *Suck it up, Petra.*

I quickly run my fingers under my eyes, hoping to wipe away any leftover mascara smudges from the day.

Our readers were used to seeing us like this, though. Unpolished and real, usually in the middle of the night when inspiration (or in my case, frustration) struck. Nora and I used to go live on a whim all the time, mostly because we had smaller fan bases that were much more positive.

But the bigger I started getting, the meaner the questions became. And that was before the latest drama with my leaked text exchange.

For a while, our lives were a regular thing, so much so that we started monetizing them and counting on the paycheck to cover a few bills. Our late-night live videos were surprisingly popular on TikTok, gaining us more readers than any marketing strategy ever had. Writers tuned in because we were honest about the creative process—how hard it can be, how frustrating it is to write a sentence that feels right one minute and wrong the next. We talked about the days when we wanted to quit, and it seemed to resonate. I believe our transparency gave people comfort, made them feel like they weren't alone in their struggles. And it wasn't just writers—readers loved it too. They got an inside look at the making of our books long before they hit the shelves. Nora and I shared just enough to keep them interested, a line here, a plot point there, dropping hints that left them buzzing with anticipation.

I guess, in a way, it was like giving them insider access, a peek behind the curtain that they wouldn't get anywhere else. They didn't even mind the spoilers—they just wanted to be part of the process.

But then, a year ago, I stopped. Nora still goes live, but it's just her now.

"No TikTok, I promise," Nora says. "Just your Facebook group, and your group is private, so unless they're in the group no one will see this."

I can hear her hope building, though mine is laced with pure dread as I pull my laptop in front of me.

"Nora," I say in a pleading voice. "I don't think I can—"

"Just focus on me." Nora's voice cuts through my thoughts, calm and reassuring. "And on the camera. I'll vet every single question, Petra. You'll see how easy and familiar this is, and it'll make you feel so much better. You know better than anyone that nothing motivates us more than the readers. And you've cut yourself off from them for way too long. This is going to help you write, I promise."

I take a deep breath, try to smooth my hair a little, and open my group. I wait as Nora cues up the live video and invites me to join.

After getting a glimpse of my shadowy face on the screen, I jump up and flip on the kitchen light so my screen won't be so dark. The harsh overhead light flickers for a second before illuminating the room, casting long shadows against the walls. It's not flattering, but it'll do.

Just as I sit back down, we're live.

There's no countdown, no time to second-guess my appearance or what I'm going to say.

When Nora and I first started doing these live sessions, it felt a little awkward—like we were performing for an invisible audience. The pressure to be entertaining, insightful, or even just coherent was always there, however mild it was. But now, after a year of only Nora being on-screen, and my long absence, that pressure feels like it's going to make me combust.

"And . . . we're live!" Nora says. "You guys, I was finally able to nail Petra down with her busy schedule! She's here!"

I wave. And love that she makes it seem like I've been too busy for these, when all I've been is too terrified.

"Petra, I have missed you so much, you have no idea. How's life? Anything interesting to share?"

We both laugh, knowing the questions were rhetorical. Everyone knows how my life has been. But I answer with "Oh, you know. Same ol' same ol'."

"I know you're having a writer's getaway," Nora says. "The place looks new. Did they remodel the one you usually stay in?"

I look behind me and around me, holding the laptop to give readers a view of the place. "Nope. Had to pick one on the opposite side of the lake this time. But look at this place. It's insane."

"Wow. Should have invited me," Nora says.

"You know we never work when we're together."

"Yeah. Your fault, though. You're always turning on some addictive murder series, and then we get caught up in watching every episode, and before you know it, our days are up and vacation is over."

"Vacation," I say with a laugh. "I wish. I can't remember the last time I took a vacation."

"Oh, don't sound spoiled," Nora says. "You're in a sleek rental that isn't your home. I don't care if you're working or not—at least you aren't somewhere worse. Like here, in my apartment, having to listen to my neighbor fight with her ex over the phone every hour. Speaking of struggle, how is the writing going?"

I shrug, feeling the burden of my lack of progress settle in again. "I haven't even been here for a whole day yet, but I can just feel my stagnation on the horizon. Eighteen months and I barely have twenty pages."

Her brow furrows, and she tilts her head, her voice dropping into a more serious tone. "You need to talk through it?"

"I was about to go to bed when you called," I admit. "Already shut off my brain for the night."

Nora groans dramatically, throwing her head back. "I was hoping for a chapter or two."

I smile, despite myself. "You and me both."

Nora waves off my concerns with a dismissive hand. "You're way too hard on yourself."

I sigh, the familiar self-criticism rising to the surface. "I'm my own worst critic. Or at least I used to be."

She rolls her eyes at me, something she's done a hundred times when I get like this. "Did you at least decide on character names yet?"

"I did get that far." I shift in my chair, feeling a little proud of the progress, as small as it is. "Cameron is the main love interest of the heroine. He goes by Cam. The heroine will be Reya."

Nora's eyes light up. "Cam and Reya," she says, testing the names out. "I like those. Are they married, or do we get a meet-cute?"

"Both, in a way. Cam is married," I say, hesitantly. "At least in the outline I wrote almost two years ago."

Nora's eyebrow rises. "Oh. Unexpected. A triangle?"

I hesitate, glancing off-screen for a moment as if the answer might be hiding somewhere in the shadows. "I don't know. That's how I had planned it, but . . . I might change it. You never know." I originally outlined this story before the backlash from the adaptation, and I think that's part of what has me blocked. The fear that maybe I don't know what I'm doing when it comes to writing about things I haven't experienced.

"No, no, no," Nora says, leaning forward toward the camera, her expression an animated betrayal. "You know love triangles are my favorite. I want the triangle." She's whining now.

"Let's just hope I get at least one character fleshed out, much less three. Then we'll talk."

"Deal. Okay, let's take a question," Nora says, her eyes squinting as she scans the screen. Like she suggested, I have the chat box minimized and leave the sifting up to her.

"Here's one. Ally Panzano wants to know why this one has taken you so long to finish. '*You've always been a fast writer*,'" Nora says, reading off the question.

I lean back in my chair, wondering how to delicately approach this one. "If you're looking for complete transparency, I'd have to say . . .

the public attention. I'm not used to it. I don't like it. Not even the positive attention."

"It's true," Nora confirms. "She squirms just as much when she's complimented."

"I've always used writing as both an escape and therapy, and when you're in it and enjoying it, you aren't thinking about what comes after you finish writing. The book releases, the book tours happen, the interviews begin. I've never really found that stressful because I've always enjoyed the tours and release days. To an extent. I've never enjoyed the publicity, but the requests have been manageable. But now that my public image is amplified even more, everything that comes after the writing feels more fraught, so I stress about it more than I used to when things were less chaotic. The idea of finishing a book and writing *THE END* doesn't feel like it'll be an accomplishment. It actually fills me with fear that I'll have to enter that next phase of publicity. And that's what scares me now, because the publicity requests and content of the interviews have changed. And not everyone is born with a natural ability to speak in front of a camera, especially when you're being asked to speak on more than just your books."

Nora smiles at me. "Thank you for your vulnerability, Petra. That was a really good answer. Very honest. Okay, here's another one. *'Why did it sound like you're hesitating to write the love triangle in this new book? Is it because of what happened with the love triangle being cut out of the adaptation?'*"

"Is that a real question from a reader, or is that a *Nora* question?" I ask, raising a brow at her.

"It's a real one, I promise," she says, laughing.

I'm surprised at how I'm not hating this so far. It feels like the old days a little, and with each moment that passes, I start to feel more at ease.

"I'm not sure. After the last one, I obviously took the criticism to heart. This book I'm writing was meant to be a love triangle also, even though it's very different in every way. But I've never been in a love triangle, and they say write what you know. Maybe that's where I went wrong with the last book. I guess I find it difficult writing something I've never experienced," I say.

Nora lets out a laugh, a sharp burst of disbelief. "Bullshit," she says. "Your bestselling novel was about a woman who fell in love with an ex-convict. You've never dated an ex-convict."

"Exactly. And several reviewers said it was unrealistic."

Nora shakes her head, the look on her face a mixture of exasperation and fondness. "First of all, stop reading your negative reviews. Second . . . almost every negative review calls the book, or the characters, *unrealistic*. It's the go-to term for reviewers who didn't like something. I personally don't need every single thing in a book to be realistic. Dragons aren't realistic, but *Fourth Wing* is killing it on the charts."

"That's intentionally unrealistic," I point out. "It's called fantasy for a reason."

"Romantasy," she corrects. "Whatever. I can still recognize a good story when I read one. Realism is overrated. Sometimes people just want to escape into something that feels impossible, like it could never happen in real life. That's the beauty of fiction. Why do you think Lifetime and Hallmark are successful channels? They're escapes."

"Can we even call them *channels* anymore? Is that outdated? What are they now, apps? Services?"

"Don't get me started on how much I miss DIRECTV—it'll age me," Nora says. "Either way, the Lifetime and Hallmark storylines are some of my favorites. I could watch a cheerleader get murdered by a jealous mother a million times, and it still wouldn't get old."

I smile, but still feel the familiar tug of doubt. "You know what I really think it is? The primary reason I'm struggling with my writing?"

"Do tell," Nora says.

"I want the story to feel *real* when I'm writing it. But I'm not sure anything can feel real if I haven't lived it. Maybe I need to switch to fantasy and give romantic suspense a break. Either that, or *I* should take a break and go live a little. Do some dangerous, suspenseful shit. Get more life experiences under my belt."

"The feeling people get while reading is what matters," Nora insists, her tone more serious now. "*Real* doesn't always mean it's something you've lived. It just has to make people feel like it's possible. That's what you do, Petra. You make people believe in the impossible."

I nod, letting her words sink in, even though I'm not quite convinced. But that's the thing about Nora—she always believes in me, even when I don't believe in myself. And maybe that's enough to keep me going for another day.

"What do you know about realistic versus unrealistic? You've never dated an ex-con either," I tease.

Nora laughs. "That's what you think."

I smile, but inside I'm battling the usual frustration. I wish I could believe the numerous five-star reviews over the negative ones. The praise is right there, outnumbering the criticisms, but sadly, I seem to focus on the negative way more than Nora does. It's as if the negative comments hold more truth, like they're somehow more honest or insightful, even though logically, I know that's not true. Nora has always been better at brushing off the criticism, at trusting her instincts and her readers. Me, on the other hand, I tend to let the negative voices live rent-free in my head. But also, thanks to the notoriety the film brought to my career, I receive a lot more online scrutiny, so there is a difference. I used to have the same attitude as Nora.

"Maybe you should have an affair so you can really nail the emotions of your characters in this book," Nora says teasingly. "Find a married man who reminds you of Cam and sleep with him."

I laugh, but there's a part of me that cringes a little at how freely she just said that in front of who knows how many readers watching us live. My heart flinches, a familiar tremor of fear in relation to how one casual comment could be misinterpreted, taken out of context and used against us for clickbait. I can see it now—the headlines tomorrow will say something like **PETRA ROSE WANTS TO FUCK A MARRIED MAN!**

Nora never seems to filter herself, and it's one of the reasons I love her, but it also keeps me on my toes, especially now. "Where am I going to find a hot cop while I'm secluded in the middle of nowhere?"

"He's a cop? Wow, spoiler alert." Nora grins like she's got the perfect solution. "Maybe you should go somewhere a little less secluded. Start writing at Starbucks. Cops love coffee."

"Maybe you should go to sleep," I suggest. "It's late in New York."

"There are two hundred people firing off questions at us. Let's answer a few first," she says, glancing at the numbers ticking up on the live feed. Her fingers scroll through the flood of comments and questions popping up on her screen. I fix my gaze on her face, avoiding even looking at the number of viewers. I hold my breath, waiting for the inevitable harsh word, the cutting remark that will prove my fears right. But Nora's expression remains bright, unbothered. She's a pro at this, even if it's just our private group. She's shielding me, I realize, just like she promised.

Her eyes light up when she sees one that grabs her attention. "Here's a good one," she says, leaning forward toward the camera. "This person asks, '*Do you really believe a writer needs to personally experience a situation before they're able to capture how a character would truly respond? Isn't that what imagination is all about?*'"

Nora looks at the camera expectantly, raising her eyebrows at me as if to say "*This one's yours.*" I lean forward and fold my arms over the table, taking a moment to really think about it. The question feels heavier than most of the ones we get during these live sessions. It's a question that has been haunting me for the past year, echoing in the silence of my cabin. And this one is a hard one to address because it feels more like a jab than a question.

"Impostor syndrome is a tough thing to navigate," I say with a sigh. "Books on writing tell authors to let our imaginations run free, but those same books tell us to write what we know. Well . . . what if we *don't* know? But we want to write it? And then we get it wrong?"

"But there's really no wrong, is there? Every human responds differently to situations," Nora says, her voice still calm, a steady anchor in my rising tide of self-doubt.

"I feel like I certainly got it wrong," I say. "Look at the last year of my life."

Nora raises a surprised brow. "Well. Since you brought up the elephant in the room," Nora says, "I'd like to be able to address this if that's okay with you."

"Go for it. I'd love to hear what you have to say."

"We write *fiction*," Nora says. "For entertainment. I don't understand how and when the fun got flipped on its head. You wrote a book, and that should be praised. Hell, you've written dozens of books. Fun, entertaining, sometimes emotional books. Why has the backlash gotten so severe for authors when a reader doesn't agree with them, or hates their book, or their adaptation? It's a *book*. It's a *movie*. It's not brain surgery. We aren't saving lives."

"Some might argue against that," I say. "I mean, I get what you're saying, and I agree with the first part of what you said. That it doesn't feel as fun now that we're getting reviews in more forms than just ratings on Goodreads and Amazon. Now people make videos and dedicate entire social media accounts to reviews, so we see it more. Readers are more involved and have more impact, but that's also a positive thing. One good review that goes viral can change an entire author's life in a lot of positive ways. But I think you're wrong about books just being for entertainment. I personally think books and movies can be very powerful tools. They can change minds, behaviors, thought processes. And yes, they *can* save lives. I do believe reading can save lives."

"Interesting," Nora says. "Do you think books can *ruin* lives?"

What a great question. I'm not sure I'm prepared to answer it, but Nora gives me space to think about my response. "There are absolutely people who think books can ruin lives. That's why books get banned. Do I agree with them? Not with banning books. But I do worry that some readers, especially the younger ones who are reading books meant for adults, don't quite know where to draw the line between fiction and reality. We've seen how the behaviors of a character we intentionally wrote to be evil can occasionally be excused by a reader. Does that mean the reader would excuse those behaviors in real life? I hope not."

Nora slaps her hand on the table in agreement. "Yes! I swear, the number of people pleading for me to write a sequel to redeem that awful character from my first book makes me so sad for humanity," Nora says. "Don't get me started on the complexities of humans and their morals. It fascinates me how one person's experience and interpretation when reading varies so much from another person's experience who is reading those same words. I'll get emails from readers telling me a book was way too vulgar, and in the same day get an email from a reader complaining that the same book wasn't edgy enough. It's all so subjective. And confusing to navigate, especially when you're reading these opinions that come through to you all day. We're up, we're down, we're back up, we're down again. And sometimes, the same people who say books shouldn't be banned are the same people making a living off of saying certain books should never have been written. And then they go on to review in detail all the reasons why the book shouldn't have been written and why the author shouldn't be an author, but then their next post is a rant about the banning of books again. Make it make sense! Which is it? Ban the books or just beat the author down until they can't write anymore? And then some of them have the audacity to tag us in their rants as if we want to read about why we should quit our careers!"

Nora takes a deep breath after that tirade.

I don't know what's got her riled up, but I have a feeling not all the questions have been as safe as the ones she's read out loud.

"Thanks for letting me get that out," she says with a laugh.

"You're welcome. Maybe we should go back to another reader question before we lose all our readers," I tease.

Nora looks into the camera. "You know that wasn't directed at any of you guys," she says. "We love and appreciate our readers. We just don't necessarily want to be tagged in the hate. Now, back to the question at hand. I forgot the question at hand," she says.

"Should we write what we know, basically," I summarize.

"Oh yeah. I had a good answer for this before the rant. But yeah, sure, we could describe emotions and reactions better if we lived through each situation we ever write about. But how boring would books be if all authors did was write the things they've experienced and felt? It would be so limiting. I'm not here to write a biography. I do this to use my imagination. It's as much of an escape for us as it is for you guys."

"Agree," I say. "But I think every writer questions this themselves. Right?"

Nora waves off my comment like it doesn't apply to her. "I don't question it," she says confidently. "We're storytellers. Our job is to imagine lives beyond our own. If we had to live everything we write about, we'd be too busy having affairs with hot cops and chasing down murderous mothers of cheerleaders to actually sit down and write the books."

I chuckle at her candor, the tension in my shoulders easing just a fraction. Nora's eyes skim the screen again, and she reads off another question, clearly enjoying this back-and-forth.

"Here's a fun one: *If given the chance, would either of you willingly experience all the things your characters have ever gone through? Like the tornado that killed . . .*" Nora stops reading the question and says, "Spoiler alert, not finishing the rest of that sentence. But . . . *hell* yes," she says adamantly. "I think a tornado would be exciting. And I just finished writing a book about a hockey player falling in love with his agent. Sign me up. I'll take that romance any day."

"Ditto. Sign me up. For the hockey player, not the tornado."

"What about Carrie's life?" Nora asks, referencing her favorite character of mine. "Would you live that one?"

I put that poor character through hell, but I can't say I wouldn't have liked to experience it before writing it. It does make me wonder whether that book could have been even better if I truly knew the misery she was feeling. "You know what? Yes. I would do anything if it meant I would be a more confident writer. A *better* writer. I'd live through all my stories if it meant you guys would enjoy them more. Believe them. Five-star them."

There's a playfulness in my voice about the five-star part, but I'm being very serious. If living through these dramatic, heart-wrenching moments could make me a better writer, why wouldn't I? Sometimes I wonder if I'd get closer to the real emotions I'm trying to capture if I let myself live a little more recklessly. My current life is boring, predictable, and not at all worth writing about.

"Well," Nora says. "Next time you're in New York, we'll go cop hunting and see what happens."

We both laugh, but the question persists in the back of my mind long after that section of the conversation moves on. A writer asks Nora if she'll continue a series she says she stretched out two books too long. A reader asks us when we're going to write a collaboration.

"Never," we both say immediately.

"We have too many solo deadlines as it is," Nora says. "Also, that's the kiss of death for authors. It's rare to find two authors whose friendship survives it."

"Yes, we like our friendship too much to risk it."

We answer four or five more questions, with Nora still expertly filtering. I watch her face, her eyes scanning the comments, and occasionally she'll give a tiny, almost imperceptible shake of her head before moving on to the next question. She's keeping her promise. People aren't saying anything rude, or if they are, I'm blissfully unaware.

This really *is* easier than I thought. My responses are still a little more curated than they used to be, but the initial tightness in my chest is starting to loosen. I feel like the more I get back into this, the more candid and relaxed I'll become.

Nora is carrying the conversation, drawing me in with her infectious energy, and the familiarity of our banter slowly begins to resurface. The ease of our old live sessions, the feeling of just talking to Nora, starts to overshadow the awareness of the thousands of eyes watching.

I find myself relaxing into the rhythm, focusing on Nora's questions, on the friendly tone of the comments she reads aloud. It's like a tiny, safe bubble, a controlled exposure to the world I've been hiding from. Maybe this is the answer. Maybe doing things like this, gradually easing back into the public eye on my own terms, in a space that feels safe and familiar, will actually help. It's not the public forum I dread, anyway; it's the lack of control, the vulnerability to untamed negativity. But here, with Nora as my shield, I'm almost enjoying it. The conversation about realism, about the importance of imagination versus experience, even the playful jabs about dating cops . . . it all feels like stepping stones back to the comfortable routine I once had.

"Okay, I have to ask this one," Nora says. "Alex Brown wants to know if you'll ever do another movie adaptation since this last one seemed to be stressful."

"I hope so," I say with honesty. "I did enjoy that the book was being adapted. I just didn't enjoy the process, and how many people I had to work with and speak to. Writing a book is a solo mission until the editing phase, but working on a film is like welcoming a hundred people into your office with you every day. I bowed out of that as fast as I could. It was not for me."

I do sometimes wonder—if the result had been different, and there was no fallout, would I have felt differently about the process? I guess I'll never know, and neither will readers, because I'm never giving that adaptation a platform again. Not even to explain my side of things, or why I texted Allister what I texted him.

Because yes, Caleb was cut from the film, and yes, I did send that text. But it was the reasoning *behind* me sending that text that I still grapple with. Caleb was integral to the original story. I fought for him at first when they mentioned cutting his character. I argued his necessity, but not with the fire I usually have.

The truth is, I didn't trust myself enough. I thought the people in Hollywood who have made countless movies knew better than I did. At first, I did what I could, tried to articulate Caleb's importance and depth, but there was a certain detachment as I advocated for him in those endless production meetings. I presented my case, explained his arc, but deep down, a part of me felt like a fraud, fighting for a character with words born from feelings of inadequacy and incompetence.

In one of the meetings, Allister brought up several of the negative comments regarding Caleb's character, reading them out loud to the entire table of creatives. He said, and I quote, "*The character was written poorly in the book. He can't hold up to the brevity of the script. It could be detrimental to this film.*"

I didn't hear much after that. I was so mortified after that meeting, I went home and started contemplating the character more in hopes I could come up with reasons to fight for him harder in the next meeting.

Some reviews hinted at a lack of emotional depth in his character, or that he felt less vital than the others. There were murmurs on forums, questions about why his storyline felt underdeveloped compared to the rest.

Of course, in the midst of all that were all the people who absolutely loved and adored Caleb, but their words were whispers to me, and the negative words were more like screams.

My issue has never been with accepting criticism. My issue is that I tend to believe the criticism is the only truth, and find it much more difficult to believe the positive feedback.

By the end of that night, I was convinced the people in that room, including Allister, were right. That they knew better than I did about people *I* made up in *my* own head.

I caved over a text exchange with Allister. In the next meeting, Caleb was ultimately deemed expendable, a narrative casualty, and I couldn't shake the feeling that my own lack of conviction, possibly born from a lack of lived experience, played a role in his demise.

I just thought I didn't write him well enough. And I'm still not convinced I did.

These thoughts are still swirling in my mind, loud and persistent, when Nora wraps up the video. The conversation about "living the story" has opened a new avenue of self-doubt, focusing the spotlight squarely on my perceived shortcomings.

Yet, paradoxically, the live session itself wasn't the nightmare I anticipated. The fear I carried thanks to past experiences feels a tiny bit lighter now. Nora, in her unflappable way, proved that with the right safeguards, the reconnection with my readers doesn't have to be terrifying.

I attempt a smile for the camera, tell the readers good night, and then give Nora a quick, tired farewell. But the moment I close my laptop, a wave of relief washes over me, so intense it almost feels like physical release. I sit in the quiet, staring at the blank screen, and the doubts about my writing keep gnawing at me, a persistent little worm in my brain.

However, the broader fear of the internet, of the public, feels less like a monster under the bed and more like a grumpy old man who's been effectively muzzled. Maybe this private group, this controlled environment, is exactly what I needed to ease back into the book world.

A baby step, perhaps, but a step nonetheless.

I turn off the lights, the soft click of the switch echoing in the stillness of the cabin. I double-check the locks on the doors, the habit of someone who's spent enough time alone to know it's better to be safe than sorry.

The cabin is silent, save for the distant sound of the lake lapping against the shore, but I know that this is usually the time when the noise in my head is the loudest. It's like my inner critic decides to take up permanent residence, reminding me of every flaw, every scathing review, every scene I've questioned, and now, every time I didn't fight hard enough for a fictional character.

But for the first time in a long time, there's a faint whisper of hope, a tiny voice suggesting that maybe, just maybe, I can find my way back to the words. The possibility that a little controlled exposure to my readers, combined with the solitude, could be a good thing. It feels like a revolution, albeit a pocket-size one.

As I head to my bedroom, I think about tomorrow. I hope it'll be a more productive day, that I'll wake up with a clearer mind and a fresh perspective on this love triangle. And perhaps I'll be a tiny bit less afraid of the online world, thanks to Nora and a carefully vetted live stream that didn't spontaneously combust.

It will be okay.

CHAPTER FOUR

"It will be okay," I repeat to myself as I tear the plastic off my second 5-hour ENERGY shot of the day. It's my writing ritual.

Well, it's not so much a ritual as it is a really, *really* bad habit.

I avoid any type of soda or other carbonated beverage because it upsets my stomach, but for some reason, I can shoot a 5-hour ENERGY shot first thing every morning and it doesn't have a single negative effect on me. It just puts the pep in my step that coffee otherwise would. What makes it worse, though, is that by lunch, I convince myself I need five *more* hours of energy, so I'm up to two a day now.

I'm not sure it works that way—that two of them will give me ten hours of energy—but I've conditioned my brain to think it does, and now I can never be fully convinced I'm at my best until I've consumed both, and I can't be productive until I have them. Sometimes I drink them at the same time, which means soon, I'll start adding a third one later in the day.

Which, by all definitions, is an addiction.

I'm just waiting to give them up until either my heart gives out on me, or I retire, but as long as I'm here and forced to still work, 5-hour it is.

I prefer the strawberry banana flavor. They're all pretty terrible, but it's just a shot, so I hold my breath and down my second shot of the day. I toss the empty bottle into the trash can just as someone knocks at the front door.

My first instinct is to duck for cover, but my second instinct is that of a more mature adult. I head to see who's at the door, hoping it's just Louie and not someone new, but when I glance through the peephole, I'm not met with Louie's face. Instead, I come eye to eye with lots of bright-orange . . . stuff.

I just see a lot of orange, so I back up for a moment to let my eyes adjust. I look out the peephole again, and whoever was standing so close to the door has backed up now, and I can make out a head.

It's a woman with a lot of curls. Bright-orange curls hanging down to her shoulders. She's older than me, probably a little older than my mother. She's wearing a long silk dress, with a matching shawl covered in purple flowers. I can't tell if it's a nightgown or a fashion choice, but I do know that she's probably Louie's wife. Just a wild guess based on her age, the fact that she's here, and the pan of food she's holding.

If I hadn't had ten hours of energy shots already today, I'm not sure I could find it in me to open the door, because the way she's dressed combined with her hair makes me think she is not a quiet introvert. Luckily, I have the energy to meet someone new. I'm also curious if her hair is natural, so I open the door to greet her and to get a better look.

"Hi, hi!" she sings. Her voice is exactly as I imagined it—a little bit too loud and a lot chipper. And her hair is definitely not natural. That color is a conscious choice. But it works. Somehow.

"Can I help you?"

"You met my husband when you checked in." Her voice sounds solid and trained, like she could probably sing and project on a stage. "Just seeing if you need anything!"

"Hi. No, I'm good, thank you."

"Good, good," she says. I open the door wider, and her eyebrows twitch in excitement just a little bit at the thought of being invited inside. She holds up the tray. "Brought you some goodies."

"Oh. Wow."

She hands me a tin pan of something. "Brownies," she says. "Not the special kind. Sorry."

"Probably for the best," I say. "I'm not getting any work done as it is. The last thing I need is a cannabis-induced nap."

"Marigold," she says, reaching a hand toward me. "But please, call me *Ma*ri. Never Mary. Never Marie. *Mar*-ee," she says, enunciating. "I tried to make Gold work for a good year, but Gold doesn't flow well with my husband's last name. Longsetter. Gold Longsetter. Sounds like a dog breed."

I laugh, unsure if I should. "Nice to meet you, Mari. I'm Petra."

"Petra Rose. I know who you are. We watched that movie you wrote."

I can feel my chest heating up. If she watched the movie, and she knows my name, it makes me wonder what else she's heard about me. "Well, I didn't write the movie. I just wrote the book it was based on, but—"

She dismisses my next thought with a wave of her hand. "Yeah, I work in Hollywood—I know all about how these things run. Your idea, your book, *your* movie. That's how I see it, anyway." She motions with her head. "Can I come in? Won't stay long, I promise."

"Um. Sure." I open the door wider, and she makes her way in, her heels clacking on the concrete floor. She sighs as she makes a circle, taking in the kitchen.

"I just love it in here. I tried to get Louie to let us move in after the remodel, but he said it makes for the better rental." She pauses her circle and looks straight at me, her dress coming to a stop a few seconds after she does. "Guess he was right, because it attracted a big-time celebrity."

"Oh. I wouldn't say I'm a . . ."

"Not you. Not to say you *aren't* a big-time celebrity, but I wouldn't gush over you that way. It would be improper. I was talking about Michael Showalter. He stayed here a few years back. Before the remodel, but still, I'll give Louie the credit anyway because I'm a good wife, but Michael stayed here two whole weeks and even left a five-star review with his actual name on it. It's the review we highlight on our website now."

She can see on my face I have no idea who Michael Showalter is, and I can tell she can tell because she rolls her eyes, waving a hand. "I forget, you're a writer, not an actress. He's a director. Big time. Well, *medium* time. Either way, he wrote the review right there in our guest log," she says, pointing to a guest log sitting on the credenza beneath the television. "Said it was the best vacation he's ever had. It's on page thirty if you want to read it."

Mari motions toward a barstool for permission to sit, so I nod. She slides it out and takes a seat. "Did Louie tell you I'm an actress?"

"He started to talk about it, but I think the conversation got derailed." I walk into the kitchen. "Would you like something to drink?" She doesn't seem like she's keen to leave immediately, so the least I can do is be hospitable to this woman who would be *the* most unrealistic character if I wrote her straight into a book.

"Got any wine?" she asks.

"I do. Red, is that okay?"

She nods. "Me and Louie lived in Los Angeles most of our lives. We met there. He was a gripper, and I was an actress. I still act, but mostly just stuff for the ID channel. You know those murder-type shows? The short documentaries?"

"I do," I say, pouring her a glass. I slide it to her. "They're my favorite pastime."

She picks up the wineglass with the elegance of an old Hollywood actress. "I do the reenactments. You know how in the documentaries they'll be talking about a woman who gets murdered by her grandkids and they have those silent reenactments with people who pretend to be the murderer, or the murdered, or a detective? That's me, I've played dozens of different characters. I've done so many of them, I'd probably get recognized if I still lived in Los Angeles."

When I don't respond, or laugh, she pegs me with a pointed stare. "You are in your head, girl. That was a joke," she says, taking another sip of wine. "Shockingly, and contrary to what it may seem, I'm not that self-absorbed to think I'd be recognizable, although most people in the industry do think that about themselves. Boy, do I have stories I could tell you about some of these people you see on your television every day. I won't, because I've signed too many NDAs throughout my career, but if you get me drunk enough . . ."

She says the last line like a tease. A dare to pour her more wine. "Have you ever done any movies or shows I'd know?" I ask. "Or do you mostly stick to reenactments?" I'm just trying to keep up with her at this point so that I don't seem so quiet.

"Still waiting for my big break," she says. "You never know, lots of actresses have their big breaks late in life. Although, some people in the industry think once an actress starts to take the smaller roles, your chances of a big-time career are over, but I'll do anything for money. Any kind of proper acting job, anyway. I won't do the other stuff, you know, the improper stuff they give away for free on the internet now. But I'll do just about any other role to not have to work a nine-to-five. I've gone my whole life being able to pay bills with my art. A lot of actresses, they don't get their big break *or* become a household name, but they refuse to take on the roles that pay the bills in fear it'll crush their dreams. So they just die with all that rejection in their hearts and absolutely zero pride. Not me. Give me a prop, a wig, and a paycheck, and you've got yourself a happy actress. You ever seen that show called *I Survived...*? The one about the people who don't die, but they reenact how they *almost* died?"

"Yeah," I say, surprised I'm still following along. "Were you on it?"

"That's how I got started doing these kinds of roles. They use the actual people who survive in their episodes, along with actors, but lucky for me one of the ladies who survived a car wreck and then spent six days hanging upside down in a creek looked a lot like me, so I got her part and had to hang suspended in a car for eight hours every day while we filmed the episode. With breaks, of course—no one could actually safely hang upside down that long. Well, except for the lady who survived it, I guess she did. Anyway, it was the hardest part I've ever had to do, but I got paid the most for it. And because I was so professional, those producers have used me quite a lot since then, on a lot of their different shows." She takes a sip of her wine, and as she's sipping it, she starts to flap her other hand so fast, her bangles jingle.

"I'm so sorry," she says, setting the glass on the bar, waving her hand in apology. "I never shut up. Just tell me to leave when you want me to leave. Otherwise, I'll be here all night."

Oh, God. Please no.

I smile, despite the dread I'm feeling inside. "You're fine," I say, lying.

It's as if she can sense it, because she swigs the rest of her glass of wine and stands up. "Petra, if you knew how to hide your expressions better, I might have believed you wanted the company and stayed. Don't be polite to spare my feelings, or *any*one's for that matter. If you don't speak your feelings, your feelings don't exist. I'll get out of your hair."

"I'm sorry, it's just . . . I have so much work to do."

"Honey." She walks straight up to me and grips my shoulders. "If there's anyone who understands, it's me. I know how it is to be an artist. You are at the mercy of your muse." She pats my cheek with a cold hand. "You are so pretty. Successful *and* attractive—it is everything I dreamed of being. I kind of hate you." She skirts around me and walks to the door. "It was lovely to meet you. Loved your wine. Please text me a picture of the brand—I'll send you my number. Holler if you need me. And if you want to watch any of the stuff I've been in, I can send you my info. You never know when you might need an orange-haired sixty-year-old murderer in one of your movies."

"Sounds good," I say, laughing. And bewildered.

She swings open the door, leaving it for me to grab as she walks out onto the porch. "I know, I'm a lot to take in, but you'll miss me once I'm no longer here. I'm the type of person who seems overwhelming up front, but once you get to know me, I'm . . . well. *Still* overwhelming, but at least you'll know me." She begins to descend the steps.

"Mari?" I call after her.

"Yes, hon?" she says, spinning back around to face me.

"I think you totally could have gone by the nickname Gold. It fits you."

She stares at me thoughtfully a moment, then says, "Nah. Can't have a crazy name with this personality. At least one part of me needs to be tame."

And with that, she walks down the stairs and toward the road.

"I'll be back another day for the brownie tray!" she yells.

I close the door and make my way over to the dessert. When I pull the lid off, the smell of freshly baked brownies fills the air around me.

Two 5-hour ENERGYs and an entire pan of brownies before lunch.

Yes, please.

CHAPTER FIVE

No.

Something isn't right.

I sit up straight in bed, my heart hammering loud and wild in my chest as I slip the face mask off my eyes. The air in the room feels thick, the kind of suffocating quiet that follows an unexpected jolt from sleep. My mind races, trying to figure out what woke me. Was it a noise? A dream?

Whatever it was, it was disruptive enough to yank me out of a deep, blissful sleep, and now I'm wide awake, my senses heightened, my body tense with a rush of adrenaline.

It's probably Mari, here for more wine after two days of silence since her visit.

I'm still trying to regain my bearings when I notice the lights. Red and blue flashes are cutting through the darkness of the room, splashing across the walls like some kind of warning.

They're disorienting, casting long shadows that dance with each pulse of light, and for a moment, I can't tell if I'm dreaming or if this is real. My bedroom is on the west side of the cabin, so I can't see much from where I'm sitting, but the lights keep coming—urgent, rhythmic, and impossible to ignore.

There's a window directly behind my headboard, so I twist around and pull the curtain aside to get a look at what's happening outside. But all I can see are those flashing lights radiating from the front yard. I can't see any vehicles from my vantage point, just the constant pulse of red and blue illuminating the trees.

My mind immediately races to worst-case scenarios—was there an accident? A break-in? Why would the police be here, in the middle of nowhere? Is it Louie?

A loud knock at the front door snaps me out of my thoughts, making me flinch. My heart jumps in my chest, the sudden noise propelling me out of bed. The pounding is relentless, echoing through the cabin like thunder. I slip on my robe with shaky hands and grab my phone, my pulse quickening with each step toward the front door.

I check the time on my phone. It's almost five in the morning. The sun should be coming up soon.

I flip on the front porch light, the brightness flooding the small space in front of the cabin, and peer through the peephole.

The sight that greets me is unexpected. It's a police officer, standing a couple of feet from my door. His stance is casual, but there's an air of urgency in the way he cranes his neck, looking over his shoulder toward his patrol car.

The flashing lights from the car are so bright that they cast him in silhouette, making it difficult to discern his features. His profile is outlined by the harsh glow of red and blue, and for a second, I feel a strange disconnect, like this scene is happening to someone else and I'm just watching it unfold. My mind races with questions.

I hesitate for a moment, gripping my phone tightly, my fingers hovering over the screen. Should I call someone?

No, it's too late. Or too early. Either way, I can handle this.

It's probably just a misunderstanding—a wrong address, maybe. But that doesn't stop the unease from settling deep in my stomach as I take a breath and reach for the door handle.

With one last glance through the peephole, I unlock the bottom lock first, wondering what on earth could have brought a police officer to my quiet, secluded cabin in the dead of night.

My thoughts spin out of control as I stand here, hand on the dead bolt, hesitating for a moment longer before I finally release it. Even though I unlock the door, I leave the chain latched, opening it only a few inches. A small sliver of space, just enough to see out, but not enough to let anything—or anyone—inside.

Being a writer comes with a constant sense of distrust, no matter what uniform someone might be wearing. I've created too many plot twists, written too many villains disguised as heroes, not to assume the worst in every situation.

My brain automatically goes to the darkest places—*What if he's in a fake police car?*

For all I know, this guy could be posing as an officer, flashing fake credentials just so I'll open the door and make myself vulnerable. Too many crime stories, too much stolen valor, too many psychological thrillers. I've been conditioned to be suspicious of every scenario.

But still, curiosity and concern push me to at least hear him out.

When the officer hears the door creak open, he shifts his gaze toward me, locking eyes with mine. The flashing lights from his patrol car are still making it difficult to see his features clearly, distorting his face in alternating washes of red and blue and shadows. My eyes are still heavy with sleep, making the whole situation feel surreal, like I'm caught between a dream and reality.

But even with the disorienting lights, there's one thing I can tell for sure—this is not your stereotypical donut-and-coffee-for-breakfast kind of cop.

He's tall, broad shouldered, and muscular, the kind of guy who looks like he spends more time in a gym than a precinct. The sight of him standing here, so authoritative and composed, makes me suddenly hyperaware of my own appearance. I'm still in my robe, underdressed and vulnerable, a detail that makes me pull the robe tighter around my body.

I have no idea why he's here, but part of me, maybe the writer in me, can't help but appreciate the timing. If I had to imagine what Hot Cop Cam from my book would look like, this guy would be it.

My brain catalogs the moment, storing away the image of him for later use. *This is the face you need to put on Cam,* I think, a small smile tugging at the corner of my lips despite the odd circumstances.

The officer holds up his badge, the metal catching the porch light for a moment. I squint, my eyes landing on his name and then on the glint of a wedding ring on his left hand. *Of course he's married.* Not that it matters, but it's another detail my overactive mind clings to as I add to the list another similarity between this guy and my character.

I feel like I just found my muse.

"Sorry to disturb you, ma'am," he says in a scratchy deep baritone that seems to vibrate through me. "I'm Officer Nathaniel Saint."

I stare at the badge, reading his name again, even though it's already etched in my memory. My heart is still racing, but now it feels like a different kind of racing, equal parts nerves and something else I can't quite name. I bring my hand up to my throat, pressing it against my skin as if I can physically calm my own heart down.

As Officer Saint lowers his badge, putting it back into his pocket, I realize this isn't some dream or figment of my imagination.

This is real.

There is a police officer standing at my door in the middle of the night, and that can only mean one thing: *Something bad has happened.*

Panic surges through me as my thoughts immediately jump to my family. Did something happen to someone I care about? The cold rush of dread washes over me, making it hard to breathe as a thousand horrible scenarios flash through my mind.

As if sensing my unease, Officer Saint softens his voice, his tone smoothing over like he's trying to reassure me. "There's nothing to worry about," he says, his voice gentler now, more calming. "I'm just here to inform you that there was an incident that occurred on this road tonight. I just have a couple of questions if you don't mind. Protocol."

I let out a shaky breath of relief, my tension easing a little at the words.

Everyone is safe. No one I love is hurt.

I nod, feeling a wave of gratitude wash over me, and unlatch the chain lock on the door. The officer isn't here to deliver bad news, just to ask some questions. I can handle that. But then my mind wanders to Louie and his wife, Mari.

"Are the neighbors okay?" I ask as I open the door wider. I'm met with a cool breeze that makes me even more acutely aware of how underdressed I am. The night air wraps around me, and I instinctively cross an arm over my chest, feeling exposed. I gesture toward the kitchen, inviting him inside.

"They're fine. Just left their place."

I sigh in relief, but am still confused. "Come in," I say, my voice quieter now, as if the weight of the situation is starting to sink in.

As Officer Saint steps inside, I notice just how tall he is. He's at least five inches taller than me, maybe more. He takes up more space than his body requires, his presence commanding but not overbearing. I close the door behind him, still feeling a little disoriented, but thankful the night's chill is now shut out.

"What kind of incident?" I ask, my voice steadier now, though my mind is still buzzing with unanswered questions. I motion toward the kitchen table, but he declines my offer. "What happened?"

"This shouldn't take long," he says, remaining near the door.

This is not exactly how I pictured my night going, but then again, I guess that's the nature of plot twists. And now that I know everyone is safe, I welcome this intrusion. It's the most dopamine I've had in years.

I stand a few feet from him, keeping a cautious distance between us, unsure if it's from instinct or the strange, almost surreal feeling of having a police officer standing in my cabin. He remains close to the doorway. He seems aware of the tension, the delicate balance of not wanting to overstep while still delivering whatever news he's here to share.

I can't help but wonder how old he is. I'm thirty-four, and I look every bit of it, give or take a couple of years. But with him, it's hard to tell. My eyes are still trying to adjust to being awake, to the lights outside, making his face shift in and out of focus. He could be younger than me, late twenties, maybe, but then again, he could be older.

There's something experienced in his expression that makes me think he's older than me, though. A lack of gentleness in his eyes that suggests someone who has been exposed to too much of the world's harshness. That could be years of experience at a job like this and not at all an indicator of his age.

But then again, it could be a hardened, trained expression, something he's perfected in his line of work. A calm demeanor and reassuring looks aren't requirements for a job like his. Police officers probably learn to mask their own emotions when delivering difficult news, which is why most of them seem so serious.

The officer's eyes scan the room for a moment, briefly taking in the surroundings of my cabin, before they land back on me.

There's a slight pause, as if he's choosing his words carefully. "Do you know a man by the name of Don William Puttman?" he asks, his tone professional but cautious, like he's testing to see if the name means anything to me.

I shake my head, frowning slightly. The name doesn't ring a bell. "No," I say, and he seems to relax a little when I give him my answer. There's a visible shift in his posture, like a weight has been lifted. He leans against the doorframe, his hands resting at his sides in a more casual stance.

As I watch him, I can't help but take a few mental notes. He's *perfect* for Cam. It's like the universe knew I needed inspiration and dropped this officer on my front porch at the perfect moment.

His posture, his voice, even the way his uniform hugs his frame— all of it is exactly what I've been searching to find the words for. I haven't felt like writing character descriptions with the creative fog hanging over me, but seeing him standing here, in the flesh, is sparking something. I feel a strange, urgent need to get this interaction over with so I can go straight to my laptop and start typing.

"There was a police pursuit that ended on this road," he explains, motioning toward the road outside, where the lights are still flashing in the distance. "We've secured the scene, but we're going to have officers nearby—possibly on your property—for the next hour or so. I just wanted to come by and let you know there's nothing to be concerned about."

I nod, trying to process what he's saying.

A police pursuit? On this road?

The rural isolation of the cabin makes it seem impossible that something so dramatic could happen here, in the middle of nowhere.

Before I can ask more questions, he continues, "And of course, to see if there's a reason the victim was heading in this direction. It is a dead-end road. But since you don't know him—"

"Victim?" I interrupt, the word catching in my throat.

The officer nods, his face darkening a little as he glances away, clearly not thrilled about delivering this part of the news. "Yes, ma'am. He, uh . . ." There's a discomfort to him that's unsettling. "It was self-inflicted."

Oh.

I feel my stomach drop, and I instinctively wrap my arms around myself, a subconscious effort to ward off the sudden chill that seems to have swept through the room. I blow out a slow, shaky breath, trying to wrap my mind around what he's just said. *Self-inflicted.* Someone came this close to my cabin—this close to *me*—and ended their life.

"Someone just . . . killed themselves? Near here?" I whisper, the words sounding hollow as they leave my lips. I don't know why I repeat them out loud. Maybe saying them helps me believe it, or maybe I'm hoping there's some mistake, that he'll correct me and assure me it's not as bad as it sounds.

But the look on his face tells me otherwise.

He nods again, his expression softening with sympathy. "He'd been to prison before and recently broke parole . . . I'm sure he knew he had warrants and if he got caught, he'd have to go back, so he . . ."

I put up a hand and nod to cut him off. He doesn't need to finish the sentence. I know how it ends.

I swallow hard, my mind still struggling to catch up with this new reality. The quiet of the cabin, the stillness of the night—it feels wrong now, tainted somehow. I've always searched for solitude, for peace, but tonight it feels like a place where something dark has taken root. Something I won't be able to shake.

The officer, sensing my distress, gives me a moment to process. "We'll be out of your way soon," he says gently. "Just wanted to make sure you were aware of what was going on and to see if you had any information that could help us. Any ties to the victim that we should be aware of before we notify next of kin."

I shake my head again, feeling numb. "No. I don't . . . *didn't* . . . know him."

"Okay," he says, his voice calm and steady. "If you need anything, just let one of us know. We'll be close by."

I nod, barely registering the words.

Tomorrow, I'll write about this. I'll try to make sense of it through my characters, through their emotions. But tonight, all I can do is stand here, trying to comprehend the fact that someone came so close to me, so close to this quiet, safe place, and made the decision to end their life.

"I may need a statement," he says, his voice steady, professional, but with an underlying gentleness that doesn't quite match the somber situation he just explained. "But we don't have to get that tonight. I can send an officer by tomorrow if you don't mind. It's protocol. We're asking both homeowners on this road for information."

"Yeah," I say, nodding. "That's fine. I'll be here all day. I'm not a . . . I'm just here for a visit. I don't own this place." I have no idea why I'm explaining that I'm not the homeowner like it's going to help me get out of a murder I didn't commit.

"Well. Enjoy your stay. Despite . . . this." He dips his head in a slight nod, preparing to turn and leave, but then he pauses. He hesitates for just a second, and I see something flicker in his eyes before he turns fully back to me. "Are you here alone?"

I hate that question. It's such an innocent inquiry on the surface, but there could be more to it. There's no good way to answer it. Sure, he's a cop, and maybe I should feel safe answering him honestly, but he's also a man. A complete stranger, standing at my door in the middle of the night.

My thoughts tumble over each other as I attempt to figure out how to respond. A lie about a husband in the bedroom seems smart in theory, but with a police investigation happening just feet from my cabin, lying to a cop doesn't seem like the brightest idea. Yet admitting that I'm alone feels like inviting vulnerability, like putting a target on my back.

I must look torn, because the sudden understanding in his expression becomes evident. Before I can answer, he speaks up again, his tone softening, as if he senses my unease.

"Not that I'm assuming you can't take care of yourself," he adds quickly. "But . . . just be cautious. If you have conversations with people in town, make sure to give the impression you aren't out here alone. Wear a wedding ring when you're out and about if you can."

As he's opening the door, his words hit me in a way I didn't expect. This town, this quiet little place where I've repeatedly come for solitude and peace, has always felt like a sanctuary. A place where I could escape, recharge, and write without interruption or fear. But the way he's talking now makes it seem like there's more beneath the surface. It's unsettling, like I've been missing something all this time.

"Should I be worried?" I ask, my voice quieter than before. "Is this a bad area?"

He's now standing in the open doorway. He glances out into the yard, his gaze momentarily drawn to the flashing lights still illuminating the trees. Then he looks back at me, his eyes steady but unreadable. "No area is perfect," he says after a beat, the words careful and diplomatic. He tips his hat again, signaling the conversation is over. "You should always be cautious. Sorry to interrupt your night. Someone will be in touch tomorrow."

He turns to leave, heading across the porch that leads to the stairs, but something inside me panics. I don't know why, but I feel a sudden urge to stop him, to keep him here just a little longer. Maybe it's the shock of everything—the dead body so close to my home, the strange advice he just gave me about pretending not to be alone. Or maybe it's just the raw fear settling into my bones.

Either way, before I can stop myself, I call out, "Wait."

He pauses on the bottom step, turning around to face me again. There's a look of concern in his eyes now, like he knows why I stopped him, even if I can't quite put it into words myself. I stand there, gripping the doorframe, feeling small and unsure, like a child asking for reassurance after a bad dream.

I don't know why I called after him. I just feel . . . scared. This man shows up to tell me a guy killed himself, and now he's leaving, and I'm supposed to just . . . go back to sleep?

"I'm sorry," I say, embarrassed I look so scared, and embarrassed I asked him to wait. I wave a hand, letting him know I've changed my mind. "It's just a lot to take in."

He takes a slow step back toward me, his expression softening as he speaks. "There's not much else I can do here," he says gently. "I'm needed back at the scene. But I'll make sure there are extra eyes on your place tonight. You'll be fine."

His words are meant to reassure, but the cold gust of wind that sweeps over me makes it hard to believe. I wrap my arms tighter around myself, trying to hide the chill that has settled deep in my stomach. I've always felt safe on my writing retreats, but after the last several minutes, that sense of security has been chipped away.

"Okay," I whisper with a nod, but my voice is unconvincing, barely more than a breath. The officer can see right through my concern, and for a moment, I wonder if he's reconsidering leaving me here alone.

He ascends the last steps and comes back to me, pulling something out of his pocket as he approaches. It's a business card. He hands it to me, and I look down at the bold print on the top: **Detective Nathaniel Saint**. Beneath his name are an email address and two phone numbers.

"I didn't mean to worry you," he says gently. "The top number is my cell. If you need anything at all, don't hesitate to call me."

I clutch the card in my fist, a small comfort in the midst of this surreal situation. "Thank you," I murmur, my fingers curling around the card as if it holds some kind of protection.

"How long are you here for?" he asks, his eyes searching mine with genuine curiosity. "I'll make sure an officer drives by a couple of times a night for the duration of your stay."

"A few weeks," I reply, feeling a little embarrassed for some reason. There's something in the way he looks at me, like he's trying to figure out why a woman my age would be holed up alone in a cabin for so long. "I'm a writer," I explain quickly, hoping that will suffice. "I stay in this area a couple of times a year, usually in the month leading up to a deadline."

His eyebrow lifts, a hint of surprise and admiration in his expression. "A writer," he repeats, as if testing the word. "What kind of books do you write?"

"Mostly romantic suspense," I say, feeling oddly self-conscious as I admit it. "And the occasional short story, but . . ." My voice drifts. "Sorry, I hate talking about my job. It's awkward."

He gives me a small smile, his lip twitching slightly. "What's your name?"

For a second, I have the wild urge to tell him my name is Reya—the name of the character I've been writing about. The urge is so strong that I almost blurt it out, but I catch myself just in time. I can't lie to a cop. Instead, I give him my real name. Begrudgingly.

"Petra Rose."

He smiles a little wider, but not from familiarity. He nods as if he's committing it to memory. "I'll be in touch tomorrow, Petra Rose."

I watch him as he walks down the length of my driveway, his figure eventually swallowed up by the blinding patrol lights. He folds himself into a midnight-black car, only visible because of the lights.

Once he reverses and rejoins the activity down the road, I close the door and lock it behind me. I lean against it for a moment, my heart still racing, and glance down at the business card in my hand. *Nathaniel Saint.* Even his name sounds like it belongs in one of my books.

He could definitely be Cam.

Despite the time and the strange events of the night, I feel a sudden burst of inspiration. I walk straight to my laptop, the unexpectedness of the events pushing me forward. The details of Detective Nathaniel Saint swirl in my mind, and I can't resist the urge to write them down.

I recall everything about him—his voice, his presence, the way he made me feel both uneasy and comforted at the same time.

The words pour out of me like they haven't in a long, long time. Somehow, the fear, the uncertainty, and the strange energy of the night have all worked together to crack open the creative block I've been struggling with.

Nathaniel Saint has become Cam, and with every word I type, the story starts to flow again.

I cannot believe tonight just happened.

CHAPTER SIX

"You are not going to believe what happened last night," I say, practically vibrating with a mix of disbelief and exhilaration, the phone pressed tight to my ear. Sunlight streams through the kitchen window, but my mind is still replaying the bizarre, utterly unexpected encounter that somehow, miraculously, jump-started my brain.

"Oh good, something dramatic," Nora says, ever the enthusiast for chaos. "Tell me everything. Did you finally get to page twenty-one?"

"Something infinitely better." I can practically hear Nora's ears perk up. "I had a visitor. A very, *very* unexpected visitor. And . . . he was a *cop*."

A beat of silence. Then, a dramatic gasp from Nora. "A cop? Petra, what did you *do*? I swear, if you're writing your next book from jail, I am not sending you care packages."

"No, nothing like that," I assure her, already picturing her imagining me in an orange jumpsuit. "There was a police chase that ended near my rental. Some convict. But he shot himself in the road, and then a cop knocked on my door to see if I knew him. At, like, five in the morning. I almost died, I was so scared. But oh, my God, you should have seen him."

"The cop?" Nora asks. "Or the dead guy? There was actually a real-life dead guy? Jesus, Petra. Did you see a body?"

"Well, *real-life dead guy* makes no sense, but yes, it actually happened. I'm not talking about the dead guy, though, I'm talking about Cam. The cop."

"HIS NAME WAS CAM?"

"*No.* It's just what I call him because he's exactly who I'm picturing as Cam now."

Nora's voice drops to that conspiratorial whisper she uses when she's truly invested. "This is crazy. See? The universe is on your side. Was he hot? Because if it's a cop, and it's rural, there's like a fifty-fifty chance he looks like he either hunts his own dinner in a fitted flannel shirt, or he can't jump a fence."

I lean against the counter, a genuine smile spreading across my face. "Nora. He was . . . *so* hot. And his name is even hot. Detective Nathaniel Saint." I let the name hang in the air, relishing it.

Another gasp, even louder this time. "Stop it. That is such a book-boyfriend name. You have to be making this up. You probably fell asleep at your keyboard and dreamt him."

"I swear it happened," I insist, pushing off the counter and pacing the kitchen. "He was tall. And had these intense eyes. And the way his uniform fit . . . Ugh. My brain just immediately went, '*Hello, Cam. Meet Reya's leading man.*' It was like a sign, Nora. Like the universe decided to send me an actual living, breathing muse."

"Your muse!" Nora crows, a triumphant note in her voice. "I knew it! The universe *does* love us! So, did you, like, get his number? Did you flirt? Did you offer him a cup of coffee and accidentally spill it on his very attractive uniform so you could help him take it off?"

I roll my eyes, though I'm still grinning. "No, you lunatic. I was too busy trying not to hyperventilate. But after he left, I couldn't stop thinking about him. And then, I just *wrote*. I wrote pages, Nora. Actual, coherent pages."

"No way," she says, her tone shifting from playful incredulity to genuine surprise. "You're not pulling my leg? You actually wrote something?"

"I'm serious," I say, pulling up the file on my laptop. "I'm sending you the pages now."

There's a pause on Nora's end, the sound of her typing, then a small "Ooh!" of surprise. "Petra! This is almost ten thousand words!" Her voice is practically giddy now. "See? I told you. You just needed a little reconnection to the book world to kick that block to the curb. And now karma's dropped a hot cop in your lap. I think you're getting your mojo back."

"I guess so," I admit, feeling a warmth spread through me that has nothing to do with the sun. It's the warmth of words flowing again, of a story finally taking shape. "Writing just feels so . . . *right*, suddenly. Like something has been unlocked. I forgot how exciting it is."

"You unlocked a payment from your publisher soon, that's what you unlocked," she says. "Okay, so here's the crucial question. Is there a Ring camera? Do you have any security footage? Because I need a visual. For research purposes, obviously."

I sigh dramatically, leaning my forehead against the cool surface of the refrigerator. "Believe me, I wish there was a camera. Or that I had thought to subtly, discreetly, *incognito*-ly snap a picture of him."

The lingering image of him, framed by my cabin doorway, feels almost like a dream now, a vivid mirage. And while the words on the page are a fantastic start, a small, selfish part of me craves that visual proof, a physical anchor to the man who seemingly broke my curse.

"I have to go," I say, already feeling the pull back to my laptop. The well of inspiration, so recently dry, is now overflowing. "I have to jot more down before he vanishes back into the ethereal realm of 'hot cop muses.'"

"Go, go! Don't let Cam escape. And seriously, if you get any surveillance footage, you know who to call."

"You'll be the first," I promise, already picturing myself hunched over the keyboard. Just as I'm about to end the call, there's a sudden knock on the door. *Could it be?*

"Okay, gotta go," I say.

"Wait," she says, and my finger pauses on the screen while I head to see who is at my front door. "This means you're on for another live stream, right? Readers will go apeshit over this."

A tiny flicker of the earlier anxiety returns, a whisper of doubt. But then the image of the detective, tall and compelling, flashes in my mind, and everything in my life feels a little bit more manageable. More salvageable. "Fine," I sigh, a smile touching my lips. "As long as you vet everything and read all the questions again."

Another knock at the door.

"Wouldn't have it any other way," she says. "Good luck!"

I end the call and look through the peephole, but my hope that it might be the cop is diminished when I see Mari standing at the front door.

I sigh, but open the door anyway. "Hey, Mari." I motion for her to come in. She's probably here for her brownie tray, so I head to the counter where I set it after washing and drying it.

"You get any sleep with all that ruckus last night?" she asks.

I shrug. "Enough." I hand her the tray, but instead of heading toward the door, she walks over to the table and pulls out a chair.

I guess I'm having company.

She flicks her dress out so that it billows over the chair before she takes a seat. "How about those cops?" she asks. "Wasn't too happy to see them at our door, but they sure were easy on the eyes."

"I only met one of them," I say.

"I hope it was the hotter one," she says. "Well, they were both good looking, but the tall one, my goodness. This road hasn't seen that much action since that group of swingers booked the place three summers ago."

I never know what's going to come out of her mouth, I swear.

Mari notices the business card the officer left. It's sitting on the table between us, so she picks it up, tapping it against her finger. "Yes, this one," she says. "The tall one. Nathaniel Saint."

"Do you know him?"

"Nah, I keep away from authority as much as possible. Never know with those guys. I keep out of most of the city and county stuff unless some dumbass on the city council is trying to suggest a law to ban rentals on the lake. Twice they've tried that, and twice me and Louie have gone and put a stop to it. This is our income, and I'll be damned if I have to go get a nine-to-five. What a nightmare that would be." She feigns wiping away sweat. "Working away at some desk job that rots my soul until artificial intelligence deems me unnecessary before I'm even eligible for retirement, so I'm forced to rely on the hope that there's a niche market on OnlyFans for an aging wannabe actress with hair like a Cabbage Patch doll. No thank you."

She drops the business card back on the table but is still staring at it when she says, "If I didn't see the dead body for myself, I'd think I dreamt it, but they talked to both me and Louie for a good half hour."

"You . . . saw the body? *What?*"

"Heard the commotion. I'm nosy. Don't worry, they got it all cleared out. Only thing left over from last night that I saw on the walk over was some spray paint markings in the road. Happened right in front of this house, you know. I was kind of expecting to see an outline of him on the asphalt, just like they do in the shows I work on, but they didn't do that. Probably because it wasn't a murder and they got it on dashcam since they were in pursuit, but still. Would have been cool to see."

Cool is not the word I would use to describe that, but okay. It is so hard to keep up with her; I don't know how Louie does it. Maybe he doesn't. Either way, her reminder of last night makes me tense up, despite her effervescent personality.

"Straight out of a crime novel," she continues. "Too bad you don't write suspense, Petra. That could have been some good motivation."

I do write suspense. "Mari, what kind of books do you think I write?"

She shrugs. "Romance? I don't know, I should probably read one. Which one do you recommend?"

"None of them," I say honestly. "They are suspense novels, though, but there are so many other books I'd recommend to you if you like that genre."

Mari swats at my arm. "Stop that self-deprecation. It is so unattractive."

I didn't even realize I was being self-deprecating. I call it honesty.

"Let's try having this conversation again," she says. She straightens up, eyeing me. "Petra, which of your books do you suggest I read?"

She's right. I never answer this question with pride, so I commit to at least trying. Maybe it will improve my current attitude toward my career.

"Start from the beginning," I say, feigning confidence. "The release order is on my website. If you like the first one, you'll be able to see my writing progress as you work your way through the books."

Mari grins. "That's better. I'll visit your website. What is it? The Pitiful Petra dot com?"

She laughs at her own joke, but then says "Kidding" before I have time to find the humor in it. "You just act so pitiful when it comes to your career. I'm gonna compliment that pitiful out of you before you leave here," she says as she stands. "Let me know if you ever need a shopping break. I'm going estate hunting in the morning if you're interested."

"Not sure I need the distraction yet," I admit.

"I'll text you before I leave, just in case," she says. She grabs her pan and heads toward the door. "Maybe we'll get lucky and Louie will have a heart attack so we have an excuse to call the cops over here again."

"Jesus, Mari."

"A *mild* one," she says, dismissively. "I don't want him to die. Who would drive me to Los Angeles for all my auditions?" She winks at me and then closes the door behind her.

I stand up and lock it, then walk back over to the table.

I pick up the business card sitting next to my laptop. I scroll my thumb over Detective Saint's name, wondering what people call him. There are so many possibilities, but I imagine I'd call him Saint if I knew him on a more intimate level.

Do people call him Nathaniel? It seems too formal, too stiff for someone who carried himself with such confidence and ease.

Maybe they call him Nathan, a little more approachable, relaxed. Or maybe he's just Nate to those closest to him. Or is he simply *Detective* to everyone?

Whatever people call him, I've been anxiously waiting for him to show back up. I should have asked Mari if they mentioned to her that they might return for a statement.

Surely, he'd need to take my statement, right? Last night, he said he'd be in touch today, or that *someone* from the precinct would be, and a part of me has been counting down the hours, expecting to hear the knock on my door any minute before the workday ended. But as the afternoon dragged on and the sun started to sink lower in the sky, I realized it was already nearing six o'clock, and I still hadn't heard from him.

Just one knock, and it was Mari instead of the man I was hoping it would be.

Maybe they decided against asking the residents for statements after all. Maybe, in the light of day, they realized it was a waste of time, that the case was open and shut. Like Mari said, the man who died took his own life. Isn't much more to investigate.

The thought feels logical, but it also leaves me with an odd sense of disappointment. I have a million questions about the events of last night, and not just for my own peace of mind.

For a writer, this is a rare opportunity. A chance to talk to a real detective, to ask him the kinds of questions that could add a layer of authenticity to my book. How often do I have a muse at my door, straight out of my work in progress?

And yet, the day is slipping away, and it seems like that opportunity might not come.

Still, part of me doesn't want to let it go. What if I text him? Just to check in, to see if they still need my statement. I could frame it as a polite inquiry, but it would also be a subtle way to get him to respond, to reestablish that contact. And if nothing else, maybe it would open the door for me to ask some of the research questions that have been building in my mind since last night.

My fingers hover over my phone screen for a moment, debating if this is a good idea. Finally, I look at the business card phone number and type out a quick message.

> Hi. It's Petra Rose. Do you guys still
> need a statement from me?

I hit send before I can second-guess myself. The text is straightforward, professional, but also casual enough that it won't seem out of place if he responds.

I'm not sure what I'm expecting. Maybe a delayed response, or a formal reply from one of his colleagues from a different phone number. But to my surprise, my phone vibrates almost immediately. His response comes back faster than I anticipated, and there's something about that speed that makes my heart skip a beat.

> We've been short-handed today.
> Sorry about that. If it's not too late, I
> can swing by on my way home.

I reread his text, my stomach swirling at the thought of seeing him again. There's something casual yet considerate in his tone, like he's apologizing for being late to an unscheduled appointment, while also offering to make it up to me. And though it's all business on the surface, I can't help but feel a surge of excitement roll through me at the thought of him stopping by, even if it's just to take my statement.

> Sounds good. If you have a few minutes while you're here, I have questions about some scenes I'm writing. I could really benefit from picking the brain of a police officer.

I send the message quickly before I can overthink it. It's true—I do need some insight for my book, and having an actual detective to talk to is an opportunity I can't pass up. But if I'm honest with myself, it's more than that. There's a part of me that just wants to see him again, to spend a little more time in his presence, to feel that strange mix of curiosity and attraction that he sparked the first time he showed up at my door.

> I'm all yours. Be there in an hour.

His response comes almost immediately, and it's that first sentence that makes my breath catch. *I'm all yours.* It's a simple phrase, probably meant as a professional gesture, but it hits me in a way I didn't expect. Excitement rolls through me, warm and electric, as I read it again.

I don't even hesitate. I immediately rush to my bedroom to change clothes. I glance at myself in the mirror, realizing with a bit of embarrassment that I've already changed three times today, each outfit picked with the possibility in mind that he might come back. It's ridiculous, I know. I don't normally bring many cute clothing items when I hole up in a cabin to write. My usual wardrobe consists of sweatpants, old

T-shirts, and a few hoodies I rotate depending on the weather. I'll pack maybe one or two jeans and shirts that I use in case I get a wild hair and go to the grocery store. The most flattering thing I have with me that doesn't scream *trying too hard* is a sundress that could easily pass as something I'd lounge around in on a lazy afternoon.

I slip it on, smooth it down, and decide to go barefoot to keep the look casual. I pull my hair up in a messy bun, just loose enough to look effortless, and put on the slightest touch of makeup. Just enough to give my skin a subtle glow, to make it look like I haven't tried at all. It's a delicate balance, one I don't often concern myself with, but tonight feels different.

I sit at the kitchen table, trying to focus on the questions I want to ask him about my book while I wait for his arrival. I jot down a few actual procedural questions I have, but then write a few fake questions I don't actually have, framing them in a way that makes it seem like I'm being productive, like this is purely for research purposes. But it's for entirely selfish reasons.

Last night, after he left and I wrote several chapters, I was filled with a euphoria I haven't felt in years. There's something about putting a real-life face to my fictional character that made the story flow effortlessly. I've always imagined Cam in a vague, abstract way, but now that he's based on someone who actually exists—someone I've met—it feels like the words are coming to life in a way they haven't before.

The knowledge that Cam is now inspired by Detective Nathaniel Saint has done wonders for my confidence in this story. It helps minimize the nagging fear I always have that readers will call my work unrealistic. How could it be unrealistic if I'm writing Reya's reactions to Cam based on my own reactions to Detective Saint? I've never felt more in tune with my character, and it's all because of him.

When the knock finally comes, my heart leaps into my throat. But instead of rushing to answer, I force myself to pause. I stand on the other side of the door, my hand hovering over the handle, and I count to thirty. I want it to seem like I'm preoccupied, like I haven't been waiting all day for this moment.

Taking a deep breath, I finally open the door, ready to see where this next chapter takes me. I try to seem collected, determined to maintain some semblance of professionalism. But the moment I see him, all my composure slips away.

I'm shocked to see him out of uniform. Instead of sporting the crisp, authoritative look I've come to associate with him, he's dressed casually, and I do exactly what I told myself I wouldn't do. I check him out.

My eyes can't help but scan him from head to toe, taking in every detail. He's wearing faded jeans, the kind that look soft from years of wear, with a few paint splatters on them that give him an effortlessly rugged look. His T-shirt, snug enough to show off the lean lines of his torso, has a fist up in the air and the word **Gonzo** printed across it. A Hunter S. Thompson T-shirt. I wonder if that was deliberate, if he's making some kind of subtle, intellectual nod toward my writing career, or if it's just a coincidence. Either way, it catches my attention, and I can't deny that he looks even better out of uniform than I could have imagined.

"Nice shirt," I say, holding the door open a little wider, trying to sound casual even though my heart is still racing.

He grins, a slow, almost teasing smile, but he doesn't reveal whether the shirt choice was intentional or not. His grin is infectious, and for a moment, I find myself caught up in the easy confidence he radiates.

Now that I'm seeing him up close in the daylight, his age is easier to pin down than it was last night when shadows distorted his features. He's definitely older than me, but not by a lot. Maybe four or five years, which would put him in his late thirties. There's something about him that feels grounded, experienced, but without the weariness you often see in people who've lived through too much.

"Did you get any sleep after I left?" he asks, stepping inside the cabin like he's done it a hundred times before, his presence filling the room.

"Not much, but I'm okay," I reply, closing the door behind him, my voice a little lighter than I intended. "You?"

"Not any, but I'm okay," he says, flashing that same slow smile, the one that feels just a little too knowing, a little too intentional. I don't know if he means for it to come off as seductive, but there's something about the way he holds my gaze that feels . . . different.

And I don't know what to do with that. Normally, I can hold my own in moments like this, especially when it comes to flirtation, but the fact that he's wearing a wedding ring keeps me in check. I don't flirt with other women's men. I've always drawn a firm line there.

But then again, this isn't about me. *Reya*—my character—*would* flirt with him. That's how her affair with Cam begins in the book, after all. She latches on to every flirtatious smile he throws her way, turning it into a game, letting it pull her deeper into the affair that eventually consumes her.

As I stand here, watching Detective Saint move through my kitchen, a part of me wonders how much writing I could get done tonight if I let myself slip into Reya's skin for a little while.

What if I became her, just for a moment?

What if I allowed myself to step out of my own reservations, to lean into the flirtation and see where it takes me? It might inspire me, might help me push past this creative block and meet my deadline.

There's a strange thrill in the idea of letting go, of becoming my character just long enough to capture her essence on the page.

The detective is making a slow spin in the kitchen, his eyes scanning the high ceilings and the deceivingly modern style of the cabin. "I've always wondered what the inside of this place looked like," he says, his voice filled with genuine admiration. "It wasn't at all what I expected when I walked in last night. This might be the nicest cabin on the whole lake."

"I usually stay on the other side of the lake," I reply, gesturing toward the wide windows that overlook the water. "It has the best sunset views. But this one is really nice." *Too* nice.

He nods appreciatively, glancing toward the large windows overlooking the lake. It's dusk now, so there's a warm glow being cast over the room. "Is it not two-story? It looks multilevel from the outside."

"Nope," I say, shaking my head. "Just the one. All the rooms have ceilings this high."

He gives an impressed nod, his eyes still scanning the space as if he's taking mental notes. And I can't help but watch him, my mind wandering again to Reya and Cam, and how easily this interaction could slip into something more if I let it. I force myself to stay grounded in the moment, but the line between fiction and reality feels thinner than ever.

He brings his eyes back to mine, locking me in his gaze with an intensity that makes my pulse quicken. "It's gorgeous," he says, his voice low and casual.

I nod in response, trying to keep my cool, but I'm not sure he's talking about the house anymore. There's something in the air that shifts the atmosphere. Neither of us speaks for a moment, and the silence between us becomes thick, almost palpable. I can feel it pressing against my skin, making me more aware of every breath, every movement. My mind clamors for something to say, anything to break the tension.

"What name do you go by?" I ask him, desperate to keep the conversation going. "Nathaniel? Nate?"

He tilts his head slightly, a faint smile playing on his lips. "Saint, actually."

Oh, I nailed it.

"Saint," I repeat softly, more to myself than to him. The name lingers in the air between us, and I can't help but think about how perfect it would be for a character.

Saint—it has a certain strength to it, an edge that makes it stand out more than the typical names I've used. It would make a better character name than *Cam* by a mile. But that would be too weird. Cam is already beginning to look exactly like this guy in my mind. I can't make his name the same too. It would be too much.

"So," I say, shifting the conversation back to safer ground, "you need a statement from me?"

Saint doesn't answer right away. He stares at me quietly for a moment, like he's weighing his words before he speaks. "Not anymore," he finally says. "It's all on dash- and body cam. Nothing to dispute."

Those words jar me for a moment. Reminding me that with the advancement of technology, there are probably many things recorded digitally for eternity that no one would want a record of. *That poor man.*

But also, I have no idea what he did that made him a wanted man. I almost open my mouth to speak up and ask for more details, but Saint makes me nervous with his ease.

He leans against my kitchen island, crossing his legs at the ankles, looking so effortlessly breathtaking that I suddenly feel completely out of my element. There's a confidence about him that makes me feel like I'm stumbling over my own thoughts. But then I remind myself—*Would Reya feel out of her element right now?*

No, she wouldn't.

Reya would be composed, in control. She would take whatever flirtatious energy was simmering between them and use it to her advantage. She wouldn't back down.

"If you don't need a statement," I ask, crossing my arms casually, "then why are you here?"

He quirks an eyebrow at me, a hint of amusement flickering in his eyes. "You said you needed to pick my brain."

Oh, right. I did say that, didn't I?

I nod, swallowing the lump in my throat as I try to remember what questions I planned to ask him. But now that he's standing right in front of me, my mind feels like it's short-circuiting. Every carefully crafted question I had seems to vanish into thin air. I don't want to look down at my list like an amateur, so I scramble to come up with something—anything—to keep the conversation from veering into awkward territory.

"Why do you wear a uniform if you're a detective?" I blurt out, mentally kicking myself for how weak the question sounds.

"It's a small town," he replies, unfazed by my flustered state. "I only do detective work when it's needed. Most of the time, I patrol, so I have to be in uniform."

I nod as I search for a follow-up question, but none comes to mind. The silence creeps back in, and I can feel it growing between us as I chew on my lip, trying to think of something else to say. But then, before I can manage another weak question, he speaks up again.

"I have a confession," he says, his tone suddenly more serious.

I blink in surprise, tilting my head slightly. "You do?"

He nods, and for a moment, I feel the air shift again, like whatever he's about to say might change the dynamic between us. "I didn't sleep when I got home, but it had nothing to do with my job."

My brow furrows slightly in confusion. "Why couldn't you sleep?"

"I googled you," he says, his tone matter-of-fact, as if it's the most natural thing in the world. "Watched a lot of your TikTok videos."

Heat floods my face, and I instinctively cover my cheeks with my hands. "Oh, God. Not those."

He laughs, a deep, easy laugh that seems to fill the entire cabin. "You and your friend . . . what's her name?"

"Nora," I mutter from behind my hands, still mortified.

"Yeah. Very entertaining," he says, clearly enjoying my embarrassment. There's something playful in his voice that makes me want to hide and laugh at the same time. "Why'd you stop? I couldn't find any newer ones."

I lower my hands, feeling the flush creep down my neck. "I just . . . it's been a rough year. We did one in my private group the other night, but I don't venture onto TikTok anymore."

"Well, that's a shame," he says, his gaze never leaving mine. "In your text, you said you wanted to pick my brain. About what? You writing about a cop?" He says it with a sexy emphasis.

"I am, actually," I reply, feeling the heat in my cheeks intensify.

His lips twitch into a small smile. "What a coincidence."

I can feel the embarrassment climbing up my neck, spreading across my face like wildfire. "Yep," I say again, my voice barely above a whisper. "But to be fair, my character was a cop long before last night. This book has been in the works for over a year and a half, unfortunately."

He chuckles softly, and the sound of his laughter sends a shiver down my spine. There's a moment where our eyes meet, and I feel something in our look. The tension that's been simmering beneath the surface suddenly feels more real, more electric. And for just a second, I wonder what Reya would do in this moment.

Would she let herself lean into the friction? Would she allow herself to blur the lines between what's fictional and what's real? I'm tempted to find out, but instead, I smile, feeling both flustered and exhilarated. And guilty. We aren't two single adults standing in a room together. This isn't innocent fiction.

"What's your question?"

"I have lots, actually. A lot of . . . cop questions. I don't even know where to start."

"What kind of book is it? Romance?"

I nod. "Romantic suspense. A love triangle. And the married cop is part of that triangle because he falls for a witness. It gets . . . messy. I just . . ."

He waits quietly for me to finish.

"I don't know anything about cops. Or love triangles, apparently."

"Not sure I can answer questions about a love triangle. I've never been in one. But anything else is fair game." His voice is low and curious, like he's genuinely interested in my answer. He grins, and I can feel that smile slide right into my stomach, settling there like a slow-burning flame. It's the kind of smile that makes you forget how to breathe for a second.

I'm still stuck on the fact he watched my old videos. I can't believe I didn't think to make them private on TikTok after all the drama. Which means he's seen me drunk, spouting off ridiculous ideas, laughing until I snorted wine out of my nose. I'm mortified just thinking about it, but at the same time, there's something intriguing about the fact that he's here, standing in front of me, bringing it up as if it's the most natural thing in the world to Google search someone you just met.

"Yeah, I've never been in one either," I say, trying to downplay my embarrassment while still engaging in the conversation. "I've been second-guessing that whole part of it, but I do have questions that might come up about your job if you wouldn't mind answering them as I go. I'm sure the more experience you have as a cop, the better you get at it over time, right? You learn things on the job that you can't learn in a classroom. Things I won't be able to find on Google."

"True," he says, his smile softening a little as he nods in agreement.

"Writing is like that," I continue, the words coming easier now. "If I lived through something, I could probably make it more realistic when I put it into words on paper. There's only so much you can imagine before your lack of experience starts to show. And I've never been a cop, so . . ."

"Or in a love triangle," he adds.

Saint breaks our eye contact for the first time since we started this conversation, his gaze drifting down to his arms, which are folded across his chest. I follow his line of sight and see that he's staring at his left hand, specifically at the wedding ring on his finger. He starts to twirl the ring absentmindedly with his thumb, and I can't help but wonder what's going through his mind.

That move makes my stomach tighten, not just from embarrassment but also from the sudden realization that this conversation is skirting perilously close to what might lead into inappropriate territory.

Maybe that's why he's here.

"This book you're working on," he says after a beat, his eyes lifting back to meet mine. "What are the main characters' names?"

"Cam is the cop," I reply, feeling a strange thrill at the fact he's asking so many questions. "Reya is the female protagonist."

"And who is the third?"

"Cam's wife. Cam is the one having the affair, but Reya feels guilty because she doesn't want to be the other woman, but she's just too . . . intrigued by him."

"Are there specific things that happen to Reya in the book that you've never experienced?" His voice is steady, but his question dwells, thick and heavy. "Or are you still outlining?"

Holy shit. This conversation is really going there. I can feel the heat creeping up the back of my neck, and suddenly I'm not sure if I'm ready to have this conversation with him. Not like this. Not while we're standing so close, not while the air feels charged with something I can't quite name.

I need a drink.

Without saying anything, I walk around him, moving toward the cabinet to grab a glass. "I need wine for this conversation," I say, my voice a little breathless. I turn to face him, raising an eyebrow. "Want some?"

He shrugs, a slow, easy movement that somehow makes him seem even more relaxed. "I'll take a glass," he says, his gaze never leaving mine.

I grab the open bottle of wine I broke into for Mari from the refrigerator, feeling the coolness of the bottle against my skin as I pour two half glasses. When I turn to hand him his glass, we're closer now. He's still leaning against the kitchen island, and I'm leaning against the sink, but our feet are just inches apart, and the proximity sends a shiver down my spine. He takes the glass from my hand, his fingers brushing lightly against mine, and for a moment, I feel frozen in place.

He takes a sip, his eyes still locked on mine, watching me over the rim of the wineglass. There's something in the way he watches me that feels different now, more intense, like we're no longer just talking about the book. It's as if the conversation is a stand-in for something else, something unspoken but undeniably present.

I don't sip as delicately from my glass. I take a huge gulp, the wine sliding down my throat in a rush as I try to steady myself. I set the glass on the counter next to me, my hand lingering on it as I stare down at it, trying to gather my thoughts.

"Reya is very different from me," I begin, my voice a little softer now. "I don't want you to think I took inspiration for her character from my own life."

"I'm sure you took *some*. Would be impossible not to, right?"

"I suppose. But I do intentionally make my characters different from myself. It's fun living vicariously through them. She's only twenty-six, but she's lived a busy life. Already out of law school and practicing, so when she meets Cam, she isn't the most experienced with men. All her time has been put into becoming a badass attorney, but he's the first thing that makes her nervous." I glance up at him, my heart thudding. "Their attraction is intense. But . . . as you know, he's married." My eyes inadvertently glance down at his ring and then back up again.

Saint nods slowly, his expression unreadable as he sips from his wine again. He lowers the glass to his chest and holds it there like it's a shield. "How does that make Reya feel?" he asks, his voice quieter now, more probing, as if he's asking me something more than just a plot detail.

"Jealous," I say immediately, the word slipping out before I can stop it. "Disappointed."

His gaze darkens just a fraction, and I wonder if I've said too much, if I've let too much of myself slip into the story. But the way he's looking at me like he's searching for something in my answer makes me feel like I'm not the only one unsure how far we're going to take this conversation.

For a moment, the air between us feels impossibly charged, the mass of his question still hanging there. We're not just talking about Reya and Cam anymore. There's something more personal woven into this conversation, something that neither of us has said aloud, but we both know is there.

"Do they know each other very well?" he asks, his voice softer now, pulling me even more into the moment.

"Not at all," I reply, shaking my head. "Not in the beginning."

"So this attraction . . . it's strictly physical?" His eyes are searching mine, his question hanging in the air, heavy, almost tangible.

"For now," I admit, my voice quiet as I feel the tension between us grow.

I have no idea what's happening here.

Are we still talking about the book? Or are we talking about us now? It's as though the conversation has taken on a double meaning that neither of us is acknowledging outright.

Now that I've been picturing Cam as Saint in my head, it's impossible to separate the two. For a writer, it's a strange feeling—to be standing so close to a real-life version of your character. It's like something I created has come to life, and that thought sends a rush of adrenaline through me.

I take another drink of wine, feeling my heart pounding so loud I'm sure Saint can hear it. I'm trying to keep my breathing steady, but it's difficult.

"How does their affair begin?" he asks, his tone calm but curious, like he's genuinely interested.

I swallow hard, knowing that the answer to this question will take us even deeper into a hazardous place. "A kiss," I say, my voice barely above a whisper. "Cam loves his wife, but he's never felt such a strong physical attraction to anyone like he does to Reya. So one night . . . when he's at Reya's house on business . . . he lets his weakness take over. And he kisses her. But in the middle of the kiss, he feels guilty, so he pulls away from her and storms out of the house."

"Without apologizing?" Saint's eyebrow rises, and I can tell he's intrigued by the emotional conflict.

I nod, feeling my pulse race even faster. "Cam is a tortured soul," I explain.

Saint nods slowly, thinking it over. His eyes stay locked on mine, and then he asks, "And that's never happened to you? You've never been kissed by a man who is married to another woman?"

I shake my head, my voice quiet now. "No," I say softly. "And now I feel stuck when I try to write Reya's reaction." I take another sip of my wine and then continue. "How would Reya react after that? Would she get angry at Cam for kissing her, even though she wanted it? Would she cry because he stormed out without a word? Or would she feel triumphant—like she won?"

Saint tilts his head slightly, his eyes narrowing as he considers my question. "That does sound like something you would have to experience before you could really nail the emotions."

"Exactly," I say, feeling a surge of validation, even as my heart races.

We stare at each other for a long, quiet moment, and my heart might be pounding louder than when I was woken up by police lights in the middle of the night.

Then, he does something I'm not expecting—he pulls his bottom lip in and chews on it for a moment, a classic move straight out of the novels I write. The sight of it makes me want to laugh, but the tension is too real, too thick, and I wonder if he realizes how perfectly he's fitting the role of my fictional hero right now.

Is he biting that lip on purpose? Has he read a romance novel?

There's a sudden intrusive buzzing sound that makes Saint stand up straighter. He pulls his phone out of his pocket and glances down at the screen. His expression changes slightly, and when he looks back at me, his eyes are serious. "It's my wife," he says.

The words hit me like a splash of cold water, and I try not to let the disappointment show. I set down my wineglass, my fingers trembling slightly. "You should probably answer it," I say, trying to sound casual, unaffected.

Saint also sets his wineglass on the counter beside him, his eyes still locked on mine. "You're right. I should answer it."

But he doesn't.

Instead, he tosses the phone onto the counter, and before I can even process what's happening, he closes the gap between us. In an instant, his hand slips behind my head, and his mouth is on mine.

The kiss happens so suddenly, so unexpectedly, that I gasp. His lips are warm, soft, and when his tongue slides into my mouth, it sends chills rolling down my spine. I press myself against him instinctively, my hands moving up to the sides of his neck as his lips close over mine.

He tastes like mint and merlot, a combination that sends my senses reeling. I know immediately that this is how I'll describe Cam's kiss in the book—this taste, this feeling, this moment.

His phone is still buzzing away on the counter, but all I can think about is the way he chose this kiss over answering her call. I was right, at least about that feeling. Reya would feel triumphant, like she'd won something she didn't even know she was fighting for.

But the triumph comes with a heavy side of guilt, and that feeling starts to creep in almost as quickly. I can't ignore the fact that his phone is buzzing because his *wife* is calling.

His literal *wife*.

And I won't even allow my mind to start dissecting all the things *I* should feel guilty for.

The phone finally stops vibrating, and in the silence that follows, the only sounds are the soft, intoxicating hum of his mouth moving against mine and the quiet moan that escapes from me without warning. His hand slides down to the small of my back, pulling me closer, and I press myself into him, lost in the heat of the moment.

But then, just as quickly as it began, the phone starts buzzing again, jerking us both back to reality.

Saint pulls away from me, his breath heavy as he presses his forehead to mine. I gasp for air, my chest rising and falling as I try to catch my breath.

No kiss has ever left me this breathless, this affected.

When I open my eyes, I see that his are still closed, as if he's trying to hold on to the moment for just a little longer.

Did I really just allow that to happen?

I'm awful.

The phone keeps buzzing, an insistent reminder of the reality we're trying to ignore.

And then Saint releases me and grabs his phone, his expression unreadable, and without another word, he walks to the door.

The door slams behind him, and I stand here, feeling the weight of the silence in the cabin. He filled me with so many emotions in that brief moment, only to rip them away just as quickly. Now, all I'm left with is this aching feeling in my chest—an emptiness I wasn't expecting.

I ache for more of that kiss. More of his flirtation. More of that triumphant feeling.

I hear the gravel crunch beneath his tires as he pulls away from the house, and even after he's been gone for several minutes, I'm still standing in the same spot, touching my lips with my fingertips, trying to process everything that just happened.

The reaction that surprises me the most right now is my smile. If I were to have written Reya and Cam's first kiss last night, I never would have thought she would smile after he left the way he did.

But I'm smiling. Despite the guilt I feel for the betrayal, I'm somehow smiling because it doesn't feel like I've done anything wrong. It's research. *Right?*

Without thinking, I walk straight to my computer and open it. For the second night in a row, I sit down and immediately begin typing.

I am never telling a soul about that kiss.

CHAPTER SEVEN

I just told Mari about the kiss.

I didn't mean to. But she showed up here unannounced wearing floral overalls. And she's been drinking a mimosa from a YETI cup, so she seems harmless and bored.

She came for a visit just as I was needing a breather from the most recent all-nighter I pulled, so we came out here to the front porch to sit on the patio furniture, and the conversation just ended up here. Right here, with me saying "It was just a kiss," and her just staring at me in amusement.

"Oh, my," she says.

"I know," I say.

I can't believe I caved that easily. To her, not to the kiss. But she was being nosy, asking me about seeing a mysterious black car in my driveway two days ago. I explained to her that it was the detective, and he had stopped by to take a statement. But when I was telling her, I don't know what happened. I just couldn't hide it. I was blushing, I couldn't stop smiling.

I became a flailing idiot.

Then, out of nowhere, she accused me of sleeping with him. "*You're porking the porker!*" she said.

I became defensive, but instead of making a full denial, I said something like *"No, I'm not! I swear, it didn't go that far! It was just a kiss."*

That's when she said, "Oh, my."

And I responded with "I know."

And now here we are. Staring at each other.

She sips from her YETI cup, a long, constant sip. "Well. Good for you. I've been married to Louie since I was seventeen. It wasn't until I was in my fifties that I realized my lips had never touched another man's and likely never would at that point because I was in my fifties and Louie was healthy as an ox. And to be honest, it made me kind of sad. Because what if Louie is a terrible kisser? What if we aren't even doing it right? How would we know when we've only experienced each other?"

She's staring off into the distance, focused on nothing in particular.

"Now my youth is gone, and the thought of Louie putting his tongue in my mouth makes me want to walk right out there to the spot where that young man ended his life the other night and do the same exact thing."

"Jesus, Mari."

"Have zero regrets, Petra. Kiss *all* the men. And the women, too, while you're at it. Because there are some of us in the world who never got to do any of those fun things."

Her YETI is empty now. She's trying desperately to get the last drop to empty onto her tongue.

"At least you and Louie have had a long marriage. Not a lot of people get that."

She waves me off with a flippant hand. "Yeah, yeah. I know. Wouldn't change a thing, blah blah blah."

I laugh. "Have you ever kissed a costar? For a role?" I ask her.

"A couple of times, but those don't count. Makeout scenes are actually terrible. You have some sweaty director in a chair five feet away yelling *action* at the two of you, and the heat from the lights is making you both sweat, while the guy you're being forced to pretend to want to kiss has been a whiny little bitch for the last two solid weeks and you'd rather be strangling him with your hands than your tongue."

"Sounds awful."

"It is very, *very* hard being an actress. Okay, going home. Out of alcohol." She stands up, but I remain in my chair as she walks down the porch steps. "And don't worry, I won't tell anyone you smooched the cop. Hell, this is my third mimosa today—I probably won't even remember it happened by the time I make it home."

"Thank you."

As Mari is walking away, she says, "And yes, I am possibly an alcoholic, but I'm too old for interventions, so don't even try."

"I won't. I promise. Enjoy your next mimosa."

"I will. Enjoy your next makeout."

All I can do is laugh at that. It feels good to laugh, because the last twenty-four hours have been getting stressful again.

I walk back into the house and take a seat in front of my laptop. The writing was going well for like an entire day after Saint kissed me. But then day two came, and I still hadn't heard a word from him. The silence started to get the best of me, even though he owes me nothing. Not even a text.

But it's almost as if I need another boost of him to get back into my groove. I've been trying to live off the memory of the kiss alone. The way his lips moved against mine, the feel of his hands on me, the unexpected thrill of it all. It's a kiss that has taken root in my thoughts, refusing to let go, lingering in the quiet moments. Which has literally been every moment since he slammed the door.

At least I was productive after. I wrote several chapters, words pouring out of me like they hadn't in weeks. I even rewrote some of the notes I've taken over the past year and a half to make Cam more like Saint. Every time I sat down to type, I saw Saint in my mind—his face, his voice, his presence. Cam took on new dimensions, becoming a character that felt more real, more tangible, because I had someone to model him after. It felt exhilarating, watching the pages fill with a story that was suddenly alive in a way it hadn't been before.

But before Mari came over, I had been staring at this blinking cursor taunting me again as I struggled to find the words.

I know what needs to happen in the story, but the energy from the kiss has faded, leaving me with the familiar frustration of writer's block. It's as if the high from that moment has worn off, and now I'm left wondering if I can even recapture it again without him.

I talked to Nora last night, but I didn't tell her about the kiss. Other than Mari, who knows next to nothing about me or my life, I'm never telling anyone. That is definitely something I want to keep private. I've always been a private person, and this . . . well, this feels too personal, too complicated to share, even with my best friend.

I write under my real name, but just my first and middle name. My last name is Andrews, but readers don't know that. I've never worried too much about my personal life being revealed to them. They know very little about me. I have the version of myself I portray to the readers, but none of them know if I'm dating or married or single or a mother or a lonely cat lady. I don't put anything out there beyond my writing, and I want to keep it that way. It's always been a kind of shield, keeping my real life separate from the persona I present to the world. My readers get the stories, but they don't get *me*, and that's how I like it.

Which is why—as much as I trust Nora—I would never tell her about my kiss with Saint. I feel too guilty, and she's one of the only true friends in all areas of my life. I'd hate to taint her version of me, whatever that may be.

I'm more worried about how other people would feel about my actions than how I feel. Is this really any different from two actors kissing for the camera? It's art.

Obviously, a spouse would never be forgiven for kissing someone else based on the excuse that it's research for a book, but it sure as hell makes it easier to forgive myself that way. I feel very little guilt compared to the moment it happened, thanks to all the clever ways I've excused it. And I don't know what that says about me. Whether it means I'm cold and detached—or is it simply that I've compartmentalized what happened as part of my process, something separate from real life?

In fact, I feel so little guilt, I'm starting to wonder how far I can take this thing with Saint. I've picked up my phone several times to text him again, but each time I chicken out.

Cam and Reya have kissed in the book, but I'm having trouble writing about the relationship they develop because I've never had feelings for a married man. I've never felt like the other woman. There are so many ways a relationship with a married man would differ from a more traditional relationship. Not only would you not be able to go public with it, even to your closest friends, but you would also have to go to great lengths to keep it private.

What would that feel like? To love a man who can only love you part-time?

To be the one left behind, always waiting for stolen moments, knowing that someone else gets the best of him while you only get the leftovers?

It's a feeling I can't quite grasp, but I know it's something Reya would be wrestling with in the story. It's a layer of complexity I haven't fully explored yet, and I know it's the key to making the relationship between Cam and Reya feel real.

I've been at war with myself over whether or not to call him. On one hand, it feels reckless, like I'm stepping into dangerous territory. On the other hand, it's *work*.

I settle on a compromise with myself.

I'll text him.

I keep in mind that his wife might see this message, so I stay professional. I don't want to raise any red flags. Just a simple, innocent request.

> This is Petra Rose. I have a research
> question if you have time for it.

I stare at my phone after I send the text, half expecting him to respond immediately like he did the last time I texted him. But this time, the dots don't appear. He doesn't text me back right away, and the silence stretches out longer than I expect.

I watch the phone for a moment, waiting, but when nothing happens, disappointment creeps in.

He's had time to think over what he did, and he's starting to regret it.

I stare at my computer for several minutes, wondering if I shouldn't have sent the text. I *know* I shouldn't have sent the text. But I feel more disappointment that he didn't answer right away than I do guilt from sending it. I know I'm walking a fine line here, but the pull of curiosity is stronger than my sense of caution.

I need to busy myself, so I go to the kitchen to cook dinner and leave my phone on the table. I make a salad and grill a chicken breast, trying to focus on the task at hand rather than the gnawing sense of anticipation building in my chest.

I eat my entire meal while staring pathetically at my phone. Each bite feels like it's dragging time out even longer.

I guess he really does regret that kiss.

Maybe he's trying to distance himself, to draw a line in the sand that I've already crossed. The thought stings more than I expected it to.

I take my plate to the sink and begin rinsing it, but I almost drop it when I hear my phone buzz. I turn off the water and rush to my phone, my heart racing with a mixture of excitement and anxiety. I can feel a swirl of excitement roll through my entire body when I see it's a response from Saint.

Saint: Are you having writer's block again? More than happy to help. ;)

Holy shit. He even added a wink.

I wasn't expecting that. I wasn't even really expecting him to respond, but that reply proves that we're both on the same page after that kiss a couple of days ago.

> Me: Yeah, I guess you could say that. After you left the other night, I wrote several chapters. But today I'm stuck.

Saint: What's tripping you up?

> Me: I'm not sure I know how it feels to be the other woman. I have no idea how to describe things between Cam and Reya because I have no idea how often she would be thinking about his wife or the future of their relationship when they're together.

Saint: Are Cam and Reya in love?

> Me: Yes. Very much in love.

Saint: So you're wondering how two people who are in love would navigate a normal night together, when one of those characters is married?

>Me: Yes. Exactly that.

Saint: It sounds like you would need to experience that firsthand. Research can only go so far, I'm assuming.

>Me: Experience has definitely proven helpful in the recent past.

Saint: It would be rude of me not to help you. I can be there in an hour.

>Me: I would appreciate that.

I calmly set my phone back down on the table, but my reaction is anything but calm right now. My heart is racing, my hands trembling with anticipation. I want to scream. This entire situation is insane. I can't even believe I've gotten myself involved with this guy, but again—it's for research. That's all. *Research*.

I only have one hour before he gets here. One hour to shower, dry my hair, brush my teeth, make my bed, and clean up two days' worth of complete chaos. I move through my routine in a blur, my mind spinning with a thousand different thoughts, each one louder than the last.

I spend the better part of the next hour worrying more about how I look than about the state of the cabin. My reflection in the mirror becomes a battlefield of indecision. Hair up or down? Light makeup or bare faced? Casual or a bit more put together? It's ridiculous how much thought I'm putting into it, as if the way I present myself could somehow control the course of the evening. But I can't help it. Every detail feels like it matters in a way it hasn't before, like how I appear might influence the direction of my career.

My heart is racing as I change my outfit for the third time, settling on something that toes the line between casual and deliberately chosen. A fitted sweater that hugs my curves but not too much, jeans that look good but aren't trying too hard, and just a touch of mascara to make my eyes pop. It's all calculated to look effortless. Why are women so pathetic sometimes? Men don't have to do a damn thing other than show up.

By the time I finish getting the dishes cleaned and put away, I hear the familiar sound of gravel crunching beneath tires. *He's here.* A surge of nerves mixed with anticipation floods through me, and I quickly finish the last sip of the wine I've been nursing for the past hour. It doesn't help calm me down as much as I'd hoped, but it gives me something to focus on other than the fact that he'll be at my door in seconds.

When the knock finally comes, I take a deep breath, trying to compose myself. I pause for a moment before heading to the door, wanting to seem as calm and collected as possible. When I open it, Saint stands there in full uniform, but there's something about the way he's looking at me that makes the moment feel anything but professional. He's holding a change of clothes in his hands, and I catch myself staring at them before I look up to meet his eyes.

"I didn't have time to run back to the station to change," he says, his voice carrying a casual familiarity. "Mind if I do it here?"

I shake my head, pointing behind me toward the hallway. "Bathroom is through that door."

He doesn't wait for further invitation. He steps inside with that same devilish grin I've come to associate with him, a grin that sends a spark of heat through me. Without missing a beat, he steps closer, his hand slipping around my neck, and before I can even process what's happening, his lips are on mine. The kiss is sudden, consuming, like it's the most natural thing in the world. I respond instinctively, my body moving toward him, meeting him halfway as if this kind of greeting is completely familiar to us now. The feeling of his mouth on mine pulls me into a daze, a moment where nothing else exists but the heat of the kiss and the weight of his hands on me.

He backs me up two steps, his mouth never leaving mine, and kicks the door shut behind him with an easy motion. "I can only stay an hour," he murmurs against my lips, his breath warm on my skin. "I wish I could stay all night."

I blink, pulling back slightly, my mind trying to catch up to what's happening. *Is he in character right now?* The way he's kissing me, the way he's speaking—it's as if he's channeling Cam. But I don't know if that's intentional or if I'm projecting. The line between Saint and Cam is becoming increasingly muddled, and I'm starting to wonder if he's doing it on purpose. This kiss—this greeting—feels like something Cam would do at this point in the story. But would Saint? Under normal circumstances, I doubt it. But in this moment, nothing feels normal.

Saint sets his clothes on the counter and heads straight for the refrigerator, pulling out a bottle of wine with an ease that suggests he's done this before. He grabs the glass I was drinking from earlier, refills it, and slides it across the island toward me. Then, he pulls another glass from the cabinet and fills it for himself.

The whole scene feels surreal, like we've slipped into an alternate reality where this is just what we do. Share wine, exchange kisses, play out a story that might not even be ours.

"How was your day, Reya?" he asks, the name of my character slipping from his lips as if it's always belonged there. The shift in tone, in context, makes me realize with certainty that he's completely in character right now. I have to bite back my smile at the realization.

"It was good," I reply, picking up my glass and taking a small sip. "How was yours, Cam?"

He walks toward me, his presence overwhelming the small space between us. He's so tall, I have to tilt my head back slightly when he stops in front of me. He touches my chin with his finger, tipping my face up toward his. "I haven't stopped thinking about you," he whispers, his voice low and intimate, just before he brings his mouth down on mine again.

Good God, my knees feel like they might give out under the weight of that kiss. His lips press against mine with a hunger that leaves me breathless, and for a moment, I lose myself in the sensation. When he pulls back, his eyes searching mine, he adds softly, "I'll be right back."

He heads for the bathroom to change clothes, leaving me standing there, dazed and a little dizzy from the kiss. My mind is racing, trying to process what just happened—and what might happen next. Does he expect me to pretend I'm in love with him? Is this all part of some role play he's initiated, or is there something more happening here? The uncertainty is exhilarating and terrifying all at once. I don't know how this will play out, but the anticipation is coursing through me.

When Saint emerges from the bathroom, he's no longer in his uniform. He's opted for a simple navy T-shirt and jeans. He walks over to the table and casually lays his police uniform and gun on top of it, and the sight of them sends a shiver down my spine. It's a reminder of the reality he's left behind, and the role he's chosen to step into now.

He moves toward me with purpose, his hands finding their way around my waist before effortlessly lifting me onto the island in front of him. The ease with which he moves, the way his body fits so perfectly against mine . . . it's straight out of a book. His lips find my neck, and I close my eyes, letting the sensation of his mouth on my skin wash over me.

He's making me dizzy.

I lean my head to the side, allowing him more access to my neck, my skin tingling under the slow, deliberate slide of his tongue. I can feel his left hand tracing a path down my thigh, pulling my leg up around his waist as he moves closer, pressing himself against me. It's a strange mix of control and tenderness, and I can't help but wonder if this is how he is with his wife.

Is this the way he kisses her, the way he touches her?

I push the thought away, refusing to let it take root. Right now, he's here. Right now, his mouth is on my neck, and I need to focus on that.

"Tell me something," he whispers against my skin, his voice sending shivers down my spine.

"Mmhmm," I mutter, barely able to form a coherent response.

"What kind of guy is Cam?" His question is laced with curiosity, but his lips never stop moving against my skin.

I open my eyes, the reality of the moment sinking in.

If he's asking about Cam, does that mean he's kissing me as Saint right now? Is this real, or is this part of the game we've been playing? *God, I hope it's real.*

"He's . . ." I pause, trying to gather my thoughts as his tongue slides precariously close to my ear. It's hard to focus with the way he's making me feel, but I manage to speak. "He's good, but rough around the edges. He's controlling. Jealous. Has a temper."

Saint pulls back just enough to look me in the eye, his expression thoughtful. "He wouldn't hurt Reya, would he?"

"Never," I say, my voice soft but certain. "He's madly in love with her. Tries his best to protect her."

"Tries?" Saint's brow furrows, his gaze questioning. "Does that mean he doesn't always succeed?"

I shake my head, my breath catching in my throat. "Not always."

He rubs his thumb over my bottom lip, his eyes darkening as he stares at my mouth. I love the way he looks at me in this moment, the intensity of his gaze, the way it makes me feel seen in a way I've never felt before. I want to capture this feeling, write it down, describe it in detail, but I'm afraid that if I wait until later, I won't be able to capture the fullness of it. The way his eyes make me feel like I'm the only thing that matters.

"Does anything bad happen to Reya in your book?" he asks, his voice low, but full of genuine concern.

"Yes," I whisper. Normally, I wouldn't spoil the plot for anyone, but in this moment, I don't care. Saint isn't just anyone, and I doubt he'll ever read my work.

"What happens to her?"

"Well. A lot, actually. She loses her best friend. There's an attempted kidnapping. A car chase. Someone breaks into her house."

Saint's eyes narrow in concern. "Does anyone ever hurt her?"

"Yes," I admit. "She gets hurt toward the end of the book. The person who breaks into her house . . . after he ties her up, she realizes her arm is broken."

"Does she know who is doing these things to her?"

"She doesn't."

"Why do these things keep happening to her?"

"Reya is a lawyer. She has evidence that this character is trying to locate."

Saint runs the backs of his fingers over my cheek as I speak. He seems so interested in my answers, it makes me wonder if he's planning to act any of these scenes out. *Is that why I'm telling him about it? Because part of me hopes he does? Do I actually want to know what it's like to be kidnapped? To have a broken arm?*

No. That would be taking things a little too far. I'm not so sure I'm willing to go that deep for research.

"What happens next?" he asks. "How does she find out who is doing all this?"

I clear my throat. "I'm not sure. I haven't gotten that far into the story yet."

He pulls back farther, shifting his weight slightly on the island, though my leg is still wrapped around his waist, keeping us intimately connected. His thumb continues to stroke my hip, a steady, comforting rhythm. His gaze softens, losing some of the intensity it often holds, becoming surprisingly empathetic.

"You know, for someone who writes such compelling stories, you seem hesitant to talk about your own." His voice is quiet, almost gentle. "Maybe even embarrassed."

"What do you mean?" I ask, feigning ignorance, my voice a little too high.

He doesn't let up. His eyes, surprisingly perceptive, search mine. "I don't know. When you talk about your story, or your career, you just seem embarrassed."

Wow. Isn't he an astute one. I sigh. "*Embarrassed* doesn't feel like the right word. But yes. You're right. It's hard talking about myself."

"Has it always been? Or is it just since the adaptation controversy?"

I give him a look that must be full of surprise, because he immediately shoots me back a reassuring glance.

"Look, I know I barely know you at all," he says. "But it's weird, because I feel like I kind of *do* after watching all your videos. And the you I saw in those videos just isn't the same you standing in front of me."

"Ouch. I'm more disappointing in real life?"

"Disappointing and disappoint*ed* are two very different things. You are far from disappointing, Petra."

I push off the counter and pace for a moment, not sure what he wants from me. "I don't like this conversation. I liked pretending you had no idea about me or the noise online."

"You're hard to scroll past. Even out here in the middle of nowhere, we all have cell service."

"It's not really something I like to talk about," I murmur, looking away, staring at the polished surface of the island, anywhere but at him. The thought of revisiting the vitriol, much less talking to him about it, makes my chest ache.

"I get it," he says, his voice softer now, almost soothing. "I shouldn't have brought it up. I just can't imagine it's easy, having your passion picked apart by strangers. And on top of that, having them feel like they're entitled to more than just your words on paper. They feel entitled to rip *you* apart, without even having spent a single second in the room with you." He pauses, and when I glance at him, he's watching me with a look of legitimate concern. "How are you handling it? Are you okay?"

The directness of his question catches me off guard. The way he says it, as if he genuinely *cares*, is disarming. Tears prick at the corners of my eyes, a surprising response to his empathy. "Well, it hasn't been fun," I admit, the words barely a whisper, forcing them out. "I feel like the whole past year broke something inside me. I haven't been able to write anything meaningful." I look up at him, my eyes pleading. "Until you kissed me."

A slow smile spreads across his mouth. "It helped?"

I nod. "A lot."

With that, he kisses me again, soft and quick, then wraps his arms around me. He gently caresses my shoulder with his thumb.

"What did you used to love about writing?" he asks.

"Everything. I've just always gotten a thrill out of putting words to paper."

"So it's the act of writing, not necessarily the act of being read?"

"I mean, it's nice when people want to read what I write, but it's not why I write. I write for my own enjoyment. It's therapy for me. It's what makes me happy."

"Then why haven't you been writing?"

The question is so simple, but so complex. Saint moves his hands to my shoulders, pushing me away just enough so that he can look me in the eye.

"I'm serious. If it makes you happy, why aren't you doing it?"

"I just didn't think my career would ever take off like it did, or that people would have such passionate feelings toward what I do in my spare time. It's the aftermath I don't really like. And it's impossible to get away from. I fear that any move I make from here on out will always become a headline. I think that's why I've had writer's block, because in reality, I'm a little bit scared to finish the book and give it to the world."

"Then don't give it to anyone. Just write it and keep it for yourself."

"Have to pay the bills," I say flatly. The hard truth behind the dream breaks through the kindness of the moment. "I'm sure I'll still sell books when I release another one, which is why I'm writing. But my desire has changed. My audience has changed. I think that's what makes me the saddest. I feel like I've let down everyone who used to admire me." I separate myself from him and put my hands on my hips. "But I'm just not the type to try and change people's minds. If me defending myself will require me to speak ill of someone else, I'd rather just take the loss."

Saint is staring at me with what looks like admiration. "There you are," he whispers, gently tucking my hair behind my ears.

His words, simple yet profound, land with an unexpected weight, cutting through years of self-doubt and poisoned thoughts.

"I want you to write," he says. "*And* I want you to publish. I know I'm just one person, but I want to read everything you've written and everything you haven't written, so even if you're only writing for you and me, let that be enough to finish at least one more book."

A warmth spreads through my chest, a sensation that has nothing to do with physical touch and everything to do with genuine connection. It makes me uncomfortable, so I cut through it with humor. "And you promise you'll buy it? I need the royalties. The whole dollar."

He laughs. "I'll buy ten copies," he jokes.

"Wow. Baller."

I realize, as he kisses me again with a smile, that he sees me. He truly sees me, beyond Reya, beyond Cam, beyond the initial physical attraction. He sees Petra, the struggling author, and he's offered me a listening ear instead of just another nosy inquisition.

A different kind of attraction sparks within me, a deeper, more personal fascination. I wrap my arms around his waist.

"Thank you," I whisper. This conversation has been liberating in so many ways.

He smiles, a soft, genuine smile that reaches his eyes, making them crinkle at the corners.

"Will you let me read some of it?"

The question takes me completely by surprise. No one but Nora reads my first drafts. They're my messiest, most vulnerable thoughts. "You want to read my book?" I ask, incredulous.

"I mean, I am helping you research. And if it helps your process to know that someone else is invested in the story . . . I'd be honored."

My heart gives a surprising lurch. The idea of him, Saint, reading my words, seeing the raw, unpolished beginnings of Reya's story. The parts of her that are so clearly me and the parts of Cam that are so clearly him—it's terrifying. But it's also exhilarating. It's a bridge between our fantasy and my reality, a sign of a deeper engagement. He's not just playing a character; he's investing in my art, in *me*.

"Maybe," I say, a shy smile finally breaking through. "Okay." The thought of his eyes on my words, of his mind engaging with the world I'm building, suddenly feels like the most powerful inspiration of all. This is more than just research now. This is a collaboration.

He grins, and then kisses me. And just like during our first kiss, his phone begins to vibrate. He doesn't even flinch. He just kisses me even deeper, ignoring the incoming call.

With every vibration of his phone, he pulls me tighter against him as if he's trying to drown out the noise with my touch.

"You should get that," I whisper, pulling away.

We both know it's his wife.

He reluctantly steps away from me and pulls his phone out of his pocket. He carries it to the front door and takes the call outside.

I watch him through the window. He's gripping the back of his neck as he speaks to whoever is on the other end of that call.

I wonder what her name is. How long they've been together. Does he have children?

The call doesn't last long.

He heads back toward the house, so I walk away from the window. When he's back inside, his expression is regretful. He walks past me and scoops up his uniform and gun. He doesn't say a word. He just grips my face with one hand and kisses me, almost possessively.

Then he leaves.

I'm left speechless, standing alone in the kitchen.

I don't know what just happened, it occurred so fast.

Was that part of his act? I'm getting reality and fiction confused. Was he doing what he thought Cam would do in that situation? Or did Saint really feel guilty enough after that phone call that he just left without a word?

I have no idea what was going through his head, so all I can do is focus on what's going through mine. I take my computer to the bedroom with me, full of new ideas and new feelings and new thoughts.

I write until I fall asleep.

CHAPTER EIGHT

I've been writing since the moment I woke up.

Saint is very good for my productivity. That is a proven fact.

My phone vibrates on the table beside me. I'm so deep into my story, I'm afraid to pause and look at it. Sometimes when I'm in this kind of writing frenzy, the world outside my writing fades into the background, and it's too risky to jump back into it. I ignore the text for half an hour, until I finish the chapter.

When I finally glance at my screen, I see it's from Saint.

What are you doing tonight?

I blink at the words, my pulse skipping. The casualness of the text doesn't match the density of the thrill it sends through me. Is he offering to come over again? To go out? Even a simple phone call from him would make this bored heart of mine flutter in a way it shouldn't.

There's an alarming allure to his attention.

I stare at the screen, hesitating for a moment. My fingers hover over it before I finally type back a response.

> Writing. Unless you have an idea for research.

It's a playful reply, one that keeps things ambiguous enough, but the tension beneath it is unmistakable. I press send and wait, chewing my bottom lip. The silence feels long even though it only lasts seconds. His response buzzes through my phone almost immediately.

> Do your characters ever make risky moves and go out in public?

The words seem innocent enough, but I know better. Is this a dare? An invitation? The thought sends a rush of adrenaline through me, mingling with the slow, creeping guilt that always accompanies thoughts of him. If Saint is planning on following through with whatever I say next, I'll make it work to my advantage. I use an actual scene I've written in the book.

I respond with a text that reads **Cam works up the courage to take Reya out on a date, but he's nervous someone may recognize him. So they end up eating in his car.**

The thrill of the idea pulses through me. I know this is a step into something potentially more lethal than what we've done before. We've flirted and crossed lines, but a *date*? It feels different—bolder. We're treading into territory neither of us should be exploring.

But that's also the pull, isn't it?

My pulse is pounding as I consider the implications. Before I can overthink it, another text from Saint lights up my screen.

There's a restaurant I'd like you to try, he texts. **It's in the next town over. You in the mood?**

The thought of going out in public with him, even in another town, feels like too much of a risk. But his words prove he's playing this game with me, and the logic of us going to the next town over makes sense for both Cam in the book and Saint, who has a wife and probably friends and coworkers who would recognize him here.

He's taking a risk for me. I like it, so I text him back.

When and where?

As soon as I send the message, the nerves kick in. My stomach flips in that heady mix of excitement and guilt. I'm not just thinking about crossing a line—I'm planning it. And I want to. More than anything, I want to.

The reply is quick and decisive.

Meet me at the Blue Lantern. 7 pm.
I'll be at the bar.

I know the place; I've passed it many times on my way to and from this lake. It's perfect for keeping a low profile, for blending in.

See you then.

I try throwing myself back into my story after the text exchange, but my thoughts keep drifting to what this evening will hold. This isn't just a random encounter. This is planned. It's a decision.

By the time six o'clock rolls around, I'm dressed, my heartbeat pounding in my chest like a drum. I've opted for something simple—a blouse and jeans—but I've never felt so self-conscious. It's as though every piece of fabric clinging to my skin is a reminder of what I'm doing. Of the secrets I'm keeping.

Once I'm in my car and backing out of the driveway, an unsettling fear slips over me. There isn't a single person in the world who knows where I'm heading right now.

I don't usually put myself in these positions, so I'm not sure what to do. Who to text. I'm almost to the end of the long asphalt road when an idea comes to me.

Mari.

I pull into their driveway, but before I even get out of the car, Louie is walking outside.

"Everything okay, Petra?"

I nod. "Everything's great. Just wanted to speak to Mari real quick."

Louie seems a little disappointed that I'm not here to ask him a question about the house. He nods, then yells, "Mari! Writer renter lady is here for you!"

I can hear Mari make a noise from outside my car, and then she billows out onto the patio and into the yard like a ghost gliding across the pavement. "Petra!" she says.

Louie is still standing within earshot, so I eye him in a way that lets Mari know I don't want him to overhear me.

"Get lost!" she yells over her shoulder. Louie disappears into the house. "What is it?" Her hands are clasped giddily beneath her chin, her fingers wriggling.

"Nothing salacious. Calm down. I'm just going to a work meeting and wanted someone to know where I am."

"A work meeting. Okay. Where will you be? Who will you be with? What time should I expect you home?"

"Him," I say in a whisper. "The Blue Lantern. Start to worry if I'm not home by eleven."

"Oh, that place is really good. Get the burger. Sounds basic, but trust me."

"Thank you."

"Anytime," she sings, twirling her silk dress with her as she heads back toward her house. She waves over her shoulder as I'm climbing into my car.

I feel better. Safer.

But not home free. My mind is racing with what-ifs the entire drive to the restaurant. *What if we're caught? What if someone sees us?* But with every anxious thought comes the undeniable thrill of being seen. Of someone noticing, but not quite catching on to what's really happening between us.

I pull into the parking lot of the Blue Lantern at exactly 7 p.m. The restaurant is tucked into a row of other restaurants and bars, unremarkable but cozy enough. It's perfect for what we're doing. I park at the back, taking extra care to make sure no one can see my car from the street. It's a rental, and no one would even notice me or my car, but I try to imagine what Reya would be doing in this situation.

My palms are damp as I grip the steering wheel. I sit there for a few moments, my breath shaky, before I finally gather the nerve to get out of the car.

I've never had to worry much about being recognized until recently. I've always had a decent-size following, but it's rare that people would actually approach me and know that I'm Petra Rose, the writer. I'm not sure normal society outside the tight-knit book world really pays attention to what the authors who write the books they read look like.

Social media has changed that for my generation of writers, though. The handful of times I got recognized in the first few years of my career, it was always by someone who followed me online because they read my books. It would happen more if I was in a bookstore, or in a town where readers and authors were there for a book convention and happened to see me in passing. Up until these past couple of years, I'd honestly have been shocked if someone recognized me in this town.

But it's different now. I'm not just an author. I'm a . . . whatever they call people like me. People who have reached such a level of either success or infamy, or both, that they get recognized even by people who aren't readers.

I'm glad I keep my personal life offline, at least. I could be in public with any man or woman in the world, and no one would think twice since I never post about whether or not I'm married or whether or not I have children.

The risks are high for Saint tonight, though. I keep that in mind as I walk toward the entrance and push open the door.

The restaurant is understated—low lighting, quiet booths, and a long bar that stretches along the back wall.

The low murmur of conversation around me makes me feel anonymous. People are engrossed in their own lives and their own company and pay very little attention to who is walking in or out the door.

I find Saint at the bar, already seated, his back to the room. It's strategic—smart. He's already ordered a drink, his fingers wrapped casually around the glass as he watches me approach in the mirror.

My nerves fade a little when I see him smile in the mirror across the bar. It's a small, knowing smile, like we're in on something no one else could possibly understand.

We're supposed to blend in here, just another pair of strangers sitting side by side. My pulse quickens as I walk toward him. He doesn't turn when I approach, but I see the smirk tugging at the corner of his mouth in the reflection of the bar mirror.

"Late," he says in a teasing tone as I slide onto the stool next to him.

"And not even fashionably," I counter.

He gives me a quick, direct once-over, his eyes dark with amusement. "I beg to differ."

The bartender approaches, a towel slung over his shoulder, his gaze flicking between us as he waits for our order.

Saint leans forward slightly, his forearms resting on the bar, and with a low, confident voice, he orders another old-fashioned. The word comes out smooth, probably like the drink he's just finished. It's simple, but there's an intensity behind the choice that matches him perfectly.

The bartender nods, acknowledging the order, and then turns to me.

I take a moment, swallowing down the nerves that seem to be sitting heavy in my throat. "I'll have a glass of Sauvignon Blanc," I say, opting for something light and crisp. Understated, like I'm trying to make this feel as normal as possible, even though my insides are twisting with a mix of excitement and anxiety.

As the bartender turns away to prepare our drinks, I feel Saint's gaze on me. I glance over, and his eyes are already on mine, a subtle smirk playing on his lips. It's casual on the surface—the kind of scene that wouldn't raise suspicion if anyone were watching—but the air between us is thick with the kind of tension that can't be easily ignored.

"You look . . ." His eyes sweep over me. "Incredible."

His compliment warms me up, more than the wine could even accomplish. "Thank you," I say.

He adjusts himself so that his thigh is pressing against mine. "How did the court case go?"

I tilt my head, confused, but only for a second. *Reya is a lawyer. He's in character.*

I grin. This is exciting. "We won. Unanimous verdict in less than two hours."

"I wouldn't have expected anything else," he says.

I love this game. Too much. "What about you? How was your day?"

"It's better now," he says flirtatiously.

The bartender returns, setting down a short glass of whiskey for Saint and a tall-stemmed glass of wine in front of me. "Enjoy," he says before walking away, leaving us alone in our little bubble.

Saint lifts his glass, swirling the amber liquid inside it before taking a slow sip, his eyes never leaving mine. I do the same, lifting my wine and taking a small, measured sip, trying to calm the rapid beating of my heart.

It feels like everyone in the room knows what's happening between us, even though logically I know no one is paying attention. But the secrecy, the unspoken understanding of what this meeting is really about, makes it exciting. I wish I was taking notes right now.

Saint takes another sip of his whiskey, his eyes still holding mine over the rim of his glass. After he sets it back down, he leans a little closer, his voice low but casual. "How was the drive over?"

I raise an eyebrow and smile, feeling the tension loosen just a bit. "You mean the thirty minutes I spent rehearsing what to say when I saw you, then driving in circles around the parking lot trying to convince myself not to walk in?"

His lips twitch into a smirk. "You did seem a little flustered when you walked in. I was beginning to think you might pull a U-turn back to your car."

I let out a soft laugh, shaking my head. "Oh, I almost did. You should've seen me sitting in the car, giving myself a pep talk like some motivational speaker on a bad day. *'You can do this, Petra. It's just a casual drink, no big deal.'*" I mimic the exaggerated gestures of a pep talk, rolling my eyes at my own ridiculousness.

Saint grins, the amusement dancing in his eyes.

"Petra, is it?" he asks, a twinkle to his eye. "I thought your name was Reya tonight."

Saint's grin widens as he leans in, the air between us buzzing.

My stomach drops as I realize my mistake. Sometimes I forget we're playing a game when he speaks to me, but that's all this is. A game. It's not about me, not about Petra and her guilt, but about Reya, who would embrace this kind of reckless thrill without hesitation.

I can feel the heat rising to my cheeks as I fumble for a response. "My bad. Reya." I force a laugh, trying to play it off like I didn't just slip up, but the awkwardness is impossible to hide.

Saint raises an eyebrow, clearly enjoying my discomfort. "Are you forgetting who you're supposed to be right now?" he teases, his voice low and laced with amusement. "Reya wouldn't be apologizing. Reya is a badass, remember?"

I look down at my glass, suddenly feeling like he's way better at this than I am, and I'm the one who is supposed to have the imagination. "You're right. I just—" I pause, swallowing the embarrassment.

He chuckles softly, the sound rumbling in his chest. "You're overthinking it." He glances at me, seeing the hesitation on my face. He offers up a gentle smile as he leans in slightly. "And if it's guilt making you feel this way, don't let it. Your actions aren't a factor in my marriage. I made the choice to be here. That's on me."

His words are surprisingly reassuring. "You don't . . ." I struggle to find my question. "You don't feel bad?"

His eyes narrow as he thinks about my question. "I do. But my marriage is . . ." He takes a sip of his drink and then gingerly sets his glass on the bar. "Complicated," he says dryly. "But that's for me to figure out. When I'm with you, I just convince myself I'm doing a good deed. Helping you with research. Every good writer needs to research." He washes away any trace of guilt on his face with a slow grin. "Who am I to deny you your muse?"

I literally do not know if I'm speaking to Cam or Saint right now. I don't know how he does it—pretends so well. And if he isn't pretending . . . he's convincing. Because I am so much more at ease than I was five minutes ago.

Every brush of his knee against mine sends another jolt of awareness through my body. We may be sitting at a bar, trying to keep this casual, but nothing about this feels casual at all. I don't know that I've ever felt more thrilled on a date before.

My pulse races. His proximity is intoxicating, and I know I'm playing with fire, but the danger of it only fuels my attraction. I'm acutely aware of how easy it would be for someone to recognize him. Or me. But it's also rousing, knowing we're on the edge of something forbidden.

That's actually not a bad book title contender. *The Edge of Forbidden.* I grab my phone and type it into my notes before I forget it.

When I look up from my phone, I notice Saint's posture shift. He's suddenly more rigid now as his eyes flicker toward the entrance. At a couple who just walked through the door. I saw them out of the corner of my eye but don't want to turn around.

"What's wrong?" I ask, lowering my voice.

"It's nothing," Saint says, gripping the back of his neck. "False alarm." He eases up, but only a little. Then he turns to me. "I have a dilemma."

"What's the dilemma?" I ask him.

"I'm hungry," he says, scanning the restaurant discreetly. "But the bartender told me before you got here that they only serve food at the tables, not at the bar. However, I'm not sure sitting at a table with a gorgeous woman who is not my wife will look very good if I actually do see someone I know." His gaze moves from scanning the restaurant and comes back to me. "I was wondering if you wouldn't mind if we got food to go and ate in the car. Not the ideal date, but . . ."

I want to smile, because he's playing out the scene in my book with pure perfection. I nod in understanding, because Reya does understand. She understands it so much, I think she would almost rather cancel the date altogether, because in no way, shape, or form is what we're doing okay. But instead of objecting to what we're doing, I say, "Let's do it."

"Maybe you should wait outside," he says, standing up. "I can get our food and meet you at your car."

I stand up with him, grabbing my purse. "I want a cheeseburger. No tomatoes. French fries." I down the rest of my wine. "I parked in the back."

"Perfect," he says. "See you soon."

<hr>

"Where'd you go to law school?" he asks.

The question makes me laugh because I'm a writer, not a lawyer, but that's why we're here. *To pretend.* I have fun with it. "Harvard. I'm super smart," I say. "Genius level. Scientists want to study my brain."

Saint laughs. We're sitting in my car, and while I'm doing my best to eat in a civilized way, eating from to-go containers in a small car and trying to keep the mood alive is anything but easy.

Turns out we both like salty ketchup, so Saint opened several packets and poured salt directly onto the ketchup, and we're taking turns dipping fries into it, making small talk as Cam and Reya. It has actually been fun. I've never seen him so at ease.

"Where'd you go to cop school, Cam?"

"Oh, you know," he says. "The, um . . . academy. The cop academy."

I laugh way too hard at that. "Where did *Saint* go to cop school?"

"LAPD, baby."

"Maybe that's where Cam should go, then. I don't think I've written much of his history yet." Right before I take a bite of another french fry, I say, "Tell me something interesting."

"Interesting?" he asks. "Have I been boring you so far?"

"Of course not," I say, laughing. "Just . . . tell me something real. And unique."

Saint takes a sip of his water. He insisted we both order waters to go so we'd be sobered up before heading back to our respective places for the night.

He clears his throat and sets his drink back in the cup holder. "I have a brother," he starts, his voice slipping into something lighter, almost playful. "He's got one arm."

I raise an eyebrow, intrigued but cautious. "Oh?"

"Yep," he continues, "lost it in the army five years ago. He was standing guard next to an armored car, and boom—gone."

I blink, unsure whether to laugh or gasp. He watches me, a smirk tugging at his lips, like he knows exactly the effect this story is having. "It's true," he says. "It was awful at the time, but he's got a great sense of humor about it now," he says, his eyes glinting with mischief. "He likes to tell people that his lack of armor cost him an arm in the army."

I can't help it. I laugh, the absurdity of it washing over me. But then doubt creeps in. *Is he messing with me?* Is this an actual thing that happened to Saint's brother, or is he making this up? I squint at him, trying to read his expression. "Wait, is that even true?"

Saint's face remains perfectly neutral. "It's absolutely true."

"So that's not something I can write into the book?"

"Please don't," Saint says immediately. "That would be way too close to home." He wipes his mouth and closes his to-go box. "Now look who keeps forgetting to be in character," he says. "I'm telling you stories from my real life. Not very helpful to the writer who needs content she can use."

I love that he's slipping out of character. "It's harder than it seems to be someone else," I say.

Saint watches me closely. "You do make it difficult not to be myself."

That sentence makes my mouth run dry. I take a sip of water and help him start bagging up all the trash. Once we've cleaned up our space in the car, he exits and walks over to a trash can and dumps it all in. But when he walks back toward the car, he walks to the driver's side, where I'm seated. He opens the car door with that quiet confidence of his, extending a hand toward me. As I stand, he doesn't let go.

Instead, with a slow, deliberate motion, he guides me closer to the back of the car, adjusting us so that my back presses gently against the closed door.

And then his mouth connects with mine. The kiss is soft, almost reverent, like he's taking his time to savor every second, as if each touch, each breath, means something more. There's no rush, no game. It truly feels like it's just him and me right now—no roles, no walls.

It's the kind of kiss that makes a person feel seen.

But then, as if a switch flips, I feel him stiffen. The softness of his kiss begins to withdraw, replaced by something more restrained. His hands, which have been holding me so gently, suddenly freeze in place. I pull back slightly and see it—the way his gaze flicks around, scanning the street like he's just remembered we're not alone. We're out here, in public, exposed. It's as if the mask he let slip for just a second is quickly being put back in place.

He takes a step back, his posture rigid now, his hand falling from my waist. The warmth that was there just moments ago cools, leaving behind the sharpness of reality. His eyes flick back to mine, a brief apology hidden somewhere in the tension of his expression.

"I should go," he says, his voice quieter now, more controlled. He steps away, giving me space. "I'll be in touch, Reya," he adds, almost as an afterthought, like he's forcing himself to say it before he walks away.

I want to stop him, to ask him for more, entreat him to stay with me just a little while longer, but the words get stuck in my throat. I just watch him retreat, slipping back into the Saint I'm used to. The man who always seems to be running from something, even when he's standing still.

I pull out my phone after having that thought and jot it down as a note for my book. *The man who always seems to be running from something, even when he's standing still.*

CHAPTER NINE

"*'The man who always seems to be running from something, even when he's standing still'*?" Nora practically yells the line back at me. "Petra, this is so good! I am so invested in this story, and you sent me one chapter! When will you have more?"

"I have over ten chapters," I say. "Forty-six thousand words."

"Are you serious? You've written forty-six thousand words?"

"Yep."

"That's like half a book!"

"I know. I'm so relieved, but I'm scared to get too cocky. I might jinx it."

"Are you happy with what you've written so far?" she asks. "You're not going to toss it and start over and confuse me by changing the entire plotline?"

She knows me so well. "So far it's a keeper," I say. "I'll send the rest to you if you want to read more of what I have."

I'm curious what she'll say if she can find the time to read it. I don't know if the reason I like what I've written so far is because of the whole muse aspect I've still kept hidden from Nora, or if I just like Saint so much that I'm confusing my trash writing with my exhilarating feelings for him. It would be good to have an outsider's opinion.

"Absolutely you better send it, right now, while I'm on the phone."

God, I love her. I don't know if she's actually excited to read this, but she knows how much confidence her excitement lends. I open the file and attach it to an email while she waits, and then I hit send.

"It's rough," I say.

"I know, I know, it sucks, it's trash, you have to flesh it out more," she says. "I do this for a living, too, you know." I hear her download the file after it comes through. "Still untitled?" she asks, looking at the first page.

I'm still not sure what the book will be called, so right now I just have the literal word *Untitled* as the working title. "Not yet. I have a list of contenders, though."

"Okay, starting it now. Love you, bye." Nora ends the call, but her rush to start reading everything I've written so far perks me up. I was about to crawl into bed when she called, but now I feel like crawling into bed with my laptop.

I don't know why, but whenever I know someone is reading one of my works in progress, I feel like I have to start from the beginning and read it like I'm them, not knowing where the book is heading, looking at it with a fresh pair of eyes. I especially love doing this when I know Nora is reading, because she sends me live updates over text as she reads.

This is probably my favorite part of writing. The peer support.

My least favorite part is the dread I feel knowing she may very well come back and tell me the manuscript isn't working. That I still don't know how to write a love triangle, even though I'm risking so much by playing a part in one.

I plop down onto my bed with my laptop and open it as I adjust the pillows. I've had my phone on Do Not Disturb since being on my date earlier, so I'm surprised at the number of messages that begin popping up on my laptop as soon as it wakes.

It's Mari. U didn't text by 11.

Petra, it's 11:03.

It's 11:06 are u dead?

11:09 now I'm getting worried

Ok I'm coming to u

Nvmd. Just saw you drive by. Guess ur alive.

Unless he's wearing your skin and driving your car

 I can't believe I forgot to message her. I called Nora as soon as I walked in the door and forgot all about Mari. I immediately respond and let her know I'm safe in bed, and then I put my computer on Do Not Disturb so I can hopefully get some work done while still running off the creative fumes of my conversation with Nora.

∼

I fell asleep in bed with my laptop open. It happens a lot. I'll wake up in the middle of the night with the familiar weight on my chest, satisfied to know that I worked until I couldn't write another word.
 I can feel its cold edge pressing into my ribs when I attempt to roll over, so I push it away, hearing it slide across the blanket to the other side of the bed. The screen light flickers for a second before I reach over and close it, and then the room goes dark.
 Too dark.
 I open my eyes wider, suddenly nervous to move. I don't know why. I don't think anything woke me, and I don't hear any unfamiliar noises.

That's the problem, though. It almost feels more than quiet—it feels like there's a huge absence of noise. I don't hear the ceiling fan. I don't feel the air circulating. I don't hear the hum of the air conditioner.

I squeeze my eyes shut and try to convince myself to fall back asleep. *Just go back to sleep.*

But something is off. I can't place it at first, but there's an eerie stillness in the air. The house is *so* quiet, like the world outside has gone mute. *Too dark.* My heart begins to race. *Too silent.* An instinctual alarm is going off in my chest. *Too alone.* I blink a few times, trying to shake off the drowsiness, but the unease only intensifies.

I open my eyes fully, and my gaze is immediately drawn to the bedroom door. I don't know why. Maybe it's the feeling that I'm not alone, that something is waiting.

And then I see it.

A shadow.

It's filling the doorway—dark and unmoving, blending into the blackness of the room but still distinguishable in its shape. The silhouette of a person. I can't make out any details, but it's there, and it's watching me. A cold wave of terror crashes over me, weighing down on my chest like a vise grip.

This can't be real.

For a moment, I'm paralyzed, unable to move, barely able to breathe. My body freezes in fear, my muscles locked tight as I stare at the figure in the doorway. I want to scream, but it's like one of those nightmares where you try to call for help, but no sound comes out.

My throat feels tight, my voice trapped somewhere deep inside me.

I reach for my phone instinctively, my fingers fumbling on the bedspread, desperate to find it in the darkness. My heart is pounding so hard it feels like it's going to explode out of my chest. I can't think. I can't focus on anything except the shadow, which is now *moving.*

The figure lunges forward, and in that split second, my body finally reacts. A jagged scream rips from my throat as I scramble to the other side of the bed. My legs tangle in the sheets as I try to pull away, to escape.

But I'm not quick enough.

A hand—large, strong—wraps around my ankle with a brutal grip, yanking me backward with such force that I lose all sense of balance. My hands claw at the blankets, trying to find something to hold on to, but it's useless. I slide across the bed, my body dragged toward the figure. My phone slips from my fingers, tumbling off the mattress with a dull thud as it hits the floor.

I'm crying now as my chest heaves with panic. The hand around my ankle tightens, cold and unrelenting, pulling me closer to the edge of the bed. I kick out with my other leg, desperate to break free, but it's no use. I'm trapped, helpless.

In the back of my mind, a thought flashes: *Is this Saint?*

But no—this feels worse. This feels like a nightmare I can't wake up from.

My body is racked with adrenaline like I've never felt before. "Stop!" I scream. I plead with whoever this is.

Could it be the owner of the cabin?

No. Louie wouldn't be this strong. It can't be him.

Terror surges through me, sharp and electric, every nerve on high alert. My heart pounds so violently in my chest, I'm sure it's about to burst. My breaths are coming out in quick, ragged gasps, each one more desperate than the last.

"Saint, if this is you, please stop. *Please.*"

My pleas fall on deaf ears. I try to recall everything I learned in self-defense class—the techniques, the moves, the strategies to fight back—but there's no time to think. No time to react. Everything I learned feels distant, like a memory I can't fully access.

Move, Petra. Do something!

Before I can even try, I'm being yanked off the bed with such force that I can barely process what's happening. My feet flail wildly, searching for something—anything—to anchor myself to, but there's nothing. The ground seems to slip out from under me as I'm dragged across the floor, the rough fabric of the carpet burning against my skin. I let out a scream full of terror, but it's cut short as a hand clamps over my mouth, silencing me in an instant.

Please be Saint. Please be Saint.

The thought shoots through my mind like a lightning bolt, and I hate myself for it. Why am I hoping it's Saint? *Why?* Even if he's taken our little game too far and he's here, breaking into my house in the dead of night just to scare me, his actions are still horrifying. They're still inexcusable.

But deep down, I know why I'm hoping it's him. Because if it's Saint, then at least I know who it is. I know what this is about. I can reason with him, maybe. I can remind him of the boundaries, the unspoken rules we've created in this twisted thing between us.

But if it's not him . . . the alternative is much, much worse.

I kick my feet against the floor, struggling to get any kind of leverage. My body twists, fighting to find an escape, but he's moving too fast. Too strong. Every time I think I'm gaining some ground, his grip tightens, and I'm dragged farther, helpless against the force pulling me across the room. My fingers claw at the carpet, searching for anything to grab onto, but it's useless. I can't stop him.

"Please," I cry, my words useless. Saint wouldn't be this rough with me. Even if he were here playing out a Cam-and-Reya scene, he'd be mindful of my fear. Mindful of his grip.

Whoever this is isn't thinking about me and my comfort at all.

The house is so dark. Darker than normal. The kind of darkness that presses in on you, suffocating and all-encompassing. I can barely see two feet in front of me, but as I'm dragged through the hallway and into the kitchen, I notice something that sends a chill down my spine. The faint glow of the appliances is gone. All the little lights normally blinking from the microwave, the stove, the fridge, are out. Completely dead.

The power's been cut.

A fresh wave of panic surges through me. The realization hits me like a punch to the gut. Whoever this is, they didn't just show up uninvited. They planned this. They made sure the house was in complete darkness, that no one could see or hear what's happening. They've covered their tracks. *I'm alone.*

I start to scream again, but a hand comes down on my mouth. Hard. Stifling.

All the shades are drawn, blocking any light from the outside. There's no one to see, no one to help. My stomach twists painfully as I fight against the arm wrapped tightly around me. He's got both of my arms pinned now with just one of his, locking me in place, making it impossible to move. I'm trapped. Completely at his mercy.

Suddenly, the hand over my mouth is removed, and for a split second, I gasp for air, choking on my fear. This is my chance. I have to figure out what's happening. Who this is. *I need to know.*

"Saint?" My voice comes out in a trembling whisper, barely audible through the sobs that are threatening to break free. The sound of my own desperation sends a shock of humiliation through me, but I can't stop it. "Saint, please." I can't believe I'm saying his name, begging for him, but I have to know.

Is it him?

I try to turn my head to look at the figure behind me, to catch a glimpse of his face, but the moment I attempt to move, he forces my head forward with a brutal shove.

Too strong. Too rough.

His hand clamps down on my jaw, holding me in place, and my body vibrates uncontrollably under his grip. He's so close now, so close I can feel the heat of his breath on my skin, the oppressive weight of him pressing against me. He brings his mouth to my ear, and for a moment, I stop breathing. I freeze, waiting for whatever comes next, hoping—*praying*—that I'll hear something familiar in his voice. But the silence is worse than anything he could say.

But then a chilling, deep voice cuts through it. "Don't. Fucking. Move."

I'm slammed down hard into a chair, the impact jolting through my entire body.

That didn't sound like Saint.

My breath leaves me in a sharp, panicked gasp, and the shock of it makes everything feel more surreal. Is this someone else entirely? Am I actually in real danger?

Tears spill down my cheeks, sliding into my mouth. I can taste the salt as I sob.

The uncertainty wraps itself around my throat, making it even harder to breathe. *Was that Saint?* Since I can't recognize his voice, the fear bubbling inside me only grows stronger, more suffocating. My heart pounds so hard I'm afraid it might stop.

I try to jump up out of the chair—somehow willing myself to escape—but I'm not fast enough. Before I can even get my feet under me, hands clamp on my wrists with bruising force, shoving me back down. The grip is so tight it feels like my bones are being crushed. I wince in pain, but my mouth is quickly covered with a strip of tape. The adhesive sticks instantly, pressing tightly against my lips, sealing off any chance of screaming for help. I can feel the tape pulling at my skin, trapping me in silence.

Please let this be Saint.

I don't know why I'm still hoping it's him, because at this point it doesn't matter. Even if it's Saint, I'm in pain and I'm scared and I'm crying. But the thought of it being someone else—someone with worse intentions—makes my blood run cold.

My arms are yanked behind me with such force that a sharp, stabbing pain shoots through my shoulder, up my arm, and straight to my spine. I cry out, but the sound barely escapes my throat before it's swallowed by the tape. The muffled noise is all I can manage as my hands are tightly bound together behind the chair. The rough texture of the rope digs into my skin, burning with every movement.

I wince, gritting my teeth behind the tape, trying to ignore the searing pain radiating from my wrists. The rope bites into my skin so hard it feels like it's cutting through, like I'll start bleeding at any moment. *How did this happen? How did I get here?* The panic is overwhelming, but I try to focus—try to think of something, *anything*, that will help me get out of this.

I manage to get in a few desperate kicks, my legs flailing out in a last-ditch effort to break free. My feet connect with something solid—a body, maybe his legs—but it doesn't slow him down. He grunts, and for a split second, I feel a surge of triumph, but it's short-lived. His hands clamp down on my ankles with brutal force, pinning them to the floor long enough to secure them with more rope. I fight, I thrash, but it's no use. My feet are tied to the legs of the chair so tightly that I can't even wiggle my toes without feeling the strain.

Tears spill from my eyes, unbidden and uncontrollable. The more time that passes, the less control I have over my body and mind. My vision blurs as the tears mix with panic, making everything seem distorted, more chaotic.

This is real. This is actually happening.

There's no way Saint would let this game go this far, I tell myself, trying to cling to some shred of hope. He wouldn't let this happen. He wouldn't let me be in this much pain.

For the first time since I woke up just minutes ago, the cold realization sinks in: *I might not make it out of this.* For the first time, I truly feel like my life is in danger.

My body goes still. The adrenaline that had me thrashing and fighting just moments ago begins to drain away, leaving me numb and paralyzed by fear. I try to stop the tears, knowing they won't help me now.

I need to calm down. *I have to think.*

My breath comes in shaky bursts as I force myself to focus.

Think, Petra. Think.

I can't move my hands, can't even flex my fingers without the rope digging into my wrists. My legs are equally trapped, every slight movement sending sharp pain up my calves. I'm completely bound to the chair, every inch of me immobilized.

What do I do?

I hear noises behind me—things crashing to the floor. The sound is sudden, violent. I jump at each crash, my muscles tensing involuntarily. My ears strain to pick up every sound, trying to figure out what he's doing. I can hear drawers being yanked open, slamming shut, one after another. Panic grips me again, but this time it's icy cold, settling deep in my bones.

Is he looking for something? A knife?

The thought chills me to the core, my mind racing with horrible possibilities. I can barely breathe as the minutes stretch on, filled with the chaotic noises of his search.

What is he planning?

The longer the noise continues, the more my heart sinks. I'm stuck, powerless, with no way to defend myself or even see what's happening behind me. Every crash feels like a countdown, like the seconds ticking away before he makes his next move. I pray he's not finding whatever he's looking for. I pray he's not preparing for something far worse.

Just when I think I can't bear the tension any longer, a new sound cuts through the air. The front door opens.

It doesn't close.

I can hear footsteps fading away. The door is still open, though. I can feel the cold, the outside breeze creeping into the house. I don't know if he's coming back. I listen quietly. The cool air brushes against the back of my neck, sending shivers down my spine. Each gust feels like an intrusion, a reminder that I'm still vulnerable, still at the mercy of whatever comes next.

The silence in the house is suffocating. I hear nothing but the faint whistle of wind filtering through the door and the quiet sound of my own ragged breaths, mixed with muffled sobs. My chest feels tight, and each breath is a struggle as I try to keep the hysteria from bubbling over. I sit there, tied to the chair, my heart pounding in my ears, and for a moment, it feels like time has stopped completely.

I squeeze my eyes shut as tightly as I can, trying to block out the world around me. *Please let him be gone.* The words are like a chant in my head, a desperate plea. I haven't set foot inside a church in years, but in this moment, I pray harder than I ever have before. *God, please. I'll go back. I'll make up for all the services I've missed. Just let him be gone. Please, don't let him come back.*

The prayers come in waves, fast and urgent, tumbling over each other in my mind. I pray that somehow, by some miracle, he's already left. That he's walked out that door and disappeared into the night, never to return. I pray that I'll find a way to free myself, to wiggle out of these ropes and run. *I need to survive this.* I don't know how long I've been praying. Minutes feel like hours, and the terror makes every second stretch into an eternity. My mind is racing, but my body is still frozen in fear.

Eventually, I start to move. It's a small, tentative movement—just a slight wiggle of my wrists to see if there's any give in my bonds. The sharp burn of the rope against my skin is immediate, but I push through it, hoping that maybe, just maybe, I can find a way to slip free.

My hands are sore, my wrists raw from the tightness of the knots, but I keep trying. *I have to try.*

I spend what feels like an entire hour rubbing my wrists against each other, loosening the rope little by little. Eventually, I can feel it starting to give. I can also feel the painful scratches formed on my skin as I work my right hand out of the rope. As soon as it's free, I start to sob. I untie the rope from my other hand, and then I pull the tape from my mouth with a loud gasp.

I work on my legs next. It doesn't take as long now that both my hands are free. As soon as I can stand, I try, but I collapse to my hands and knees. There's still too much fear and shock running through me, I can't even walk to the bedroom. I crawl, crying, until I reach my phone.

Just as I feel a sliver of hope—just as my fingers begin to dial the number 9—I hear it.

Footsteps.

Oh, God.

My heart, which had just begun to slow down, leaps into my throat, and the panic rushes back, stronger than ever. Every muscle in my body tenses, and I freeze in place, holding my phone against my chest as the footsteps grow louder.

He's coming back.

I feel like my entire body is vibrating with fear. *I can't do this. I can't face him again.*

I start to crawl my way toward the closet, holding my breath so that he won't hear me in the bedroom. But then, through the pounding of my heartbeat in my ears, I hear a familiar voice coming from outside.

"Petra?"

I freeze in place, and for a moment, I'm not sure if I heard right. But then I hear it again, clearer this time.

"Petra!"

Saint.

The sound of his voice cuts through the fear, and my heart feels as if it plummets to the floor. There's concern laced in the way he says my name, an urgency that fits the situation but still doesn't match the terror I'm feeling. The front door swings open farther, and I hear it slam against the wall, and before I can even process what's happening, Saint is suddenly here, across the room, kneeling right beside me.

His presence overwhelms me. I don't know whether to feel relieved or even more afraid.

He looks at me, and his eyes widen when he sees the state I'm in. I'm shaking, my eyes are wild, there are tears streaming down my face, and I am absolutely terrified. His face hardens, but there's something else in his expression now.

Anger?

No. *Concern.*

Without a word, he rushes back into the kitchen, and I can hear him pulling open drawers in a frantic search for something. I listen to him, my mind racing, trying to piece together what's happening. He walks into my bedroom, but it's still too dark to see. I catch a glimpse of the glint from the knife. He's back by my side in an instant, kneeling down as he begins to cut through the rope still tied to my left ankle.

The rope falls away, and the sudden release of tension makes me gasp, my arms and legs still throbbing as blood rushes back to my limbs. But I'm not relieved. Not yet.

Seeing Saint sends a fresh wave of emotion crashing over me, and the tears I had been trying so hard to hold back come pouring out uncontrollably. They aren't just tears of fear anymore—they're tears of everything.

Tears of confusion, of frustration, of relief, and of dread all at once.

Saint reaches up and gently pushes my hair out of my face, but instead of feeling free, I feel more trapped than ever. I can't speak. I can't find the words to explain the mess of emotions swirling inside me. All I can do is cry, sobbing harder now than I did when I was being dragged through the house.

Saint places the knife on the floor beside him, and his hands hover near me, as if he wants to comfort me but isn't sure how. "Petra," he says softly, his voice calmer now, but I can't respond. I don't even know if I want to.

My mind is spinning. I have so many questions, but none of them make sense right now. All I know is that he's here, that he came back, and that somehow, I'm still not safe.

There's no reason he would show up here at this time of night. *None at all.*

"Please. Tell me what happened," he says.

He did this. I know he did. There's no other explanation.

No one else would know where I am. No one else would know how to get in, how to cut the power. Only someone like a cop would know these things.

My body trembles as I try to push the thought away, but it clings to me, suffocating in its certainty.

Saint pulls me to my feet, but I fall limply against him, too weak to do anything but shake. Too upset to beat him against the chest, which I so feel like doing. The burning sensation in my wrists from the tightness of the rope is overwhelming. I instinctively rub my wrists, but the pain is too much, so I stop. Saint wraps his arms around me and says my name with such worry.

"Petra. It's okay. I'm here."

I'm reeling from the realization that *he* is the one who caused this. *He* is the one who put me through this nightmare.

"Stop *pretending*!" I scream. I push against him, my hands slapping him in the chest. The sting is sharp, but it's nothing compared to the emotional pain flooding through me. He tries to grab my wrists, to stop me from hitting him, so I take a wide step back, and then I cover my mouth with my hands, trying to hold back the sobs that are bubbling up uncontrollably. My chest feels tight, my breathing shallow. The tears come harder now, and I can't stop them. I don't even try.

"Petra, it's me. Saint," he says, his voice gentle, soothing, as if he can fix everything with those two words. "I'm here. You're safe."

Safe.

The word feels hollow. Empty.

There's nothing safe about this. About him.

I feel the rope still touching my ankle, so I immediately start kicking at it, desperate to get it away from me, to rid myself of any reminder of what just happened. My feet shake as I kick, my body still trembling uncontrollably. The sensation of freedom should bring relief, but it doesn't. I feel trapped in my own skin, trapped in this moment that I can't escape.

Saint reaches out for me again, his arms coming up to wrap me in an embrace, but the sight of him reaching for me makes something snap inside me.

I don't want him to touch me.

Without thinking, I shove him away—hard. And I do it again. And again. He starts to take steps backward, but I move with him, pushing him over and over toward the door. It's an instinctive reaction, fueled by anger, confusion, and sheer terror. I push him with all the strength I can muster, wanting nothing more than to get him away from me. My hands shake as I do it, my breath coming out in ragged gasps, but I don't care. I can't believe he thought I'd be okay with any of this. *How could he think this was what I wanted?*

I don't give him time to react. I don't even look at him once I have him out of my bedroom. I just turn and slam my bedroom door with him on the other side of it, and I run toward my bathroom, my feet moving faster than my mind can keep up with.

I slam the bathroom door shut as soon as I'm inside, my fingers fumbling for the light switch on the wall. I flip it on, desperate for the comfort of light, but nothing happens. The room stays pitch black.

The realization that he actually turned off power to the house sends another wave of panic crashing through me. My fingers tremble as I reach for the shower faucet and turn the handle to as hot as it will go. The sound of the water splashing against the tiles is the only thing I can focus on now, the only thing keeping me from falling apart completely. I strip off my clothes with shaky hands and step into the shower, my breath coming in shallow, panicked bursts as the hot water hits my skin.

The water is close to scalding, but I don't care. I let it beat down on me, hoping—*praying*—that it will somehow wash away the fear, the confusion, the overwhelming sense of betrayal that's consuming me from the inside out. I close my eyes and lean against the wall, trying to steady my breathing, but nothing is helping. I'm gasping for air, each breath more frantic than the last.

This isn't happening. This can't be happening.

It's too dark.

CHAPTER TEN

It's too bright.

I squeeze my eyes shut, but the entire bathroom is suddenly flooded in bright white light.

Rather than calm me, it only makes things worse. The fact that the power is back on—just like that—proves one thing. *Saint* was the one who turned it off in the first place. He was in control the entire time. He's the reason I was left in the dark, terrified, alone.

And then I hear it—the soft knock on the bathroom door.

"Petra?" Saint's voice is muffled through the door, but I can hear the gentleness in his tone, the concern. It's the same voice he's always used with me, the voice that once made me feel safe. Now, it only makes me feel more trapped.

"Get . . . out," I manage to choke out between sobs. I try to sound angry, but my voice betrays me. It's thin and weak, filled with fear instead of fury. *I should be angry.* I *am* angry, but right now, all I can feel is scared.

The door creaks open, and I feel my stomach drop. My legs are shaking so hard, I can barely stand. My heart is pounding so loudly in my chest, I'm sure he can hear it.

"Petra," he says softly, stepping into the room. His voice is calm, soothing, but it does nothing to calm the storm raging inside me. "Petra, I'm sorry. I thought—"

"You thought I wanted you to *attack* me?" I scream, my voice cracking with emotion. I shove the shower curtain aside, using part of it to hide myself, but I need to look him in the eye. Tears continue streaming down my face as I glare at him through the haze of water and steam. "Are you out of your fucking mind?"

He sighs heavily, his shoulders slumping as if my words have physically hurt him. But I don't care. I don't care if he's sorry. I don't care if he regrets what he did. He crossed a line, a line I never thought he would cross, and there's no coming back from that.

I yank the shower curtain shut, and then I close my eyes, trying to block out the confusion, the whirlwind of conflicting emotions. *Did I think he'd never cross this line?*

Or did I ask him to do this?

My thoughts scatter in all directions as I search for some logical explanation, a reason why Saint would take things this far. I replay every conversation, every look, every word exchanged between us, desperately trying to make sense of the situation. But no matter how hard I try, I can't find anything that justifies this.

No. I didn't.

I didn't ask for this. I didn't ask him to break into my cabin in the middle of the night, to terrify me, to tie me to a chair. *All I did* was tell him about the book, share the inner workings of my writing process. It wasn't an invitation to scare the living shit out of me. It wasn't supposed to be an open door for him to step into my life and confuse me so badly that I thought I was about to fucking *die*.

But here we are, and I can't help but wonder . . . *Did he assume I wanted this?* Did he think I was asking for this? For him to take over my life, my space, my thoughts?

Did I confuse him?

I don't even know what to think anymore. I'm so wrapped up in the emotions of everything since he walked into my life, in the intensity of what's been happening, that I don't trust myself to make sense of any of it.

Do I even have the right to be angry at him for doing this?

The thought stabs at me, sharp and cruel. I hate that I'm questioning myself, hate that I'm doubting my own feelings. But the truth is, I don't know if I have the right to be angry.

Somewhere deep inside, a small, shameful part of me wonders if this is what I hoped for. If, on some subconscious level, I craved this chaotic dark thrill.

Did I subconsciously want this to happen?

The question burns through me, leaving a trail of guilt and confusion in its wake. I don't want to believe that I did. I don't want to think that I somehow invited this madness into my life. But the doubt is there, clinging in the corners of my mind, whispering that maybe, just maybe, I'm responsible for all this.

I lean against the shower wall, letting the water cascade over me, mingling with the tears that won't stop falling. I feel so small, so lost in this moment, trapped between wanting to lash out and wanting to curl up and disappear.

My sobs are quieter now, more resigned.

Did I even lock the front door last night?

The thought hits me like a punch to the gut.

No. I didn't.

I *know* I didn't.

After Saint and I parted ways, I was so consumed by the rush of inspiration, so eager to get everything out of my head and onto the page, that I took my laptop to the bedroom as soon as I got home and I wrote until I couldn't keep my eyes open anymore.

I've been going on writing retreats for years, and in all those nights, I've *never* forgotten to lock my doors. But last night . . . last night, I did.

I left myself exposed, vulnerable. And now, standing in this shower, I'm paying the price for that mistake.

My hands are covering my face, my fingers trembling as I try to pull myself together. But then I hear it—the sound of the shower curtain being pulled back. My heart leaps into my throat, and I freeze, too terrified to even look. I don't want to see him. I don't want to face him, not like this. But I can feel him standing here.

I'm angry. *God, I'm so angry.*

I'm embarrassed, humiliated by the way things have spiraled out of control. But beneath it all, I'm still scared—*terrified*, even. I feel so powerless, and the last thing I want is to confront the man responsible for all this.

"God, Petra." Saint's voice breaks through the sound of the water, soft and full of remorse. "I am so sorry."

His words hang in the air, but they don't offer the comfort I need. He doesn't get to apologize. Not after what he's done. Not after the way he's crossed every line. But even as my mind screams at him, as I tell myself that I should hate him for this, my body betrays me.

I can't stop crying. I can't stop shaking.

I keep my hands over my face, not wanting him to see me like this, but I can feel his presence getting closer. I'm shocked when I feel the water shift, and then his arms wrap around me, gently pulling me against him. I can feel the wet fabric of his clothes pressing against my bare skin, and for a moment, I'm too stunned to react. He's stepped into the shower with me, fully dressed, his clothes now soaking wet, but his arms are holding me tightly, as if he's afraid to let go.

I don't understand why I'm allowing him to do this. I don't understand *anything* anymore.

I should push him away. I should scream at him, yell, do something to make him understand how *wrong* this all is. But instead, I stand here, leaning against his chest, my body trembling, my sobs muffled by the fabric of his shirt. As much as I hate myself for it, as much as I want to punch him, to make him feel even a fraction of the fear and confusion I've felt, I can't deny that in this moment . . . I need him.

I need him to hold me. I need to feel like someone is here, like someone cares.

I think this might have been a terrible miscommunication.

The thought offers a small sense of solace, something to hold on to in the midst of this emotional storm.

"When you told me about your book," Saint begins, his voice softer than I've ever heard it, "I thought you were asking me to—"

I shake my head quickly, interrupting him before he can finish. "I know," I whisper, my voice hoarse from crying. I'm too exhausted, too emotionally drained to rehash every detail of what happened. "I know," I say again, because in a way, I do know. I *did* ask for something—I just didn't know it would unfold like this.

I lower my hands from my face, letting them fall naturally around him. My arms wrap around his waist, pulling him closer, and I press my cheek against the wet fabric of his shirt. The heat from his body seeps into mine, and for a moment, I let myself feel comforted by his presence. I can't tell if that makes me weak or if it's just what I need right now, but I don't let go. I hold on tighter.

"I don't know if that's what I was asking you," I admit, my voice barely above a whisper. "What we've been doing . . . it's confusing. I barely know you, and then this . . ." My words trail off as the load of everything settles on my shoulders. The whirlwind of emotions, the passion, the fear—it's all too much. I barely recognize my own feelings anymore, let alone understand what I've been asking of him.

Saint presses a soft kiss to the top of my head, and then he just holds me. Quietly. Steadily. No words. Just the warmth of his arms around me, the steady rhythm of his breathing against my hair, the feeling of being anchored after having been adrift for too long.

We stay like this for several minutes, the sound of the shower cascading around us, washing away the tension in small, soothing waves.

My tears finally begin to subside, and I take a deep breath, pulling away slightly to look up at him. His eyes are filled with remorse, and I can see how much he regrets what happened, how much he wishes he could take it back. There's a tenderness there that tugs at something deep inside me.

He lifts a hand to my face and gently brushes his thumb under my eye, wiping away the smudges of mascara that have streaked down my cheeks from all the crying. His touch is so soft, so careful, and it's in this moment that I realize he wasn't trying to hurt me. He never wanted to scare me. He just . . . misunderstood. Like I did.

He was just trying to help me. To push me into a feeling I've never experienced before.

"I'm sorry," he says, his voice thick with sincerity. "Truly. That night, I thought you were going into detail about what happens to Reya because it was your way of . . . I don't know. Giving me instructions."

For the first time since I met him, I feel embarrassment coming from him.

I nod slowly, feeling the stiffness between us start to loosen, the fear dissolving into something softer. "Okay," I say, my voice fragile but certain. "Just . . . make sure I'm actually asking you to do something before you do it from now on. Don't assume." There's a slight tremor in my voice, a residual trace of the panic I felt earlier, but I mean what I say.

His expression softens even more. "I promise." His hand remains on my cheek, his thumb gently stroking the skin there, as if he's trying to reassure me, to ground me in this moment. He searches my eyes, and then he asks, "Do you want me to leave?"

The question hangs in the air, and for a split second, I consider it. Part of me thinks I should tell him to go. That I need space to process what just happened, to get a handle on my emotions. But I can't bring myself to say the words. As much as I was terrified of him a few minutes ago, it wasn't *him* I was scared of. It was the character he was playing. The situation we both created, however unintentionally.

I can't fault him for that. Not entirely.

I shake my head, quickly, instinctively. "No," I say, my voice soft but firm. "But can we just . . . I don't want to pretend tonight." I'm too tired to keep up the charade. I don't have the energy to slip into the roles we've been playing. Tonight, I just want things to be simple and real.

Saint nods, understanding flashing in his eyes. He pulls me back against his chest, his arms wrapping around me again, and whispers, "Okay. Let's just be us."

Just us.

That shouldn't make me feel as good as it does. After everything that's happened, after the fear and confusion and all the lines we've crossed, I shouldn't be able to find comfort in those words. But somehow, I do. A warmth spreads through me, something unexpected but welcome. His words seep into me, soothing my anxiety, and for the first time since he stepped into this shower, I feel a little bit of peace.

"I'm sorry," he says again, pressing his lips to my forehead. "So sorry."

"I know," I reply. And I do know. I can feel his remorse in every touch, every word, and while I know it's not enough to erase what happened, it's enough for now. Enough to help me breathe again.

I start to orient myself more to the situation. I realize just how bright it is as I stand here, water dripping off my skin under the downpour of the shower, acutely aware of every inch of my body exposed in front of him. Other than a few heated kisses, I'm not sure I've experienced enough with this man to feel comfortable being completely naked under his gaze, especially in the bright light of this bathroom. It's an odd vulnerability that I can't shake.

How am I supposed to get out of this shower without his eyes being fully on me?

As if he can sense the shift in my mood, Saint lifts his gaze away from me with surprising gentleness, like he's attuned to my every thought. Without saying a word, he reaches out of the shower for a towel hanging on a nearby hook. The movement is fluid, practiced, as though he's done this a thousand times before in a thousand different situations, always knowing exactly what to do to ease whoever he's with. He turns off the water, and his touch is careful when he wraps the towel around me. It's not just the towel that feels like a protective layer, but also the way he handles me. Soft. Noninvasive. Respectful.

Such a huge contrast to mere minutes ago.

He leans in and presses a gentle kiss to my forehead, long enough to feel reassuring but not overbearing. Then, just as quietly as he wrapped me in the towel, he steps out of the shower, leaving me with the privacy I need.

The moment he's out of the shower, he pulls his soaking-wet shirt off and glances down at it, his brow furrowing as if he's suddenly at a loss for what to do next. It's a small, humanizing moment, one that makes me realize he's not as infallible as I sometimes imagine him to be. Even Saint, with all his control and confidence, doesn't know what to do with a wet shirt.

I step out of the shower carefully, wrapping the towel tighter around me, and reach into the cabinet to grab him a fresh one. "I'll dry your clothes," I say, handing him the towel. "A towel is the closest thing I have to something that'll fit you."

He nods, giving me a small smile that doesn't quite reach his eyes. I slip out of the bathroom, the feeling of control creeping back into my chest as I wait for him to open the door and hand me his wet clothes. There's something oddly satisfying about knowing he's reliant on me right now, that he can't leave before his clothes are dry. In a strange way, it gives me a sense of power.

When he finally hands me the damp bundle of fabric, I take it to the laundry room and toss his clothes into the dryer. The mechanical hum of the machine is almost soothing, a stark contrast to the erratic pounding of my heart just moments ago. *He can't leave yet,* I think, and the thought brings a subtle sense of relief. He'll have to stay longer than he has the other times he's been here, and for reasons I can't entirely explain, I want him to stay. Even after everything that just happened.

I reenter the kitchen after exiting the laundry room and find Saint standing at the stove, the towel tied low around his waist, his broad back facing me as he sets a teapot on the burner. The sight of him like this, so casual, almost domestic, sends a ripple of warmth through me and helps to ease my anger even more.

"Want some hot tea?" he asks, glancing over his shoulder at me with a gentle expression.

"I'd love some," I reply, my voice softer than I expected. I'm still wearing nothing but a towel, the fabric damp against my skin, and for a moment, I feel a bit more exposed than I'd like. But there's something about the sight of Saint—*this version* of him, vulnerable in nothing but a towel, in the middle of my kitchen—that makes me feel strangely at ease. It's not the same as before, when I felt like I had to hide. Now, the playing field feels more even.

While he focuses on the tea, I slip into the robe I wore the night he first showed up here. It's familiar, a layer of comfort that feels just right for this moment. The memory of that first night flits through my mind—how exposed I felt, how nervous I was in front of him. Now, it feels different. The power dynamic has shifted somehow. And now that he's the one standing here half naked, with nothing but a towel wrapped around him, I feel more . . . comfortable. Even despite the awful misunderstanding between us, I feel more in control now. His position of vulnerability helps me shed the fear that consumed me earlier.

Oddly enough, putting on anything more than this robe would make me feel *overdressed*, like the moment calls for simplicity. I tighten the belt around my waist, letting the fabric fall loosely over my skin as I walk back into the kitchen. The scent of the tea begins to fill the room, warm and inviting, and I lean against the counter, watching as Saint finishes preparing it.

I catch his eye, and for the first time since that terrifying moment in the shower, I feel a sense of calm settling between us. Maybe it's the quiet intimacy of the kitchen, the low hum of the kettle, or the fact that for once, there are no pretenses, no games.

It's just us.

Saint and Petra.

I use the time it takes him to prepare the tea to regroup. I head back to the bathroom and look in the mirror, and my hair is a frightening wet mess. I blow-dry it and then pull it up into a knot on top of my head. When I go to put the blow-dryer back in the drawer, I see my bottle of Xanax. I sigh with relief and open the bottle and swallow one.

When I walk out of the bedroom to rejoin Saint in the kitchen, he's pouring two cups of tea.

Saint without a shirt is exactly how I described Cam in the book. Rippled muscles across his back; a narrow waist; tanned, smooth skin.

I'm going to need to go back and rewrite how I described his arms, though. Now that I know the astounding strength in them, I'm aware what I have written does not do them justice. I fought with everything I had earlier, and he reacted like I wasn't even trying. Knowing he would use that strength to protect me feels comforting.

Saint slides my cup of tea toward me. "Here you go," he says, handing me the mug. Our fingers brush as I take it from him, and for a split second, I feel that familiar spark, the one that's always there between us.

"Thanks," I say, lifting the mug to my lips and taking a sip. The tea is hot, almost too hot, but the warmth spreads through me, steadying the frayed edges of my nerves.

We stand here in the kitchen, sipping our tea, both of us wrapped in towels, and for a moment, it feels like the most normal thing in the world.

The Xanax is kicking in, and it's exactly what I needed after what happened.

Saint is watching me while he takes a slow sip of his tea. I want to ask him so many questions, but I also prefer the mystery that surrounds him. I know very little about him other than his name and his occupation. But if I ask too many questions, the answers might contradict all the ways I've built his character up in my mind.

Saint sets his tea on the counter and then takes my cup from my hands and does the same. He slides his hands down my back until both of his hands are gripping my ass. Then he lifts me and sets me on the counter next to the stove.

He takes my hand gently, lifting it toward him as his eyes drop to my wrist. His fingers trace over the red marks left by the rope, and the contrast of his warm, tender touch against the remnants of restraint sends a shiver over me.

He lifts my other hand, repeating the same motion, his thumbs running back and forth over the sensitive areas where the rope dug into my skin.

There's a softness in his eyes as he studies my wrists, a rare moment of vulnerability from him, and I can feel his concern. "Did I hurt you?" he asks quietly, his voice low, almost cautious, as if he's afraid of my answer.

I shake my head, my voice steady. "I'm fine."

He doesn't look convinced. He tilts his head slightly, his brow furrowing as his eyes narrow with skepticism. "Be honest," he urges, his gaze penetrating, searching for the truth.

"I'm fine," I repeat, firmer this time. I can see he still isn't entirely convinced, so I soften my tone, offering reassurance. "I'll be fine." I offer a reassuring smile, but I'm still somewhat coming to grips with the night. With how easily I've forgiven him.

I think it's because I'm just now realizing what he's given me. As both a reader and a writer, I tend to lean more toward the darker side of suspense and romance. The kinks some readers and writers are into can make even me blush.

But even the darkest of books have an audience that enjoys them. And even though as readers, we wouldn't want to live out some of the fantasies we read about, it doesn't mean we don't enjoy reading those things.

I did not enjoy what Saint did tonight. But I do appreciate that he was trying to give me the experience he thought I was asking for in a safe way. Aside from being tied up, I was never in any actual danger. He just thought I wanted to feel like I was.

What's strange is that it feels as if he did those things in a book and not in my real life. We forgive our characters for much worse than we'd forgive our friends and lovers for, and I feel like I'm lending him the forgiveness I'd lend a character rather than an actual person in my life.

This entire night has been surreal, but I feel his remorse and I can accept it and I can take what happened and I can use it. I will definitely be using it.

Knowing how Reya is feeling in that moment has given me a whole new level of respect for her fear. For the actual pain she endures.

The red marks are still fresh on my wrists, and I can feel the slight sting when I flex my hands, but it's nothing I can't handle. They'll fade in a day or two, nothing that would leave lasting harm. I've endured worse in the heat of passion, moments where pleasure and pain blurred together. He wasn't trying to hurt me. He was following the script, playing the role we both fell into.

The game I started.

At least . . . I *think* I started it.

A part of me isn't even sure anymore, but I know I want him here. I know I don't want him to stop. Every emotion I just went through is one I want to type into my laptop this very moment. I want to describe Reya's fear, the strength in the stranger's hands, the way Reya's voice betrayed her when she needed it the most.

I almost want to thank Saint for giving me that.

Almost.

"I think you might be crazy," I whisper.

Saint laughs quietly. "Yeah, well. I'm still here, so which one of us is crazier?" He brushes a strand of wet hair off my cheek. "Petra, are you sure you don't need some alone time? I would understand."

"No. Don't go." I want more of him, more of whatever this is between us. More time with him. More attention. More gentleness, specifically.

But mostly, I want more experiences with him that will make me love writing again. I would never want to repeat what happened earlier. It was far too intense and raw, but the experience itself, it's feeding a curiosity inside me. I can't help but think of other ways he could pull emotions out of me in a way that will help me believe I lived through them.

His gaze is more heated now, simmering with something unspoken, but I can tell he's holding back. There's a restraint in the way he looks at me, like he's waiting for me to make the next move, leaving the choice in my hands. It's a shift from before—earlier he had the control, guiding the scene, but now . . . now he's leaving it up to me. I can sense his hesitation, his awareness of how fragile this moment is.

I lift my hand slowly, and my fingers brush lightly over his lips. His breath catches slightly at the touch, and the feel of his mouth under my thumb ignites a warmth that spreads from my chest down to my core. I trace the outline of his bottom lip, savoring the softness, the subtle parting of his mouth under my touch. His eyes darken with desire, but still, he waits.

I lean forward, closing the space between us, and press my lips to his. His kiss is slow, gentle, as if he's testing the waters, unsure how far I want to take this. But I can feel the tension beneath his restraint, the way his body leans into mine ever so slightly, as if begging for permission to go further.

I decide to give it to him.

I slip my tongue into his mouth, deepening the kiss, and he responds instantly. His arms wrap around me, pulling me closer, but still gentle, still careful, as if he's making sure I know I'm the one in control this time. The kiss grows more intense, more heated, and I can feel the fire between us building with every passing second.

There's no longer any hesitation.

His hands slide down my back, his fingers pressing into my skin, and I feel my body arch toward him, craving his touch. The restraint from earlier has vanished, replaced by something raw and real. This isn't about playing roles anymore. This is just us, Saint and Petra, two people caught in the heat of a moment that neither of us wants to escape.

He's standing between my legs now, and his towel leaves very little barrier between us, so I feel him harden almost instantly.

I wrap my legs around him, and that's when he takes my control of the kiss away from me. He cradles my head with his left hand and deepens the kiss, then pulls me to the edge of the counter with his right hand so that I'm mostly being held up by him.

I let my head fall back as he drags his mouth down my throat. I close my eyes, dizzy beneath his touch. I feel his fingers at the knot I've tied on the robe.

"Can I?" he whispers.

I lift my head and look at him, then nod quietly.

His eyes fall to my chest, and then he unties my robe. I lift up a little as he removes it and pulls it away. He tosses it over his shoulder, sucking in a small gasp of air as he looks at me, then runs his fingers down the center of my chest.

I can't help but stare at his wedding ring as his hand moves to cup my breast.

Are my breasts prettier than his wife's?

Am *I* prettier than his wife?

He takes my nipple in his mouth, and I fist my hand into his hair, pressing his lips against my breast even harder. He sucks and bites without a trace of the gentleness he's been displaying since I got out of the shower.

The hungry side of him has taken over, and his mouth is suddenly all over me—moving between both breasts, then to my neck, then back to my mouth. I can barely keep up with the parts of me he's focused so intently on before he moves on to another part of me.

He lifts me off the counter and holds me against him, one hand wrapped around my lower back and the other cupping my ass while his tongue is deep in my mouth.

I'm glad he's carrying me right now, because I think I'm too dizzy to walk.

He drops me on the sofa, pulls his towel away, and then lowers himself on top of me. "Do I need a condom?" he asks.

I'm on the pill, and I know I'm good not to use one, but how do I reassure myself that he is? I barely know him, and my decision-making skills have not been great tonight. I'm naked beneath a man who made me cry from fear earlier.

My hesitation in answering him gives him what he's looking for. "My wallet. Be right back." He crosses the dark room, and I hear him rifling through the wallet. I even hear him tear the wrapper as he's making his way back to me.

And then he's back on top of me, condom in place, his mouth pressed against mine again. He returned so fast, I didn't even get a good enough look at him to determine whether this is going to hurt.

I've never had that before—the kind of sex women have in the books I write. Every man I've ever been with has been of average size, so I've always had to imagine what it would be like to be fucked by a man who is so big, it actually hurts.

As soon as I wrap my legs around him, it's clear that I won't have to imagine it any longer. I can feel the intimidating length of him rubbing against my thigh.

When he repositions himself so that he can start to slide into me, I wince.

His mouth is feathering mine, back and forth. "Just say *stop* if you want me to stop, okay?" The gentleness in his voice coupled with the reassuring look in his eyes makes me putty beneath him.

He begins to push the rest of himself into me, and I close my eyes, savoring every second of this. I pay attention to the pain, to the pleasure, to the noises we're both making. I imagine how I'm going to describe this when I write it all down.

Painful, yet satiating.

Sensual, yet animalistic.

We find our rhythm almost instantly, and I stop thinking about how I'll describe this. All I can think about is how good this feels. Those thoughts are occasionally mixed with worry about the current state of my morals, but that worry is easy to pack away when Saint kisses me.

I could get used to this.

So used to this.

That thought terrifies me as my moans echo through the house.

CHAPTER ELEVEN

The click of the front door closing is still echoing in the house when I wake. I immediately look around the living room, sitting up on the couch.

Saint is gone.

I walk to the living room window and watch, hidden behind the curtains, as his dark car pulls out of my driveway and disappears down the street. A strange mix of relief and an unsettling emptiness settles in my chest. He always leaves.

I wait. One minute. Then two. The urge to know, to see, to understand who he is and where he comes from gnaws at me. It's an intriguing itch, one I know I shouldn't scratch, but I can't help myself. And if I stand here long enough to talk myself out of this, it'll be too late.

I hurry to my room and pull on the one sundress I packed, throw on some flip-flops, and then grab my keys, my heart thrumming a frantic rhythm against my ribs.

The sun is low as it rises in the east, painting long golden shadows across the street. *This is a bad idea,* my logical brain screams. *He'll see me.* But the other, more insistent side, the one that's been captivated by Saint since he first walked into my life, pushes me out the door.

My car feels like a glaring beacon as I back out of the driveway. I drive quickly down the road, assuming he turned left to go toward town. I drive quickly still, another minute, until I spot what looks like his car. I keep a good distance behind him as we travel, trying to blend in with the sparse morning traffic. My grip on the steering wheel is tight, knuckles white. Every passing car is a mini panic attack, every turn a potential reveal. I just want to know where he goes, where he lives. Maybe, just maybe, I'll catch a glimpse of her, the wife. The woman who holds the other, *real* part of his life.

Fifteen minutes creep by. He's taking a route I don't recognize, leading me farther away from the sanctuary of my cabin. My stomach churns with a mix of anticipation and dread when he turns onto a county road. What will I see? What will I learn?

Will I regret it?

Then, as soon as I make the turn, the brake lights of his car catch my eye, bright red against the green of the trees. He is already pulled over.

He's already outside his car.

He's waiting for me.

My breath hitches. *How did he know? How did he even see me?* I'm scrambling for a plausible reason for being on this street, in this neighborhood.

He's standing by the driver's side, looking directly at my car with crossed arms as he leans against his own. There's no mistaking the stern set of his jaw, the narrowed eyes. My heart sinks. *He definitely knows.*

He gestures for me to pull over. It's just a quick motion of his head, but I feel like a small child caught with my hand in the cookie jar.

I pull over and shift into park as he pushes off his car and begins walking toward mine. I press the button to roll down my window, and the whirring sound of the glass descending seems impossibly loud in the sudden quiet.

"Get out, Petra." His voice is low, commanding. Not angry, not yet, but with an undeniable sternness.

I hesitate, frozen by a potent cocktail of shame and fear. My cheeks burn. He sees my reluctance, and with a sigh, he opens my car door and reaches for me.

Before I can protest, he has me. One strong arm loops behind my back, the other under my knees. He lifts me, effortlessly, as if I weigh nothing. The suddenness of it, the unexpected intimacy, steals my breath. My hands instinctively grip his shoulders. My body feels surprisingly light, almost buoyant, as he carries me to the front of my own car.

With a practiced ease that makes my stomach flip, he sets me down on the hood, my legs dangling, the bottoms of my thighs sticking to the metal, warm from the heat of the engine.

His hands brace against the car on either side of my legs, trapping me between his arms. He leans in, his face close, his eyes dark with an unreadable intensity. The scent of him fills my senses.

"You better stop digging." His voice is a low rumble, a warning.

I can feel the heat radiating off him, the solidness of his chest so close to mine. My pulse quickens. "I . . . I just . . ." I stammer, my voice thin, pathetic.

"You already know I'm married." It's not a question. It's a statement, a reminder, heavy with unspoken implications.

My gaze drops, unable to meet his. Shame washes over me, a hot tide. "I was just curious about you," I whisper, the words barely audible. They sound hollow, even to my own ears. A lame excuse for something far more complicated.

He sighs, a slow, deliberate exhalation that stirs the hair at my temples. "I thought we had an agreement." His words are firm, a boundary drawn in the air between us.

My eyes flicker up to his. "I wasn't going to do anything. I just wanted to see where you go when you aren't with me. Where you live."

"It's not your business," he says.

"I know. I just . . ." I can't articulate myself right now. Men rarely, if ever, leave me speechless and nervous like Saint does.

I look back at his face and ask the one question I'm most curious about. "I just want to know things. Things that will help my book."

"Like what?" he responds, his voice flat.

"Are you happy?" The question slips out before I can stop it, a desperate plea for some crack in his carefully constructed facade.

His jaw tightens almost imperceptibly. "Yes." The word is clipped, definitive.

A bitter taste floods my mouth. "Then why are you cheating on your wife with me?" The accusation hangs in the air.

His eyes narrow. "You *asked* me to." The bluntness of his reply stings. It's a cold dose of reality. And it's true. I did, maybe not outright. But I definitely initiated it, fueled by a reckless desire for something I knew I shouldn't want.

"But do you feel guilty?" I press, my voice rising slightly, desperate to find a chink in his armor, a flicker of guilt, anything.

"Are you really asking these things because of your book? Or should I be worried you're about to cross a line?" His tone is bordering on condescending. It makes me feel small, insignificant, just another secret to be kept among so many other secrets that he tucks away.

"It's not fair to her," I argue, a sudden fierce protectiveness for the woman I don't even know rising within me. "*I* feel guilty and I don't even know your wife." I don't even know what I'm doing or why I'm saying this. I just want to know what he feels, I guess.

He pushes back from the car slightly, enough to break the intense physical contact, but not enough to release me from his gaze. "Then I'll stop coming over if that's how you feel." The words are delivered without emotion, a simple statement of fact, but they hit me like a physical blow. The thought of him not coming to the cabin, not filling that space in my life with his presence, sends a cold dread through me.

My breath hitches. He sees the reaction in my eyes. His gaze softens, a fleeting moment of something akin to understanding, or perhaps pity. He leans in again, closer than before, his voice dropping to a near whisper.

"I'm a good husband outside of what she doesn't know. But if you're starting to question doing the things she doesn't know we're doing, then maybe we should stop doing those things."

His hands, which have been bracing him while we speak, now move. Slow, deliberate. They slide from the hood of the car, over the thin material of my dress, and settle on my thighs. A jolt, electric and potent, shoots through me. My skin prickles under his touch. My breath starts to come in short, shallow gasps. His fingers move, a light, teasing caress, up my inner thighs. My body responds before my mind can even process it, a familiar warmth spreading through me, a primal ache.

"Would you like to stop doing these things my wife doesn't know we do?"

His eyes, dark and heavy lidded, meet mine. I shake my head. "No. Not yet." I can see the desire there, mirroring my own. The air between us thickens, charged with an undeniable tension. Our breathing grows heavier, ragged, almost synchronized.

"If you want to know the truth, I feel like a complete asshole," he murmurs, his voice rough with suppressed emotion as he continues to caress me, moving up my thigh.

"Maybe you are," I whisper back, my own voice hoarse, barely recognizable. The shame is still there, a dull throb, but it's being eclipsed by a different, more urgent sensation.

"My wife deserves better," he says, his voice a low thrum against my skin as his hands continue their slow, intoxicating dance on my thighs, moving higher.

"Petra deserves better," I counter, the words surprising even me. A flicker of defiance, a quiet reclaiming of my own worth, even in this messy, complicated situation.

A faint, almost imperceptible smile touches the corner of his lips. It's not a happy smile, more of a weary acknowledgment. "Petra. You deserve *so* much better." His fingers slip inside my underwear, and then into me.

I gasp.

His other hand, strong and sure, spreads my legs wider on the hood of the car. My dress rides up, exposing my skin to the cool air, but I barely register it. My senses are consumed by him, by the intoxicating pull of his presence.

I gasp again, my back arching off the hood and into his hand. He leans down, his mouth finding mine, silencing any protest, any sound, with a deep, consuming kiss.

It's raw, it's urgent, it's everything I shouldn't want but crave with a desperate intensity. The fact that we're outside on an open road, the shame of a potential approaching car, it all fades away, replaced by the sounds coming from me.

Saint watches me, exposed on the hood of my car, as I completely come apart in front of him. His eyes remain dark, but as I tremble against his hand, there's a flicker of something new there. Something he only wishes he were pretending.

When my breathing slows, Saint pulls his hand away, never breaking eye contact with me.

My legs are aching and my body is still tingling. My mind is a whirlwind of emotions. Shame, desire, confusion, a surprising surge of defiance. "Where will you tell her you've been all night?" The question tumbles out, breathless, a desperate attempt to grasp at some tangible piece of his other life, to understand the woman who shares him.

He sighs, a deep, heavy sound. He pushes off the car, creating a small distance between us. "Stop asking questions about her. I don't like thinking about her when I'm with you."

"Do you like thinking about me when you're with her?" I ask, my voice small, vulnerable.

He looks away, staring out into the middle distance, his jaw tight. "No. But I do it anyway. And it doesn't feel good to feel good about someone who isn't my wife." His voice is flat, yet the words themselves carry a profound weight. He turns back to me, his gaze direct, unyielding. "Go back to the cabin, Petra. Don't follow me. You won't like what you find."

Then, he turns and walks away. He doesn't look back. He gets into his car, starts the engine, and drives off, leaving me alone, exposed on the hood of my car, the morning sun casting long, lonely shadows around me.

I do what he says. I go back to the cabin and I write.

CHAPTER TWELVE

For two days, I wrote.

I didn't hear from Saint at all after he left me at my car two days ago. No texts, no visits, no surprises. I was okay with it, though. I got so much written. I was still reeling from the fear of being tied up, and then I was still buzzing from the emptiness he left me with after what happened on my car.

I've barely eaten, I've been writing so much. I was so fired up by the way his hands had gripped my hips on that car, the way he was being such an asshole. I loved it. I loved feeling vulnerable.

That's new to me, and I'm surprised by how much it turns me on.

I channel my energy into the manuscript, typing away on my keyboard at a speed I'm not accustomed to.

> Every detail replayed in my mind of us on the couch, vivid and undeniable. Before he left, Cam fucked me again, on my bed. It wasn't rushed or frantic like the first time. It was slower, deliberate, as if he knew we wouldn't see each other for a while. His hands moved over my skin like he was memorizing it, like he was committing the feel of me to memory.

> The room had been bathed in darkness, the only sounds our shared breaths, the creak of the bed, and the occasional murmur of his voice in my ear.
>
> Even now, I can feel the imprint of his fingers on my waist, the discrepancy in the temperature of his body against mine.
>
> I don't know where he told his wife he was last night—possibly working a night shift—but he said he'd be back again this afternoon. That's how these things go, I guess. Sneaking moments, lying to someone we vowed our lives to, all in the name of something we pretend we can't resist. I should feel guilt clawing at me, but instead, there's this strange mixture of anticipation and dread swirling in my stomach. Part of me is counting down the hours until I see him again, while another part of me is terrified of what might happen if this goes on any longer.

I'm ripped from my writing by a knock at my front door. I glance at the clock and see that it's barely after lunch. An odd time for Saint to show up here.

Maybe it's Mari.

I close my laptop, hoping for Saint to be at the door rather than either of the Longsetters. It would be a nice reprieve from work, considering it's been more than forty-eight hours since I last saw him. I'm starting to have withdrawals.

Maybe he is too.

I entertain changing into an actual outfit, considering I'm just in my nightgown, but that sounds like too much effort, and I'm too tired from the writing marathon to give a shit.

I glance toward the window overlooking the front yard, expecting to see Saint's car, but I immediately stop walking.

My stomach drops at the sight of the car in my driveway. That's not Saint's car.

That's Shephard's car.

Shit.

Shit, fuck, shit!

What is he *doing* here? This was supposed to be my time, my space to write, to disconnect from everything else, including my family. *Especially* my family. Oh, God. Did he bring the girls with him?

The panic sets in, rising up through my chest like a wave threatening to swallow me whole. I can't even believe this. Shephard never shows up to my writing weeks unannounced. We have an understanding. This is my retreat, my sanctuary, the one place where I'm supposed to be able to escape the real world, where I can focus on my work and nothing else.

But now, my carefully constructed bubble has been burst, and I have no idea how to piece it back together.

Just as I'm turning toward my bedroom to make sure nothing of Saint's was left behind, Chloe cups her little hands around her eyes and presses her face against the window.

"Mommy!" she squeals, her voice muffled by the glass but unmistakable in its excitement. She backs away from the window, pointing inside at me, her grin wide and full of joy. "Daddy, I see Mommy!"

Shephard is looking through the window now too. His expression is one of complete happiness, like he's giving me the best surprise in the world. He waves at me, his smile a thing I'd like to wipe off his face right now.

"Surprise!" he yells, his voice carrying through the glass, as if this is exactly what I would have wanted.

I feel like I'm walking through quicksand as I move toward the door. Each step is slow, deliberate, as I try to wrap my mind around what's happening. My heart is pounding in my chest, my pulse loud in my ears. I glance around the living room, my eyes scanning this area, too, for any signs of Saint—anything that might give away what's been going on here since I left home.

There's nothing obvious, nothing that screams *infidelity*, but the memory of him is everywhere. It lingers in the air, in the sheets on my bed, in the scent of him still clinging to my skin.

What have I done?

What the fuck was I thinking?

Saint might come back today. He'll *likely* come back today. That's been his routine during all of this. An intense day here, a break there, another intense day, another break. Today is on schedule for an intense Saint day, and that absolutely cannot happen. It jolts me, and I realize with a sinking feeling that I need to text him as soon as possible and let him know not to show up here.

My hands are shaking as I reach for the lock on the door. I hesitate for a brief moment, my fingers hovering over the handle, before I finally unlock it and pull it open.

Chloe and Andi push past their father, their little arms wrapping around me before I even have a chance to greet them properly. Their tiny hands clutch at my nightgown, their faces pressed against my legs, and for a moment, the guilt of everything I've done hits me with full force.

These weeks I spend at the lake are honestly the toughest weeks of the year for me, being away from them. I love my daughters more than anything, and yet, here I am, standing in the aftermath of these days and nights where I've pretended I'm not their mother, where I've pretended I'm not Shephard's wife.

Having these getaways allows me to write my books much faster so I can spend more time with my girls when I'm at home, but I've never had the experience that I've had this time. I've always just gone away and worked. Truly worked. I've never gone away and done something so horrid, it could destroy my family. Destroy my kids.

I kneel down and pull them in for an even better hug, my arms wrapping tightly around them as if holding them close could somehow erase the guilt gnawing at me. "We came to surprise you!" Andi says, her excitement bubbling over as she bounces up and down in my arms.

I glance up at Shephard, my smile forced but as genuine as I can muster under the circumstances. "I see that."

Shephard slips around us, his presence looming larger now that he's inside the cabin. Just as I stand back up, he leans in for a quick kiss, his lips brushing against mine in a way that feels foreign after everything I've done. "Sorry," he mutters, his tone apologetic. "They insisted I not tell you."

"It's fine," I say, my voice steady despite the whirlwind of emotions crashing through me. I hope my reaction is convincing, that he can't see through the mask I'm wearing. "I needed the break."

Shephard is holding two bags of groceries. He sets them on the counter with a sense of purpose, already moving toward the front door again before I can even process what's happening. "We're going to cook dinner for you," he says over his shoulder, his smile wide and genuine. "I'll grab the rest of the groceries." He heads back outside, and I pry the girls away from me with as much patience as I can manage.

"Mommy needs to change out of her nightgown," I say, trying to sound lighthearted as I usher them toward the kitchen. "You two start putting away the groceries."

They're too young to know how to put away groceries in a home they're unfamiliar with, of course. Andi is four and Chloe is five. Shephard and I had them back-to-back, hoping it would be easier on us to go through the toughest years all at once. Now, watching them climb onto the chairs to reach the counter, their little faces full of concentration as they pull items from the bags, I feel a pang of guilt so sharp it's almost physical. I should be better than this. I should be a better mother, a better wife. I shouldn't be living this double life, sneaking moments with a man who isn't my husband.

I glance out the kitchen window, watching as Shephard reaches into his trunk to grab the rest of the groceries. My stomach churns with a mixture of dread and urgency. I rush to the bedroom and grab my phone, my hands shaking as I open my texts to Saint. My fingers fly across the screen as I type, each word feeling like it's sealing something inevitable.

> Whatever you do, please do not come back here today.

I toss my phone on the bed and strip out of my nightgown, my heart still racing with the fear of what could happen if Saint shows up. The thought alone is enough to make my skin crawl with anxiety. I hear the buzz of his reply come through just as I'm pulling a shirt over my head.

My hands are still trembling as I grab my phone and read the text.

> Is everything okay?

I hesitate for a moment, my thumb hovering over the screen. I don't want to lie to him, but for some reason, it feels like I've betrayed him. He's never asked me if I'm married, so there's really nothing for him to be upset about. Besides, he's married too. He'll understand. He'll probably even be relieved.

> My husband and kids just showed up.

I delete all my texts from him and finish getting dressed. I slide my phone in my back pocket so Shephard won't see me preoccupied with it.

I walk out of the bedroom just as Shephard is heading into the kitchen with the rest of the groceries.

Chloe rushes over to me with a puzzle she's pulled off a shelf. "Mommy, can we do a puzzle?"

"Please?" Andi begs.

I nod and look over at Shephard. "You want to join us?" I'll do anything to pretend I'm a good wife and mother, and not the terrible human being I've been since showing up here.

"You girls go ahead. I'm going to prep."

Shephard seems at ease as he begins pulling items out of the bags. He seems to dive right into the normalcy of our routine, unaware of the chaos I've brought into our lives.

CHAPTER THIRTEEN

The rhythmic clatter of pans and the faint, comforting smell of garlic fill the kitchen, creating a sense of normalcy that feels so at odds with the storm brewing inside me. Shephard is at the stove, his back to me, stirring something in a gleaming skillet, humming softly under his breath. It's a tuneless, content sound; he's completely at ease in his role as the devoted husband and father. He's prepping dinner while I sit at the kitchen island, hunched over a brightly colored jigsaw puzzle with the girls. Andi, my youngest, giggles beside me, her sticky fingers carefully placing a piece. Chloe murmurs instructions: "No, Andi, that's a wing, not a tail!"

He's so absorbed in what he's doing, the meticulous chopping of herbs, the sizzle of oil, that he doesn't seem to notice how distracted I am. My eyes dart from the vibrant puzzle pieces to the clock, to the window, to the back of Shephard's broad shoulders.

But then again, why would he notice? I've been playing the part for years, slipping in and out of roles and characters like they were costumes I could change at will. The serene, engaged mother. The supportive, loving wife. The business-minded public speaker. I pretend to be all the things I'm supposed to be when I need to be them, while trying not to live completely in my head. I'm used to it—I've been this way my whole life. I dress the part for every other aspect of my life, but I'm the most me in the silence of my mind. But today, it feels less like I'm wearing a costume and more like I've been shoved into a suffocating straitjacket.

The humming falters. It's almost imperceptible, just a slight catch in his breath, a break in the rhythmic stirring of the pan. My gaze, which was fixed on a bright-blue puzzle piece, flicks to Shephard. His stirring slows, becomes hesitant. His head cocks slightly, his eyes narrowing as he looks out the window, a subtle shift in his focus. There's a pause, a beat of hesitation that stretches taut in the quiet kitchen, before he turns his attention fully to the driveway, his body stiffening almost imperceptibly.

Something about the shift in his body language sets off alarm bells in my head, a frantic jingle behind my ears. My skin prickles. My stomach clenches, a cold fist tightening. But I don't look up right away. I can't. Instead, I keep my eyes glued to the puzzle pieces in front of me, trying to make the disparate pieces fit into a coherent picture, even though my mind is a frantic whirlwind elsewhere.

"Mommy, found it!" Chloe crows, thrusting a yellow piece into my vision. Andi nods approvingly. The girls are giggling beside me, their little hands eagerly helping me assemble the picture of a bustling farm, their joy so innocent. Their laughter, usually a balm, feels like a distant echo in the sudden ringing in my ears.

It should be a moment of calm, of simple family bonding, the kind I tell myself I cherish. But I feel anything but calm, knowing that a car just pulled into the driveway, an uninvited, ominous presence. My hands are shaking as I place down a green piece, missing the connection slightly, my vision hazy as my thoughts spiral.

I tell myself it's fine, that everything will be fine, that it's just the neighbors, or a delivery, or . . . *anyone but him.*

But deep down, there's a gnawing unease that I can't shake, a cold certainty. It's been gnawing at me since I sent Saint that text telling him my husband and children were here. He never responded. The silence from him was louder than any roar.

I've been on edge since I sent the text, jumpy at every shadow, waiting for the other shoe to drop, for the fragile peace I've constructed to shatter.

Is this it? Is this the end of my comfortable family life as I know it? Is this where everything unravels? The scent of garlic and simmering sauce, once comforting, now feels cloying, heavy, suffocating.

I finally work up the courage to follow Shephard's unblinking gaze. My neck feels stiff, resisting the turn. When my eyes land on it, I stiffen further, every muscle locking into place. A black, unmarked car, its windows tinted, reflecting the bright afternoon like dark mirrors. It's the kind you see in movies, the kind that signals trouble, the kind that belongs to men who operate in shadows.

It's the car I followed two days ago. The car that pulled over and waited for me.

The kind of car you never want to see pulling up to your house unannounced, ever. I'm grasping for any way to rationalize this, but deep down, I already know. I know before I even see him step out of the dark vehicle. My intuition, sharp and unwelcome, screams his name.

Shephard cuts the fire to the pan and then pushes off the counter. "Someone just pulled up." His voice is low, strained, a question and a warning wrapped into one. He sees it too. He knows something is profoundly amiss.

The car door closes, a silent swing, almost graceful. The blood feels like it drains from my body, rushing from my head, leaving me lightheaded, dizzy. My vision tunnels. The world seems to tilt on its axis, a sickening lurch, the floorboards swaying beneath me. The air suddenly feels too thick, too heavy to breathe, pressing down on my lungs. My heart lurches in my chest, a violent, painful beat, my stomach dropping like a stone, the sensation of free fall. I blink, hard, once, twice, hoping that somehow I've imagined it, that my mind is playing cruel tricks on me, a residual nightmare from last night.

But it's real. He's real. *Motherfucker.*

The sunlight catches on the sharp line of Saint's jaw, the dark gleam of his hair. Saint. He's here. And he's walking toward my house. Toward Shephard. Toward my girls.

My breath hitches, lost in my throat. *What is he doing here?* The words are a desperate whisper, barely audible, directed at no one, a plea against the impossible.

"Who is that?" The question slams into me like a freight train, sending my thoughts spiraling into a maelstrom of sheer panic. Shephard's quiet query echoes in the sudden, cavernous silence of the kitchen, but it's my own internal scream. Every rational thought evaporates, dissolving like smoke; I'm desperate to find a reason that would explain his impossible presence here and doesn't involve the scorching, undeniable truth of what I've done.

I can't think straight. All I can hear is the rushing in my ears, a roaring like a distant ocean, the steady thrum of blood pounding in my veins, deafening me to the innocent giggles of my daughters still playing with their puzzle on the island.

My heart is hammering against my rib cage, a frantic bird trying to escape, its wings beating a furious rhythm.

"Do you know this person?" Shephard asks.

Suddenly, it's hard to breathe, each inhale a shallow, desperate gasp. I can feel the walls of the sterile kitchen closing in around me, the familiar comfort suddenly constricting. Every instinct screams at me to stop this, to find a way to stop him before everything unravels, before the fragile facade of my life shatters into a million irreparable pieces.

"No idea," I say, my voice steady but my shame buried just beneath it.

Shephard starts heading to the door, his steps purposeful. I want to scream at him, to stop him from answering it, to grab him and hold him back, to physically block his path, but my voice is stuck in my throat, a dry, choked whisper.

I slide Andi off my lap, almost roughly, as soon as Shephard says, "Why would a cop be here?"

His voice is more casual now, a slight note of confusion in it, like he's mildly perplexed by this unexpected visit, not truly alarmed. He has no idea what's really going on, no idea that the officer outside isn't just here for some routine check, isn't just a friendly public servant. But *I* know. I know with a sickening certainty, and the dread pooling in my stomach, a cold, viscous liquid, is almost unbearable. It tastes like ash.

My legs feel like they might give out beneath me, like jelly, but I force myself to walk to the door with Shephard, each step a monumental effort. Every stride feels like I'm walking toward my own execution, toward the scaffold. I glance out the window, my breath catching in my throat when I see Saint walking slowly around Shephard's car, circling it like a predator. His movements are deliberate, measured, a terrifying choreography, like he's taking his sweet time, like he knows the absolute, devastating power he holds in this moment, a puppet master pulling invisible strings.

I keep my distance from Shephard, putting a few precious feet between us, trying to maintain some semblance of composure, to project an image of calm.

Shephard's hand is already on the doorknob, his face still a picture of mild confusion. He pulls the door open, and it's as if I can literally see my family dissolving like a sandcastle hit by a rogue wave. The foundation we've built, the life we've shared, all of it feels impossibly fragile, like it could shatter with just one wrong word, one wrong look, one perfectly delivered lie.

I want to scream, to tell Saint to leave, to go back to wherever he came from, but I'm frozen. Paralyzed.

Why else would Saint be here? There's no good reason, no benign explanation that doesn't lead straight to the truth spilling out in the most catastrophic, painful way possible. He's here for a reason, a calculated, devastating reason, and whatever that reason is, it's going to end me.

Shephard steps out onto the porch, a picture of genial hospitality, and I remain frozen in the doorway, my hand gripping the doorframe for support, my knuckles white. My legs feel weak, like they might give out at any second, but I force myself to stand still, to hold my ground, to remain upright. I can't let either of these men see how terrified I am. I can't let Shephard know I have anything at all to feel guilty for, and I can't let Saint know how much power he holds right now.

Saint glances at Shephard, a brief, dismissive flick of his eyes; then his gaze, cold and sharp, cuts to me. The look in his eyes is hard, unreadable, like polished obsidian, but there's something in the set of his jaw, the tightness around his mouth, that makes my heart sink even lower, plummeting into the pit of my stomach.

He's in full uniform, crisp and impeccable, a perfect mask of professionalism. The badge gleams, the dark fabric of his shirt accentuating the breadth of his shoulders, the holstered gun a stark, chilling presence.

But his eyes—they're locked on me, zeroed in with an intensity like laser beams piercing my very soul. He knows exactly what he's doing, like he's fully aware of the precise chaos he's about to unleash, the emotional fallout he's meticulously planned. His jaw is hard, a rigid line, his expression severe, almost menacing, and I can't breathe. I can't even move. I am a statue of dread.

"Sorry to bother you folks," Saint says, his voice perfectly modulated, the picture of professional courtesy. But I can hear the testiness in it, a subtle, almost imperceptible undertone. He slowly brings his gaze to Shephard, his eyes lingering on me for just a second longer than necessary, a deliberate, silent promise of destruction.

Saint stops at the bottom step, his presence looming large even from a distance, radiating an unnerving power. "I'm just doing a standard patrol of the area and noticed you don't have a visitor tag." His words are casual, almost too casual, delivered with an ease that is utterly chilling.

Shephard tilts his head, confusion flickering across his face, a slight furrow appearing between his brows. "Visitor tag?" His voice is laced with surprise, a genuine bewilderment. I can see him trying to make sense of what's happening, trying to fit this odd interaction into his comfortable, predictable world. He shrugs slightly. "We've been coming here for years."

Saint nods, his expression never faltering, a perfect, unwavering mask. "New county ordinance. All vehicles traveling in and out of the area now require a visitor tag. Standard procedure, just implemented this month."

Shephard lets out a short, surprised laugh at the absurdity of needing a tag just to be here, on a public lake that isn't even an official park. His chuckle is light and dismissive, as if he's trying to brush off the strange encounter with casual humor.

I can't even fake a smile right now. My mouth feels dry, like cotton, my hands trembling slightly as I clasp them together in front of me, trying to steady myself, trying to anchor myself in this rapidly destabilizing reality.

I know Saint is lying. Every fiber of my being screams it. There's no requirement for a visitor tag in this area, and there never has been. We've been coming to this lake for years, and not once have we ever had to deal with something like this. He's playing a dangerous game.

It's a risky lie, an incredibly audacious one, that sends my mind spinning with a sickening mixture of questions and dread. What is he thinking? Does he really expect Shephard to believe this blatant fabrication? And more importantly, what's his plan? What's the next move in this terrifying chess game?

Saint has no idea how much Shephard does or doesn't know about the local laws, or how much attention he pays to minor ordinances. He's gambling on the hope that Shephard will take him at his word, that he'll be too distracted or too trusting, too polite, to question it. And for a split second, a terrifying, hopeful second, I think it might work. Shephard doesn't seem suspicious—just confused, a mild annoyance creasing his forehead.

"I didn't realize," Shephard says, his tone still casual, but there's a slight furrow in his brow as he turns around to look at me, seeking confirmation. His expression is full of mild confusion, but there's no alarm, no suspicion, no accusation. "Did *you* know this, Pet?"

I can feel Saint's eyes on me, drilling into me with an intensity that makes it hard to breathe. I feel pinned to the doorframe by Shephard's nickname for me being spoken in front of Saint.

Pet.

I swallow hard, as if every word I utter is going to betray me, to unravel the precarious lie. Saint is staring at me, hard, his gaze unwavering, and I know this is a test. He's watching to see how I'll handle this, whether I'll crumble under the pressure or play along, whether I'm a good enough actress.

This moment feels pivotal, like walking on a knife edge. One wrong word, one hesitant glance, could unravel everything I hold dear.

I nod, a stiff, barely perceptible movement, forcing my face into an expression of mild nonchalance, of detached understanding, even though inside, I'm falling apart, pieces of me splintering. I clear my throat, trying to push down the hot, painful lump forming there, fighting to keep my voice from breaking. "Yeah," I say, my voice barely steady, a thin thread of sound. "It's a new law. I . . . forgot to tell you." The lie feels heavy on my tongue, sticking there, thick and repugnant, but I push it out, praying it sounds convincing enough, praying for his belief, for my salvation.

Shephard seems to accept my explanation without a second thought. He even offers a small, rueful laugh. He tosses a hand toward me, his smile easy and relaxed, as if this is all just one big joke to him, a minor inconvenience, something to be amused by. "She forgot to tell me," Shephard says with a light laugh, the sound bubbling up as he looks back at Saint, as though he's trying to break the awkwardness, to turn this strange, unsettling moment into something normal, something lighthearted. He's hoping to get a smile out of Saint, a shared moment of masculine understanding.

But he gets nothing.

Saint's expression remains unchanged, a stoic mask. His gaze is fixed on me, unwavering, intense, dark and piercing. He's not here to laugh, not here for polite social graces. He's here to make a point. The air between us feels thick, suffocating, charged with unspoken menace, and I can't tell if he's acting, a master of deception, or if this is something darker.

Saint is still staring at me, his eyes narrowing slightly, as if he's waiting for me to crack. Every second that passes feels like an eternity, the tension stretching and pulling until I feel like I might snap under the pressure.

"I'm only here for the night," Shephard says, oblivious to the swirling undercurrents, the deadly game playing out right in front of him. He speaks calmly, still trying to be amiable, completely unaware of the storm brewing right in front of him. "My car will be gone by eight tomorrow morning. Can we let it slide this time?"

He's just trying to be polite, to resolve a minor inconvenience, to wrap this bizarre conversation up and go back to the comfortable, predictable life we've built together, completely unaware that it's all hanging by a single fraying thread.

Saint finally looks back at Shephard, his expression still hard, a chiseled mask of authority, but something in his posture shifts, a subtle easing of tension around his shoulders. He gives Shephard a tight nod, a curt, professional acknowledgment, his jaw clenched, a muscle jumping under his skin. "I'll be back in the morning to make sure the car's gone," Saint says, his voice flat, but his words are laced with something that feels like far more than just a promise. It's almost as if it's a warning, a subtle threat wrapped in the chilling formality of his professional tone. The way he says it sends an icy chill slithering down my spine, burrowing into my bones, and I know, with absolute, terrifying certainty, that he means every single word.

This isn't just about Shephard's car—it's about control. It's about letting *me* know that he's not done, that this isn't over, that I am still firmly within his grasp. Or maybe he just wants me to know he's angry that I failed to mention I have a husband. The thought is a bitter, unwelcome taste in my mouth.

Shephard looks at me, raising an eyebrow, his expression a complicated mix of bemusement and disbelief, like he can't quite believe what he's hearing, or what he's just witnessed. He doesn't say it, not out loud, but I can see it in his eyes: *This guy is crazy. This is beyond weird.* And for a terrifying, fleeting moment, I find myself agreeing with him. *He might be right. This might be pure, unadulterated madness.* But then I pull myself back, a frantic mental tug.

No, this is Saint.

This is Cam.

I can't tell.

The character and the muse are bleeding into each other like watercolors in a storm. I don't know if Saint is just playing the jealous, possessive role of Cam right now, or if he's crossed some unseen, dangerous boundary, if the character has consumed the man. Either way, the cold, sticky fear bubbling in my chest won't go away, clinging to my ribs.

As if the moment couldn't get any worse, I see a mop of orange curls on top of a silky dress making its way up the driveway.

"Are you kidding me?" I whisper, mostly under my breath, but Shephard glances at me.

"Who is she?"

"Hi!" she sings, waving a wild hand. "Just going for a stroll and thought I heard children!"

"The neighbor. Owner of the house."

Saint's eyes dart back to mine just as Mari reaches him. "Hello, there, Officer. Lovely to see you again." Mari's eyes move toward Shephard. "And who are you?" she asks, reaching out a hand as she ascends the steps. "I'm Mari."

"Shephard. I'm Petra's husband."

Mari stops in her tracks. She looks at me. Then at Saint. Then back at Shephard. Then back at me. "Oh. How fun."

Kill me now.

"I'll be heading out," Saint says, bringing me my first sigh of relief since Shephard showed up today. He tips his hat toward me, a slow, deliberate gesture, his eyes never leaving mine, drilling into me, holding me captive. "You two have a lovely night." There's something about the way he says it, that subtle curve of his mouth, like he's amused by all this, by my terror, by Shephard's cluelessness.

Then he turns and gives Mari a tip of his hat, his movements fluid and unhurried, and walks back toward his car, each step measured, like he knows exactly the impact he's having, exactly how deeply he's burrowing under my skin. He gets inside the black vehicle, a silent, predatory glide. The air in my lungs feels thin, inadequate, but I exhale as much of it as I can afford to let out.

"And who are these two?" Mari asks, gesturing toward the doorway, where the girls are now standing.

"Andi and Chloe," I say, my words clipped. "Mari, do you think you could come by another time? We were about to sit down to dinner."

She blinks several times. Too many times. "I sure can. Just wanted to introduce myself to your company." She looks toward Shephard. "If you need anything, please let me know. We're just at the end of the road."

"Sure will," Shephard says.

As soon as Mari turns, I walk back inside the cabin, my hands shaking so violently I have to press them against my sides to control them as I close the door behind us. The latch clicks with an exaggerated finality. My legs feel weak, like they might give out at any second, so I go straight for the wine rack, my trembling hands grabbing the bottle with a desperate urgency.

I pour myself a glass, the red liquid sloshing slightly over the rim. My thoughts are a jumbled mess of pure panic, searing regret, and the gnawing, terrifying realization that this situation is spiraling out of control faster than I can possibly manage, faster than I can even comprehend.

Shephard returns to the stove, shaking his head with a bewildered smile, a picture of blissful ignorance. "That was weird," he says, his voice light, tinged with amusement, like he's already dismissed the strange encounter, already moved past it and tucked it away into the "odd occurrences" file of his mind. He lights the flame under the pan again and stirs the pot on the stove, the garlic scent suddenly overwhelming, his back to me as he talks, his shoulders relaxed. "Wonder why they're getting so strict around here all of a sudden."

"I don't know," I mutter. My voice is tight, my throat constricted, dry and scratchy, but I force the response out, trying to sound as casual, as unbothered, as possible.

Shephard walks over to me, and his arms wrap around me in a warm, familiar embrace. He pulls me close, pressing a kiss to the top of my head, the scent of him, clean, comforting, *safe*, momentarily grounding me, even though my insides are still rattled, a chaotic tempest.

"I guess it's a good thing with you being out here all alone," he says, his voice soft, full of concern and love, a protective rumble in his chest. He's trying to reassure me, to make me feel safe, to be my anchor, but his words only make the panic claw deeper into my chest, a cold, sharp blade twisting. The irony is a bitter laugh caught in my throat. *Alone.* I have been far from alone.

I force a tight smile, the muscles in my face aching with the effort, nodding against him. "Yeah. It's . . . comforting," I say, the words coming out hollow, empty, devoid of any genuine emotion. I say that in my most convincing voice, the one I use for book signings and interviews, but every syllable feels like a blatant, painful lie. There's nothing comforting about any of this. Not Saint showing up unannounced, not the chilling way he looked at me, not his deliberate lie, and certainly not the looming, terrifying threat of everything I've built, everything I cherish, crumbling down around me like a house of cards in a hurricane.

It's disturbing. Profoundly, deeply disturbing.

CHAPTER FOURTEEN

The rest of the night has been much less disturbing. It's passed by without incident, actually. I held my panic attack at bay and sat through dinner, feigning normalcy. Mari hasn't shown back up, and neither has Saint. So far.

Each bite of Shephard's perfectly seasoned chicken felt like ash in my mouth. I smiled, I nodded, I asked the girls about their week at school, all while feeling like I'd just earned the World's Worst Wife and Mother of the Century award. I can feel it, a tarnished invisible medal hanging heavy around my neck.

The acute tension that clung to me earlier in the day has settled now into something deeper, something heavier. There's no easy way to release it. We move through the motions of a normal evening with the clatter of dishes as Shephard cleans up, the familiar shouts of the girls from the guest room, but nothing feels normal. It's all a flimsy stage set, and I'm a terrible actress tonight. I try to lose myself in the routine of bedtime, helping the girls brush their teeth, the minty scent a fleeting comfort, tucking them into their brightly colored duvets, kissing their foreheads as they drift off. The familiar comforts of motherhood should ease my mind, should anchor me, but they don't. They only amplify the piercing guilt.

The girls are out by nine, asleep together in the spare bedroom. I stand by their door for a moment, watching their peaceful, unsuspecting faces, my heart heavy with a guilt so profound it threatens to swallow me whole. How can I possibly reconcile myself to the fact that I've so irrevocably betrayed the life I built with Shephard, the life I treasure as their mother, to the dark, illicit secret now pulsing beneath my skin? The guilt gnaws at me, twisting my stomach into tight, painful knots, a persistent, physical reminder. But I push it down, deep down, as far as I can, burying it under layers of denial, and head into the living room.

I text Nora as I make my way toward the couch. **Shephard and the girls just showed up unannounced.** I hit send.

Immediately, she responds with **Noooooo. Asshole!**

I sit next to Shephard on the couch and chuckle at her response. She knows what it's like being a writer and in the groove, only to be interrupted countless times by people who don't get it. It's why I have to write somewhere away from home—because home is a constant revolving door. If it's not one kid, it's the other, or Shephard, or my sister, or my mother, or a UPS driver. Although, the UPS driver is usually my fault. I tend to online shop when I get emotional about work.

I get *a lot* of packages delivered.

Shephard doesn't look up from whatever he's doing when I sink into the couch. We don't feel the discomfort when the girls are in the room, but when it's just the two of us, there's a distance between us that wasn't there before, or perhaps was always there, only now it's become a yawning chasm. Since I stopped being able to write and the money issues began, we argue more than we compliment. He's lived a cush life until now.

Now, he's just stressed. All the time. When I started making better money, he took a lower-paying position to ease his stress, but he's regretting it now. He hasn't said it, but he implies it with little jabs here and there. I just ignore it. Sure, I wish I had a husband who understood the emotional trauma I've been through, but I guess both spouses end up feeling the fallout of financial burdens, so I understand that he's under stress too.

He's beside me physically, the familiar warmth of his leg brushing mine through the denim of his jeans, but mentally, emotionally, we're worlds apart, orbiting different planets. His laptop is propped on his knees, the screen casting a pale glow on his face, his fingers tapping away on the keys as he catches up on work, bills, something mundane and responsible.

He's focused, absorbed in whatever report or email he's typing up, his brow furrowed in concentration. I wonder if he senses the shift between us, if he can feel the chasm growing wider, the silence between us thickening with unspoken grievances. Or is he truly oblivious?

He has no idea that he isn't the last man I kissed. The last man to see me naked. The last man inside me. The thought sits like a cold, heavy stone in my gut.

I have the television on, the screen flickering with chaotic scenes from some show I can't even remember the name of. Distant gunfire, dramatic music. But I can't pay attention to it. The characters move across the screen, saying words I barely register. My mind is elsewhere.

I've never cheated on Shephard before. I've never even had the urge. For years, our marriage felt solid, built on a foundation of shared history, quiet companionship, and a love that, while perhaps not fiery, felt steady and true. We've had our ups and downs, of course. The usual ebb and flow of any long-term relationship. Money stresses, parenting disagreements, the natural drift of routine. But I never, *ever* thought I'd be the type to have an affair, to cross that line. It's the kind of thing that happens to other people, in other relationships. Not mine. I thought I was better than that, stronger, more grounded. But here I am, sinking under the devastating consequences of my own choices, choices I never imagined I'd make, never dreamed I was capable of.

And it was so easy. *Too* easy. I barely thought of him, of Shephard, in those moments. It was like when Saint was around, when his intensity filled the space, Shephard was out of sight, out of mind. *Why?* Why was it so simple to betray the man I vowed to cherish? The man sitting just inches from me, oblivious.

"Are you even listening?" Shephard's voice, sharper than I expected, slices through my thoughts. He's looking at me now, his laptop half closed on his knees, a flicker of irritation in his eyes.

"What?" I force my gaze from the flickering screen to his face. "Sorry. Just . . . tired." The lie is instant, automatic.

He sighs, a small, weary sound. "I was just saying, I finally got our expense report done, but I want to make sure I have every bill listed before I meet with the accountant. So if you're feeling up to it, maybe you could look over some of it before me and the girls head out in the morning?" His tone is carefully neutral, but I catch the subtle dip in his voice on "*if you're feeling up to it*," a barbed wire wrapped in concern.

A familiar resentment prickles. His moods seem to ebb and flow with the fluctuations of my career. When my books were flying off shelves, when the advances were big, he was my biggest cheerleader, and subtly, my manager, my financial advisor, taking pride in *our* success. But now, with the backlash from my last book, with the cancel culture biting hard, with my creative well feeling dry for months . . . now it's different. The pride has curdled into something else. And he acts like he's some martyr, saving us from my bad choices.

It's like he wants to own my successes, but when I fail, those are all on me.

"Money trouble is the last thing I need in my brain, Shephard," I say, my voice tighter than I intend. "That's why I came to the cabin, to try and *solve* our money issues. Going over them in detail will just make my writer's block worse."

He raises an eyebrow, a sardonic curve to his lips. "Right. Well, the well's looking a little dry, Petra, and I can't keep hoping you'll find inspiration. Good intent doesn't pay the bills. Producing something does."

"For your information, I've written over half a book since I got here. Thanks for asking. I've been in a groove until . . ."

Shephard sets his phone down beside him. "Until *we* showed up?"

I sigh. "I'm due to be home for Chloe's birthday next weekend for two whole days. I don't know why you thought it was a good idea to interrupt two more of my writing days. That means I'll get three writing days out of the whole week, tops. It's not enough, and I can't just switch it on and off."

"The girls missed you," he says, his words sharp. "Sorry you have people who love you." He stands up, heading toward the kitchen.

"That's not . . ." Ugh. I drop my hands to the couch on either side of me and groan. "That's not fair. Writing is a weird beast, and you know I work best when I have stretches of solitude. I love you, and I love my girls, but it's like you can't even get through a week without needing me to give you a reprieve. When do I get *my* reprieve?"

"How many episodes of *Love Island* have you watched since you've been here? You can't tell me you actually spend all day every day writing. I've been working, watching the girls, all while trying to figure out how to get our finances in order for our meeting with the accountant. Sorry if I can't understand how a vacation in a . . ." He looks around. "You can't even call this a cabin. A vacation in a *dream* home can in any way be torture. All I asked is for you to look at some numbers. My bad. I'll do it myself."

The jab lands, sharp and precise. It always comes back to money, to my career, to the fact that for so long, I was the primary earner. And now that I'm struggling, it's thrown everything off balance, and he isn't taking it well.

"Are you implying I haven't been working?" My voice rises, a defensive heat flushing my cheeks. "Do you have any idea how hard it is to write under this kind of pressure? With all the noise?"

He leans against the counter, crossing his arms, his expression hardening. "Pressure? Petra, you get to write stories for a living. I sit in meetings all day, dealing with spreadsheets and corporate politics, trying to hang on to my job so a fresh-out-of-college kid doesn't come in and do it for half the price. Don't tell me about pressure. And frankly, your *noise* is partly your own making. You didn't want to be more well known, and I tried to tell you letting them adapt one of your books was just going to make your life more stressful."

"So now my success is the problem? I thought my *lack* of success was the problem."

"No, the problem is you made a lot of money and now you're making none. I'm happy you're writing, but I'm a little annoyed that you're annoyed we're here. One day isn't going to make or break this book. You're being kind of a bitch."

My jaw drops.

His immediately tightens.

He steps toward me, pulling me in for an embrace. "I'm sorry. I'm so sorry. I'm just . . . I'm stressed, okay?"

In all our years of marriage, he's never once used that word at me.

"I wasn't calling *you* a bitch. Just . . . *God*. Our financial future isn't as secure as it was when you were churning out bestsellers every six months. All I asked was for you to look over expenses, and you're acting like I don't appreciate what you do for our family." He pulls back and looks me in the eye. "I just need a little help, Petra. From *my wife*."

The words hang in the air. *My wife*. The role I'm failing so spectacularly at.

He's not wrong, not entirely. He carries a burden too. But his inability to truly understand the creative block, the emotional toll of public scrutiny, feels so unsupportive. He always wants me to be the successful, unbothered author, not the messy human struggling beneath the weight of it all.

"I know," I say, my voice softening, the anger deflating, leaving behind only exhaustion. "I know. It's just . . . it's hard to switch gears. My head's not in that space right now. And with . . . with everything else." I almost say *Saint*, but the name catches in my throat, a dangerous secret.

He just sighs, releasing me. The conversation, like so many lately, dead-ends, unresolved. We're both left with our unspoken grievances, our quiet resentments. He's stressed, I'm guilty and creatively stifled, and the money situation is a constant undercurrent of tension.

I look at him, at his tired profile, and the guilt gnaws. He's not a bad man. He's working hard for our family. But the connection, the spark, the *understanding* that used to bridge these gaps, feels thin. And I just made it so much worse.

I just don't feel like I'm *Petra* here, so him showing up and bringing my real life into my creative solitude is jarring.

These writing weeks give me an opportunity to slip out of my own skin and into the skin of someone else entirely. I sometimes get so immersed in my writing, I don't just create the character; I *become* her. It's like I'm living in two worlds at once—one where I'm Petra, the struggling yet outwardly faithful wife and mother, and another where I'm whichever character I'm writing at the moment, someone who exists only on the pages of my book, unburdened by consequence.

Some call it Method writing, and I suppose I can blame my actions on that, blame it on the fact that I let myself get too deep into the story this time. I let the characters take over, let the narrative consume me, and for a while, it felt like I wasn't even in control anymore. But it doesn't excuse what I've done. It doesn't change the cold, hard fact that I made a choice, that I crossed a line I can never uncross.

I cheated on my husband, the man who just sat down on the couch again to scroll through his spreadsheets. And all I can do is hope to hell he never finds out. Because if he does, the tenuous thread our marriage hangs by will snap.

The thought of him knowing, of Shephard looking at me with that raw, wounded hurt and betrayal in his eyes, makes my stomach churn, a sickening, acidic burn. It would destroy him. It would destroy *us*, the life we've meticulously built, brick by agonizing brick.

I've always prided myself on my self-control, on my ability to separate fiction from reality, to walk the line between my imagination and my life. But now it feels like everything is bleeding together, indistinguishable, in ways I never expected.

Shephard closes his laptop with a soft, decisive click, the sound sharp and final, breaking through the heavy silence that's settled between us. It's been minutes since our terse exchange, minutes filled with the silent hum of the refrigerator and the low volume on the television. He slides the laptop off his lap and onto the couch beside him, his movements slow and deliberate, like he's considering something profound, something weighty. I can feel him looking at me, his gaze lingering, a warm, familiar weight on my skin, but I can't bring myself to meet his eyes. Instead, I pretend I'm watching the television, forcing my eyes to stay glued to the screen, focusing on the garish colors, even though I have no idea what's happening in the ridiculous show, its plot a meaningless blur.

"I didn't expect this," he says.

Didn't expect what? My stomach lurches, cold and empty.

Panic flares in my chest, hot and suffocating. For a split second, a terrifying, absolute certainty crashes over me: *He knows.* He knows. I think he's figured it out, that somehow, impossibly, he's pieced together the truth. I turn to him immediately, my pulse racing, thrumming a frantic rhythm in my ears.

"Didn't expect what?" I ask, my voice sharper than I intend, betraying my sudden, overwhelming fear.

He smiles, a soft, almost wistful expression, his eyes kind but searching, piercing through my facade. "You not being happy that we're here." He says it simply, not as an accusation, but as an observation. He's watching me closely, waiting for my response, but it's clear he doesn't suspect anything beyond what's on the surface—my creative frustration, my need for solitude.

His blindness is both a relief and a new kind of pain.

I can't relax, not really. The tightness in my chest remains. "What? Of course I am," I say, but even to my own ears, it sounds forced, hollow, a pathetic attempt at conviction. I plaster a smile on my face, twisting my lips into a semblance of ease, but I know it doesn't reach my eyes, which still feel wide and terrified.

Shephard's expression is one of understanding, but there's something bittersweet about it, a subtle undertone of melancholy. "You were in the groove and we interrupted you. I should have called first. I'm sorry. It's like we sucked you out of a dream, Petra."

I let out a short, bitter laugh, unable to help myself, the sound rough and dry. "Or a nightmare," I mutter under my breath, the words slipping out before I can stop them, a raw, uncontrolled confession. I glance at him, hoping he didn't catch the tension in my voice, the dark double meaning, but he only laughs again, a light, dismissive chuckle, completely unaware.

"You've always been way too hard on yourself," he says, shaking his head, a fond exasperation in his tone. "But it works out. Every time you come here, you leave with the bones of a brand-new book. It's your magic place. I believe in you, and I'm sorry I snapped at you. It's not fair of me to show up and put burdens on you."

He's right.

But even though the words I need to hear are pouring from his mouth, he doesn't truly realize the blood, sweat, and tears that go into every book I write, the piece of my soul I carve out and leave on the page.

To him, these getaways are mini vacations, a clever way to recharge and find inspiration, to relax and then conveniently come home with a finished story, a new product. He never asks about the agony, only the financials.

I don't fault him for that. How could I? He loves me, supports me in his own way, and he does, in his own practical Shephard way, understand that writing isn't easy. But no one can *really* understand how emotionally draining it is, how utterly consuming, unless they've written a book themselves, unless they've poured their very essence into something so abstract. It's not just the hours spent typing away at the keyboard—it's the aftermath of all that blood, sweat, and tears, and how so many people pick it apart and tell you all that effort was pointless because you're shit.

And I am. I am a shit human, in more ways than one.

I'm seated on the couch with my legs tucked beneath me, trying to focus on the steady rhythm of my breathing, trying to calm the frantic beating of my heart as the soft glow of the television casts flickering shadows around the room, onto Shephard's face.

Shephard, completely unaware of the turmoil inside me, moves with his usual ease as he reaches over and grabs one of my ankles, his touch warm and familiar, a practiced gesture. He pulls my leg toward him, gently tugging until I'm lying down, my body stretched out beneath him, just as it has been a thousand times before. But this time, something is different. Something feels profoundly, irrevocably wrong.

As he crawls on top of me, his body pressing down in a way that should feel comforting, familiar, an insatiable, overwhelming amount of guilt floods my chest. This couch is tainted by what I've done with Saint, and now Shephard is crawling on top of me, in the exact position Saint was in a matter of days ago.

The memory of Saint—his hands, his lips, his body—flashes through my mind like an intrusive thought I can't shake, a vivid, unwelcome superimposition over Shephard's face.

He kisses me, his lips soft and familiar against mine, his breath warm, but I can't lose myself in it the way I should, the way I used to. Every second of the kiss feels like a betrayal in itself, a searing reminder of the secret I'm keeping from him.

A lie pressed against his mouth.

I know the kiss won't last long. Shephard is nothing if not predictable in moments like these. He'll take it to the bedroom before things get too heated, before the passion can truly ignite, as he always does.

He's a bedroom kind of lover, methodical, careful, almost . . . ritualistic. It's the way he's always been, always contained, always planned. There's something safe about it, something comforting in its routine, its predictability, but tonight, it feels stifling, like I'm trapped in a script I've followed for too long, a play where I no longer remember my lines.

I don't know that we've ever had spontaneous sex on a couch before. The thought strikes me as odd, considering how long we've been together. Our intimacy has always followed a pattern, a rhythm we both understand, a comfortable dance. There's never been much room for surprises, for wild abandon, for spontaneity.

And yet, with Saint, everything was raw, unpredictable, charged with a kind of reckless energy I'd never felt before. The contrast between the two men, between the two experiences, is startling, a jarring shift in frequency. I can't help but compare them in my mind, even though I know it's wrong, know it's unfair to Shephard, to our history, to everything we've built. But the comparison happens anyway.

"Let's go to bed," Shephard says, predictably, his voice soft and full of affection, a familiar invitation. He kisses my forehead before pulling away, leaving just enough space between us to remind me that this is how it's always been, this careful, controlled distance. I nod, even though my mind is elsewhere, still trapped in the sticky web of lies I've spun.

"Okay," I say, forcing a smile that doesn't reach my eyes. "I'll be right there. I have some emails I need to send first." The lie slips out with scary ease.

"Take your time. I need a shower anyway." Shephard's voice is a warm, even murmur laced with a familiar, uncomplicated affection that feels like a heavy blanket draped over my shoulders. He stands up from the couch, stretching his arms over his head with a contented sigh, a soft, almost purring sound, as if nothing is wrong in the world, as if the unsettling encounter with Saint earlier was merely a quirky interlude.

As if everything is exactly as it should be, perfectly aligned in his predictable, comforting universe. His hand briefly brushes mine as he passes, a faint warmth, before he heads down the hall toward the bedroom. His footsteps are steady, even, his presence radiating an oblivious sense of comfort. But I can't take comfort in him tonight. Not now. Not after what I've done.

My skin crawls with the memory of it, the scent of *him* still clinging to me like a phantom perfume.

The bedroom door closes softly, a quiet, almost imperceptible click that echoes like a gunshot in the sudden, cavernous silence of the living room. I wait, holding my breath, straining my ears, listening for the distinct sound of the bathroom door closing behind him. I hear the faintest creak, then the unmistakable whoosh and spray of the shower turning on, a steady, rhythmic rush of water that signals I have time, a precious, stolen window. Time to do what I shouldn't. Time to fall deeper into the trap I've set for myself, a trap of my own design.

I bypass the laptop entirely, its purpose forgotten, a flimsy lie. My bare feet glide across the cool hardwood as I make my way to the back door, drawn by an invisible, irresistible pull. I unlatch the lock, the click surprisingly loud in the quiet house. I step outside and pull the screen door shut behind me.

The cool night air hits my skin like a slap in the face, sharp and biting, chilling me to the bone, but at the same time waking me up to the raw, treacherous reality of what I'm about to do.

My hands are shaking, a nervous tremor that runs through my entire body, as I pull out my phone, my fingers fumbling clumsily with the screen, almost dropping the device onto the wooden porch. Without hesitation, almost by instinct, I immediately dial Saint's number, my mind racing, a frantic carousel of emotions: raw anger, piercing guilt, and a flicker of excitement.

He answers on the third ring, a deliberate pause that makes my nerves hum with anticipation. "I figured I'd hear from you before you went to bed." His voice, when it comes through the line, is maddeningly casual, an easy, almost lazy drawl, as if he's just woken up from a pleasant nap.

"What the fuck was that?" I snap. The words come out filled with the crushing weight of everything I'm feeling.

"You're married," he snaps back, his voice losing its playfulness instantly, turning cold and hard, like tempered steel. There's no warmth left in his tone now, just an edginess that slices through me, an immediate counterattack. His words are heavy with accusation, laced with judgment, as if *he* has any right to condemn me, as if he's not the primary instigator of this entire, devastating mess, the architect of my current torment.

"So are you," I bite back, my hand tightening around the phone so hard my knuckles ache, pressing the device painfully against my ear. My voice is low, a guttural growl, barely controlled, a raw, strained whisper, as if I'm holding on to the last shred of patience I have, the final, fraying thread of my sanity.

"I never lied about it," he says, his words cutting through me like a knife, cold and precise. His tone is flat, emotionless, devoid of any inflection, like he's stating a factual truth that cannot be argued with, an undeniable, inconvenient reality.

And the worst part is, he's right. He never did lie about being married. He laid it all out, clear and uncompromising. He never pretended to be something he wasn't. *I* was the one who hid, who pretended, who built a fragile facade around my life. The realization is a bitter, metallic taste in my mouth, a self-inflicted wound.

I glance instinctively toward the living room window, my heart racing as I check to make sure Shephard is still in the bathroom, still safely hidden behind the monotonous sound of the running water. I take a deep, shaky breath, steadying myself before I speak, finding a sliver of composure amid the chaos. "I technically didn't lie about it either," I say, my voice quieter now, more controlled, laced with a calculated defiance. "You never asked."

There's a long, excruciating pause on the other end of the call, the silence stretching out between us like a vast, dark chasm. When he speaks again, his voice is lower, almost a whisper. "Are you going to fuck him tonight?"

The question hits me like a physical punch to the gut, a brutal blow that knocks the air clean out of my lungs, leaving me breathless and reeling, gasping for air. My throat tightens, suddenly constricted, but I feel the chill of arousal build in my stomach. "He's my goddamn husband, Saint. What do you think?"

How dare he ask that. How dare he make me *answer*.

"So that's a no?" The playfulness is back in his voice, instantly, a light, maddening teasing lilt returning, as if he's pushing me, testing me, seeing how far he can go, how much he can unravel me.

He isn't mad at all. Not really. This is part of the game to him, a meticulously crafted performance. He's enjoying this, enjoying my torment, my confusion.

And then, with a jolt of ice-cold clarity, a chilling realization that pierces through the fog of my anger, I realize what he's doing. Why he showed up here today to meet Shephard. Why he played up the stern, unyielding officer. He's embodying the very things I wanted Cam to be.

Controlling, possessive, jealous. He's playing the role I created for him in Reya's story, the role of Cam, the obsessive, dangerous lover.

And in this moment, consumed by a confusing, terrifying mixture of pure terror and perverse fascination, I hate him for it. And I love him for it.

I hate him for seeing through me, for knowing exactly what buttons to push, for pulling me so relentlessly into the fiction, making it horrifyingly real. He's not just playing a role; he's weaponizing my own desires against me.

Showing up at my house today was just him pushing the limits of my experience. He wanted me to know what it felt like to be scared my affair was about to be found out, but he had no desire for Shephard to *actually* find out.

"You're making me insane," I whisper. "I didn't expect you to take things this far."

I can almost hear the grin in his words. "Do you want me to stop?"

I think about that for a minute. I think about Shephard. I think about what it would do to him if he found out what I've done. What I'm *doing*.

"Just say the word, Petra. You'll never see me again if that's what you need."

A knot forms in my throat. "No," I whisper. "I don't want you to stop."

"Good," Saint says. "But if we're going to continue this, then I need a favor from you."

I close my eyes and whisper, "What?"

"When your husband fucks you tonight, get on top and pretend you're fucking me."

The call ends after he says that. My mouth is agape. I pull my phone from my ear and stare at it. Then I quickly peek through the window again, not wanting Shephard to see the look that's spread over my face right now.

The audacity.

The disrespect.

I like it.

I can't ignore the heat pooling in my stomach. Hearing him talk like that—just like Cam would talk to Reya—makes me want to go straight to my laptop and write another scene.

But it also makes me want to crawl in bed with Shephard and do exactly what Saint said. No matter how hard I try, I just can't mentally lock Saint out.

CHAPTER FIFTEEN

I locked the doors after our phone call with a series of loud, frantic clicks, as if to physically bar him from entry, to erect an impenetrable shield. Then I turned out every light in the living room and kitchen, plunging the space into near darkness, hoping to erase his lingering presence, to make myself invisible.

The house is finally silent now as I lie in bed and wait for Shephard.

His nightly routine is as familiar and predictable as the rising sun: a long, efficient shower, the vigorous brushing of his teeth, the final, obligatory check of his work email, scrolling through his phone one last time before settling in for the night. I hear the water shut off, the sudden cessation of the spray, and then the soft shuffle of his feet as he walks across the cold bathroom tiles.

The bedsheets are cool against my skin, and I'm wrapping them around me at the exact same moment Shephard walks out of the bathroom, a towel tied around his waist. He plugs his phone into the charger on the nightstand with a soft click and pulls back the covers on his side. We don't verbalize, the words hanging unspoken in the air, but we both know how things will end up.

We play our familiar marital game of winding down the night on our phones, each of us lying on our respective side of the bed, separated by an invisible wall of technology. He'll show me a TikTok he thinks is funny, a silly video that elicits a polite chuckle. I'll show him a meme I found, forcing a smile. Then, eventually, he'll reach over, grab my phone, and toss it behind me onto the bed, a subtle signal that the night is about to take its predictable turn. He'll pull me to him. We'll fuck. He'll put his headphones on and fall asleep immediately.

I feel Shephard's presence beside me, the warmth of his leg brushing against mine under the covers. It should feel intimate, connecting, but instead, it feels mechanical, a practiced proximity. We're both just going through the motions, like every other night. A quiet, familiar dance of habit and assumption.

Eventually, he does what he always does. His hand reaches over, firm and familiar, takes my phone out of my hand, and drops it behind me onto the bed, his subtle, established way of signaling that the winding down of the night is over, and the real intimacy is about to begin. He pulls me close, his body warm against mine, his lips brushing against the sensitive skin of my neck. I close my eyes, trying desperately to relax, to surrender to the familiar, but my thoughts drift elsewhere, stubbornly refusing to obey.

Shephard always starts out kissing me. Gentle, exploratory kisses. Touching me, his hands tracing familiar paths. Then he'll move on top of me and inside me. It's predictable with us, a well-worn path. I always feared it was predictable, but being with Saint and experiencing his raw, untamed intensity has proved it, cementing the uncomfortable truth.

I love Shephard. I always have. He is my steadfast rock, my quiet anchor. But sometimes, lately, it's just so . . . *boring*. The word echoes in my mind, a shameful, damning confession.

My mind flashes, unbidden, to Saint—his hands, his mouth, the fierce, unapologetic way he commands the space around him, the way he just *takes*. I shouldn't be thinking about him now, not here, not with Shephard beside me, but I can't help it. The more I try to block him out, to force his image from my mind, the more vivid the memories become, sharper, more insistent. The phantom taste of him lingers on my lips, hot and metallic, even though he isn't here, not really.

I recall the words Saint said to me earlier tonight, the taunting whisper that still vibrates in my ears. *". . . get on top and pretend you're fucking me."* The command is so clear, so precise, so utterly irresistible in its audacity.

I wait a couple of minutes, giving myself a moment to gather my nerve, to steel myself. Then, slowly, deliberately, I roll Shephard over onto his back, his body shifting beneath mine with a surprised groan. I straddle Shephard, the movement practiced, familiar, and he groans again, a deep, satisfied sound, when I take him inside me, the familiar fullness. He grips my thighs with his hands, strong and possessive, and I begin to move up and down in a slow, deliberate rhythm. I lean my head back and close my eyes, picturing the cabin ceiling, then Saint's face, imagining, with a desperate, shameful intensity, that it isn't Shephard beneath me right now, but him.

My mind races with everything Saint said, every single provocative word. I know I shouldn't, but I follow through on his instructions, his silent dare, feeling the thrilling current of it course through me, igniting every nerve ending.

Shephard has no idea. He thinks this is for him. He thinks this is *us*.

When Shephard's hand finds its way between my legs, a warm, familiar press against me, he begins to rub me. The pressure slowly builds as I pretend it's Saint's hand there, bringing me closer. I move with him, matching his rhythm, pushing faster, harder, and just before I'm about to come, just as the pleasure becomes too intense to bear, I open my eyes.

I immediately gasp, a sharp, choked sound, and can feel all the color rush from my face, draining away, leaving me cold and bloodless.

Saint is standing outside our bedroom window.

He's there, a tall, dark silhouette against the backdrop of the full moon, which shines unnaturally bright around him, casting his form in a silver halo. Part of his shadow, long and distorted, falls over Shephard's face, a chilling, dark stain on his unsuspecting features.

I'm so startled by his presence that I stop moving mid-thrust, frozen, my body seized up, my breath caught in my throat.

Shephard assumes it's because he's about to make me come, his body stiffening beneath me, his breath hitching slightly. "Almost there, baby," he murmurs, his voice thick with satisfaction. I do my best to convince him that's what has me reacting this way, forcing a small, desperate groan. The last thing I need is for Shephard to lift his head and look behind him, out the window. My gaze is locked on Saint, a silent scream building in my chest.

I keep my eyes trained on Saint, unable to tear them away, nervous he's about to do something, to shatter the glass, to reveal himself. Is he going to bang on the window? Break the glass to get to Shephard? To me? What the fuck is he doing here? His presence is a terrifying, electrifying violation.

He's staring at me with a fierce intensity, his eyes like twin points of burning coal, and I can't tell if it's because he's turned on or angry or jealous, or some terrifying combination of all three.

Saint raises an eyebrow, a slow, deliberate arch, when he notices I've frozen in place—on top of my husband—unmoving, utterly transfixed by him. He grins a little, a dark, knowing curve of his lips, then lifts an intimidating brow, gives a subtle, almost imperceptible nod, indicating I should resume what I was doing before I noticed him standing there, his silent command unwavering.

My lips begin to quiver, but it's not because of how Shephard is touching me, not from the building pleasure. It's because I'm scared. And as fucked up as this is—as perverse and wrong as it feels—I'm also, undeniably, turned on by it all. The forbidden thrill, the dangerous audacity, the sheer, breathtaking risk.

I start moving on top of Shephard again—slowly at first, then picking up speed, a frantic, desperate rhythm.

Saint's gaze scrolls longingly over my body, a possessive, hungry sweep from my hair to my hips, and seeing that raw, unapologetic need in his eyes, the feral hunger, makes me move on top of Shephard even faster, a wild, frenzied pace, responding to *him*, not Shephard.

I don't want Shephard touching me, not there, not now. His touch feels wrong right now, almost intrusive, as if it's not meant for me, not meant for this moment. So, almost without thinking, I remove his hand from between my legs, and I press it against my hip, a silent, firm dismissal. His fingers twitch slightly in protest, a faint, questioning squeeze, but he doesn't resist, simply shifting his grip to my hip bone.

When I come, I want it to be because of Saint's unblinking stare, because of his silent command, not because of Shephard's familiar hand.

I glance away from Saint for a split second, looking down at Shephard. His eyes are closed, his face relaxed in a way that tells me he's utterly oblivious to what's happening outside, to the predatory shadow falling across him, to the fact that another man is watching, claiming this intimate moment. His peaceful ignorance is both a blessing and a fresh stab of guilt.

I lock eyes with Saint again, my breath catching in my throat, a ragged gasp. His gaze feels like it's burning through me, unraveling every part of my body, dissecting me, consuming me. There's no need for him to be inside the room; his presence alone dominates everything, filling the space between us, suffocating all other thoughts.

Slowly, deliberately, I slide my hand up my stomach to my breast, tracing the curves of my body as if trying to mimic Saint's imagined touch, his unspoken desire. His reaction is immediate—he pulls his bottom lip between his teeth and bites down hard, his jaw clenching, his eyes darkening further. That move sends a fresh rush of heat through me, a current so strong it nearly makes me falter, makes my body convulse. It's like he's controlling me, commanding my movements without a word, a puppet master pulling my strings from the darkness. My hand trembles slightly as I continue to caress myself, his gaze a burning brand on my skin, and it proves harder to keep my eyes locked on his. Every time I look at him, it's like a challenge—an unspoken dare to give in, to let go, to utterly shatter.

Shephard groans beneath me, his voice low and rough, the familiar sound indicating he's close to finishing, his body tensing with effort. The sound barely registers. All I can think about is Saint, his unwavering stare, the way his lips part slightly as if he's imagining being here with me instead of Shephard, as if he's mentally consuming me.

It's overwhelming, this insidious power he holds over me, this complete, utter domination. My heart pounds, a frantic drum, and I put my own hand between my legs, desperate to finish with Shephard, to end this agonizing, exhilarating torment, but needing, desperately, to make it about Saint.

Almost immediately, the sensation hits me—a rush so fierce, so profound, so utterly consuming that I let out a scream before I can stop myself, a raw, primal sound torn from my throat. It's like nothing I've ever felt from Shephard alone, nothing even close. My entire body seizes with pleasure, convulsing, and I can't keep my eyes open a second longer. I do everything in my power not to collapse onto Shephard, my body trembling uncontrollably, my legs quaking as the feeling pulses through me in wave after wave, an endless, shattering crescendo. It's as if Saint's stare is fueling this orgasm, as though he's the one reaching into my body, commanding every surge of pleasure, every shattering ripple.

I continue to move on top of Shephard, my hand still between my legs, even after I know he's finished and I've finished, our bodies both spent. But I don't want it to be over. My body hasn't caught up yet, the sensation still rippling through me like a shock wave, a lingering tremor. My legs shake, and I feel a soft whimper escape my lips as I collapse fully onto him, unable to hold myself up any longer, burying my face against his neck.

Shephard's hands slide up my back, gentle and comforting, tracing soft patterns, as though he thinks this is something *he's* done for me, something he's given me. His lips brush against my shoulder in a soft kiss, but the touch feels distant and muted.

I roll off Shephard, my eyes darting toward the window, the space where he stood. I lift my head slightly, heart pounding, hoping to see him still standing there, but . . . Saint is gone. The moonlight filters in through the gap in the curtains, illuminating nothing but an empty yard, the stillness of the night. The sudden absence of his presence leaves me cold, like I've been abandoned mid-thought, mid-pleasure, mid-orgasm, a sudden, jarring emptiness.

I close my eyes and tuck my head against Shephard's chest, as if seeking comfort, burrowing into his familiar warmth, but it's hollow, a feigned gesture. I can feel the tears threatening to form, hot and stinging, hovering just behind my eyelids, pricking them. And the worst part is, I'm not even sure why I'm crying. I feel guilty, profoundly so, sure—but not sad. Not even close.

This is so fucked up.

That was probably the most fucked-up thing I've ever done in my entire life, crossing so many lines.

But what's worse is the undeniable truth gnawing at me, one I can't ignore no matter how hard I try to suppress it. I would do it all over again if given the chance. It felt that good. That dangerously, thrillingly good.

"You've been deprived," Shephard says, his voice thick with satisfaction, completely oblivious to the devastating reality of my experience. "That was . . . mind blowing."

I want to laugh, a harsh, brittle sound, at the word *deprived*, at his utter lack of comprehension, but I hold it back, biting my lip hard to keep the sound in, to prevent the truth from escaping.

Deprived? If only he knew how deep my deprivation goes, how long it's been festering beneath the surface, a silent, aching void, waiting for something—someone—like Saint to bring it to life, to tear open the dam. But I don't say that. I try to say something an innocent wife and mother would say in this moment to maintain the fragile peace.

"I think I was too loud. I hope I didn't wake the girls." My voice is muffled against his chest.

Shephard chuckles softly, pressing a kiss to my forehead, his breath warm against my skin. "They're heavy sleepers," he murmurs, his voice laced with contentment, before pulling away from me to grab a towel from the nightstand. I watch as he wipes it between my legs, careful and considerate. It's a small gesture, but one I've always appreciated about him—that he takes care of me, even in these intimate, vulnerable moments. It's one of the things that makes him a good husband, one of the things that used to make me feel so safe, so cherished with him.

But in the times I've been with Saint, there was no cleaning. There was no neatness. We were sticky and messy, and he didn't seem to care. In fact, he seemed to like it, a primal, animalistic acceptance. And surprisingly, terrifyingly, I liked it too.

Saint is everything Shephard isn't, and that's both good and bad. It's a chasm, a thrilling divide.

Shephard adjusts the blanket to cover us, his body warm and familiar beside mine. He rolls over onto his side, his back to me, the ultimate gesture of postcoital comfort and trust. He murmurs, "Good night."

I roll away from him, pulling the covers tighter, hugging my pillow tightly as I stare into the darkness, the faint moonlight painting shadows on the wall. "Good night," I whisper, but the word feels hollow, like it's meant for someone else.

Someone who's no longer standing outside my window.

I need to mentally buckle up, because the ride Saint is taking me on is getting way too unstable.

CHAPTER SIXTEEN

I buckle the girls into their car seats and then brush my fingers through their soft hair. Chloe wiggles a little, her usual restless energy bubbling over, a kinetic force of nature, as she fidgets impatiently with the strap. Andi, in contrast, sits perfectly still, gazing up at me with wide, innocent eyes, like twin pools of clear water.

I can feel their anticipation of resuming their familiar routines. I'm anticipating returning to my own routine I've set here. But there's also the familiar tug at my heart that always accompanies our partings, no matter how often I do it, no matter how much I tell myself I need the solitude to write. I lean down and kiss them both on the forehead, my lips lingering for just a moment longer than usual, inhaling the sweet, faint scent of sleep and childhood.

"I'll be home in a week for your birthday," I say, trying to infuse my voice with a cheerfulness I don't feel, even though the words catch in my throat like a dry and uncomfortable lump.

One week feels like an eternity right now, like I'll have so many more moments with Saint between now and my trip home for the party next weekend. And then I'll come back for another week. A final week with Saint, with my laptop, with my thoughts. I really do think I'll walk away from this cabin for good with an entire book.

Maybe it will have all been worth it.

"How long is a week?" Andi asks, her voice small and curious, a tiny, piping sound, her eyes sparkling with that endless thirst for knowledge, her innate wonder. She's still trying to grasp the concept of time.

Before I can answer, Chloe jumps in with the unshakable confidence only a five-year-old can possess. "It's only thirty days," she says matter-of-factly, her tone full of certainty, as if she's the undisputed authority on all things time related. She crosses her arms over her chest, a gesture of absolute conviction, proud of her declaration, and Andi nods, as if her big sister's word is absolute law, etched in stone.

I can't help but smile at Chloe's firm assertion, even though it's entirely, hilariously wrong. "A week is only seven days," I correct gently, knowing this will probably turn into a back-and-forth debate that neither of us will win. I tuck a stray strand of Chloe's hair behind her ear.

Chloe shakes her head, her brow furrowing in frustration, a determined frown. "No, it's thirty," she insists, her voice rising just a little, imbued with a fierce conviction, determined to make her point, to defend her teacher's wisdom. "Sometimes thirty-one. My teacher said it."

I suppress a weary laugh, not wanting to start a battle I have no interest in fighting, especially not now. I know I could patiently explain the difference between days and weeks and months, the nuances of the calendar, but my patience is threadbare. I just need them to leave, need them to be safely away from here, before Saint pulls another horrifying stunt and shows up while they're still here. The thought sends a fresh wave of nausea through me.

"Okay. Thirty days," I say, capitulating, just wanting the conversation to end, to usher them out. "Love you." I lean in one last time and press a quick kiss to each cheek.

I close their car door with a soft thud, the sound echoing in the deceptive quiet of the morning air, and I take a deep, shaky breath, knowing that the next week will feel far longer for me than it will for them, an eternity stretching out ahead.

As I step back from the car, Shephard walks toward me, his arms already outstretched for a hug, his face a picture of relief and contentment. He pulls me into a tight embrace, his warmth enveloping me, familiar and solid, and I lean into him for just a moment, trying to let the sheer physicality of his presence ground me, pull me back from the edge. He kisses my cheek, the gesture tender and reassuring, a practiced kindness, but it does little to soothe the storm swirling inside me, the relentless turmoil.

"I'm glad we came," he says, his voice soft but filled with an easy affection that, in other circumstances, would be deeply comforting. To him, this visit was just a nice break, a chance to reconnect as a family, a chance for me to "get back on track," for him to remind me that I'm not alone out here, struggling in the shadow of my career's recent decline. "Maybe last night was the inspiration you needed to finally kick-start things again," he adds with a smile, his eyes twinkling with a hopeful optimism that feels completely out of place.

He has no idea. He doesn't know how sickeningly right he is, but for all the wrong reasons. Last night did bring me inspiration—just not the kind he's imagining, not the kind that would ever see the light of day in a book for general consumption. The thought brings a fresh wave of guilt rising in my throat, thick and suffocating, but I swallow it down, forcing it deep inside where it can't hurt me right now, where it can't betray me.

"I'm glad you came too." I force a quick, almost perfunctory peck on his lips, trying to keep the facade in place, to keep the flimsy walls from crumbling down around me. I step back as he climbs into the car, the girls already waving eagerly from the back seat, their small hands pressed against the glass. I plaster on a wide, practiced smile and wave back. I keep waving until the car disappears down the winding gravel driveway, until I can no longer see their small faces pressed against the windows, until the last glint of chrome vanishes beyond the trees.

The moment the car is out of sight, my smile drops, evaporating from my face like smoke. The relief I feel is instant. A sharp, exhilarating rush.

When I'm certain they're gone and can no longer hear the rumble of the engine, I turn and head back into the house. I'm moving on autopilot, my steps quick and purposeful, almost frantic, my mind racing with one singular, overwhelming thought: *I need to call Saint.* It's not a question. It's a primal, desperate need.

He's all I've been able to think about since last night, his audacious presence lingering in my mind like a dark, intoxicating shadow I can't shake, clinging to my thoughts, weaving through every fleeting moment of false calm. I need to hear his voice again, to ground myself in whatever this terrifying, exhilarating thing is between us, this dance that feels utterly out of my control.

I don't get far. The moment I open the door, I'm left frozen in place.

Saint is somehow standing right in front of me, having materialized as if from thin air, his tall, imposing frame blocking my path completely, filling the doorway. His eyes, dark and piercing, are locked on mine with an intensity that makes my skin prickle.

A million questions flood my mind all at once, a chaotic, unbidden torrent. *How did he get inside? I locked the doors last night, I was so careful! How long has he been here? Has he been watching me? Watching Shephard?*

I feel utterly exposed, incredibly vulnerable, like the very walls of my supposedly safe space have been irrevocably breached, and I have absolutely no control over what happens next. The familiar, quiet cabin suddenly feels like a cage.

Saint doesn't say a word. He doesn't need to. His presence speaks volumes as he keeps his gaze on me while he steps aside to allow me to pass. Without warning or an invite, he follows me inside, then shuts the door with a startling slam. The sound of the lock echoing in the otherwise silent room seals us in. His hand moves quickly, with a chilling efficiency, as he continues to the next lock, a sharp twist of the dead bolt, the thud reverberating through me. Before I can even process what's happening, he grabs me and pushes me against the door. The sudden force of his body presses against mine, pinning me to the solid wood, trapping me, and I can feel the radiating heat from his skin, the raw, barely leashed power in his touch, in the taut muscles of his chest against my own.

He grips my jaw with one firm hand, his fingers digging into my skin just enough to make my breath hitch, and then his mouth crashes against mine in a hard, possessive kiss.

There's no gentleness, no hesitation, no tender exploration. His kiss is a claim, a brutal, undeniable reminder of the power he holds over me, a force that both terrifies and thrills. And despite the fear thrumming through my veins, I feel myself melting into it, my body betraying my mind, responding with a desperate hunger of its own.

I don't know what it is about this twisted game we're playing that I love so much, this push and pull of control and surrender. But rather than shove him away, rather than fight him, which is what every shred of my responsible, married self screams I *should* do, I moan, a low, guttural sound, and pull him closer, my hands instinctively gripping his shirt, clinging to him like a lifeline.

I think it's the reckless, careless danger surrounding Saint's actions that draws me to him, the thrill of walking so close to the edge. He takes risks that Shephard never would, not in a million years. He puts me in uncomfortable, exhilarating situations, pushing my boundaries, shattering my complacency.

And he clearly enjoys every single second of it. His pleasure is almost as intoxicating as his touch.

Saint pulls back, tearing his mouth from mine with a soft, wet sound, and presses his forehead to mine, his eyes still burning into my soul. His breath is warm against my face, a ghost of a whisper. "Get in the shower and wash him off."

The command, delivered in that low, intimate tone, hits me like a physical blow. It's so shockingly, surprisingly insulting, so utterly possessive and demeaning, that my immediate response is pure, unfiltered defiance. "Fuck you," I snap, the words spitting from my lips before I can even think.

He grins, a flash of white teeth in the dim light, a predator's smile. Without a word, he grabs my wrist, his fingers firm but not bruising, and pulls me with a deliberate, unyielding force in the direction of my bedroom, toward the bathroom. "Don't worry, I will," he murmurs, his voice dark with promise. "But not until you wash him off."

He gets me all the way to the bathroom door, the porcelain gleam of the sink visible, before I try to defend myself, to regain some agency, some shred of dignity. The rational, self-preserving side of me wants to run from him, to escape this intoxicating vortex he's created. But the overwhelming majority of me is consumed by a morbid curiosity, a thrilling anticipation of where this will lead, how far he's willing to push. I pull my wrist from his grasp, the gesture more symbolic than effective. "You're insane," I whisper, my voice laced with a genuine awe and terror.

He pulls me into the small bathroom, the space suddenly too confined, too intimate, and then, with a shocking tenderness amid his strength, he grips the back of my head, his fingers tangling in my hair. "And you fucking love it," he says, his voice a low, gravelly rasp, right before his mouth comes down on mine again, harder this time, more desperate. And like the whore that I am, I kiss him back with just as much urgency, just as much desperate need, my own body demanding the punishment and the pleasure.

He's unbuttoning my jeans while he kisses me, his fingers quick and adept, surprisingly gentle, making short work of the button. When he gets them unzipped with a soft rasp of metal, he tears his mouth from mine, his breath ragged, and kneels in front of me. His dark eyes burn into mine as he expertly removes my jeans and then my panties, pulling them down my legs, urging me, silently, to step out of them. My balance is precarious, but I obey, stepping out of the small heap of denim and lace. Then he's standing again, pulling my shirt over my head, stripping me bare under his relentless gaze.

He reaches into the shower, turns on the water, and then looks at me, his gaze intense, expectant. "Get in, Petra." The command is soft, yet absolute.

I love that he doesn't call me Reya in this moment. When he says my name, my *real* name, it makes it seem like he really is jealous, truly possessive. That raw, masculine jealousy inexplicably emboldens me, fuels a defiant thrill. I step into the shower, the cool spray hitting my naked skin, just as he starts to remove his own clothes, shedding them with a fluid grace.

I know he locked the front door. I saw him do it. But Shephard could still come back. What if he forgot something? What if he realizes I'm not in the living room, that I didn't grab my laptop? If he forgot something and came back . . . The thought flashes through my mind, a fleeting spark of terror, a necessary adrenaline rush.

My thoughts are broken, fragmented, as Saint steps into the shower with me, his warm, naked body pressing against mine in the confined space. He grabs the showerhead and pulls it off the holder with a soft click. He places it between my legs, aiming the nozzle, and I gasp, a sharp, involuntary intake of breath, because the water is still stunningly cold, a frigid shock against my most sensitive skin.

"What are you doing?" I ask, my voice thin, almost a whimper, shocked by the sudden, visceral intensity of it all, the sheer, brazen audacity.

He presses his mouth to my ear, his breath hot against my wet skin, the words a low, guttural growl that vibrates through me. "Washing him off your cunt so I can eat it."

His words, crude and utterly depraved, make me physically shudder, a deep, involuntary tremor that racks my entire body. I lean my head against the cold, tiled shower wall, surrendering to the sensation, to his sheer will, and in that moment, in the face of his desire, I forget all about Shephard. All about my husband, about the lies, about the life I'm betraying.

Right now, it's just . . . *Saint.*

CHAPTER SEVENTEEN

Saint, Saint, Saint. He is a beautiful specimen.

The sun beats down, a warm, benevolent weight on my skin, as I watch him navigate the boat across the glittering expanse of the lake. He's a natural, his movements fluid and strong, utterly at ease behind the wheel. He's shirtless, his back a canvas of lean muscle, glistening with a fine sheen of sweat. Every flex, every shift of his shoulders, is a stark, captivating display of power, a visual rhythm that makes my breath catch in my throat. He's so undeniably sexy out here, untamed and free.

And in return, I, too, feel free. I lean back against the cushions of the boat, the worn fabric warm beneath me, and try to lose myself in the pages of my book, a psychological thriller that feels far less unsettling than my own life right now. But my eyes keep drifting, drawn inevitably to Saint. He glances my way often, his gaze a hot brand on my skin, and occasionally, as he moves past me, adjusting a line or checking a gauge, he leans down to press a quiet, lingering kiss to my hair, my temple, the corner of my mouth. Each touch is a silent claim over me.

"Need any help?" I ask, my voice a little breathless, as he passes by again, his hand brushing my arm. The words are automatic, a reflex from years of partnership, of being the one who always offers.

He laughs, a low, dismissive sound that isn't unkind. "Relax, Petra. You work too much." He says it with a casual ease, a simple observation, and the words resonate with a surprising depth. I remember Shephard's voice, the subtle barbs, the undercurrent of judgment when I *don't* work, when I try to rest. "*The well's looking a little dry*," he said, a veiled accusation, making me feel guilty for not churning out content, for not always being productive, for my artistic struggles. Saint, with that simple sentence, offers a liberation I didn't realize I craved. He sees my exhaustion, not my failure.

The sun is getting hotter, and I can feel the beginnings of distinct tan lines forming where my tank top ends. With a decisive shrug, I pull my top over my head, exposing myself to the wide-open sky. I feel Saint's eyes on me immediately, a familiar heat, and he lets out a low, appreciative groan, a raw, visceral sound that hums through the air. But he doesn't say anything annoying, anything that feels cliché or objectifying, none of the cheap compliments or possessive remarks most men would offer. He just watches, his gaze intense, possessive in its own way, and utterly silent. It's more powerful than any words.

After a while, the wind whipping his hair, the sun glinting off his shoulders, he finally comes to sit down next to me, the boat swaying gently beneath us. He props an elbow on his knee, his body angled toward me, his presence a warm, magnetic force. The silence stretches between us, comfortable for him, electric for me. I can't hold back the question that's been gnawing at me, a persistent ache in my chest.

"Do you regret this?" I ask, my voice barely above a whisper, gesturing vaguely between us, meaning *this*—the affair, the betrayal, the secrets we share.

He considers it for a long moment, his eyes scanning the horizon, his expression unreadable. Then he turns to me, his gaze direct, unflinching, honest to a brutal degree. "I wish it wasn't an affair, Petra," he says, his voice low, tinged with a quiet regret that surprises me. "But no. I don't regret being with you. Not for a second."

The words hit me with a jolt. He wishes it wasn't an affair. That implies a desire for something more, something legitimate. And that, in turn, makes me think of his wife, the woman he's still married to, still talks to daily. It feels like more of a compliment to me, a heady rush of validation, but simultaneously, a profound insult to her, to his marriage. It's a cruel, delicious irony.

A different kind of question forms on my tongue, one that feels even more intimate, more intrusive than the last. "Do you . . . do you have kids?" I ask, my voice soft, almost hesitant, crossing a line I'm not sure he wants me to cross.

He doesn't answer immediately. He just looks at me, his gaze suddenly shuttered, almost cold, like I've asked something deeply inappropriate, like it's crossing a sacred boundary to ask him these things. The sudden shift makes my heart sink.

"You know *I* have kids," I press, the quiet desperation in my voice betraying my need to know, to understand him beyond the passion. "I want to know more about *you*."

He finally breaks eye contact, looking out at the glittering water again. His voice is flat, devoid of emotion, almost dismissive. "I didn't ask about your family. They just showed up. It's different." His implication is clear: My life, my family, my circumstances, were simply presented to him. He didn't seek them out, didn't intrude. But his, his are off limits.

A knot of frustration tightens in my stomach, but I bite back the retort, sensing a fragile barrier I shouldn't push. I go back to reading my book, pretending to be absorbed in the plot, but the words feel like staring at a blank page.

Then, just when I've given up, when the silence feels like it will stretch forever, he starts to open up, his voice barely audible above the gentle lapping of the water against the hull. "We tried for years," he says, his gaze still fixed on the horizon, his face a mask of distant pain. "To have kids. Failed IVF cycles, false positives, miscarriages . . . it was hell." His voice cracks, just slightly, on the last word. "Turns out, after all the testing, it was me. Not her. *I* couldn't have kids."

I sit up straight, startled, my book sliding unheeded from my lap to the boat deck with a soft thud. *Shock.* The vulnerability in his tone, the depth of that revelation, takes my breath away. "Oh, Saint," I whisper, my hand instinctively reaching for his arm, a gesture of comfort.

He flinches, just slightly, at my touch, then continues, his voice softer now, tinged with a deep sadness. "She started to resent me. I could feel it. The quiet anger. The unspoken blame for taking her dreams away. We separated six months ago."

My mind reels. Six months? So recent. My heart aches for him, for the quiet devastation of that dream. And then, another thought, a more selfish one, emerges.

Why did he let me believe he was in a happy marriage?

"You didn't tell me any of this," I say, my voice trembling with the revelation.

He turns to me, his dark eyes meeting mine.

"I still wear my wedding ring. I still feel married. Where, in the space between you needing a muse who is a married man and me explaining my messy break, could I have fit all that in? Besides, you needed the full experience, Petra," he says. "And I've had fun with it. The guilt, the secrecy, the forbidden thrill. You needed to feel it all, to live it, so you could feel better about your writing. To get the fuel you needed for Reya."

A cold dread washes over me, mixing with a strange, dark understanding.

"Do you want the marriage to work?" I ask, the question tumbling out before I can stop it in a desperate need for clarity. I'm searching for a shred of normal human emotion in this chaotic game.

He looks back at the water, his gaze distant. "Of course," he says, simply, quietly. "But I don't want to tie her down. Or prevent her from having other children. From pursuing that dream with someone else."

His voice holds a profound sorrow, a selflessness that's almost unbearable, given what he's just admitted to me.

"Do you still live together?" I ask, pressing for more details, trying to piece together the shattered fragments of his life, to understand the man behind the persona.

"No," he says, shaking his head. "We don't. But we talk almost daily." He pauses, then turns back to me, his eyes searching, vulnerable in a way I haven't seen them before. "She's having trouble moving on. But so am I." He shifts, his knee brushing mine. "Do you . . . do you have any advice?"

The sudden vulnerability, the genuine plea, takes me by surprise. And for a moment, I see him not as Saint, the intriguing, manipulative muse, but as a man in pain. But the answer is automatic. "No," I say, shaking my head, my voice flat. "I don't. I don't know how to move on, either, even though sometimes I want to." The words are true, agonizingly so. "But you don't have kids," I add, almost without thinking, a reflexive defense, a way to diminish his pain in comparison to mine, to make mine somehow more valid. "So maybe it isn't as hard for you."

The moment the words leave my lips, I regret them. His face hardens instantly, a subtle but profound shift. His jaw clenches, his eyes darkening, and he pulls away from me, the distance suddenly vast between us. It's like I took his infertility, his deepest wound, and diminished it, trivialized it with a careless, thoughtless comparison to my own self-inflicted marital woes. The accusation, though unspoken, hangs heavy in the air.

"I'm so sorry," I whisper, my voice filled with immediate, genuine contrition. "Saint, I didn't mean it like that. I just . . ." I trail off, unable to find the words.

He holds up a hand, stopping me, his expression still etched with pain, but softened slightly now. "It's okay," he says, his voice strained.

"I'm not going tit for tat about this, but not being able to have kids at all is a hell of a lot harder than divorcing someone you have kids with."

He's right. His pain is immense because his dreams were shattered by something beyond his control. Mine . . . mine would be shattered by my own hand, simply because of boredom. It's difficult to leave any relationship if there's not a huge betrayal, especially when children are involved. Boredom and annoyance are likely not grounds for a divorce, but I'm worried that's where it starts. The thoughts of escape. This glimpse of what my life could be like without Shephard.

It used to feel like his presence was air, lifting me up and making me lighter. Now, for whatever reason, he just feels more and more like a weight. Something else I have to carry to keep us all moving forward.

Saint looks out at the water again, his jaw working. Then, his voice lowers, almost to a confession, chilling me to the bone even in the warm sun. "When I was watching you say goodbye to your girls, when Shephard was there . . ." He pauses, and I hold my breath. "I was angry, Petra. So angry." He turns his eyes to me, and they burn with an unsettling intensity. "I wanted you to get caught, so you'd leave him, so I could have what he takes for granted. What he barely sees anymore."

The confession is a dark, dizzying plunge into his psyche, revealing a level of calculated malice that should repel me. But instead, a perverse thrill shoots through me. He wanted to destroy my life, to claim it for himself. And he almost did.

He leans in, his hand cupping my cheek, his thumb tracing my jaw. His eyes, burning with a mix of fury and desire, lock onto mine. And then, his lips descend, hard and hungry, claiming me completely. The kiss is fierce, a primal embrace of chaos. And then, right there, on the open water, beneath the broad, indifferent gaze of the afternoon sun, we have open sex, or maybe it's the beginnings of making love, unashamed, a defiant act of rebellion against everything we've just confessed and every boundary we've shattered.

We pull into the small cove, the water lapping gently against the hull as Saint expertly maneuvers the boat toward the rickety wooden dock. The sun, lower now, casts long, stretching shadows across the water, painting the sky in hues of orange and purple. We don't speak, the quiet after our intense coupling thick and heavy.

As we begin the process of tying up the boat, securing it to the weathered pilings, our movements synchronized and efficient, a familiar anxiety begins to prickle at my skin. The real world, the one I've temporarily escaped, is rushing back in, demanding its due. My hands move mechanically, coiling a rope, but my mind is already back in the cabin, drifting further, to my house, to Shephard, to the delicate facade I have to maintain.

"I have to go home this weekend," I say, the words feeling brittle, almost like a confession, the sudden return to mundane reality jarring.

"What? I thought you had another two weeks booked."

I avoid his eyes, focusing instead on the knot I'm trying to tighten. "I don't leave until Friday, and it's just for two days. It's my daughter's birthday. I need to be there."

Saint pauses, his large hands still on the rope, his movements ceasing. I feel his gaze on me, steady and intense, but I don't look up. The silence stretches, taut with unspoken questions, with the reality of our separate lives.

He just nods. A single quiet nod. No questions about Shephard, no protestations, no demands. Just that simple, heavy acknowledgment. It's both a relief and a subtle disappointment. Part of me, the part that craves his intensity, wanted a fight, a plea, a sign of his possessiveness. But he gives me none. He just accepts it.

When the boat is securely fastened, the ropes taut, he steps onto the dock. Instead of releasing my hand, which had somehow found its way into his during the tying process, he tightens his grip, coming to a pause.

I follow his gaze to the opposite side of the water from where we docked, and when my eyes lock onto what made him freeze, I squeeze his hand until it slips from mine.

Oh, God.

Saint is in the water before I can even fully process what I'm seeing. But there she is, just twenty or so feet from the shore, floating in the water. Mari, with her bright-orange hair, face down, her arms limp, skimming the top of the water.

"Mari!" Saint yells, swimming toward her. I step closer to the edge of the dock, wondering if I should go call the police, or yell for Louie, or jump in and help him. But I'm just frozen as I watch.

"Mari," I whisper. "God, no."

Saint reaches her, both his hands gripping her waist to flip her over. As soon as he does, I hear a piercing scream.

But it isn't coming from Saint.

It's coming from Mari, who is wearing goggles and beating Saint over his head with her snorkel. "I. Know. How. To. Swim. You. Dumbass!"

Oh, my God.

My entire body sighs, and I feel all the blood that rushed to my head suddenly drop to my feet. I'm so shocked that I have to lower myself until I'm sitting cross-legged on the dock.

"I'm so sorry," Saint says. "It looked like you needed help."

Mari motions to her body—to the bathing suit she's wearing—and then pulls the goggles off her eyes. Her wet curls are matted over half her face. I've never seen her so mad. "I had a snorkel literally sticking up out of the water! I'm in a bathing suit! Aren't detectives supposed to know what context clues are?" She starts marching toward the shore, water splashing all around her. "Can't even get a peaceful swim out here anymore," she mutters.

I can't help but laugh at that.

"I hear you laughing, Twinkle Twat," she calls over her shoulder at me.

I laugh at that too. Then I glance over at Saint and see he's slowly making his way back to me, sopping wet. But there's a smile tugging at his lips.

He pushes himself up onto the dock until he's sitting next to me. "You gonna put that in your book?" he asks.

"Absolutely."

"Can you rewrite it so that I actually save her?"

"Absolutely not."

Saint laughs, pulling off his shirt. Then he grabs my hand and helps me to my feet. His fingers intertwine with mine again, just as they were before he tried to save a perfectly fine woman from drowning. His hand is warm and strong. My anchor.

We walk back to the house in silence, the gentle creak of the old planks beneath our feet the only sound disturbing the quiet afternoon.

Aside from the sound of water dripping from his soaking-wet clothes.

His presence beside me is still powerful, still electric, but the silence between us now feels different. It's not the comfortable, easy silence of shared pleasure, but a charged, knowing quiet, filled with the unspoken reality of everything we confessed on the boat.

The fact that he's married, but he's also available, feels like a big change.

I can't help but insert images of him into my future, wondering what it would be like to no longer be holding the weight that is Shephard.

CHAPTER EIGHTEEN

Oh, my God, he is so heavy. "Shephard! Get off me!"

He was trying to catch a rogue football but tripped over the firepit and landed right on top of me and my chair. I try pushing him off my lap, but he's having trouble straightening himself up. He's probably had too many drinks today, but it's a party. I don't blame him.

"Kev, help," Shephard says, reaching for our neighbor. Kevin finally helps him regain his balance to stand up, but before Shephard runs away to rejoin their game of front-yard football, he leans in and kisses me on the side of the head. "Sorry, babe."

"You're good. Go kick some ass."

The sweet, chaotic sounds of my daughter's birthday party fill the front yard. Laughter bubbles up from the kids, punctuated by the pop of a balloon. Then Shephard's booming voice, carrying over the general conversations. "You've got to be *kidding* me!" he yells. I watch as he falls onto his back in the grass, clutching his forehead in some defeated gesture. Two of the other neighbors are celebrating their win against him and Kev.

A fresh round of giggles erupts as the girls run past me. I can hear Nora in the seat next to me, laughing at whatever conversation she's having with my neighbor Esther.

It's a symphony of normal. Of safe.

This is what I love about my life with Shephard. These weekends in the front yard, cooking out, having margaritas while the kids play in the cul-de-sac. Every sun-drenched second here feels like a shield, which is strange, since the cabin feels like a shield from *this* life.

If only I could have both forever. Alternate between the chaotic thrill of Saint and the chaotic normalcy of my family.

But no one can truly have it all without eventually losing it all.

"Where are you?" Nora asks, leaning in, her voice low. "Thinking about the hot cop?"

My gaze snaps guiltily in her direction. She's grinning.

"What? No." I respond like she literally meant Saint, but I know she's only asking if I'm thinking about my book. *Guilty much, Petra?*

"Wait a second," Nora says. "I know this look. Petra, did you delete everything? I swear to God, if you changed any of what you sent, I'm going to steal your laptop, recover it, and publish it myself."

"I didn't!" I say defensively. "I haven't deleted anything, I swear."

She sighs. "Okay. Good. It's just that every time I've tried to talk to you about what you sent, you change the subject. I thought maybe you didn't want to admit that you trashed it."

"No, I'm just in wife-and-mom mode this weekend. Not thinking about the book at all."

"That's fair," Nora says. "No work talk at the party." She holds up her red SOLO cup for a cheers, so I hold mine up too. "To a weekend of not working," she says.

"And to getting to see you in person for the first time this year," I add. We click our cups together, and her attention soon drifts back to the conversation she was having with Esther.

I take a sip of my iced tea, watching Andi chase a rogue balloon with a shriek of delight. "Mommy, look!" she yells, her tiny hand outstretched. I'm smiling, about to call out a reply, when my gaze drifts, almost idly, toward something that's caught my eye at the end of the street.

I almost overlook the vehicle at first. It blends in for the most part. But when my eyes lock in on it, I realize it's almost camouflaged by the dense shade of the old oak trees lining the curb. It looks like it's been swallowed by the shadows, deliberately.

My breath hitches, catching painfully in my throat.

My iced tea glass slips from my damp hand. I immediately try to recover it, but watch helplessly as it falls quietly onto the grass with a thud, going unnoticed by everyone around me.

No. It can't be. He would not drive this far.

But the sheer, undeniable presence of that car, even from this distance, screams his name.

A knot of icy anxiety tightens in my stomach, quickly followed by a hot, furious surge of anger that makes my hands clench into fists.

The nerve.

He was so mad when I dared to follow him, when I stepped even a toe into *his* real life. And now he's here, a silent, dark sentinel, watching *me* in mine? The sheer hypocrisy of it burns, a searing flame in my chest. I want to march down that street, to confront him, to demand, *"What the hell do you think you're doing here?!"* My jaw clenches, the joyful symphony of the party suddenly feeling discordant and tainted.

I try to ignore it, but it's hard to pretend I'm not being watched in the very element I keep so hidden from the rest of the world. My eyes keep flicking, almost involuntarily, to the end of the street, to that dark, menacing shape lurking beneath the oak trees. It's like a predator observing its prey.

I refuse to feel like prey in my own home.

When everyone's attention is diverted by a particularly boisterous game between the men, I seize my chance. I steal away from the group but make it look like I'm heading inside to use the restroom. I slip around to the side of the house and then pass through Esther's backyard. When I'm sure I've gone far enough for no one to see me, I merge onto the sidewalk. My steps are purposeful, aimed straight for his car. Each stride is deliberate, like marching into the lion's den. I keep glancing back to make sure no one is watching me, but everyone is paying attention to everything else.

I go around the back of the car so that I don't risk being seen. I can hear the click of the locks on the doors, which further solidifies it's Saint.

I open the passenger door and can see his arm, his hand gripping the steering wheel, his thigh. The air inside the car is cool, a stark contrast to the muggy summer afternoon. I slide into the passenger seat. My hands grip my thighs, my knuckles white. My voice, when it comes, is a strained whisper that barely hides the roar beneath.

"I thought homes were off limits," I demand, my gaze fixed on his profile. He's looking straight ahead, at my house, at my family, a silent, very unwelcome observer in my domestic world. His stillness is infuriating.

He turns his head slowly, his eyes finally meeting mine. There's no apology, no explanation, just that familiar, unsettling depth. "It's different now." His voice is low and calm.

"How is it *different*?" I challenge, my arms crossing over my chest, a defensive barrier.

He shifts, turning more fully toward me, his elbow resting on the center console. "You're in danger."

My brow furrows. "Danger? What are you talking about?" A cold trickle of unease joins the anger.

"Reya, you've received death threats. I can't let you go unprotected."

Good fucking God.

I stare at him, a snort of disbelief escaping me, sharp and involuntary. "I'm at my *home*. This is my *daughter's birthday*. I don't have time for this shit, *Saint*."

"Reya," he says.

"Stop calling me that! This is ridiculous. You've found a flimsy reason to intrude on my personal space, and I'm angry."

He holds my gaze, unwavering, his expression unreadable. And then he finally breaks character, leaning his head back against the headrest. He allows an expression to finally reach his eyes, and maybe I'm just hoping, but he actually looks a little remorseful.

But then the asshole has the audacity to grin. "Petra," he says, finally using my actual name. "Relax." He tries to slip a reassuring hand up to my neck, but I push it away.

"Do not tell me to relax when you're literally sitting outside my home."

He seems genuinely surprised by my reaction. He angles toward me a bit more. "Are you worried I'm here to confront your husband?"

"I honestly have no idea what you're capable of. It's fucking terrifying."

He immediately drops the whole act, no more grin, no more cockiness. He transforms back into the Saint I had on the boat, his eyes reassuring, his posture comforting. "Petra," he repeats. His voice is quiet, almost a plea, the barest hint of vulnerability in its tone. "I would never do that."

"You need to leave," I say, my voice firm, despite the tremor in my hands that I desperately try to hide.

"Wait. Just wait a second," he says, grabbing my hand.

"No. I can't function with you here. I need you to leave. This is not okay."

He doesn't argue further. He just watches me for another long, silent moment, those dark eyes dissecting me. Then, a slight, almost imperceptible nod.

Nothing else needs to be said between us. I grab the door handle, my fingers fumbling slightly, and step out, the sounds of the party rushing back in, louder, more vibrant, almost overwhelming after the contained silence of the car.

I walk back toward the house, every muscle in my back tense. I finally hear him start the car and pull away.

I walk straight into the house and to the bathroom. I lock the door and do everything I can not to have a complete meltdown.

This is my *home*.

I think he might be crazy.

I think *I* might be crazy.

CHAPTER NINETEEN

I am. I'm crazy.

Because what sane person would return to the location where she's vulnerable to a man who drove two hours to sit outside her house without permission?

Me. That's who. But my God, I've never felt anything like this. It's a constant tug, like a thick rope loops from my chest to Saint's, and I'm constantly being pulled until I'm too exhausted to fight that pull.

Following attraction and intrigue over instinct and common sense is a very good description of crazy.

The hum of the road beneath my tires is the only consistent sound in the oppressive silence of the car. My hands grip the steering wheel, knuckles white, a mirror to the tension coiling in my gut. The sunlight feels harsh today, glinting off the evergreens that line the winding drive. Every mile closer to the cabin feels like a tightening spring, a coil of dread and anticipation.

It's been a whole day since I told him to leave. He hasn't reached out since. Not a text, not a call, not even a cryptic emoji since he drove away.

My phone, lying face down on the passenger seat, feels useless to me. I've checked it a hundred times, hoping for a flicker of something, anything, just to know he's not a phantom, that he really did have the audacity to show up at my house and it wasn't a fever dream. The silence of my phone screams.

My jaw aches from clenching. I told myself I was coming here to finish work, but deep down, I know I'm coming because he's here and I'm not done with him. Because I've been pulled into his orbit and never want to be pushed out.

The turnoff appears, a gravel road whose crunch beneath my tires is starting to feel like the sound of coming home. The familiar trees close in, tall and silent, casting long shadows. My breath hitches. *Please, don't let him be there. Please, let him be there. I realize I'm begging for two very different things right now. I am so confused.*

But then, as the trees thin and the small clearing where the cabin sits comes into view, I see it. His car. Dark, imposing, just like yesterday, but this time parked brazenly in my driveway, a territorial flag planted on my property.

He's here. Of course he's here.

The anger from last night, temporarily dulled by the frantic morning, flares back to life, hot and immediate. He showed up at my *home*. The home I share with Shephard, with our girls. The audacity. The sheer, terrifying audacity. And now he's just . . . waiting for me? As if I owe him something? My hands tighten on the wheel so hard my fingers ache.

I am so happy he's here. I am so angry he's here. I'm mad at myself for wanting to run into his arms, while simultaneously feeling the need to blacken his eye.

I steer my car slowly, carefully, pulling up behind his. The engine clicks as I cut the ignition, the sudden quiet amplifying the frantic thumping of my heart. I sit here for a long moment, gripping the steering wheel, just breathing, trying to get my racing thoughts under control. I'm not in the mood for sex. I'm too angry for that. But I am in the mood for conversation. Maybe even an argument. A fight. A way to put all this to an end and somehow be okay with it.

I push open the car door, the sound a loud creak in the still air. The wood porch, the scent of pine and damp earth—it all feels alien, tainted, as I make my way toward the front door. My hand hovers over the doorknob, hesitating. What will I say? What will he say? Will he demand something? Will he act like nothing happened?

I open the unlocked door to my rental, slowly, carefully, as if expecting a wild animal to spring out. The interior is dim and cool. My eyes scan the living room and kitchen until I find him.

He's standing at the stove, his back to me, the faint scent of herbs and tomato sauce already wafting through the air. He's wearing faded jeans and a dark T-shirt, the fabric stretching taut across his shoulders. One hand is sprinkling something on top of a dish; the other rests casually on the counter.

The picture of domesticity, completely at odds with the man who invaded my life, my home, last night.

And good God. He's wearing socks. Why am I a sucker for a guy in a clean pair of socks?

He turns slightly, just enough for me to see the profile of his face, focused, intent on whatever he's making. My gaze travels lower, to the dish he's preparing. It's a glass dish layered with what looks unmistakably like pasta, rich red sauce, and creamy white.

Lasagna. He made lasagna.

The savory and comforting scent hits me fully. It's a jarring contrast to the tension in my body, to the raw anger that still simmers. *Lasagna.* As if this night is normal. As if he's not the man who just left me after violating my personal space. He's just . . . *cooking* for me.

He looks up then, slowly, as if sensing my presence, but without surprise. His dark eyes meet mine across the kitchen. There's no fear in them, no apology, just a quiet intensity that sends a fresh ripple of unease through me. He doesn't say anything. He just closes the bag of Parmesan he's holding and gestures with his chin toward the table set for two.

"Dinner's almost ready," he says, his voice low, calm.

I walk to the table, my movements stiff, like those of a doll on strings. The table is neatly laid. Two plates, silverware, even linen napkins. A bottle of red wine stands uncorked. He plates the lasagna, thick, generous slices oozing with cheese and rich sauce. He sets one plate in front of me, then takes his own seat opposite me. The silence stretches, thick with unspoken words, with the chaotic memories of last night. The comforting scent of food feels like a cruel trick.

I pick up my fork, but my appetite is nonexistent. I prod at a piece of pasta, then set the fork down. I can't eat. Not yet.

He watches me, his expression unreadable. Finally, he sighs, a quiet exhalation. "Look, Petra," he begins, his voice softer, "I'm sorry. You're right. I crossed a line."

"You showed up at my *house*, Saint. My family's *home*."

He doesn't flinch. His gaze is steady, unwavering. "I know. But let's not forget who followed who first."

"I live two hours from here! You drove two hours and parked outside my home and watched me and my husband and my children for God knows how long."

"It was just half an hour."

"Jesus Christ. *Semantics*."

"I only did it because I wanted you to feel truly *alive*. I thought it might be fun, or that it might shake something loose. Inspire you in some way."

I stare at him, disbelief battling with a minuscule flicker of understanding.

"Adrenaline is a powerful muse," he says simply. "And to be honest, I think you need more adrenaline in your life. I've met your husband."

The dig makes me angry, but also forces me to suppress a laugh. I hate that he can make this moment feel more human with his humor. I want to be fully mad at him. I wanted an argument.

I push my plate away, the thought of food too much for the moment. "We're being too risky." I can't completely put the blame on him. I was a part of last night, too, as angry as I am that he showed up to begin with. I did start the game of cat and mouse when I tried following him to his own home. But I never would have parked. "You're putting my marriage at risk. That's not a game."

He holds my gaze as he takes my hand. "You're right. We should have laid out strict rules before starting this whole thing. I got caught up in the moment. It won't happen again. But my purpose here, my role, is not to unravel your life in any way. It's to help you write. And have a little fun while doing it. That's all."

I look away from his face then, down at my hand, resting clenched in his. *He does not want to threaten your marriage,* I tell myself. It's a statement that should bring relief. And it does, a little. But beneath it, a tiny, rebellious part of me, a part I barely acknowledge, feels a perverse twist of disappointment. *It would be nice if he did.* A dangerous thought, hot and shameful, flares. Maybe if he *were* a threat, if Shephard had to actually *fight* for me, if there were a real, tangible risk, then Shephard would value me more.

I think he appreciates me, but I worry he sees me as a mold that any other female could fit. Nothing scares me more than being ordinary. I'm not sure he sees all the special parts of me, and that just makes me sad.

"Are we good?" Saint asks. His thumb brushes softly across my wrist. "It's your last week here. I promise I won't pull any more stunts."

I nod. Saint nods.

And I guess that's that. Another crisis averted. Another red flag folded up and tucked neatly away in a closet.

Saint releases my hand and takes his fork, digging into his lasagna. But I'm not quite ready to eat yet.

"What happens after this last week is over?" I ask Saint.

"Whatever you want to happen."

"Can I trust you won't show up at my house?"

Saint smiles, but it's a reassuring smile. Not a cocky one. "I know what this is, Petra. What we're doing. I think you're the one who keeps forgetting it's a game. And if you never want to see me again, you never will. But, you aren't retiring, and I imagine you'll be back at this lake again. The ball will always be in your court."

Oh, God. The idea that there's not a clear finality to what we're doing fills me with dread. Not because I wouldn't want to see him again someday after I pack up and leave, but because if I don't end this with a clear goodbye, he's more than likely all I'll be thinking about when I'm back in the real world.

I don't want the ball to be in my court. I don't want there to be a ball or a court.

Why the hell do people cheat? This is fucking stressful!

Saint reaches for the bottle of wine. "I read what you emailed me," he says as he pours. "Read it while I sat watching your house yesterday. Before you caught me."

I squirm uncomfortably in my chair. I don't know that I want to hear his thoughts.

"Petra," he says, his voice softening, a deep resonance that makes the air thrum. "I don't know why you aren't the cockiest writer in the world. You're so great."

The unexpected compliment disarms me, while also making me laugh. I blink, meeting his eyes again. "Um. Thank you?"

"Seriously, though, I couldn't put it down. Just seeing how you interpret the moments we've had together was the best reading experience I've ever had. The language you use, the way you craft a sentence—it's all so powerful." He sips his wine, his gaze thoughtful.

I don't know why his words are making me blush like I'm in grade school. "Thank you. But you can stop now. This is so awkward."

He reaches across the table and takes my hand, brushing a thumb over mine. "Take the compliments. The old Petra used to take the compliments. I told you I watched all your videos. I've seen who you used to be before the notoriety, and it makes me sad that that part of you is gone. I wish I could have known the version of you before you started believing everyone *else's* version of you."

His words hit me hard.

I miss that version too. Not that I thought more of who I was as a writer, but I definitely hadn't been jaded yet, or worn down.

I miss the passion I used to have. I miss the interaction with my readers. I miss the book releases, the signings, the trips to other countries. I used to have so much fun with it all. I used to wake up ready to see which of my friends were online. Or I'd wake up wanting nothing more than to dive back into whatever manuscript I was writing.

Now I just lie in bed, dreading what each workday will bring, what awful email will set the tone for that day, what nagging thought will prevent me from opening my manuscript.

"I wish I could find that again," I say, more to myself than to Saint.

"I wish you could too. This kind of writing, what you do . . . it's intensely personal, even when it's fiction. You pour yourself onto the page. And the more famous you get, the more success you find, the more people think they own a piece of that. Of *you*. And they're going to be louder, and it's going to come from every angle, but what do you think happens to them when you disappear completely?"

"They get what they want?" I reply.

Saint shakes his head. "No. They get nothing. They just move on to the next book. The next author. The next movie. The next popular thing. Because hating you and loving you is a fad that they *will* move on from. Every single person will move on from this experience but you. You're the one stuck in it forever, because it's yours. It's your life, it's your name, it's your passion. And you need to control what you allow in, because what you allow in will control what you're able to put back out."

He pauses, allowing his words to sink in. His thumb moves in circles over the back of my hand, a gentle, reassuring rhythm.

A strange calm settles over me. A feeling of being truly understood in a way Shephard rarely manages.

"Thank you," I say. It's all the words I can muster without tearing up.

Saint's words aren't just flattery; they resonate in a way I've always hoped to feel, but have never had articulated to me before. He validates what I'm feeling without dismissing it. Without telling me I should just be grateful to have a career. He makes me feel like my internal struggle is real, and that I'm actually strong enough to overcome it.

"You know you don't need me, right?" He says the question like it's a statement. "You wrote stacks of books before I showed up at your door. And I believe you'd still finish this book even if I didn't show up at your door. If anything, I'm a distraction to your writing, not a muse."

I shake my head. "I'm going to have to disagree with you on that."

Saint pulls his hand from mine, a faint warmth lingering on my skin. He gestures to my plate again, a small, encouraging smile on his lips. "You need to eat. And then, we get you back to work."

I pick up my fork, and this time, the scent of the food doesn't feel jarring. It feels . . . grounding. I take a bite. The flavors explode on my tongue—rich, savory, deeply comforting. It's perfect.

By the time dinner is over, the last of the surviving light of dusk has faded, and the cabin is bathed in the warm glow of the lamps. The half-empty lasagna dish sits between us, a testament to the meal. More importantly, the tension that tightened my shoulders for days has eased, replaced by a quiet sense of purpose, a strange, burgeoning lightness. He has made me feel incredibly good, incredibly valued. Not as a sexual conquest, but as an artist, as a person.

He stands up, collecting the plates.

"I'll clean up," I say, taking the dishes from him. When I reach the sink, I can hear him gathering his things behind me. I spin around, sad to see him preparing to leave.

He walks to the door while shoving his phone into his pocket. "I'll text you tomorrow."

"You're leaving?" I ask, walking toward him.

He nods, but wraps an arm around my waist when I reach him. "I am. You've got a book to finish this week." I don't want him to leave. He leans in, and for a fleeting second, I brace myself for a passionate kiss. But it's a soft, chaste, gentle press of his lips against my forehead.

"Sleep well, Petra," he murmurs, his voice a low caress. "And write fiercely."

When he opens the door to leave, the wind whips my hair around my face. The temperature has dropped several degrees, and the tops of the trees are swaying. I watch as he rushes to his car, the sky bursting with a bolt of lightning just as he opens the door.

A storm is coming.

CHAPTER TWENTY

A storm has arrived.

Her name is Mari.

Her umbrella made it inside before she did, but now the wind has picked up her orange curls, and they're flying in a circle above her head as we both go to push the door shut. The wind is coming directly against the front of the cabin, making the storm seem worse than it is.

It has been howling and thundering on and off for two days now, but I absolutely love this weather. Nothing puts me in a better writing mood than a good thunderstorm.

"Phew, it's windy!" Mari shakes some of the rain off her. "This one's a doozy," she says, sliding out of her boots.

"No one says that anymore." I grab a spoon out of the drawer so that I can eat the yogurt I just opened.

"Says what?" she asks, plopping down at the table.

"*This one's a doozy,*" I mimic.

"Oh, shut up. I'm sixty."

"The new thirty."

"Then what does that make you, a toddler?" she asks.

I laugh, just as my phone vibrates with an incoming call. I stick the spoon in my mouth and pick up my phone, and I answer it as soon as I see that Saint is calling. I take the spoon out of my mouth.

"Hi," I say, my voice cheerful.

"I'm coming over tonight," he says, his voice instantly familiar and commanding. No question, no polite inquiry, just a statement of intent.

"When?" A rush of heat floods my cheeks.

"I get off at six."

"Do you want me to cook something?" I can see the curiosity eating at Mari as she listens in to the one side of the conversation she can hear.

"Up to you," he replies. I sense a subtle test in his words. As if he's thinking, *Who are we going to be tonight?*

"What's your favorite food?" I ask, hoping it's something I can cook well.

A beat of silence, then a low chuckle. "Whatever you love to cook, Reya." The name that used to bring me a thrill when I heard it suddenly makes me frown. It's an affirmation of the fantasy, a subtle invitation to step deeper into our game, but I was really hoping he was just coming over as Saint tonight. But whatever gets him here.

"I'll have something ready, Cam," I say teasingly, forgetting that Mari is listening.

Good God, now she thinks I'm screwing *three* men.

"You think I can stay the night?" he asks.

"I think we can arrange that."

"Good." Before he ends the call, just as I'm about to say goodbye, he says, "Hey, Reya?"

My breath catches at the low whisper of his voice. "Yes, Cam?" I respond, the character name slipping from my lips automatically, an echo to his.

"I love you." The words are soft, convincing, and even though he's just pretending to be a character, playing the role I created for him, it feels like he's just said it to *me*. A raw, illogical piece of me believes it, hungers for it.

A warm, undeniable blush spreads from my neck to my hairline. "I love you too," I whisper back, quickly, the lie feeling more real than any truth I've spoken in days. The call ends abruptly, and I can't even look Mari in the eye.

I simply set my phone down on the table and take a bite of my yogurt. I can feel her staring.

"Someone coming over?" she asks.

I nod. "Saint."

"Honey, you do realize you called him by the wrong name, right? Twice."

"It's a nickname. You of all people should know how those work."

"I thought *Saint* was his nickname. You can't have two nicknames."

"He can do whatever he wants."

"You're feisty today," she says, snatching the yogurt from my hand. She grabs the spoon from me, too, and then proceeds to take a bite.

I scrunch my nose. "Eww."

"Trust me. I've had much worse," she says, and takes a second bite. "What are you going to cook for the man?"

I momentarily forgot. "Shit. I don't know. I need to go to the grocery store."

"I have a chicken recipe he'll love. It's a real doozy, Petra. A *doozy*. You hear that? A fucking *doozy*."

I laugh. "Send it to me."

I think I might miss Mari after I leave too.

I pass a gas station on the drive to the grocery store. A small worn-down place with faded signs and a single pump. The kind of place you wouldn't think twice about passing on the road, but today it catches my attention. I've been wanting a local newspaper. Something to ground me in this strange, isolated town. I should probably fill up on gas before my drive back to Sacramento in a few days too.

I pull in to the gas station and park, step out of the car, and feel the sting of the return of raindrops hitting my skin. I run into the store before getting gas, the bell above the door jingling as I step into the dimly lit interior. The smell of stale coffee hits me as I take a few steps toward the counter, scanning the shelves for any sign of a local paper. I wonder if they even sell newspapers here. This town is so small, I wouldn't be surprised if they don't.

I've been wanting to read about the incident that occurred the night Saint showed up at my cabin. The night that changed everything. The memory of it still lingers, like a scene from a movie that I keep replaying in my mind. I thought about adding it to my book, weaving it into the narrative to give it a sense of realness that only true experiences can provide.

I tend to change a lot of scenes during the rewrite phase, and I'm tempted to rework the scene where Cam and Reya meet. I'd like it to more accurately reflect what actually happened between me and Saint. Maybe it would add depth, something more visceral, something the readers could connect with on a deeper level.

At this point, I'm almost positive Saint will finish the book, considering he read half the rough draft. It gives me even more reason to insert real stuff that's happened between us into the pages.

I've never written something knowing the person who inspired it would read it. But then again, I've never written something inspired by an actual person before.

I finally find a rack with the newspapers near the register. There's only one choice of newspaper on the stand, other than *USA TODAY*, and it looks like, from the dates listed at the top of it, they only put out one paper every month. Makes sense with this town being so small.

I flip through it, scanning the headlines, but I can't find anything about the police chase that ended in a suicide.

I check the dates on the paper again and recalculate the date I first showed up here. This paper came out a few days after I showed up, so it should be here, but I don't find it while flipping through it again a second time. Maybe they didn't write about it at all, in order to keep up the facade of this town being a safe space for the few tourists.

The thought leaves me unsettled. Surely something like that would make the news in a town this small. Or maybe I skimmed over it, too distracted to focus. I flip through the pages again, my eyes scanning for any mention of the incident.

I glance over the rack again, wondering if the newest edition has come out yet.

I take the newspaper to the counter and hand it to the clerk. He's a bald man who looks to be in his fifties, his face weathered from years of standing here. He barely glances up as I place the paper on the counter, his eyes still fixed on the register as he punches in the price.

"Is this the most recent one?"

"Yep."

"Do you have any copies of last month's paper?" I ask him.

"Nope."

A man of few words. "What day does the new paper come out?" I ask, hoping maybe there will be more information in the next edition.

He shrugs, his expression bored, as if the question is too mundane to warrant much thought. "Lennie delivers them, so there's no telling. He might bring them Saturday night or he may wait until Monday." He says that like I should know who Lennie is, like Lennie is some kind of legend who transcends this town. "Why? You gonna be in the paper or something?" His eyes finally flick up to meet mine, a glint of curiosity in them now.

"No. Just looking for more information on the police chase from a few weeks ago." I try to keep my voice casual, but there's an edge to it, a hint of anxiety I can't quite hide.

The man punches some more buttons on the cash register, his fingers moving slowly over the keys. "That'll be one dollar and twenty-five cents," he says, not looking up. Then, as if it's an afterthought, he adds, "What police chase?"

I hand him five quarters, dropping them into his outstretched palm. "I can't remember the guy's name. It was a police chase that ended in a suicide on one of the roads a couple of miles away." My voice is quieter now, the words feeling strange in my mouth.

"What road?" His tone shifts, a trace of disbelief creeping into his voice.

"Hunter Trail," I reply, the name of the road sounding foreign to my ears now, like it belongs to someone else's life.

The man chuckles, the sound deep and rumbling in his chest. "If there was a police chase and a suicide on Hunter Trail, I woulda heard about it," he says, shaking his head like it's the most absurd thing I could have said.

The door to the store chimes, and we both turn to see another customer entering. It's Louie. I'm relieved to see him. He'll be able to help.

"Hey, there, Petra!" Louie says with genuine joy. "How's the writing going?"

The clerk, sensing an opportunity to share the strange conversation we've just had, speaks up before I can respond. "Louie, you heard of any police chase or suicide in the last couple weeks? Specifically on your road?"

I pause, my breath catching in my throat as I wait for Louie's response. He looks from me to the clerk, a puzzled expression on his face, before he laughs, shaking his head. "Not around here," he says with a chuckle. "We haven't had a self-inflicted death since 2014. Been even longer than that since we had a police chase."

The words hit me like a punch to the gut. I feel my insides begin to buzz with anxiety, my mind racing as I try to make sense of what I've just heard.

How could that be right? I was there. I saw the police lights, I talked to the detective. *This can't be happening.*

I shake my head, my voice weak as I speak. "But . . . it *did* happen. The road your house is on, Louie. In the middle of the night. A detective came to my door . . ." My words trail off, the confusion thickening in my mind. "Your wife even knows about it."

Louie looks me up and down, his eyes narrowing slightly. "A detective? We don't have detectives."

"You from Los Angeles or something?" the clerk asks. "You a reporter?" There's a note of suspicion in his voice now, as if he's sizing me up, trying to figure out who I am and why I'm asking these questions.

"No," I say, my voice barely above a whisper. "I'm a writer . . . fiction. Not a reporter."

"She's been staying in our remodel," Louie says proudly.

My hands are shaking as I reach into my purse and pull out my phone, the weight of the confusion and fear hitting me. My fingers tremble as I scroll quickly through my camera roll, searching for the photo I've been hiding. Two nights ago, I took a selfie of me and Saint, a moment of weakness, a moment I wanted to remember. I hid it in my phone, tucked away where no one would find it.

I hold the phone up to Louie, my hand shaking as I show him the picture of Saint. "Is this guy a police officer in this town?" I ask with an unsure tone.

Louie takes the phone from me, his brow furrowing as he stares at the picture. After a long moment, he laughs, the sound harsh and mocking. "We have two policemen who patrol this area, and both of them only *wish* they could look like this man."

The blood drains from my face. *This can't be right.* I feel a wave of nausea rise in my stomach, my mind spinning as I try to make sense of what Louie just said.

"No. He was at your house too. He spoke to both of you about the accident." Did Mari fail to mention that Louie has dementia or something?

Louie is looking at me like *I'm* the one with dementia. "Show Bill," he says. "He's the closest gas station to the lake, so the man has probably been here to the store for gas."

The weight of my confusion is pressing down on me, making it hard to focus. My heart is racing, and I can feel the sweat beginning to form on the back of my neck. I hold the phone up for Bill, the clerk, desperate for answers.

"Do you know who this is?" I ask, my voice trembling slightly as I try to keep my composure. The photograph of Saint on my screen feels like the only tangible piece of evidence I have, the only thread that ties all this together.

Bill shakes his head, his expression calm but indifferent, as if this is just another mundane conversation in a long string of them. "Don't know his name," he says flatly, but then his eyes narrow slightly as he looks more closely at the screen. "But I've seen him." He grabs my phone and a pair of glasses and inspects it even more. "Yep. Yeah. That's a face that's hard to forget. Tall guy. Drives a black car. But don't know him." He hands my phone back to me.

I latch on to that small morsel of information like a lifeline, my mind racing to make sense of it all. "Where did you see him?" I ask, leaning in closer. "Here?"

My grip tightens on the phone, my knuckles turning white as I wait for his response, hoping that what he says next will finally start to make sense of this twisted situation.

Bill nods slowly, his brow furrowing in thought. "Yeah, if it's the same guy I'm thinking of," he says after a pause, as if he's piecing it together himself. "He's come in a couple times in the past few weeks. I reckon he's staying in one of the rentals because I've never seen him before." His tone is casual, but the words hit me like a punch to the gut.

This doesn't line up with the story Saint told me at all, with the way he described his life here.

"Maybe he's new to the area?" I say, trying to rationalize all this, grasping at straws to make it fit. "Maybe he just started working here as a detective." My voice sounds weak, even to my own ears. I'm trying to convince myself as much as I am Bill, but deep down, I can feel the cracks beginning to form, the doubt creeping in.

If Saint just started working here, why wouldn't Louie or Bill know him? Why would they be so adamant that he doesn't work around here?

Louie, who's been standing nearby, senses the shift in my demeanor. His eyebrows draw closer together in concern, and he steps forward. The air between us feels heavy, thick with the weight of unanswered questions. "Petra, I don't know who this man is to you, but I can assure you he is not from around here. And he definitely does not work around here. Not as a cop. Not even as a security guard. Not even at Taco Bell."

"We don't have a Taco Bell," Bill says.

"That's why I know he don't work there," Louie responds.

The certainty in his tone makes my stomach turn. Louie's eyes are sharp, searching mine for some kind of explanation, but I have none to offer. "Me and Bill know everything about everyone in this town," he continues, his voice firm but not unkind. "Unless they're here on vacation in one of the cabins." His words hang in the air like a warning, a truth I'm not ready to accept. "But I own most of those, and he's not one of my current guests."

If they know everything about everyone in town, and they don't know Saint, then where the hell did Saint come from?

I shake my head, refusing to believe what Louie's telling me. And that, coupled with the fact that I thought he knew Saint, but now he's saying he doesn't, makes me question my own sanity. My heart is pounding in my chest, and the questions are swirling faster and faster, making it difficult to think straight. If Saint isn't a detective, what is he?

My mind backtracks, sifting through every conversation we've had, every detail he's shared about his life.

How could he have lied so convincingly?

Where did he come from?

How could I have been so blind?

I glance between Bill and Louie, my pulse racing, my hands shaking. How do these two not know who he is? They're acting like Saint doesn't exist, like the man I've been spending my nights with is some kind of ghost. But he's real. I've kissed him. I've touched him. I've slept next to him. He can't just be a figment of my imagination.

The questions begin to pile up, one after the other, overwhelming me. Why was the police chase not written about in the paper? That night was real—there were flashing lights and a detective at my door. I can still see it all in my mind, clear as day.

How could something like that happen and there be no trace? How could Louie, who lives on the same road, not have heard about it? How could he not have met Saint when Mari was woken up by the same commotion?

I feel like I might be sick from all the unanswered questions, the uncertainty tightening around my throat.

Without another word, I push open the door and rush outside, back into the storm. I can hear Louie calling after me, his voice full of concern, but I don't turn around. I walk straight to my car, my hands trembling as I fumble for my keys. The sound of the car door slamming rings in my ears, but I barely register it. My mind is too full, too chaotic to focus on anything other than making it to the cabin.

I don't bother getting gas. I can't think that far ahead right now.

I only have one thing on my agenda as I drive.

Mari.

CHAPTER TWENTY-ONE

"Mari!"

I'm yelling her name as soon as I slam my car door. I run toward her cabin, hoping she can clear up all the confusion swirling inside me.

I bang on the door. "Mari, open the door!"

"One second!" I can hear her rustling around inside her house. The floorboards creak as she makes her way to the door. When she finally opens it, I'm met with a look of shock.

"Petra?" she whispers. "You look like a drowned rat. Come inside, honey." She steps aside, but I don't enter her house. I don't trust her, or Louie, or Saint, or even myself right now.

"Saint," I say, breathless.

She raises a brow. "Did you burn his dinner?" she asks.

"No. No, I just need to know I'm not going crazy." I wave a hand toward the road. "That night . . . when the man . . . in the road . . ."

"When he killed himself?" Her response is blunt. Almost harsh. But it brings me a huge sigh of relief that at least she knows what I'm talking about.

"Yes! It happened, right?"

"Of course it happened." She tilts her head, a look of concern spreading across her face. "Are you okay?"

"No. I don't know." I begin pacing her patio. "I was at the gas station, and Louie didn't know what I was talking about and it's not in the paper and they said he wasn't a detective and—"

"Slow down, honey," she says, stepping out onto the covered patio with me. "I think you need to take a seat."

I shake my head. I don't have time to sit and chat with her. If she's about to confirm that Saint does exist and Louie just has dementia, then I still have to contend with Saint coming over tonight, and I never even made it to the grocery store to buy the ingredients for the recipe Mari gave me to try.

"So he's real, right? He's a real detective. I'm not going insane."

Mari's eyes flicker from mine toward the driveway. The sound of an approaching vehicle becomes evident over the sound of rain hitting the roof. I turn around, and we both watch as Louie pulls into their driveway.

"Shit," Mari says.

"He doesn't remember," I say, turning back to Mari. "Louie has no recollection of Saint ever coming to talk to you guys about what was happening that night."

"He's a . . . heavy sleeper. I may not have woken him up." Mari smiles and pats my shoulder. "Okey dokey. You better get back. You've got company coming tonight."

Louie has exited his truck and is making his way over to us. Mari looks nervous. It makes me instantly uneasy how she's trying to dismiss me. Someone isn't being honest.

"Mari?" I say to her.

"Mari!" Louie yells.

"Shit," Mari mutters.

Louie is standing next to us now. He points at me while looking at Mari. "Did she ask you about it?"

"About what?" Mari says.

"The police chase."

"Oh. Yes."

"Mari remembers," I say to Louie.

"Remembers what?" Louie says, his attention still on his wife.

Mari looks very uneasy. "It was nothing. Just some cops asking about an incident that happened a few weeks back."

"Petra said someone died. And you didn't think to tell me about it?"

"Mari, you told me that two cops came and spoke to you *and* Louie about it."

Louie's hands move to his hips, and he tilts his head at Mari. "What in the hell have you gotten yourself into this time?"

"Nothing," she insists. Every single inch of her is screaming that she's lying.

Louie throws up his hands as if he knows this too. "I don't want to know. If there's a body, I don't want to know."

"There wasn't a body," Mari says to him defensively. "Not a real one."

Not a real one?

"Yes, there was," I said. "You told me you saw it."

Louie grabs the front door and opens it, but before he walks inside, he looks at Mari with a very serious expression. "I'm going in the house. I want no part of this. But whatever it is, you better tell this woman the truth, because we need that rental money and I am not getting sued over whatever wacko stunt you're pulling."

Stunt?

Sued?

"Louie, wait!" I say, pleading. But he disappears inside and slams the front door. Now I'm just out here with a very guilty-looking Mari.

I'm on the verge of tears. "Tell me whatever it is you aren't telling me," I say to Mari. "If you don't, I'm calling the police, and I'll ask them myself."

"What would you even ask them?" Mari says. With that question, she takes a seat in one of the two rocking chairs that flank her front door. She looks up at me, and it's as if her entire demeanor changes right in front of my face. "You going to ask them if the man you're having an affair with actually exists?"

The way her response so easily spills out of her makes me shiver. "Mari, please. I feel very scared right now. Please just tell me what the hell is going on."

Mari sighs, and then gestures toward the other rocking chair. "Sit. This might take a minute."

"I don't want to sit. I want you to speak."

"Sit and I will."

"Just fucking *tell* me!" I yell. I can't take this another second!

Mari's eyes widen in response to my outburst. "Fine," she says. "Okay. Well . . ."

My body is trembling so much, I have to fold my arms over my chest to give myself some sort of anchor. But I'm not sitting down in this crazy woman's chair until she tells me what the hell she knows.

"I apologize for what I'm about to tell you. I really do. But you have to understand how bored I get sometimes. Louie pulled me away from Los Angeles out here to the middle of nowhere, and nothing fun ever happens. I could sit in my chair for two solid weeks without speaking to another—"

"Get to the point, Mari," I say. I can't take a second more of her rambling.

"Fine," she says, huffing. "He paid me off."

My mind takes a moment to wrap around those words and what all they could mean. "Who paid you off? For what?"

"Saint. Cam. Whoever he is. I caught him out there in the road that night he told you there was a police chase. There was no police chase."

A tear spills down my cheek. I wipe it away angrily, upset that my sadness is breaking through my anger.

"At first, I saw the police lights and thought something actually happened. I almost woke up Louie, but decided I'd just go outside and walk down toward your place to have a look for myself. And that's when I saw the guy. He was setting out fake police lights in the road. There weren't any actual cops. No body. Just lights. He had some on his car. He put a couple on a tree out by your house."

I finally concede and decide to take a seat. I plop down in the rocking chair, afraid my legs won't hold me up for another second, as I listen to her continue.

"I confronted him. I'm not scared of people, and he was on our road being suspicious, so I asked him what the hell he was doing. I caught him red-handed. I told him I was going to call the cops, and that's when he came clean. Said he knew you, and reassured me that he was just playing an innocent prank. I didn't feel comfortable with that, so I demanded to know more. He showed me the lights and offered to show me his identification. Told me he was just there because you're a writer and that you work better if things happen to you that you're writing about. Hell, it sounded like a reasonable explanation, and he didn't seem to be threatening. Promised I could wait out by the road until he left to make sure he didn't kill you. He said he was just there to give you inspiration for your book. That it's something you two worked up."

"He said I knew about it?"

Mari nods. "Yep. I mean, he didn't go into detail about how much you knew, but he said you asked him to scare you. And like I told you before, I know how it is to be an artist. Sometimes we gotta do things to get the juices flowing. I just figured it was some kind of kink, or a fetish that was between the two of you. I tried to mind my business, but I also wasn't going to just let some stranger kill you. I did wait until he left."

I rub my temples with my fingers, attempting to navigate everything she just said. That night was the first night I ever met Saint. He pretended not to know I was a writer. But if what Mari is saying is true and he already knew who I was . . . he's been lying to me this entire time. This stranger has been lying to me and fucking me, and I have no idea who the hell he is.

"Why didn't you call the police? Or tell *me* about it?" I am so angry at Mari, but the majority of my anger is with Saint. Or maybe myself. *How could I have been so stupid?*

"I threatened to. Trust me. I told him to get the hell off my property. But then he went and made an offer I couldn't refuse."

"An offer?"

"I believe I told you the first time I met you, before that night even happened with him, that I take any acting job if it pays. He offered to pay me to keep my mouth shut and just go along with his story if you asked me about it."

I feel like crying. Screaming. "You took *money* from him? To lie to me?"

"Well, it sounds bad now," she says. "But that night, it was exciting. And it's not like I just walked away. I stood there while he was at your place, and he wasn't there for very long. I made sure he didn't kill you before I took the money."

"So generous," I spit. I am so angry with her, my head is throbbing.

"He paid me to pretend. It seemed like something a writer would get a kick out of, so I didn't think it would harm you in any way. I love pranks, but I love money more than I love pranks, and when you put the two together with a man that good looking, how do you expect me to turn that down?" She's looking at me like she's expecting my forgiveness. My understanding.

"You have no idea what you've done," I say to her. Another tear falls from my eye, and she actually looks remorseful.

"It's why I came by the next day," she says. "I did feel bad. I wanted to check on you, but you seemed fine. And then you kept inviting him over. You told me you kissed him and you seemed happy about it, so I figured you two do this sort of thing all the time."

"I don't—" I shut up. I owe her zero explanation. She owes me a million apologies.

"I had no idea you were married. And it's not my business, but I did find it interesting when your actual husband showed up. But again, I stayed out of it. Just came over because I was curious and wanted to see what the three of you had going on over here. Your husband didn't seem to know about him, though, and I didn't know if that was part of the act. But like I said. I stayed out of it."

"Who is he, Mari?"

"Who? Saint?"

"Yes. If he isn't a real detective, who is he?"

Mari shrugs. "Now that's probably where I went wrong. I should have taken a better look at his identification. I was being honest when I said I stay away from the authorities in this town, so I wouldn't recognize any of them. I don't know anything about the guy, or if he's even a police officer at all. I'm just an innocent bystander."

"No, you're a guilty participant, Mari!" I stand up, exasperated. Hurt. "I can't believe you would do this. That you *allowed* it. It's . . . cruel. It's cruel and dangerous, and you should honestly be so ashamed of yourself."

I feel so stupid. So betrayed. I wipe the rest of my tears away with my shirt.

"For what it's worth, I am sorry. I hope you didn't get hurt, or taken advantage of, at least."

I can't stand being here with her anymore. I want to shake some sense into her. "You allowed a complete stranger to walk inside my cabin at five in the fucking *morning*, Mari! Of course I got hurt! Of course I was taken advantage of! By him *and* by you!"

"Now, Petra. I can see why you're mad, but you can see my side of it, right?"

"Don't even try to get me to play devil's advocate. You're an awful person. You can go fuck yourself, you absolute fucking . . . doozy!"

I've started to walk away from her when she says, "That's not really how that word is used, but . . ."

"Oh, *fuck off*, Mari!" I open my car door. "I want a full refund!" I slam my car door and put my car in reverse. I glance back at her as I'm pulling onto the road, and Louie is back out on the patio. They're arguing.

Not my problem. I still have a few hours before Saint is scheduled to show up, so I'll figure out all the pieces Mari couldn't put together for me. I also still have time to pack and get the hell out of here.

I floor it and head straight for my cabin.

I need my laptop.

CHAPTER TWENTY-TWO

My laptop has been zero help.

When I searched the name Nathaniel Saint, I came up with nothing that would apply to this man. Absolutely nothing. A few dead ends—some obscure references to old obituaries, and even a couple of ancient business listings—but no social media presence, no birth records, no marriage licenses. At least not for a Nathaniel Saint younger than eighty years old.

He lied about his name. I know that much now.

The realization hits me like a ton of bricks, cold and heavy. Every conversation, every touch, every moment we spent together runs through my mind like a distorted film reel. My leg is bouncing wildly under the table, my nerves completely shot.

How could I have missed this? I feel like a fool, like I let him walk right through my life, leaving chaos in his wake, and I never even questioned it.

I'm on edge, so I stand up and begin to pace the length of the room, hoping that activity will help me focus, hoping that somehow, if I keep moving, the puzzle pieces will start to come together. But the more I think, the more scattered everything feels. My mind spins in circles.

If Nathaniel Saint isn't his name, how am I supposed to figure out what his real name is? How do you track down someone who doesn't want to be found? I have nothing to go on. No concrete information. I feel like I've been living in a dream, completely unaware that I didn't even know this man's real identity.

I rack my brain, trying to recall if he ever gave me any clues. Something I could latch on to now. But I've never even asked him what his wife's name is. Why didn't I ask more questions? Why didn't I dig deeper? It's as if I let myself get wrapped up in this fantasy without any regard for reality, and now I'm paying the price.

Wait. *The picture!*

I freeze mid-pace, a jolt of adrenaline coursing through me. The selfie I took with him. Maybe I can use that. Maybe I can do an image search on Google and find something that will lead me to who he really is.

I rush back to my laptop, practically throwing myself into the chair. My fingers tremble as I unlock my phone and find the image buried in my private folder. The picture of us together, both smiling, his arm draped casually over my shoulders. It feels eerie now, knowing that the man in the picture isn't who he said he was. I quickly email the image to myself, my heart hammering in my chest as I open my inbox. The seconds it takes for the email to appear feel like an eternity, but once it's there, I click on it without hesitation.

I download the image, my hands shaking as I do, and then upload it into a Google image search. I sit there, my breath coming in shallow bursts as I wait for the results to load, my eyes glued to the screen. The tension is unbearable, a knot tightening in my stomach with each passing second. I need this to work. I need answers. I need to know who he is.

I hit a dead end. Google image search won't work on faces. *Fuck.*

I lean back again in my chair to think up another idea as I stare, helpless, at my screen. After a minute passes, an ad pops up, offering to do the search for a fee. It's the first time I've ever been happy to see a pop-up ad.

I instantly click on it, fill out the information on the website, and pay the fee, knowing full well I'm probably being scammed and my identity is about to be stolen. But I'll risk the fishy website for the truth.

Several images are returned to me, and I scroll through them closely, but none of them are of Saint. They're all men who vaguely resemble him—some with similar bone structure, others with similar facial hair—but not him. I keep scrolling and scrolling, my frustration mounting, my hope slipping away with each failed match. It feels like every click is another dead end, another step further into this maze of lies.

And then, suddenly, I see a picture that makes my heart drop into my stomach.

A picture that looks just like him.

My pulse quickens, my hands sweating as I hover over the image, too scared to click but too desperate not to. *Please be him,* I think, my mind repeating the words like a mantra. *Please be him.*

With a shaky breath, I click on the picture. The page it takes me to is a Facebook profile, but the page is private. Most of the information is locked away, but the name isn't. *Eric Kingston.* I stare at the name, my mind racing, the letters blurring together as I try to process what I'm seeing. The only thing available to the public is profile pictures—pictures that confirm without a shadow of a doubt that this is the man I've been calling Saint.

Saint is Eric Kingston.

Who is Eric Kingston?

There's no history, no background—just this name and these pictures are all the profile allows me to see. What kind of man goes to such lengths to hide who he really is? My fingers hover over the mouse, itching to click through his friends list, to find something more, but there's nothing to click on. It's all locked away behind privacy settings. I'm left with nothing but his face and a name I've never heard before.

The reality of the situation crashes over me. I close my eyes and blow out a shaky breath, trying to steady myself, but it's no use. The questions swirl around me like a storm, relentless and unforgiving. Who is Eric Kingston, and what does he want from me?

I close out of the private Facebook profile and move my mouse to hover over the tabs open on my browser. I need answers, and I'm not stopping until I find them. Without hesitating, I open up Google. My fingers fly across the keyboard as I type in the new name. *Eric Kingston.* I hit Enter, holding my breath as the search engine returns several hits.

I scroll through the results, scanning the names and descriptions, hoping something will jump out at me. I feel like a detective piecing together clues, but every step forward feels like I'm uncovering more of a truth I might not want. I want to know, but I'm terrified to know.

Finally, I come across a link for an Instagram profile with that name, my heart skipping a beat as I click on it. But as the page loads, my hope deflates almost instantly. *Private.* Again.

I curse under my breath, leaning back helplessly in my chair yet again, feeling a blanket of frustration settle over me. It's like every door I open slams shut before I can get a good look inside.

But then I notice something on the Instagram profile that catches my attention. The display name lists a middle name: *Merrell.* That's new. It's another piece of the puzzle, another breadcrumb on the trail that leads to who this man really is.

Eric Merrell Kingston.

I repeat the name silently to myself, committing it to memory, feeling a rush of anxiety mixed with determination. My pulse quickens as I realize how deep I'm getting into this. I reach for my wallet, my fingers fumbling as I take out my credit card again. If there's one way to get to the bottom of this, it's through a background check. I can't rely on social media alone. I need more concrete information—something that will give me more than a profile picture or a few vague details.

I open a background check website, the kind that promises a full report for a fee, and enter the information. I don't know what I'm expecting, but I know I need to see this through. I can't back down from this search now, not after everything I've learned. My knee is bouncing wildly under the table as I wait for the results to load, every second dragging on like an eternity.

When the page finally loads, I'm overwhelmed by the sheer number of results. *There are so many Eric Kingstons.* My eyes dart across the screen, trying to sort through the flood of names and profiles. Each one feels like a possibility, but none of them fit the image of the man I've been with. I scroll and scroll, looking at all the potential matches, growing more frustrated by the second. And then, I see it. One of them has the middle name *Merrell.*

It's him.

I click on the profile so hard I'm afraid I might've just broken my trackpad. My heart leaps into my throat as the page loads. I hold my breath, feeling like everything I've been searching for is right on the other side of this click. When the page opens, I see that it's a LinkedIn profile.

His résumé has popped up in front of me. It's all there, laid out in neat little sections, each bullet point revealing more about the man I've been sharing a bed with. I scan the page, my eyes racing over the details. He's not a detective. He's not even in law enforcement.

Eric is a fucking *screenwriter.*

I blink, stunned, as I process the information. He's supposedly worked on several film projects, some of which I've actually heard of. My mind is reeling.

I scroll farther down the page, taking in more of his résumé. But nothing on this page reveals that he's a detective. There's no mention of law enforcement, no indication that he's ever worked in that field. My brain is struggling to make sense of this conflicting information.

Maybe he's undercover? The thought feels far fetched, but at this point, I'm grasping for explanations. Maybe he gave me a fake name because he's not allowed to use his real one.

Maybe he's deep in some undercover operation, and the reason there was nothing in the paper about the suicide and police chase is that it's all classified. Maybe it's something he wanted to keep out of the public eye, something too sensitive to be made known. It could explain why there's been such a shroud of secrecy around him.

No, then him paying off Mari wouldn't make sense. Him planting fake police lights around my yard. Even an undercover detective wouldn't do that.

I realize I'm grasping at straws. Every theory I come up with feels like a stretch, but I can't stop myself from thinking them through. *I have to make sense of this.* As long as there are still straws to grasp at, I'm going to hoard them.

What have I gotten myself into?

I open up a new tab, my breath catching in my throat as I stare at the information in front of me. There it is—a phone number listed for Eric Kingston, bold and clear against the white backdrop of the web page. I pull up the contact information for Saint in my phone, my hands trembling as I compare the numbers.

I glance between the laptop screen and my phone screen, willing them not to match, praying that this is just some bizarre coincidence. But no. *It's a perfect match.*

The realization hits me smack in the chest, knocking the air from my lungs. My phone slips from my hand, tumbling to the floor with a dull thud, but I barely register the sound. I stand up so quickly my chair nearly topples over. I pick my phone up from the floor and slip it into my back pocket, then take two steps away from my computer, as if the glowing screen has suddenly become threatening, as if the truth staring back at me might physically hurt me. The room spins around me, my thoughts racing in frantic circles.

Why would he lie to me about who he is?

It makes no sense. Nothing about this makes sense. If he's a screenwriter, does he have connections to people I know? Is he connected to the adaptation that I wish never happened? Is he connected to Allister McFuckity Fuckface?

How did he even know I was here? How did he know, before meeting me, to tell Mari that we were doing something related to my writing? I thought that was *my* idea, *after* I met him.

I replay it all in my head, searching for clues, for signs that I missed—signs that this man wasn't who he claimed to be. But all I'm left with is confusion, a thick fog of unanswered questions clouding my thoughts.

I turn back to the screen, my eyes scanning the information. His address is listed in Los Angeles. *Los Angeles.* Hours away from here, miles from the small town where he claims to live. My stomach twists into a tight knot. *Why would he pretend to live here?*

At this point, I don't care about the why anymore. I don't care about anything except getting out of here. The panic rises in my chest, thick and suffocating, and all I know is that I can't stay here another minute. I feel like I'm trapped in a nightmare, one I can't wake up from. The walls of the cabin seem to be closing in around me, the silence suffocating.

I need to leave.

Now.

Adrenaline is surging through my veins as I rush to my bedroom. I don't even stop to think about how best to gather my stuff. I just act, my movements frantic and desperate. I yank my suitcase out from under the bed. My fingers fumble with the zipper. There's no time to be methodical. I don't bother folding anything. I pull open the closet, grab handfuls of clothes, and toss them into the suitcase without a second thought. Shirts, jeans, shoes—it all goes in, crumpled and chaotic.

I throw open the dresser drawers and empty them in seconds, piling more clothes on top of the mess I've already made. The fabric bunches together, wrinkling under the weight of my toiletries as I toss them carelessly on top. Shampoo, face wash, toothpaste—it all lands in the suitcase in a jumble.

The whole time I'm packing, I can feel the tears welling up in my eyes. I'm crying now, the sobs quiet but uncontrollable, my shoulders shaking as the reality of the situation crashes down on me. The burden of everything I've done, everything I've let happen, feels unbearable.

How could I have been so reckless? How could I have been so blind?

I swipe angrily at my tears, but they keep coming as I struggle to think clearly. My hands are shaking so badly that I can barely grip the charger as I pull it from the wall. The cord slips from my grasp, falling to the floor with a clatter, and I choke back a sob as I shove it into the suitcase. My chest feels tight, my breathing shallow, and I feel like I might fall apart completely. *How could I be so careless?*

The question echoes in my mind, over and over again, but I don't have time to dwell on it. I don't have time to think about everything I've done in the past few weeks, the lies, the betrayal. It's all too much. I grab my car keys off the dresser, the metal cool against my palm.

I know I'm leaving half my stuff lying around the cabin, but I don't care. I don't care about anything except getting out of here. Every instinct in my body is screaming at me to run, to put as much distance between me and this place as possible. I can feel my heartbeat pounding in my ears as I rush toward the bedroom door, my breath coming in short, shallow gasps.

I walk into the kitchen, my mind spinning, the panic still fresh in my veins. *And then I scream.*

The instinctual sound rips from my throat, but it does nothing to change the scene in front of me. Saint doesn't even flinch. He doesn't turn around at the sound of my voice, doesn't react at all. Instead, he's standing at the table, his broad shoulders stiff, his back to me, staring down at my laptop screen. The very same screen that, just moments ago, revealed the truth to me about who he really is.

My heart constricts as I realize what he must be looking at.

I take a scared step back, instinctively retreating into the doorway of my bedroom, my thoughts a chaotic whirl as I try to map out any possible escape route. My eyes dart to the window. Could I make it out before he reaches me? The window isn't that far, but it's partially blocked by the bed. I'm not sure I could get through it fast enough. The only other way out of this cabin is through the front or back door, and for both, I'd have to pass Saint.

I can feel the terror building in my chest, making it hard to breathe. My hands are trembling as I bring them up to my mouth to stifle the cry that threatens to escape. I can't let him hear my fear, but my body betrays me, shaking uncontrollably with each shallow breath.

Saint doesn't move for a moment, but then he reaches out slowly, deliberately, and places his hand on the laptop. I watch, frozen, as he gently shuts it, the click reverberating in the deadly quiet of the room. It feels final, like a door slamming shut on any hope I had of getting out of here unnoticed.

He begins to turn around, his movements agonizingly slow, like he's savoring every second before he faces me. My heartbeat continues to thunder in my ears as I take another step back, inching deeper into my bedroom. When his eyes finally land on me, they don't meet mine right away. Instead, they fix on my suitcase. His jaw clenches, the muscles in his face tightening as he processes what that suitcase means. His hands curl into fists at his sides as he shakes his head slowly, deliberately.

"You're leaving?" he says, his voice low and controlled, but I can hear the undercurrent of something darker simmering just beneath the surface. His tone isn't one of curiosity. It's an accusation, filled with disbelief and something far more dire.

His gaze is pressing down on me, but I can't look him in the eye. I try to force the words out, but they come out as a whisper, barely audible over the pounding of my heart. "You aren't a detective."

The accusation hangs in the air between us, heavy and charged with the realization of everything I've uncovered. For a moment, Saint doesn't say anything. He doesn't try to deny it, doesn't attempt to explain. Instead, he lifts his eyes from the suitcase to my face, his expression unreadable. The silence stretches on, thick and suffocating, and the longer it goes on, the more terrified I become. I would rather he yell at me, berate me, anything but this cold, quiet stare.

His eyes bore into mine, piercing through the distance between us like those of a predator assessing its prey. His face remains expressionless, his body unnervingly still, but there's something in the way he looks at me that chills me to the bone. It's the kind of quiet that feels more piercing than any words could be, like he's calculating his next move, deciding what to do with me now that the truth is out.

I try to take another step back, but my legs feel like they've turned to lead, unmovable. I'm trapped, and we both know it. I don't know what to say, or how I could defuse the tension. No clever words come to me. The silence between us is louder than my scream, louder than any sound I've ever heard.

And then, "Why did you look me up?" He takes a small step toward me, his eyes narrowing slightly. "Why couldn't you just leave it alone?"

My throat is dry, and I swallow hard, trying to find my voice. "You lied to me." I'm embarrassed by the audible fear when I speak. "You lied about everything. I needed to know."

His expression doesn't change, but something flickers in his eyes. He takes another step toward me, and I instinctively take a step back, my back pressing up against the doorframe. I can feel the cold wood against my skin, and the realization that I'm cornered sends a fresh wave of panic through me.

"You needed to know?" he says, his voice dripping with contempt. "And what exactly did you think you were going to find?" He takes another step forward, closing the distance between us, his presence looming over me like a shadow. "Did you think knowing the truth would change anything?"

I shake my head, my breath quick and shallow.

"What are you going to do about it? Tell your *husband*?"

My mind is screaming at me to run, to do something—anything—but my body won't cooperate. I'm frozen in place, trapped in this moment, with no way out. I feel the tears welling up in my eyes, but I blink them back, refusing to let him see just how scared I am.

"Are you . . ." I swallow hard, the fear making it difficult to speak out loud. My voice trembles as I force out the question that's been clawing at the back of my throat since the moment I saw him standing there. "Are you going to hurt me?"

He shakes his head immediately, his expression one of almost offended disbelief. "What? No." He answers me as though the question itself is ridiculous, as if I've completely misunderstood the situation. How could he possibly think my reaction right now is ridiculous? *How can he not see how terrifying this is for me?* I'm standing in the middle of a nightmare, and the man I thought I knew is a complete stranger. I have no idea who he is. *None.*

His name, his job, his life—it's all been a lie. And now, there's nowhere to go, and I'm painfully aware of how close he is.

I slide my hand into my back pocket, praying that I can unlock my phone without him noticing. My fingers fumble, slick with sweat, as I try to remember which side button to push to call an emergency number. I can't let him see what I'm doing. I feel like I'm balancing on a cliff. One wrong move, and everything could fall apart.

I take another step back, slipping from the doorway and into my bedroom, trying to create more space between us, but it feels futile. "Why did you lie to me?" My voice cracks on the last word, a mixture of fear and anger laced into it. I need answers, but more than that, I need him to stay back. To give me time.

He takes a step forward instead, closing the distance between us once again. His expression is unnervingly calm as he says, "It's what you wanted, Petra."

The audacity of his words hits me like a slap. I can't help but fume at that response, my fear momentarily drowned out by a flash of rage. "*It's what I wanted?*" I repeat, incredulous. "I didn't even know you existed before you showed up here pretending to be a detective!" My voice rises with each word, frustration bubbling over. "I know nothing happened out on the road that night. You lied about everything, and you told Mari you were here to help me write. How would you even know to say that?" The accusations and questions spill out in a rush, each one more desperate than the last.

He tilts his head slightly, narrowing his eyes at me, like he's weighing how much to tell me. The gesture is chilling, his calm composure making everything feel even more surreal. "Do you not remember your words two nights before I showed up here?" he asks, his voice eerily soft.

My words? What is he talking about? My mind scrambles to make sense of his question, but nothing clicks.

The confusion must be plain on my face, because he takes another step toward me, his eyes locked onto mine, and says, "Your live video." His tone is deliberate, like he's explaining something simple to a child. "You said you wished you could experience the things you write about. You said your character was a cop. I *brought* that to you."

The words are heavy and disorienting. *This makes no sense.* I try to process what he's saying, but the pieces don't fit together. If he showed up here pretending to be a cop because of the live video . . . that means he knew who I was before he ever walked through my door. *He was watching the video as it was live? Two days before I even met him?*

Which means . . . he's been following me? He's in my private group?

My stomach churns with the sickening realization that this wasn't some random encounter. He's been planning this. Watching me for God knows how long. *How long has he been following me online?* The thought makes my skin crawl.

My hand is still in my back pocket, my fingers desperately trying to figure out how to reach 9-1-1 on my phone without looking at it. I keep talking, my voice barely above a whisper, hoping he won't focus too much on the arm behind my back. "How long have you been watching me?" I need to keep him talking, need to buy myself time.

"Since the beginning." His tone is casual, like he's discussing the weather, but the words send a chill down my spine. "I already told you I've seen every one of your live videos. I just left out the fact that I watched them as they happened."

I cover my gasp with my hand, the horror of what he just said sinking in. He's been watching me for years, and I thought he just found me. I bring my hand to my chest, trying to steady my breathing, but the fear is overwhelming.

"Do you even have a wife?" I ask, my voice small, as if I'm afraid of the answer.

He shakes his head, smirking slightly. "Marriage isn't really my thing."

The simplicity of his answer makes me feel so naive, as if I should have been able to tell he wasn't being honest. The lie about being married, the infertility, that was just another layer to his deception, another way to manipulate me. He's been building this elaborate facade, and I fell for every bit of it.

I see it the second it happens. His gaze drops to my arm, the arm I've been trying so hard to hide behind my back. The moment of realization washes over his face, and my stomach drops. *He knows.*

Without thinking, I spin around and rush toward the bathroom. I can hear him moving behind me, his footsteps quickening as he realizes what I'm trying to do. My hands fumble for the bathroom door. My entire body is shaking, but I have to get the door locked. I have to make the call before he gets to me.

I don't make it.

Just as my fingers brush the cool metal of the doorknob, Saint's grip clamps down hard on my arm. The force of it nearly pulls me off my feet, and before I can react, he yanks me back, the air rushing out of my lungs in a sharp gasp. My heart feels like it's about to explode as I watch in horror while he rips my cell phone from my hand. Time slows, the adrenaline coursing through my veins, as I helplessly watch him glance down at the screen. His face tightens with anger when he sees the emergency number already pulled up, though not yet connected.

I was so close.

"I haven't done anything wrong, Petra!" His voice is sharp, laced with fury, as he tosses the phone behind him with a careless flick of his wrist. The sound of it hitting the wall makes me flinch. The next thing I know, he's pushing my shoulders hard enough that I stumble and fall back onto the bed. I scramble, crawling frantically toward the headboard, trying to put as much space between us as possible. My mind is screaming at me to keep moving, to find a way out, but I'm cornered.

Saint stands at the foot of the bed, his hands flexing at his sides, his jaw clenched. The look in his eyes is unrecognizable, a mix of betrayal and fury. "What would you even tell them when they showed up here?" His voice is mocking, dripping with disdain. "That I role-played too well?"

"You've been *impersonating* a *cop*!" I shout, my voice shaking with anger and fear. Every word is like venom on my tongue. I can feel the rage boiling inside me, mixing with the terror, making my body tremble uncontrollably.

Saint throws his hands up in exasperation, letting out a bitter laugh. "You *wanted* me to!" His voice rises, frustration boiling over as he glares at me. "Your online Q&As are like an open invitation into your life! You've told your readers for years what lake you come to. You let the whole world know when you're here alone. You even answered my question when I asked if you would be willing to do something like this. You said, '*I would do anything to be a better writer.*'"

The realization hits me like a punch to the throat. *Oh, my God.* My pulse stutters in my chest, and I stare at him, wide eyed. He's the one who asked that question? *He thinks I was asking for this?*

My stomach twists in revulsion as the reality of his delusion sinks in. "That wasn't an invitation to show up here and lie to me," I snap, my voice cracking under the pressure of holding back tears. I want to scream, but my voice feels small, trapped under the crushing realization of just how far he's taken this fantasy.

Saint's eyes flash with something darker. His tone becomes flat, almost indifferent, as he says, "We've both been lying, Petra. You aren't innocent in this."

I shake my head, my body rigid with anger. "You attacked me in the middle of the night!" I spit the words at him, my fists clenching the blanket beneath me, knuckles white with tension.

"You *asked* me to!" he shouts back, his voice booming through the cabin, echoing off the walls like an accusation.

I shake my head adamantly, my whole body trembling with rage. *He's not turning this around on me.* I didn't ask for this. Just because I said in a live video that I wanted experience does not mean that was an invitation for him to actually locate me and act out some twisted fantasy he concocted in his head.

"You pretended to be someone you're not," I say through clenched teeth, my voice barely contained.

"So. Did. You," he counters, his voice cold and matter-of-fact. There's no apology in his tone, no recognition of the madness of what he's done. He looks at me as though we're equal, as if my desire for authenticity in my writing somehow justifies his actions.

"Stop saying I asked you to do this," I say, my voice breaking under the strain. My hands shake as I grip the bed tighter, trying to ground myself, trying to stay calm, but I can feel myself unraveling. "What we agreed to do together is different from what you chose to do on your own."

"Is it?" His voice is like ice, unflinching, and he takes a step closer, his eyes narrowing in challenge.

"I never lied to you, Saint!" I yell, my words desperate, grasping for some shred of control in this spiraling situation. "You knew who I was before you showed up here!" My voice cracks again, but I don't care. I need him to understand that this isn't the same—that he crossed a line.

He grips the back of his neck, his frustration mounting, his face twisted with anger. "You didn't lie? Petra, you're *fucking married*!" he roars, his voice filled with accusation as he closes the distance between us in three long strides. I instinctively scoot to the other side of the bed, trying to keep space between us, my pulse pounding in my throat.

"You're a *wife* and a *mother*," he spits, the words sharp as a blade, "and none of your readers know that. *I* didn't know that. You pretend to be someone you're not *every day of your life*!" His words cut deep, striking at the soul of the part of myself I keep private, the people I've carefully kept separate from my public persona.

I feel the sting of his words, but I refuse to let him twist this around. I won't let him make me feel guilty for something that has nothing to do with what he's done. "That's not the same," I whisper, my voice trembling, my eyes wide with fear and anger. But even as I say it, I feel the weight of his accusation bearing down on me, forcing me to question myself, if only for a fraction of a second.

He stands at the edge of the bed now, towering over me, his eyes dark and unreadable. I can't shake the feeling that something terrible is about to happen. I'm trapped, and we both know it.

I slide off the bed cautiously, my feet hitting the cold floor as I try to create some distance between us. We're on opposite sides of the bed now, a temporary barrier between us, but it offers no real protection. My heart races, my mind grasping for a way out, but every path leads back to the same conclusion. I can't outrun him.

"Can you blame me for trying to keep my life private?" My voice wavers as I speak, but there's a desperation in it. "Look what happened with the little information I did put out there."

My words hang in the air, but they don't seem to faze him. He starts to move, slowly, deliberately, walking around the bed like a predator closing in on its prey. My pulse quickens as I realize the bed is no longer a safe barrier—it's just a flimsy, meaningless divide between us.

My back presses against the wall, the cool surface grounding me in this terrifying reality. *There's nowhere to go.* And now he's right in front of me, looming over me with that same unnerving calm.

My mouth is so dry I can barely swallow, my palms damp with sweat. I feel like a cornered animal, powerless, helpless. I know I'm no match for him physically—he already proved that when he grabbed me so easily. I force myself to keep my gaze on him, even though every fiber of my being wants to look away, to shrink into nothingness.

"We're no different, Petra," he says, his voice softer now, almost coaxing, as if he's trying to make me believe it. His height makes me feel even smaller, even more vulnerable. His voice lowers further, like a whisper of temptation. "You needed inspiration. I gave that to you in more ways than you could have possibly contrived inside that head of yours."

He leans in, his breath hot against my ear, and I feel my skin crawl at the proximity.

"And you *loved* it," he breathes into my ear, the words dripping with satisfaction. "You're welcome."

The room feels like it's closing in on me, the walls shrinking as I squeeze my eyes shut, trying to block out the reality of his presence so close to me. But there's no escaping it. I can still feel him there, his breath brushing against my cheek, his body so close it's suffocating. A tear slips from the corner of my eye, and I bite my cheek to keep from sobbing. I feel the slow, deliberate path the tear takes as it travels down my face and reaches my jawline.

I flinch when I feel his finger brush the tear away, the touch intimate and invasive. It sends a fresh wave of revulsion through me. He hasn't stepped back, hasn't given me even a sliver of space to breathe. I'm shaking now, but I force myself to stay still, to show as little of my fear as possible.

I'm not convinced I'm safe. *I don't feel safe.* But I'm also not convinced he has any immediate plans to hurt me physically. There's a terrifying ambiguity in the way he's behaving, like he's playing a game with rules only he knows. But knowing now that he's not actually married—that he's been lying about every part of himself—puts everything in a different light. It changes the stakes. He has nothing to lose if this affair comes to light. Nothing.

But me? *I have everything to lose.*

The realization falls hard around me. My marriage, my family, my life—everything could crumble because of this.

I thought I was in a bad place before showing up here, but after the awful decisions I've made these last few weeks, I have sunk to a new low. I haven't just reached rock bottom—I've burrowed myself through the rock and am now sinking into the earth's mantle, on my way to the core. Down, down, down I fall.

In the midst of my spiraling thoughts, it comes to me. A title for this book. *Woman Down.* Because that's what I am. How I feel. It perfectly describes the trajectory of my life, which will more than likely mirror Reya's. If I survive this, that is. The book may never get finished because I have no idea if I'm safe or doomed right now.

I swallow hard, the lump in my throat painful as I force myself to meet his gaze. I can't tell if he's enjoying the power he holds over me or if he's as lost in this twisted fantasy as I am.

"Are you going to tell my husband?" I ask, my voice barely more than a whisper, the question heavy with fear. It's the one thing that could ruin me completely, destroy everything I've worked so hard to protect. If he tells Shephard, it's all over.

He looks almost offended by the question, his brow furrowing as if the very idea is beneath him. "Do you really think I'd do that to you?" His voice is sharp, almost angry, as if he can't believe I would even suggest it. But I can't trust him. Not anymore.

"I have no idea what you're capable of," I say quietly, the truth of my words hitting me hard. I don't know who this man is.

He's quiet while his eyes trace every inch of my face as if he's trying to memorize it, trying to burn this moment into his mind. His gaze lingers on my mouth, his lips parting slightly, and for a brief second, I'm reminded of his taste. I want to spit the taste out. I want to delete it from my memory. I want every reminder of his touch and his mouth gone from my mind completely.

Saint leans forward, just a little, and brings his hand up to touch my trembling bottom lip with his fingers, the gesture almost tender. It's as if he's longing to kiss me again, a thought I can't even fathom how he could be having right now.

"I'm capable of a lot of things," he says softly, his voice thick with meaning. "But destroying you isn't one of them."

But you have.

I'm struggling to maintain control of my reactions, to keep my face neutral, my body still, but I'm beginning to think I might make it out of this cabin alive. I just have to keep my cool.

"Do me a favor, Petra," he says, his voice dropping lower, almost a whisper. "When you finish this book, dedicate it to Saint, because he fucked that story out of you."

His words hit me like a slap, and I gasp—an instinctual, visceral reaction. But it's not fear that makes me gasp. No, it's something much darker, something far more unsettling. I gasp because I shouldn't be feeling what I'm feeling right now, but my body reacts in the complete opposite way from my mind.

My intellect is screaming at me to protect myself, to run. But my nerves and the warmth building in my stomach are craving the opposite. My body still wants him to touch me, to kiss me, to fuck me.

I hate myself right now. I hate that I feel like two different people, warring over a monster. *What is wrong with me?* Why can't I just run? Why can't I push him away or do something other than stand here, frozen under his gaze?

Quit being stupid, Petra! This isn't a fucking book.

"I want to leave," I whisper, my voice barely audible. The words come out shaky, more uncertain than I intended. It's the truth—I *do* want to leave. My mind does, anyway.

He's still staring at my mouth, his fingers grazing my lips with a touch so light it sends a shiver down my spine. His eyes flick back to mine, locking me in place with a gaze so intense it feels like he's seeing right through me, like he knows exactly what kind of battle my body is waging against my conscience.

He completely ignores my request, as if I never said it, and instead, without warning, his tongue dives into my mouth with a heat that steals my breath away. The heat blends with my terror in a kiss that is equal parts passion and desperation, and for a moment, I'm stuck in it.

I *don't* want to kiss him back. I *don't* want to give in to the pull of him. But my body betrays me, my lips moving against his as if they have a mind of their own. I feel the familiar rush of adrenaline, the desire coursing through me, and it scares me, like I'm not in control of my actions.

Petra, you are smarter than this. Stronger than this.

I press my hands against his chest, pushing him away from me with all the strength I can muster.

As soon as I break contact, he pulls back with a deliberate slowness that feels calculated. He takes a step back, creating a physical gap between us that mirrors the emotional one I'm desperately trying to put in place. For a split second, as our eyes meet, I see something in his gaze that I haven't seen today—a flash of vulnerability.

It's almost as if he doesn't want me to leave. He's hoping I'll change my mind, hoping I'll stay.

But I won't. I *can't*.

He's fucking insane.

I don't waste a single second. The moment that gap opens, I move. I push off the wall, my pulse sprinting frantically as I rush toward the bedroom door. My hand flies out to grab my phone from the floor, and I snatch it up without pausing. I can feel the weight of his gaze on me, but I refuse to look back. I don't want to see what's in his eyes. I don't want to know if he's about to stop me.

I pocket my phone and grab my laptop from the table; my fingers grip it tightly as I head straight for the front door, swiping up my suitcase as I walk. My entire body is trembling, every muscle tense as I reach for the knob, praying that he won't stop me. I pull the door open with a burst of adrenaline and step outside, the rain hitting me like a wake-up call.

I don't look behind me, not even for a second.

I toss the suitcase and the laptop into the back seat of my car with shaking hands. The panic is still fresh, still raw, but I'm moving on autopilot now. I throw myself into the driver's seat and slam the door shut. As soon as I'm inside, I immediately lock all the doors. The sound of the locks clicking into place feels like a small victory, but I'm not safe yet. I shove the key into the ignition and turn it with trembling fingers.

The engine roars to life, and I waste no time. I throw the car into reverse, my foot pressing hard on the gas pedal. Only then do I dare look up, my heart beating away in my chest like a drum.

Saint is standing in the doorway of the cabin, leaning casually against the frame. His eyes are locked on mine, watching me leave with a look I can't quite decipher. There's no anger in his expression, no rage. Just something calm, almost resigned. His posture is relaxed, his arms crossed over his chest, as if he's content to just stand there and watch. But I can't shake the feeling that he's letting me go too easily, that there's something I'm missing.

I keep my eyes on him as I back down the driveway, my heart racing in my chest. I want to make sure he's not coming after me, that this isn't some sick game where he chases me down.

Right before I turn the wheel to get back onto the road, he lifts a hand and waves, the gesture so nonchalant, so *normal* for such a terrifying moment. It's as if our parting is just a casual goodbye, like two old friends, and I'm not fleeing, not running for my life with fear clogging my lungs.

My foot slams down on the gas pedal. The tires churn against the gravel, and I take off, speeding away from that cabin as fast as I can, my pulse hammering in my throat. The farther I drive, the harder the tears fall.

Every foot of space I put between my car and Saint releases more of the fear, more of the panic, until I'm choking on the sobs that have been trapped in my chest. I cry, hard, for miles.

I can't wrap my mind around what just happened. *How did I let it get this far?*

I think about Shephard. About my girls. Their faces flash in my mind, and a fresh wave of guilt crashes over me. How could I have been so selfish? How could I have put them in danger like this? The thought makes my stomach turn. *What if he decides to come after them?* What if my actions have made them targets in whatever twisted game Saint is playing?

I'm not even sure they're safe from him, or that I'm safe from him, but he's not following me, and I cling to that fact. I can only hope that his sick fantasy has played itself out, that he's satisfied with whatever he got from me and that he won't take it any further in the future. But that hope feels fragile, like something I'm clinging to out of sheer desperation.

I scream, startled, when a piercing, shrieking sound tears me out of my thoughts. My whole body jolts. For a split second, I think it's him—that somehow, he's found a way to follow me, to catch up to me. But then I realize it's just my phone.

It's just my phone.

I blow out an unsteady breath, trying to calm my racing heart. My hand trembles as I glance over at the passenger seat, where the phone is buzzing violently. Shephard's name flashes across the screen, and a fresh wave of tears stings my eyes. How could I have been so stupid? How could I have done something so terrible to a man who has been nothing but good to me?

I grab the phone, wiping at my eyes with the back of my other hand. I answer it, trying to keep my voice steady, trying to swallow the emotion that's threatening to break through. "Hey," I say, but my voice cracks, caught somewhere between a whisper and a scream.

"You okay?" Shephard asks, his voice filled with concern. The tenderness in his tone cuts through me like a knife, making it that much harder to keep it together.

I take a deep breath, forcing down the sob that's building in my throat. "Yes. Yeah." My voice sounds brittle, like it could shatter at any moment. "I just—I'm not feeling well, so I'm on my way home early."

The lie slips out so easily, but it feels like a betrayal. Another layer of deception to pile onto everything else I've done.

"Oh. Okay." There's a slight pause, and I can hear the disappointment in his voice, but it's masked by his concern for me. "I'll tell the girls. They'll be happy, but I'm sorry you're sick. Want me to make you some soup?"

Another tear spills down my cheek when he says that. How could I have done something so terrible to a man like him? A man who is willing to drop everything just to make me soup when I'm "sick." I don't deserve his kindness. I don't deserve him. I suddenly crave the boring. I want complacency. I'll happily take the mundane over whatever this shit is I'm living through right now.

"Yeah," I say, my voice barely a whisper. "Soup would be nice. I'll be home in a couple of hours."

"Be careful," he says, his tone gentle, filled with love and concern.

"I will." I take a shaky breath, wiping at my tears again. "I love you, Shephard."

"I love you too," he replies softly, and it's like a punch to the gut.

I hang up the phone, but the tears don't cease. When I come to a stop sign, I glance around, making sure there are no cars behind me. The road is empty. The world outside is quiet, peaceful, a stark contrast to the storm raging inside me. I take a deep breath, trying to steady myself as I unlock my phone screen. My fingers move quickly as I pull up Saint's contact.

Without hesitation, I block his number.

I let out a long, shaky breath, staring at the screen. It feels like a small act of defiance, a tiny step toward reclaiming control of my life. But it's not enough. Blocking his number doesn't erase what happened, doesn't erase the fear that he could show up again. I can only hope that cutting him off like this will be the end of him. *It has to be.*

I pray that whatever this was, whatever game he was playing, it's over now.

I've always known to be afraid of the obvious things like lions and bears, because those are things that present as dangerous. What I'm just now realizing is that I should have been more afraid of the things that have the capability of *pretending* they're not dangerous.

Please, let him be finished with me.

CHAPTER TWENTY-THREE

"Finished," Shephard says. He closes the book and drops it between us with a thud that sounds like a gavel banging in the quiet room.

We're both lying in bed, and I've been pretending to focus on my laptop like I'm scrolling through emails, but I've been staring blankly at the screen in front of me. I haven't processed a single thing for the last hour. I've been hyperaware of every page Shephard turned, every breath he took, as he made his way toward the last page of my latest book. The book I pray he never finds out was inspired by actual events.

There's always a certain strain in the air when Shephard reads my work—especially now, after everything that's happened. I want him to love what I create, but with this one, I just don't want him to see through me.

Shephard enjoys reading the actual book rather than an early manuscript. He loves feeling the weight of it in his hands. He has a metal bookmark he uses just for my novels.

He prefers to read the final, polished product, after I've already made all the changes. He knows my writing habits almost as well as Nora does, so he likes me to work out the kinks before he reads the full story. He likes seeing the culmination of months of revisions and edits in a final bound hardback.

I always give him the first copy a couple of weeks before the rest of the world gets to experience it.

This one is the one book I've been the most nervous to give him. And his opinion seems more important to me than ever. Maybe because I'm worried he recognized parts of me in Reya. I honestly fear that he might have.

"And?" I ask, my fingers still resting on the keyboard of my laptop, though I'm no longer pretending to type. My voice betrays me with its shakiness. If there's one thing about Shephard I admire, it's his honesty. He's never sugarcoated his feedback. I've grown to appreciate that trait even more since leaving Saint standing in the doorway of that cabin all those months ago.

Honesty feels safe. It's what I need.

I've been holding my breath for this moment, waiting to see if the truth I've hidden between the lines of the book would remain invisible to him.

Shephard pauses, turning to face me, the fabric of his silence stretching thin between us as he carefully considers his words. "It was . . ." He rubs the back of his neck, his brow furrowing in concentration. My heart clenches as I wait for whatever comes next, the seconds feeling agonizing. "It was fucking thrilling, Petra. I think this might be my favorite book of yours so far."

His words coat me like a balm, soothing the anxiety that's been gnawing at me for weeks. I feel the compliment all the way to my core, a warmth spreading through me that I haven't felt in a long time.

"Really?" I ask, the relief making my voice sound lighter, almost incredulous. I didn't realize just how badly I needed his approval until I heard it.

Shephard leans forward, reaching across me to gently close my laptop, sliding it off the bed and onto the table behind him. He moves with purpose, his gaze never leaving mine. Then, without warning, he shifts, pulling me against him with an easy grace that makes my pulse quicken. He props himself up on one elbow, his other hand moving to brush a stray lock of hair from my face. His touch is gentle, affectionate, and it makes my heart swell with guilt. *How can I even smile at him when I've done such awful things to him?*

He leans down and kisses my forehead, his lips hovering there for a moment before he pulls back just enough to look at me. "I don't know what made this one different," he says, his voice quiet, almost reverent. "But it felt . . . I don't know. I can't put it into words without insulting your other books." He pauses, smiling softly as his eyes trace my features. "It felt *authentic.*" He kisses me again, this time on the lips, tenderly, then pulls back with a mischievous grin. "Kinda turned me on, honestly."

He lowers his mouth to the spot just below my ear and presses a soft kiss there before whispering, "Who is Saint?"

My world stops spinning.

My heart. It instantly goes from a gentle thump to a thunderous pounding beneath my ribs. My breath catches, and I force myself to stay still, to not react too quickly, but inside, panic is clawing at me.

"Who?" I manage to ask, my voice so strained it barely slides up my throat.

He lifts his head, his eyes searching mine. There's no anger, no accusation—just pure curiosity. *He doesn't know.* He's asking an innocent question, but my pulse races anyway, because *I* know.

"You dedicated the book to someone named Saint," he says, the corner of his mouth twitching upward in a playful smile.

The dedication.

I close my eyes, cursing myself for forgetting about that detail. I've managed to compartmentalize so much of what happened with Saint that it hasn't even occurred to me that Shephard would notice—or care—about the dedication. But now it's staring me in the face. It's been six months since I turned in the book, and even longer since I wrote those words.

I only followed through with Saint's final request because I was afraid of what he might do if I didn't. I didn't want to risk making him angry. Or worse . . . giving him a reason to show up here. He already knows my home address, and because I've learned so little about him, I wouldn't even know how to prevent him from showing up here.

"I don't know who Saint is," I lie, the words spilling out. My voice sounds almost convincing, but I feel the falsity in it, the knot of guilt tightening in my stomach. "I held a contest for my readers," I add, hoping the lie will sound plausible. "I chose someone at random to dedicate the book to."

I squeeze my eyes shut, waiting for the tension to crack, for him to call me out on my dishonesty. But instead, he laughs—a soft, genuine laugh that makes my insides twist. "That's cool," he says, his tone light. "I bet it'll make that person's year."

I bet it will.

"Have you packed for the tour yet?"

"No. I'll get to it tomorrow," I say, relieved by the change in subject. "Sixteen stops this time, so I'll have to take two suitcases."

"Oh, big-timer," he teases. "Nora still going with you?"

"Yep." I force a smile, but inside, I feel like I'm suffocating at the thought of a book tour. At having to lie to my readers about what inspired this book, and somehow doing it convincingly. I'm scared to even do this tour, simply because it's the first tour I've done since the fallout from my adaptation. I don't know what to expect, so adding lies into the promotion makes it even more nerve racking.

I just hope people show up. And that they show up with good intentions.

The lies I've been having to tell are beginning to stack on top of each other, threatening to bury me alive. I want to tell Shephard the truth, to let it all out, but I can't. Not now.

Not ever.

Shephard leans in to kiss me again, and I let him, my lips moving against his, but my mind is far away. It's back in that cabin, with Saint standing in the doorway, watching me leave. As much as I want to forget, I know I'll never be able to escape what happened.

Shephard's hand moves to my breast, so I part my thighs to give him what I know he wants. Within seconds, he's inside me.

We have more sex now than we did before Saint came into my life. I think part of it has to do with the fact that I feel like I've betrayed Shephard in so many ways, that making love to him is my Hail Mary. If I give Shephard his favorite thing, maybe it'll erase some of the terrible things I've done.

But I also make love to Shephard more often now because when he's inside me, I close my eyes and pretend I'm being fucked by Saint.

No matter how hard I try not to, my thoughts always veer back to the thrill of everything Saint put me through. As much as I hate him and myself for what happened, I can't deny that my attraction to him was real. The feelings my body experienced during the intimate moments with him were real. And even though I live with constant guilt and regret, I'm still human. I still have depraved fantasies that will never be spoken aloud to another human. Which is why, when Shephard is fucking me, I imagine Saint in his place. Because Shephard can't read my thoughts. Because I'm human. And no matter how much of a lesson I've learned in life, I can be whoever I want to be in my fantasy.

And in this particular fantasy, I am out on the lake in the boat with Saint, and he's the one who just crawled on top of me after reading *Woman Down.*

CHAPTER TWENTY-FOUR

Today is the official release day for *Woman Down*. It's been over two years since I last released a novel. Releases normally feel like a dream, but this one sort of feels like a nightmare.

I've been through this process more times than I can remember, but this time is different. The success or failure of this particular book rests heavier on my shoulders thanks to all the guilt that came with my experience writing it.

I don't even care if it hits a bestseller list. I don't even care if people like it. I just hope I can make it through this first appearance and Q&A in one piece. If I get emotional and run offstage again, I can just imagine all the coconut Pepperidge Farm cakes I'll be consuming in my bed while I figure out a new career path.

My chest tightens with every passing moment. I can hear the faint hum of voices outside the greenroom where I'm waiting, a reminder that soon, I'll have to face that crowd and answer every question they have about the book. About anything, really.

Nora asked if I wanted the questions vetted, but I told her no. I need to face whatever is coming my way, no matter how vulnerable it makes me feel.

Nora stands beside me, her energy as bright and bubbly as ever, but today, it feels like her confidence only amplifies my anxiety. She glances at me, concern flickering in her eyes as she picks up on the storm of emotions swirling inside me. I've always been able to hide my nerves from everyone else, but not Nora.

"You've done this a million times," she says reassuringly. "Everyone in that room is here because they're happy *you're* here."

"What if that's not true? What if there are people here with bad intentions so they can get a video that'll make me look stupid and go viral, like the last Q&A I did?"

Nora grabs both my hands in hers. "Hey," she says, her voice a whisper. "You've already gone viral. You've already looked stupid. It's too late to worry about that."

Her response makes me cackle. "You're right. You are absolutely right."

The store manager finally calls my name, my cue to walk out onto the stage. Nora grabs my purse and phone from me and gives me a reassuring smile. "You've got this, Petra. Easy peasy."

I leave her backstage and step out from behind the curtains, my heart thudding in my chest as I force a smile onto my face. The bookstore manager's voice echoes faintly in my ears, something about how excited they are to host me, how proud they are of the turnout. But all I can focus on is the sea of faces, and just how many of them there are.

There are so many people. I freeze in place for a few seconds, surprised by the turnout. *People actually showed up.* And the smile that's plastered on my face might be a real one.

I take a deep breath, my legs trembling slightly as I continue making my way across the stage, the soft glow of the overhead lights doing little to warm the cold nerves pooling in my stomach.

I wave at the crowd and then settle into the chair, smoothing my hands over my lap as I try to find my center. The manager continues to speak, naming off my bestsellers, but it feels distant, like I'm watching from underwater. My fingers toy with the edge of the armrest as I prepare myself for the inevitable barrage of questions, knowing that this moment is where the real vulnerability begins.

When the manager is finished with her introduction, she instructs, "If you'll just raise your hand if you have a question, Francis will get the microphone to you."

People immediately begin to raise their hands. Francis rushes the microphone over to one of them. It's a woman who looks to be around my age, and she's wearing a shirt with a stack of books on the front of it. Other women in her row are whispering to her, so it looks like she's here with a group.

She finally makes eye contact with me, and she looks just as nervous as I feel. "This might be an uncomfortable question," she says. "But this is the first time you've done a Q&A in two years. Since the adaptation."

"Oh boy," I say, laughing awkwardly.

The woman continues. "I know, it's the elephant in the room. But you've never once spoken on it, and we're all dying to know why you agreed with the choice to remove Caleb from the movie. Could you talk about that?"

There's a quiet murmur in the room, but surprisingly, I don't mind it. I don't mind this. It's an inevitable question if I plan on writing more books, and it's better to get it out of the way first.

"Yes. I mean, not that I necessarily *want* to, but I do think readers deserve an explanation."

More murmurs rush through the room. A few excited claps.

"The truth is, I'm a writer. I write books. And when those books get adapted, it takes years, and dozens of people. And the movie side of this is a different world from what I'm used to. I don't even look at that world as part of my career, because I'm not a director or a producer or even a screenwriter. I feel like they're the experts in their field, so when their idea for their adaptation differed from what I wanted to see on-screen, and what I knew you all wanted to see on-screen, I ultimately trusted them to know what would make the better movie. Because that wasn't my area of expertise. Of course I gave my opinion, but every time I fought to keep Caleb, my words were met with resistance."

A few groans come from the audience.

"Hold on," I say. "I'm not blaming anyone. Yes, the producer, Allister, had a different vision than I did. It was his project at that point, and he chose to change the storyline, along with many other people. That's the risk you take as an author when you sell your film rights."

Someone else already has the microphone, and she immediately piles on to the previous question. "But why did you deny having a part in it? We all saw the text exchange."

I can feel heat crawling up my neck. But I knew this was inevitable, so I face it with complete honesty. "Honestly? I made the post saying it wasn't up to me because, honestly, it wasn't. If I had it my way, I would have been faithful to the book. But I lost confidence. I gave up and gave in when I should have fought harder for Caleb. And that's no one's fault but my own. For that, I'm sorry. Because for what it's worth, I am team fucking Caleb."

The audience erupts into immediate applause. I feel instant relief at the reaction, despite knowing once this Q&A hits the internet, there will be a myriad of opinions on what I just said. But finally saying my piece without throwing anyone under the bus while doing it feels good. The same can't be said for Allister, but for all I care, he can continue parading around on podcasts and calling me difficult all he wants. Because the truth is, I *am* going to be difficult if another adaptation happens. I'm going to fight tooth and nail for the story the readers supported, and I don't mind having the reputation Allister is out there giving me. It's probably better that I do. I'd rather have adaptations I'm proud of than adaptations that don't even resemble their original forms.

The woman who asked that question thanks me, but then pauses before handing the microphone off to someone else. She brings it back to her mouth and says, "You used to be more active online, but then disappeared for a while. We thought you gave up. I just wanted to say thank you for not giving up."

"I *did* give up," I say quickly, cutting off the applause. People's reactions are mixed. There's confusion on some of their faces. "I mean, I know that wasn't a question, and thank you for saying that, but I do want to clarify that I did give up."

I straighten up in my chair, preparing to continue answering the nonquestion. I don't know how to put what I want to say into words, or if I even should. It almost feels too vulnerable to be sharing with a room full of strangers, but without this room full of strangers, I wouldn't be here. So I speak honestly.

"I wish I could say I've developed an impenetrable skin being in this industry, but I haven't. Sometimes the negativity can be too overwhelming, and all I can do is hide from it. And yes, I've read the self-help books, I've tried just ignoring it, I've tried therapy, I've tried it all. But I find myself still reacting to things I read, and sometimes I need a break from those reactions. I think it's okay if you aren't someone who can just let everything roll off without it seeping into your heart just a little bit. I don't mind admitting I don't have that kind of resilience. I show up when I'm mentally capable, and I'll interact when I'm emotionally stable enough to. But my mental health is precious to me, and as much advice as people give me, nothing anyone has said to me so far has cured me of feeling the sting of a hit every now and then. And I'm sure I'll continue to give up as I move through life. But as long as I keep starting over, I'm okay with being a fallible human."

When I finish speaking, there's another loud burst of applause. The woman who asked the question thanks me, and then hands the microphone to the next girl in line. I glance off to the side of the stage and see Nora standing there, watching me with a look of pride. She gives me a thumbs-up, and her reassurance puts me a little more at ease.

"I was going to ask about the movie, too, but I guess you covered that," the next girl says. Her comment is met by a round of laughter. "First of all, I love your books. My name is Christian, big fan. My whole book club is here." She gestures toward a group of women all wearing matching shirts.

I use the break in speaking to reach for the water bottle on the floor next to my chair. I look back at the girl just as she asks her question. "I was wondering if you have any advice for aspiring writers."

I nod as I unscrew the lid to the water bottle. Just as I'm bringing it to my mouth for a sip, I pause. At first, it's just a flicker of recognition, a face in the crowd that pulls me in like a gravitational force.

But then I freeze.

My eyes lock on him. On Saint. He's sitting a few seats behind the woman with the microphone. The room around me seems to shrink in an instant, like it has just run out of air. He raises his hand with his eyes locked on mine. He wants the microphone.

The room is silent, waiting for me to answer the question I was just posed. *What was the question?*

"Google," I say, my voice strained. "Google is your best friend. Every question about writing has been answered online. It's just a matter of finding the answer that inspires you."

I take a quick gulp of the water. *Oh, God.* I feel myself starting to sweat as she hands the microphone back a couple of rows. She reaches it out toward him. *No.* He stands up confidently as he takes it from her, his presence commanding my attention, even though every fiber of my being screams for me to look away. To run.

But I can't.

My eyes lock onto his, and my breath catches in my throat at the sight of Saint. Cam. Eric. Whatever he's calling himself now. It doesn't matter, because in this moment, he's all of them, and he's none of them. He's simply the man who repaired me and then shattered me.

What is he doing here? My thoughts race, a thousand questions flooding my mind, but none of them matter as fear creeps up my spine, cold and unrelenting. I grip the armrest of my chair tighter as I fight to maintain my composure. But inside, I'm crumbling when he begins to speak.

"I just have one question," he says, his voice causing that familiar wave of turmoil beneath my skin. "Where do you get your inspiration?"

His voice cuts through the haze of my panic, smooth and unbothered, as if he isn't feeling the same havoc he's wreaking inside me. Or maybe he is. We both know he's the much better actor.

The question—innocuous to anyone else in the room—feels like a dagger aimed straight at my chest. *Where do you get your inspiration?* It's a simple question, one I've answered a hundred times before, but coming from him, it feels like a challenge, like he's daring me to reveal the truth.

I feel the anger rising, hot and fierce, bubbling just beneath the surface. How dare he? After everything, he has the audacity to stand here, in front of me, in front of everyone, and pretend like this is some game we're still playing?

Like he isn't the reason I'm scared of my own shadow?

I clench my jaw, forcing myself to stay calm, to give the answer the audience expects. But the heat in my chest only grows, threatening to spill over.

"Inspiration comes from everywhere," I say, the words feeling hollow in my mouth. "Life, people, experiences." The words are automatic, rehearsed, but I stop short of saying *you*. My voice wavers ever so slightly, and I wonder if the audience can sense the tension simmering beneath the surface. If they can feel how close I am to snapping. "Next question?" I say, tearing my eyes from his smile, looking desperately for someone who can take the microphone from him.

"I have one more," he says.

I swallow.

"Well, it's not a question, really. More of a comment. But . . . I just want you to know I couldn't put this book down. I hung on to every single word. It's almost as if I were there, in the room with you, experiencing the things these characters experienced. That takes true talent, Petra. You are very, very good at what you do."

A few people clap, but his comment was spoken so slowly, and with such intensity, I see a few people squirm or stiffen from the discomfort of it. The smirk on his face proves he doesn't give a shit what anyone else in this room thinks. He hands the microphone off to the next person, and I'm stuck, paralyzed under the spotlight.

My vision blurs, the edges of my anger creeping into my periphery, but I swallow it down, forcing myself to stay composed. I can do this. I'll be damned if I let him ruin this like I ruined my own Q&A during my last event.

That was before I truly knew what anger was, though. My anger is what gets me through the next hour, despite it being one of the hardest hours of my life.

As soon as the Q&A portion ends, I head straight to the greenroom to compose myself before the signing begins. Nora isn't in here, but I'm thankful. She would be able to see the feelings I'm having trouble reining in right now. I take several minutes to compose myself, drink water, reapply makeup since I look like I've seen a ghost.

When I finally work up the courage to walk back out, I clock Saint standing toward the middle of the line to get the book signed that he's clutching in his hand. He's already looking at me before I make eye contact, as if he was staring straight at the door, waiting to see if I'd actually walk out and finish the job despite his presence here.

I wonder if he really finished reading the book. Did he stay up until midnight last night, waiting to download the ebook? The one that holds parts of him in every chapter, every line, every word? Did he stay up all night reading the story that wouldn't exist without him, without what he did to me, without the tangled mess of our history in that cabin?

My pulse quickens, and I force myself to move, to walk to my signing table like I'm not about to fall apart. The pen feels heavy in my hand as I greet the first reader in line.

I move through each person with patience, trying to forestall the inevitable moment he reaches my table. No matter how hard I try not to look, my eyes keep drifting to his spot. He's waiting, patient, just like everyone else, but his presence is suffocating. I can feel his eyes on me the entire time, burning into my skin.

When he finally reaches the table, I feel lightheaded. I don't look up when he says, "Can you make it out to Saint?"

His voice is smooth, too smooth, like he's in complete control of the situation, as if this isn't tearing me apart inside. *Saint*. The name feels foreign on him now, but I refuse to let him retain control. I take the book, open it, and inscribe the name *Eric*.

I sign my name and slap the book shut. My final *fuck you*. I slide it back to him, still refusing to meet his eyes.

"I don't get a personalization?" he asks.

His words are a challenge laced with that familiar teasing undertone. He's toying with me, just like always. I can feel the anger bubbling up again, sharp and hot, and this time I don't try to suppress it. My eyes snap up to meet his, and for the first time, I let him see the anger, the frustration, the hurt that I've been carrying for so long.

How dare he stand here and pretend that this is just some casual encounter. That he's just another reader. How dare he show up at all.

I grab the book, and my hand moves swiftly across the page, the pen pressing hard into the paper as I add: *An absolute, complete and total stranger. May you have the life you deserve.*

I intend for the words to be a slap in the face, but he grins. That cocky smile grates on my nerves, like nails on a chalkboard. He leans in closer, his voice dropping to a low murmur that only I can hear.

"Thank you for the dedication."

I refuse to say "You're welcome" as he pauses for a reaction. I don't give him one. I look past him and motion for the next person in line to make their way to the table, indicating his turn is over and he can walk away.

I'm watching him out of the corner of my eye as he heads for the exit.

Good riddance.

Right before he reaches the door, I see him turn, and his smile brightens, but not at me. He's smiling at something else. Or someone. He lifts a hand and waves someone over.

I'm momentarily relieved to know someone else other than me has his attention.

I start to look away, but then something pulls at me, willing me to look up again. Why would he be talking to anyone here? Who would he know here?

Has he told anyone about us?

I'm craning my neck around the reader in front of me to see who it is he just waved at. I see someone making her way over to him as he walks toward her.

Nora.

She's smiling back at him with a giddiness that makes my stomach sink. The last thing I need is for Saint to fuck with her head next.

They continue walking toward each other, and I'm doing everything I can to see why Saint is trying to speak to Nora, but two more people swoop in and block my view. I'm forced to give the people in front of me my attention, but I can't help but feel an imminent urge to scream Nora's name, to warn her away from him before she falls for that smile and fake charm.

I'll be damned if he does to her what he did to me.

A fearful thought engulfs me. *Was I not the first writer he's done this to?* What if it's happened to more than just me, and he's done it to multiple writers? It sounds like something he'd be capable of, and from the looks of it, his plan is to manipulate my best friend next. If he's watched all my videos, that means he's watched all Nora's too.

Why didn't I anticipate that he'd be capable of this?

I smile for pictures as I search for Nora, but I've lost sight of them. I sign more books as I search for Saint. I look for signs of them both as I finish up the last several readers, feeling guilty they didn't have my undivided attention. But it has taken all the willpower I can muster not to run and save Nora from this monster.

When the last person in line finally leaves, the manager has two employees following behind her as she brings over leftover stock for me to sign.

"Can I take a break first?" I ask.

"Of course," the manager says. I make a beeline for the exit. I ignore my name when it's called by a reader. Not something I would ever do under any other circumstance, but I'm starting to worry about Nora. It's all I can focus on, even though my actions since seeing him wave at her have probably come off as rude to a lot of people.

I don't have time to worry about other people's hurt feelings as I make my way outside and look for her.

I almost release a sob when I finally see her. Safe. Her back is to me, and she's leaning against a car, talking to him.

Saint spots me first.

He stands up straight, pulling his weight off the car he was pressed against. Nora spins around, and she flashes her usual smile, but she also looks like I just caught her flirting with a married man.

He isn't married, honey. Far from it.

"You done already?" Nora asks. Her voice is cheerful, but also . . . rushed. She's walking toward me like she wants to escort me inside and not even introduce me to her new friend.

Saint's jaw is tense as he stares straight into me. Nora sees me clocking Saint, so she pauses her steps and stands awkwardly, feet from me and feet from him. She shoves her hands in her pockets. It makes her look . . . guilty.

Saint suddenly looks guilty too.

Why do both of them look like they have something to hide from me? Has something already happened between them? Am I too late?

I walk closer to them, hesitant. "What is this?" I ask, my eyes trading glances with each of them, waiting for one of them to speak.

Saint and Nora glance at each other with a look that indicates they share a secret.

My head is spinning. "Do you know him?" I ask her. Then my attention lands on him. "Stay away from her."

"*Petra*," Nora says, sounding shocked by my anger.

I don't give her time to make it seem like I'm overreacting. She has no idea what he's capable of, or that, if anything, I'm *underreacting*. "Stay away from her," I say to him again.

He lifts both hands in a peaceful gesture and takes a step back.

"Petra," Nora says again. "Why are you being like this?"

"He's lying to you about who he is. Do not trust him. Whatever he says, he's lying."

Nora doesn't react like I expect her to. Instead, she and Saint share another knowing look, but this one is chock full of shame. She folds her arms over her chest and looks down at the pavement.

I wait for one of them to elaborate, but neither of them does. Nora eventually peers up at me with eyes that hold a level of betrayal like I've never seen in another human.

"Eric is an old friend of mine."

The words sound like echoes reverberating around in my heart. He's . . . *what?*

It's as if my world turns gray. All the possibilities of what that could even mean are slamming into me from every direction.

"Petra," Saint says, attempting to reassure me. Or Eric. Whoever the fuck he is steps forward, but I hold up a hand.

"Don't come near me," I say to him. Then to her, "What the hell are you talking about?"

Nora sighs, and then glances toward the bookstore behind me. People are lingering, but not close enough to hear our conversation.

She lowers her voice almost to a whisper. "You were *stuck*, Petra. I was trying to help." Her voice is a plea for forgiveness, but I'm still not sure what she's done that requires my forgiveness.

How is Nora, my best friend in the whole fucking world, involved in what happened between me and Saint?

She continues by saying, "Eric and I . . ." She waves a hand at him. "After my live video with you ended that night, we were chatting online. We joked about how it would be nice if he could help get you out of your slump. And you seemed so desperate for inspiration."

I cannot believe what I'm hearing.

Every feeling and emotion I went through when I thought this was merely Saint's idea is amplified. I can feel the tears stinging my eyes.

"This isn't true," I say with a twinge of hope. "You're joking, right? If you know him, why have you never mentioned him?"

"I haven't seen him since college," she says. "We've been friends online since then. You don't know every single person in my life." She sounds defensive, but I'm the only one here with any reason to feel defensive. Or angry. Or betrayed.

The two of them should feel nothing but sheer and utter shame.

"But . . ." I can't fathom it. Nora . . . Saint. Both of them? "You're my *best friend*," I say, stepping closer. "If what you're saying is true, that you sent your *friend* to inspire me, you knowingly put my marriage at risk! You put *me* at risk!"

Nora's expression loses some of the guilt in exchange for confusion. She glances at Saint, and then back at me. "I don't think I did," she says. "All I did was ask him to show up in uniform and knock on your door so you could put a face to your character." She shakes her head, looking between us. "He agreed to ask you a question and then leave. Did . . ." Her eyes land hard on Saint. "Did something else happen?" She's finally beginning to sound concerned for *me*, rather than concerned about being caught.

"Nothing happened," he says to Nora. Then he looks at me, sincerity in his eyes. "I told her *nothing*, Petra." Saint says it quickly, as if to throw me a lifeline.

I am completely in shock. I need time to process this, but I don't know how I can do that when the person I always go to when I need to talk something through is the person I need to talk *about*.

She has completely betrayed my trust, and now she knows there's more to whatever happened, more that I haven't told her. Something big.

"It's not my business," Nora says. "But Petra, I'm sorry. I don't know what happened between you two—he said you only spoke for a few minutes—but I swear to you, that is what I'll believe. Forever. *Please* forgive me. I really was truly just trying to help. I was going to tell you the next day, but he begged me not to. And then when we spoke, you sounded like it helped, so . . . I just left it alone."

"I was there for less than five minutes," Saint says to Nora, throwing me another lifeline. He's still trying to protect our secret, despite theirs being out in the open. "I left right away. Nothing happened, I just felt bad that she got scared."

I can't even find it in myself to appreciate that he's trying to cover for me, because I'm furious. I'm embarrassed. I feel betrayed and confused and mortified, and now I'm crying and trying to wipe the tears away with quick swipes of my hands.

At least I made it until after the signing this time before having a breakdown.

My vulnerable position forces Nora to step forward and naturally try to comfort me, but I push her away. The three of us stand quietly as I try to process everything I've just learned.

Nora sent him there? My best friend?

When I finally compose myself enough to speak, I lift my chin and look at Saint. "I'd like to speak to you alone."

Nora gets the hint. She nods and walks back toward the store.

What does he want with me? Why couldn't he walk away after it happened and leave it alone? And now my best friend is involved?

I wait until I know we're completely isolated before I speak again. "Why are you here?" I say sharply.

"To get my book signed." He says it easily, a failed attempt to ease the tension. I don't laugh, so he finally straightens up and looks at me with sincerity. "I wanted to see you."

There's an ache to his voice now. He seems like he's finally being honest in this moment. I use it to my advantage because I need to know how mad I'm about to be at my best friend.

"I need the truth. What does Nora know?"

"Nothing," he says with certainty. "She's being honest. We don't even talk that often. That night of the live video just happened to be one of the nights we connected. We were discussing your writer's block, and she knew we were in the same state. She joked that she wished I could stop by and inspire you. I mean, it was a joke at first, but . . ." He stops speaking for a moment. "I'm the one who pushed her to think it was a good idea. I wanted to meet you. And then once I actually met you, I was intrigued. *More* than intrigued. So I kept it up without telling her."

I wipe another tear from my eye with a trembling hand. Seeing me cry stirs up guilt in his expression like I've never seen. He moves even closer to me, close enough that the memories of him flash through me in a heated second.

"I never meant to scare you. Or betray you. I was attracted to you, and I let it go too far. And I'm sorry. Truly." He reaches a hand up and grips my elbow gently, dipping his head so that I'm forced to look him in the eye. "I'm *sorry*."

I stare back at him, every moment we spent together spiraling through me. Apology after apology, but this betrayal is too much. This hits too close to home. Too close to Shephard. The man I almost destroyed. I owe so much more of myself to Shephard than the wife I've been to him.

"I want you to leave. And I never want to see you again."

He nods. But then he says, "For what it's worth, I would do it again in a heartbeat."

Saint might, but Saint doesn't have what I have at home. I brush his hand from my arm, and with as much resignation as I can muster, I simply say, "*I* wouldn't."

I spin and head straight back inside without saying goodbye to Saint, but it's clear this was goodbye. I don't even look back to see his expression, or watch him leave. I walk straight into the bookstore, and I don't even look at Nora, who is standing there, waiting, hopeful for any morsel of attention from me. I don't speak to her at all.

I walk over to the table where all the unsigned stock has been neatly placed, ready for my signature. I sign each book robotically, and even though I want to punch Nora square in her fucking face, she stands next to me and stacks each book neatly into a pile as I sign them.

Nora and I are staying at the same hotel, and the publisher has one driver scheduled to take us back to that hotel, but at least we don't have to share a room. I'd probably choke her in her sleep.

When the last book is signed, I thank the staff and head for the exit. As Nora follows me out of the bookstore, toward the Escalade waiting out back for us, I hear her whisper, "I'm sorry."

I climb into the car, but all I can do, after we're both seated in the back seat and heading toward the hotel, is remain silent in my betrayal as I stare out the window, holding tears at bay.

This has more than likely broken trust in our friendship forever, but it isn't Nora's fault I let things go as far as they did. She didn't set out for me to cheat on my husband.

That's something I'm realizing I was perfectly capable of doing with or without her help.

God, this is the worst night of my life.

CHAPTER TWENTY-FIVE

This is still the worst night of my life.

I haven't been able to sleep since we returned to the hotel a few hours ago. I still don't know how to feel, even after four hours of tossing and turning and poring over every second of the last two years, and this book, and my friendship, and my marriage, and every single lie Saint has told me.

I don't even know if I can stay mad at Nora forever, because I know her intentions were in the right place when it comes to my career. But for right now I need her to feel my anger enough to at least lose sleep over.

I'm sure it was meant to be harmless encouragement on Nora's part. She thought her old friend would simply swing by and knock on my door and ask me a simple question, and that his looks would spark something in me that would help me write.

But it sparked a lot more than that.

I know I'll ultimately forgive her, but it's going to take time. I just hope she never presses about what happened between me and Saint. I don't feel comfortable telling her that story, but I'm relieved to know he didn't give her any details of how far he actually took things.

How far *we* took things.

God. My brain is a convoluted mess of thoughts, and my chest is knotted with emotions.

I pull my laptop in front of me, hoping to get my mind off everything that happened tonight. I do the one thing I know I shouldn't do as an author.

I pull up my book on Goodreads.

I begin sifting through all the reviews that were left today about *Woman Down*. I don't usually do this on release day—hell, I try to avoid it for all eternity—but this book is different. *This book is personal.* I feel the need to read every review written about it because so much of it was drawn from my own experience. And for whatever reason, I need to know what people think about the relationship between Cam and Reya.

Each review feels like a magnifying glass on my soul. Every comment about Cam stirs something inside me.

> He was so dreamy.

> So protective.

> I want a Cam in my life.

If these readers only knew.

I try to imagine him—Eric—flipping through the pages, recognizing the parts that mirrored our time together as he worked his way toward the end. I know he said it was the best book I've ever written, but I'm still curious if he finished it. I don't know why I care. He certainly acted like he had, but at this point I know what a great actor he is.

There's no way he hasn't read it, though. He probably devoured it faster than Shephard did. I think that's why I'm going through the reviews one by one, looking at each username, trying to find a hint that any of the words I'm reading are his. If he was brave enough to show up at my signing, I'm sure he's left a review.

My fingers tap at the keyboard, and my eyes diligently scan my screen for an hour, but nothing jumps out at me and screams that he wrote any of the words I'm reading.

I should let it go.

Let the memory of *him* go.

Hopefully tonight really was the last of him. The book has released, I love my husband, I'm full of regret, and I need to move forward.

Just when I'm about to close my laptop and try to push the pervading thoughts of Saint from my mind forever, an email notification pops up. The sharp sound slices through the quiet.

I click on the notification, and as soon as I read the subject line, I feel a familiar heat slide down my chest and settle like a lead weight in my stomach.

Reservation Confirmation

Wait. For what?

The email is from the rental company I use to book the cabins, but it isn't for Louie and Mari's cabin. It's the west-facing cabin. The one I'd wished I was in last time.

I open the email and scan it quickly, my pulse spiking with confusion and dread. It's their standard confirmation email—polite, professional, ordinary. But the content is anything but.

The cabin has been reserved in my name for twenty-one days, starting next Friday, the week after this tour ends. My fingers tremble as I scroll down to the payment section. It's marked as prepaid.

I never made this reservation.

I never *would*.

After what happened with Saint, I vowed I'd never set foot in that town again. So how is this happening? I feel a chill crawl up my spine as I stare at the screen. I know for a fact I didn't book this.

I'm trying to make sense of it all when another email notification pops up. This time, it's from an email address I don't recognize. My pulse quickens as I click on it, fear and curiosity warring inside me.

The email is short. Too short.

All it says is I think it's time we start working on your next book, Petra.

ACKNOWLEDGMENTS

It's been more than three years since I last published a book. Three years since I sat down with characters and tried to make sense of their messes and successes. I honestly didn't know if I'd come back to writing, but stories have a way of finding you when you need them most.

Woman Down was born from a short story I wrote called "Saint," which first appeared in the anthology *One More Step*. That story lingered with me long after I wrote it, but I needed to give myself space before I could jump back into it. This book is a result of the slow, sometimes painful, but ultimately healing process that writing tends to be.

To my readers, thank you for your patience, for still being here, and for continuing to believe in my stories even when I wasn't delivering at the pace you're used to. Your grace during this time away meant more than you know.

To my incredible agent, Jane Dystel, I wouldn't be here without you.

To my amazing editor, Anh Schluep, your unwavering patience is why this book exists. Thank you for your trust and guidance.

To everyone at Amazon Publishing, thank you for giving this story a home and for continuing to support me with such care and passion.

To Tarryn Fisher. You know.

To my husband and my boys, thank you for putting my peace and happiness above all else.

To my siblings and my mom, your support has been constant and unconditional. I'm so lucky to have you all in my corner.

And to all my friends, *Woman Down* is about finding your way back, even when you don't necessarily feel lost. Thank you for giving me the time and space to do just that.

Colleen

ABOUT THE AUTHOR

Photo © Callynth Photography

Colleen Hoover is the #1 *New York Times* bestselling author of several novels, including the women's fiction bestseller *It Ends with Us* and the psychological thriller *Verity*. Her work has won the Goodreads Choice Award for best romance three years in a row: *Confess* in 2015, *It Ends with Us* in 2016, and *Without Merit* in 2017. Colleen is also a scriptwriter, producer, and co-founder of the production company Heartbones Entertainment.

Colleen currently lives in Texas with her husband and their three boys. For more information about the author, please visit her website at www.ColleenHoover.com.